MASQUE

Tor Books by Shariann Lewitt

Memento Mori
Interface Masque

INTERFACE

MASQUE

SHARIANN LEWITT

A TOM DOHERTY ASSOCIATES BOOK
NEW YORK

INTERFACE MASQUE

Copyright © 1997 by Shariann Lewitt

This book is printed on acid-free paper.

Edited by Teresa Nielsen Hayden

A Tor Book
Published by Tom Doherty Associates, Inc.
175 Fifth Avenue
New York, N.Y. 10010

Tor Books on the World Wide Web:
http://www.tor.com

Tor® is a registered trademark of Tom Doherty Associates, Inc.

Library of Congress Cataloging-in-Publication Data

Lewitt, Shariann.
    Interface masque   /   Shariann Lewitt.— 1st ed.
       p.   cm.
    "A Tom Doherty Associates book."
    ISBN 0-312-85627-X
    I. Title.
  PS3562.E987I5   1997
  813'.54—dc21   96-47121
                                           CIP

First Edition: April 1997

Printed in the United States of America

0 9 8 7 6 5 4 3 2 1

For Carol Behrman, who told me long ago that I could;
and for Peter Norton, who was my salvation

MASQUE

1

The alto sax cries sweetly just before dawn. Music blankets the streets like soft snow, tucking the downwarren in for sleep. Telling the last stragglers of the night it's time to go home, to leave an empty space before the beginning of the day. To leave a place for the music, for the old slow Delta blues that creep into the cracks in the pavement, into the cracks of the soul.

The music is alone in the dark. Melody drifts through open windows and into dreams. An improv line rides the magnetic index of the night, dancing syncopated against the steady rhythm of the databeam.

Nothing is left untouched by one heartbreak-pretty song. And then the sky fades to blue as the last notes taper away.

The blind jazzman packs up the sax and melts into the rhythms that will carry the city through the day along with the memory of the tune.

* * *

Cecilie didn't know how she was going to eat dinner, and then her mother would notice and would make her tell. And after she told them, her parents would pull her apprentice agreement from Sept-Fortune. Then she would have to find some other thing to do, to learn, to make up for the fifty work-blocks a month that her parents collected from her apprentice pay. That would be the end of the world, Cecilie thought. But she sat still, as still as the lace curtains and the matching lace tablecloth, her face as white as the starched napkin in her lap.

Dinner smelled good. Her mother settled a bowl of roasted peppers and eggplant in the middle of the table, next to the pasta. And in the kitchen waited thin sliced veal in lemon butter, and salad and pears.

Cecilie was hungry and not hungry. Her stomach had churned so badly during the day that she could hardly face dinner. Her mother sat down and her father poured the wine. Bowls passed to her and she spooned fragrant food onto her plate and stared at it.

She didn't know if she could do what was ordered. The thing was unthinkable, and yet she had been told today that it was the only route to her promotion. She didn't know if she was going to have to tell them or if she was going to die inside.

Suddenly she understood about Luisa now. Luisa had been two years ahead of her at Sept-Fortune. When Cecilie had turned sixteen and become a full apprentice, Luisa had been up for senior and very excited. Senior apprentices got real jobs and much more pay and were allowed to wear whatever they liked to the Sept-House.

Then and now, Cecilie utterly loathed the plain grey skirt and white blouse and navy blue blazer that was the uniform for apprentices at Sept-Fortune. At least when she was sixteen she had been permitted to abandon the childish navy blue kneesocks and flat shoes, so now she wore proper hose and low navy pumps.

While the uniform was hideous and humiliating, what was worse was that they were not to go masked while they wore it. Only freshly scrubbed faces revealed to the street, to any passing stranger who looked at them and studied their schoolgirl features.

Luisa had been so excited, Cecilie remembered. They had gone shopping for new clothes at the expensive shops, where Sept credit went a long way. And Luisa had bought a mask, a real grown-up mask of rose-bronze watered silk with a gold filigree pattern on one cheek.

Cecilie remembered the day Luisa had gone crazy, the day she had run shrieking out into the courtyard and her mother had to be called from work. And even Luisa's mother could do nothing at all and had begun to cry and wring her hands. The ambulance had come and Luisa had been caught and tied and sedated and taken away. No one knew anything about her.

The younger girls in Cecilie's year had wanted to send her flowers or candy. Cecilie had always been the brave one and she had asked Signora Tima if they could visit and perhaps cheer Luisa up. And when she was coming back.

Even now Cecilie could recall the perfect stillness in the room, the heavy scent of furniture polish mixed with dying cream-colored roses stuck in a glass vase on Signora's desk. "I'm afraid that won't be possible," Signora Tima had said gently but firmly. "Luisa is not at home. She's in Santa Clara's. The nuns say it is stress that broke her, and it is best if she is not reminded of the demands of her time here."

Cecilie had nodded, wondering what kind of sudden stress could make Luisa lose her mind. Only the most helpless cases went to Santa Clara's. That must mean even her own family could not keep her at home and sane. It was terrible.

And now Cecilie knew the reason and she could feel it tearing her apart inside. She envied Luisa. Being crazy was much better than having to make this choice, do what Signora Tima had insisted was merely a test.

She had sat in the same ivory moire chair that she had when she had inquired about Luisa. This time the roses were pale peach and not quite in full bloom. The top of Signora's desk was a brilliantly polished expanse of rosewood that shimmered like satin and was inlaid around the edges with something lighter.

Signora had kept her waiting. It was late afternoon, almost time to go home, by the time Signora got to her. Cecilie concentrated on sitting respectfully, her ankles crossed, her back straight, not leaning on the chair. She had waited nearly an hour and was scared and curious at the same time.

Maybe Signora was going to throw her out. Maybe her latest work was not acceptable. Maybe one of the girls had told about how she had acted at the Sept-San Marco party last week and had played with the two most appealing young men there.

Or maybe this was the summons she had been waiting for, that she was to become a senior apprentice and get to wear her own clothes and choose her own jobs from the approved list on the board. Secretly she hoped it was true. It would mean that she was the first of her year. While Julietta and Valentina were dear friends, she would be very pleased to make senior first.

Finally Signora Tima came in from her private inner office and sat down behind the desk. "Cecilie, your work has been excellent to this point. Your tutors have all recommended that you are ready to test for senior apprentice status."

Cecilie couldn't keep the smile from spreading across her face. "Thank you, Signora."

The head of the student program nodded in acknowledgment. And then her face became impassive. "The test itself, though, is not an easy thing. You know how we completed the security contract for the Bank of North America last year. You are to break into that system, get through our own key codes, and bring out the names of the bank's principals and their ownership percentages."

Cecilie could not believe what she had heard. This was not possible. To break security—especially security that Sept-Fortune had created! It was immoral. It was evil. She had been taught above all things that the Septs insured that the security of the business sector remained inviolate. That the power of the Septs rested only on how well they could perform this function.

To break security? No! Cecilie unfolded her hands and steadied herself against the edge of the desk. Maybe it was a test.

"I wouldn't break security," she said firmly. "It's against everything the Sept, my family and society have ever taught me."

Cecilie expected to see Signora's face soften. Surely the older woman was going to praise her fine sense of duty and explain that *that* was what the test had been all about.

It didn't happen. Signora sighed and leaned back in her silk-covered chair. "Cecilie, you must understand that this isn't really breaking security as you might interpret it. This is a test of our own system, how we've put it into place, how good a job we've done for the client. This hurts the client in no way. The bank will never know that you've breached the key. But we need to test our own work, and we need to test your ingenuity and expertise."

The bank will never know, Cecilie thought, *unless I fail. Then I'll set off every tracer the design team loaded and I'll be put on trial and the Sept . . .*

She looked at Signora's face again and knew the answer. The Sept would not acknowledge her. Ever. If she screwed up she went down solo. If she got in and out and brought the proof demanded, the Sept would have an audit trail on her anyway. All her life they would own her. They would be able to turn over the proof of her activity to the authorities and have her licenses pulled and perhaps get her thrown in jail.

No wonder Luisa had gone crazy. For a moment Santa Clara's was a very tempting thought. No more decisions, no more pain. Just quiet nuns and white walls and drugs to freeze the thoughts that made this life abomination.

Up until this exact moment she had always thought she wanted to belong to Sept-Fortune. What better life could she have? On top of work that consumed her there was the prestige and wealth that went with one of the most powerful Septs on the island. And there was the Sept-House itself, a beautiful palazzo with silk on all the walls and handmade carpets on the tiled floors. When she passed her Mastery in the Sept she would even have an apartment here, six rooms all to herself and much nicer than anything she could possibly afford in the city alone.

If she chose to stay in Venice, of course. Her parents had only permitted her to apply to the Septs that had student programs in Venice, and while Sept-Fortune had Houses around the world, there were only apprentice programs here and in the Vancouver House. Though sometimes Cecilie thought about taking some exotic assignments in the Fortune Houses in Singapore, or Bombay or maybe São Paulo. Many of the younger members went from location to location for several years, until they were ready to settle down. The thought excited Cecilie. There were so many possibilities open in the future. As long as the future was Sept-Fortune.

Everything, everything was tied in to her career here. She was eighteen—too old to apprentice anywhere else, and suspect besides. At her age she should have a skill or be in university. Otherwise she had nothing at all.

The old bell from the top of the Pietà building rang seven and the choir, the oldest and most notable in the city, began their final evening song. Tonight it was Bach, something cool and complex to close down the day.

Signora shook her head and closed her eyes. "You may have until tomorrow to decide, Cecilie. Do not bother to return unless you are ready to take this test. Unless you are ready to make a true commitment to us." And with a wave of the old woman's hand she was dismissed.

She hadn't felt like chattering with Julietta and Valentina, down at the stairs where the vaporetti stopped every day and picked up the apprentices and journeymen from the island where many of the older Septs had their Venice Houses. So she had dragged around the street, her eyes on the ground, hearing the laughter from the dock. Everyone else was going home, hungry for supper and eager for the evening ahead. Everyone but her.

She lingered until it was time for the last vaporetto to go. Only a few journeymen shared it with her, all of them properly dressed and masked to enter the city from the Sept island. On the island it was safer. Everyone was Sept or choir or made glass. On the mainland there was only suspicion of those who made the island trip daily. Cecilie wished she could hide behind the decency of a mask; she was certain that her misery and shame showed plainly. Julietta had always said that she couldn't keep a secret and couldn't tell a lie, that her face was as easy to read as the morning news.

At least when she got home Mama was already very busy in the kitchen and Papa was on with her older sister, Mena, who had married and moved out just last year. She was able to yell hello and slip into the bathroom and wash before anyone saw her. Maybe she could scrub some of the guilt and indecision away before she had to face anyone with talk about her day.

She sat in front of her plate, full of colorful peppers and pasta, her mouth unable to work. Papa was telling about Mena's phone call, but Cecilie could barely make sense of the sounds.

Only one thing occupied her mind, and that thing churned around and would leave her no peace.

"And so, Cecilie, how was your day?" her mother asked, as she did every night just after the meat was served.

Cecilie's mind was blank. She shrugged. "It was a day. I'll be testing for senior apprentice soon."

Her mother sighed. "Then you'll need all new clothes. I don't suppose you've saved anything out of your allowance for that."

Cecilie blinked. "But I have, Mama. You know I have a positive account. I haven't spent much since I started earning."

"Yes," her father said. "Cecilie has been very responsible with her money. I'm proud of you, that you didn't go and waste it all on going out and restaurants and hairdressers and fake nails like too many young girls. That Valentina, for example. She must be pushing negative numbers, with that new Vespa and the nails every week."

Cecilie didn't comment. She didn't do her nails like Valentina because her father disapproved so deeply, and because she thought it looked silly on Valentina while they still had to wear the uniform; she didn't have a Vespa because Valentina shared, and often picked her up when they were going out for coffee or to one of the Brother-Septs. It seemed so simple and obvious and so ridiculous for conversation.

Any conversation seemed inane. She tried to unstick her tongue in her mouth and say something. Her parents could help her, would tell her not to do something so vile as to crack her own Sept's security code. They would get angry; her father would be very righteous and her mother would tell her that there was no reason she should ever return to Sept-Fortune again. She could get a perfectly good job in her uncle's shop, selling glass to the tourists. She spoke five languages. That was worth something.

Language was essential to Sept training. What good was information if you couldn't understand it? And her mother had pushed her to this apprenticeship so young simply for the languages involved. "No matter what you do in your life, even if you never do Sept work, you will have those languages. You could become a tour guide on Murano, or teach languages, or work in Uncle's shop. You can do almost anything if you have languages."

Now the idea of being a tour guide or working in a shop made her want to gag. She was too highly skilled, too valuable, worth too much. She didn't want to live at home until she married, as Mena had, with all the rules and curfews and Mama and Papa interrogating her friends when they came to call.

Somehow she managed to nod and make the right noises while her mother gave her advice on her new wardrobe, where she ought to shop, what colors she ought to consider, what magazines she should study and how she ought to divide her budget for skirts and shoes and earrings. Her father chimed in at the mention of money, insisting that it was better to buy a few good pieces than a lot that was cheap. Yesterday this topic would have delighted her. Now, as Mama compared the various boutiques and planned a strategy, Cecilie could barely listen. She didn't know if she would survive to go out next Wednesday. It only made her more nervous.

Finally her father ended it. "The girl will want to go with her friends," he stated. "And she needs to learn to do these things by herself. She's going to be on her own soon, a journeyman at the Sept, and maybe get her own apartment with those girls."

At which her mother began to cry and her father apologized and Cecilie was able to slip out and into her own room. She closed the door and tried to find some calm. Her room had always soothed her. It was spare and small, stuffed animals on the bed and a shelf of porcelain-faced dolls that had once belonged to a great-great-grandmother her only concessions to frivolity. The apartment was high enough that she had a good view of the sky, now streaked with the liquid colors of the oncoming night. She had always loved this time of day, this place. The quiet was like that at the Sept-House or a convent, the silence of thought or the careful structure of Bach sung by one of the great choirs. Something deep where she could curl between the layers and be lost.

No comfort existed in the little room. No quiet could soothe the chattering in her head. *Do it. Don't do it. It is wrong. You have no choice. You will live with having done wrong all your life, you will know that everything you do and think and work at is dirty. You will have no life at all if you do not do it. You will have to become a shopgirl and sell things to tourists and pretend that you are ordinary. And besides, maybe you won't get caught. Maybe you can do this and deliver the goods and never have to do anything terrible again.*

It isn't even so bad, really. It isn't like I'm collecting data that could hurt our clients. It isn't like I'm going to sell it to their enemies. I'm just part of the security-testing system, is all. Even if I get caught all I have to do is explain that Sept-Fortune is making sure that all the key changes are current.

Thoughts chased each other around like kids on the soccer field until they exhausted her and she fell into a restless, fitful sleep.

The next morning Cecilie woke in her clothes. The blanket was under her and her uniform was hopeless. She smelled bad and her shoulders hurt.

At least there was something easy she could do. She stripped off the skirt and blouse, threw them and her hose and underclothes into the cleaning pile, wrapped up in her big red bathrobe and went down the hall for a shower.

The water made her feel better, or at least smell better. There was a new leaden ball in the middle of her stomach. She did not think at all, she could not think. There were only the heavy movements of getting dressed in a clean blouse and skirt. At least she had hung up her blazer when she had come in.

Everything was going too slow, was too much effort. Idly, Cecilie wondered if she had the flu. It felt like flu, like watching herself move through water and being too tired to care. All she wanted was sweet oblivion. And no one seemed to notice.

Breakfast was laid out the way it always was, coffee and frothed milk in the old ceramic pitcher her mother had brought back from a trip to Greece. Rolls in a basket, flowers in bright morning colors between the coffee and the bread. She drank a little coffee and picked at the food.

Her parents seemed oblivious of her distress. Cecilie was certain that terror was written all over her face, was clear in her slowness. She wanted to tell them about this choice, about the deadness of realizing that she had decided. She wanted to, but the words were frozen in her throat. She could scarcely acknowledge them for herself, could not really believe that she was going to go through with this.

There was still time. She would arrive and Signora Tima would tell her it was all a mistake. She would get in and there would be a message waiting for her with a big smiley saying that she'd already passed. The vaporetto could sink, the floods could come again, the Last Judgment could open up the skies before she had to break every code of decency she had ever learned.

She finished her coffee and left the roll untouched on her plate. Her father kissed her on the forehead and wished her a good day.

"And a good day to you, Papa, Mama," she said in something that resembled her normal voice as she went through the door.

The vaporetto did not sink. The Last Judgment did not come. When she arrived at the Sept-House she was sent directly to Signora Tima's office yet again. The roses on the desk had opened and one was dropping petals. A few peach petals curled on the polished rosewood as if they had been scattered by a designer for the effect.

Looking at them meant that Cecilie did not have to look at Signora's face. Or at herself. Concentrating on the colors and textures made them all so much more real, and the conversation and her own decision so much a part of the shadow.

"I am very pleased," Signora was saying as Cecilie studied the still-life in front of her. "Many girls don't understand that this promotion is the most difficult of all. Once you have been accepted as a senior apprentice you are truly a member of the Sept, not simply a student. And of course it is necessary to insure every member's loyalty. Every sister has been required to pass this same test, so we all understand."

Were you tested? Cecilie wondered. She couldn't really imagine Signora breaking even the most casual directive, let alone a stone-deep rule. And yet it seemed that Signora was saying just that.

"You will report as usual and go through your normal procedures," Signora said. "Then you will attempt to bring the information I have requested. You will not discuss this assignment; you may say it has the utmost security and you will not explain what you are doing. And when you succeed, you are to return here and hand over the proof on paper."

"Can't I just add the data to your queue?" Cecilie asked, really surprised at this request. She had never written anything official on paper, though she and Julietta and Valentina had often practiced secure communications together. And once she had received a paper letter from one of the Sept-San Marco boys. Niccolo, the one with the darkest eyes she had ever seen.

"You know nothing is truly secure in a mail queue," Signora said. "No, this is sensitive data and must be reported by eyes. No copying out, you should know that." The old woman sighed and shook her head at Cecilie as if she were the very youngest and stupidest apprentice.

Cecilie's hopes constricted in her throat. If the data was too sensitive to put in the mail, it was not simply proof that she had been and gone. It was not something innocuous that couldn't hurt the client.

If the Sept had wanted to run through security, they could have even planted their own markers for apprentices to take. That would have been very easy and straightforward, and would prove the same thing.

She could still run. The doors to the House weren't locked on the inside. She could bolt, go down to the quay and leave the island, report to the authorities.

Who couldn't care or already knew. Or were too afraid of the Septs to do anything against them. So she would be considered crazy or a liar and either sent to Santa Clara's to join Luisa or end up charged with defamation and barred from the island forever. And she would have to work in her uncle's shop or worse. They might even make her leave Venice, and the thought of that was more horrifying than any other.

"If you fail, if you're prosecuted and convicted, you will be permanently barred from all Sept interfaces and any other credentialed datasite," the signora said. "You will lose all user privileges, and will be permanently barred from anything except kiosk exchanges. So I suggest that you will need to do the best job you can. Even apprentices who were as well or better prepared than you have failed. But we have to test sometime."

Cecilie hadn't even considered that last night. There was more at stake than she had previously imagined. There was no back door out of this test, no clever solution, the way there was with software error. To be barred from the nets was to die. Without interface in the datastream she was crippled, blind and restrained. She could not survive cut off, condemned to Real Life alone.

What happened to those who had failed? she wondered. She suddenly thought of Luisa, locked deep in Santa Clara's with the nuns and the drugs and the doctors. The thought was sickening, terrifying. But so was the act that the Sept required.

She could not bolt and run.

So she went through the motions, left the office and went to her usual station, knowing that there was no reprieve. That there was nothing good anymore, and nothing at all she could trust. So now she was not only going to betray her morals, her ideals, her whole structure of the universe. She was about to betray herself.

And, Cecilie suddenly realized, it no longer even mattered. After the announcement yesterday the damage had been done and could not be undone. Yesterday she had still believed in truth and hard work and honoring her parents and the Septs. Yesterday the world had made sense. Now she knew the truth, and the truth was a cage with no escape.

2

Of the city's seven choirs, the Pietà was the greatest, maybe the greatest in all the world. Lina surely had thought so when she had auditioned, when she had begged and cried for her parents to give her not only permission but the fare to go. After two years at the Pietà she was more certain than ever that she had made the right choice.

She had music all the time, perfect and shining glorious around her. She lived and breathed music, surrounded by it the way she was by the city's shimmering golden light. And she could live this way forever, and still send funds home to her family besides. Quiet money, peace money, she thought of it. They couldn't object to her music so long as she was productive and safe.

And the Pietà above all was safe. They had their own marked masks, pale sky blue like the robes they wore. No one would touch a person in Pietà blue with the twisted gold and pearl medallion prominently displayed like the ancient chains of power that officials and generals wore around their necks. The medallions were tradition, as were the cut and color of the robes. Both dated from a time when people were known to claim that in the dark they had mistaken the blue for some other shade and killed a singer. The city fathers had been in an uproar and the medallion had been created so that there would be no such error again. To kill an enemy was commonplace in an earlier incarnation of Serenissima, the Serene Republic of Venice, but to kill a singer in one of the great choirs was abomination and treason both.

The singers themselves were sacred, inviolate. They made the music and so they could deny it, and in the past they had. Once the Pietà had been silent for a full week, when the Sept-House feud had broken into the streets and the city was an armed camp. Recordings and broadcasts had only covered the silence. They had not pierced the heart of it.

Lina fervently believed that work and love and thought and war could not exist without the music that inspired them. She had learned that this was the essential secret of the Pietà, of all the choirs, from the Maestro himself. It was the base of their power. Though she had found it odd that the Maestro had seen fit to explain something that seemed so indisputable that even a seven-year-old had no trouble mistaking it. At least, she had been quite aware of this fact when she had been seven and studying for her audition.

She had also learned that the right kinds of music could directly influence the function of the brain, though she didn't understand all the chemistry that had been presented in the lecture. For her to understand that music itself could create thought and emotion, lay the patterns down for the activity to follow, was perfectly obvious without any of the deathly dull and incomprehensible neurophysiology and chemistry that went with it.

So she had managed to ignore that part of the lecture by

imagining the piece she had to rehearse for her violin examination. Violin was much more difficult than piano or voice or even flute, and Lina considered the time far better spent. After all, she had no ambitions to become a Maestra herself. That would entail far too much chemistry for her to endure.

Still, she did understand the economics of the situation. Everyone knew that music had some kind of direct influence on brain function, and so the Sept and Merchant Houses contracted with the choirs, the smaller chamber groups and the student instrumentalists to provide the correct atmosphere. Recordings had only limited value, and a Maestro was required to choose just which pieces would produce the desired effect. True, a few very simple selections had been recorded for the shops, to encourage patrons to stay a little longer and feel relaxed and ready to part with their cash. But even the places that patronized the recording market found that over time, people became bored.

The Maestri knew as much about the brain as they knew about music, from stimulating neurotransmitters to matching erg cycles with various modes of thought. That, Lina knew, was power. No singer could deny it. The music had such dominion over her that she never doubted it affected everyone else. She knew it—but unlike some of the older and more politically ambitious singers, she had no desire to lay hands on that power. She wanted only to hear, to experience, to create that glistening ephemeral beauty.

Maestri did not always have to consider the aesthetics of the composition, only the effect. Lina thought that was ridiculous. If music could improve mental function, could induce emotional states, then it could also edify and purify those who listened. It could be a force for beauty and moral good as well as productivity.

This was something Lina desired, but she told no one. The

other Pietà singers would laugh at her, and those who studied to become Maestri would smile and shake their heads and say that she just didn't know enough, hadn't learned all the neurophysiology that was required and wasn't even interested in learning the rudiments necessary to understand.

She was a singer, a musician, nothing more—a tool that created the states that patrons requested and Maestri orchestrated. And yet when she sang, when she became part of the music, she didn't need all the years of study, the chemistry and genetics to understand the power in her voice.

Lina felt music wash through her like baptism, like prayer. Maestro had just brought his baton down and Lina closed her book. She didn't want the music to end, never wanted it to end.

"Are you coming?" Sean asked.

Lina was startled. She hadn't realized that everyone else had picked up music and bags and was trying to jam to the door, all at the same time. The immediate area around her seat was empty. She had been dreaming again.

"To dinner?" she replied vaguely. She hadn't planned on eating at home. She had expected to eat later, at the reception where their chamber group was giving a short performance. Houses that hired singers always fed them generously after the show on top of their very high fee.

Sean snorted. "No," he said, rolling his eyes in frustration. "To Café Luna. For the show tomorrow. We have to buy tickets or they'll all be gone."

Lina's head spun. Now she remembered. Sean and Eliza had told her the day before yesterday and the day before that. Café Luna was an underground club, the kind she often heard rumors of and wasn't entirely sure existed. People like Sean and Eliza liked to shock, and Lina was certain that most of what they said was what Sean had taught her to call blarney. She liked the word.

But more than just Sean and Eliza had talked about this concert. The rumor was everywhere because the show was forbidden. They were going to play jazz.

Jazz was not completely outlawed in Venice, but it was not entirely legal either. Enough research had shown that it counteracted the good of the city, according to what the Maestro had said. He hadn't said what particular good, though when she was older Lina understood that the beat she had heard was distinctly sexual and defiant all at once.

It took her a little longer to understand the real threat that jazz posed. Jazz defied authority, it stood on the outside with an attitude the Septs and city dignitaries could not abide. And so they had made it unwelcome.

Clubs were not permitted to advertise such concerts and had to pay triple and quadruple their licensing fees. They were not permitted to serve anything but wine and beer and coffee, which was not where the profit was. And so it became very risky and very expensive to put on a jazz concert. Most club owners and promoters weren't willing to take the risk for such a very small profit.

Lina had heard jazz only once, in a historical seminar when she had been too young to respond to the anger and pleasure and the anguish in it. It had been placed in with various types of African and Caribbean forms so they could note the influences and interactions. She hadn't really liked the piece, but the forbidden nature of the show enticed her. And maybe there was more to it than what she'd heard in class. Certainly Handel was radically different from Tchaikovsky.

Much as she loved the music she sang, much as she wanted to drown in Mozart and Purcell and Palestrina, she felt weighted down by it as well. There had to be other kinds of music, other kinds of ideas.

Maestro had played military marches for them when he had

taught the power they had. He had played postmodern, he had played atonal. Some of it Lina liked and some she didn't. She had never heard any of it again.

The singers were paid by the Sept-Houses to keep the intelligence level high. They were paid by the Merchant Houses to keep people buying. And they were paid by the city to keep the peace. None of that was helped by the harsh chords with difficult rhythms that she had heard only in class.

Still, Lina knew there had to be other music. She had heard about other forms, minority interests, things that made people angry or aggressive or selfish. Those kinds of music were not easy to find, and that was a good thing, the Maestro had said.

They were not forbidden. No music should be forbidden. But jazz was not well liked and so there was little money for it. Musicians could not earn a living and so they turned to playing proper music or found other contracts doing other things. Besides, from the way Maestro sneered, it was obvious that he didn't consider those people real musicians at all. Some of them couldn't even read music, he had said.

Lina had been horrified. She couldn't imagine not being able to read music. Though of course in the very early days of the Pietà, when it was still a workstation for the indigent, people had learned pieces by ear alone. Maestro always reminded them of that when he thought they were taking too much time to learn a part.

"A hundred years ago, Pietà singers could learn their parts in one afternoon listening to an old recording," he thundered at them. Lina and Eliza and Marco and Sean could all mouth the words together, they had heard them so many times, always the same thing. They had wondered if it was really true, that in the poorhouse days singers had actually managed to master the complicated harmonies of Bach or Handel by listening for a single afternoon. Older singers had smirked and told them it was impossible—just Maestro being frustrated, that was all.

"So are you coming?" Sean asked again.

Lina realized she hadn't replied to his question. It was a good question, but suddenly she didn't know the answer. She wanted to hear the new music but it frightened her. The idea of it frightened her. If they were caught, Maestro would probably put them on probation, and she could even lose her rank in the highest chamber group and be dropped a couple of notches.

It was one thing for ordinary people to go hear jazz. That might be bad and people would be suspicious, but it wouldn't ruin them. For a Pietà singer to be caught listening to suspect music would throw questions on the integrity of the choir itself.

No one could be permitted to question the Pietà. Not ever. The thought that she could bring shame on her training and her profession was more terrible than even the threat of losing rank.

"Look, if you're going to come you'd better make up your mind," Sean snapped. "I don't want to stand here all night because you can't decide."

Lina felt her face redden and she looked down at her shoes. The pointed toes were scuffed, she should have them polished. She didn't know what to answer. She was afraid.

She wanted to say yes. She wanted to go because everyone was going, and Eliza and Sean would call her a coward if she didn't. And they were the best singers in the choir, the best who hadn't made soloist quite yet. But they would, Lina thought. And she wanted to be with them. She admired them, she wanted to be part of the group.

"I want to go," she said very quietly.

The late light filtered in through the ancient rippled glass that looked out over the bridge. She could see dust motes dancing, spinning like confetti falling during Carnevale. The world was utterly, perfectly still.

"Not good enough," Sean insisted. "You either say yes or

no. You never make up your mind about anything, Lina, and if you're not going to come, just say so so I can leave and go have dinner. I have to have the money tonight for the tickets, I can't wait. Either give me money now, or forget it."

Lina closed her eyes and felt the world about to change. The risk of being caught and losing her rank terrified her, but there was some chance she wouldn't be discovered. The sure knowledge that people she admired would sneer at her was more immediate and more painful. "Yes, I'll come," she said.

Besides, if Sean and Eliza went and they were all caught together, she thought that Sean would manage to talk Maestro into being less harsh. Sean had a talent that way.

Sean raised his eyes to the ceiling again. "We're meeting tomorrow night at Café Luna at eleven," he said. "If you don't show, especially if there's trouble afterward-—" He left the rest unsaid.

"Café Luna, eleven," she repeated. But Sean had already turned to leave.

Cecilie started in the Library as she had been taught. There were separate tables for the different Septs, and private rooms as well, with doors that resembled oak with the name of the Sept lettered in gold leaf. A mere apprentice like Cecilie had never been allowed into the Sept-Fortune room, though she had often wondered what secrets lay behind that door. Probably a million masks and disguises, she'd thought, so that no one could recognize the Sept sisters about their work.

Being a mere apprentice and not truly a full member of the Sept yet, Cecilie had only a cheap mass-produced mask inside. Probably ten million kiosk users wore the same one: a plain white shiny face with a single red tear and a large red-and-white clown suit and turban that made her appear genderless. Of the generic masks, the white with red was the most popular, though white with blue and black with red were fairly common as well. All-white had been very popular two years ago, but it had gone out of style again.

"You'll always retain a catalog of generic masks," Signora Lucia had told her class years ago, when Cecilie had first been permitted trial access. "They are very useful in keeping your identity in the background. You are really quite unnoticeable in generic off-the-shelf software, even if you could write better code yourself. Most of the time you won't want the attention."

She had been disappointed that day, having dreamed of the exotic masks and costumes in the picture files—blazing, glittery, in colors as subtle as the dance of sunrise on the water. She and Valentina and Julietta had sketched and redrawn the fantasies they would choose when they were permitted grown-up masks. But the idea that they would always wear the common domino or bauta with the traditional tricorn, use the cheapest imaging where the movement flickered and the colors often tuned slightly too garish, horrified the girls.

Eventually Cecilie saw the wisdom of it. When you were tracking down deadbeats or following security leaks, it was better to be unnoticeable. And it was especially important not to be recognized as Sept—some of the time, at least. So now Cecilie saw this costume as a working uniform, no more interesting than her apprentice blazer, and far less likely to be put aside.

At least the mask and yards of fabric were only software here. She didn't have to put up with the heat and discomfort this costume would entail in the meat world. Whatever she perceived as physical sensation was very limited, and mainly pleasant. Sometimes there was the hint of a breeze, sometimes a touch of lilac or Oriental lily in the sensorium, though often those kinds of sensations were ignored. Generally she experienced only sight and hearing inside the interface. Most designers weren't good enough to include the subtle senses; most clients didn't want to pay what it would cost anyway.

The Library had been created by all the Septs, all the best of their designers working together for generations to create the finest and most intricately sensual environment. So the tables all gleamed with fruitwood inlay and the light danced across the silk moire wallpaper that changed color from grey to celadon to almost olive depending on the time of day and some random program to indicate seasonality and weather. The faint scent of carnations was layered with old leather and brittle paper to create a perfume more complex than most sold on the market, and the textures of the surfaces did not simply reproduce the originals, but captured the essence of them.

Cecilie had long since become used to the Library, though after spending time here she found that all the other constructs seemed cheap and not quite finished. She sat in one of the oversized leather chairs at the Sept-Fortune table and summoned her familiar, a bird of paradise that sat on her wrist and whispered locations in her ear.

Zizi, she called him. Zizi had been the first real piece of software she had written, and she had significantly refined him at least three times since into a personalized search engine that could be given keywords or names or even fairly intricate parameters and go-look-for data. He could search independent of her presence and save and file whatever she had requested for whenever she needed it. Zizi only appeared to her in the Library, not because she couldn't summon him anywhere but because only Sept members had familiars. Cecilie had been taught that only Sept members had the programming skills to write them, and non-Sept users had various Search Stations on the public levels.

Kiosk users were used to seeing birds and dogs, unicorns, griffins and myriad black cats wandering around on their own. But they never saw the animals interact with anything else and so ignored them. The tourists saw just more wallpaper, more extravagance for the endless entertainment of the net. When they bothered seeing the familiars at all.

And that was all they were supposed to see. Signora Lucia taught that few non-Sept users even realized there was any way to navigate besides the Search Stations. If someone did, some wild talent managed to program some crude facsimile of a familiar that might ever discover the Sept-only levels, that program would be killed immediately. The griffins and basilisks and a few of the panthers were not familiars themselves, but had originally been created as antivirus guardians. Their duties had been expanded only thirty years ago to include all unauthorized programs. In that time they had found very few offenders.

Cecilie told Zizi that she wanted the public records for the Bank of North America filed in the past year. Zizi could not get through any security pass, but was tireless in tracking down information that was available to the public, if the public knew where to look. The bird flew obediently through the mullioned window seat with colored bottle glass—well, the illusions weren't always perfect.

Then Cecilie dropped out of the interface and reestablished awareness of her own work cubby, cut the feed lines and went to Real Life. There was no use doing all the legwork before she had thought through the problem and the protocols, gotten some idea of the type of security she had to breach, and come up with a strategy for overriding the failsafes.

All security in the nets was breakable. Nothing was ever perfectly protected, utterly inviolate. That had been lesson number one when she had begun training in Sept-Fortune's specialty, security. There were one or two methods that were nearly so, but they depended on physical possession of verification keys that changed constantly. Those were expensive and clients hated using them, so the clients wound up not using any security at all. That had been lesson number two: something a client will use is better than a superior design that the client will avoid.

There were also the very large prime-number keys, which theoretically could not be broken at all. Still, Cecilie knew that even Sept-Fortune security systems had enough cracks and flaws in the finished product that there were ways into even the prime-number locks. Prime-number locks were terribly expensive as well, and very few clients wanted to pay out so much for something that was not all that much more secure.

After all, who besides a Sept-Fortune sister could possibly break any kind of professionally designed security system? The days of child hackers and wild talents getting into government systems were long gone. Most of those incidents had happened because the systems themselves had not been adequately protected in the first place. Those stories were the reason clients were willing to pay Sept-Fortune's price to make sure their secrets were protected.

Sept-Cargo worked for less, but security was only a sideline of their data-delivery services. They did a nice job for small-business and individual files, and their rates were affordable to ordinary kiosk users who felt a need for some additional protection. Large commercial entities that needed data seriously guarded were happy to pay what Sept-Fortune charged.

No, there were very few security systems that were truly secure against a Sept sister. Against some kiosk user, or the run-of-the-mill government clerk, a Sept-Fortune system was golden. Even a midlevel user from a commercial organization or a freelance datadog wouldn't be able to enter.

But Cecilie was not as harmless as any of these. That was why the Septs were so closed, so guarded, so respected and feared. They were sometimes called the net.ninja, a name Julietta had written in red paint on the concrete under the bridge near her home. They had to be ultimately trustworthy, incorruptible, beyond reproach.

And they weren't.

Then Cecilie saw it all together like a puzzle picture clear for the first time. She knew what no one else could know, and it thrilled her. Guilt came with the taste of power but couldn't erase the sweetness of the vision. Because it was power the Septs had, power beyond that of any commercial group or government.

No one owned the Septs, and no one could come close to them. Various companies and governments had tried to field their own net.ninjas, but individual talent could not make up for the generations of tradition and training the Septs had to offer.

Besides, the Septs were descended from the working groups who had created the infrastructure of the nets, and consequently had knowledge that none of the competition had. In the end, the companies and governments failed. Their best net.walkers became Sept, with journeyman-level offers and promised Houseroom at whatever location they preferred. Every major Sept had Houses in Tokyo, New York, San Francisco, Rio, London, Venice, Hong Kong, Amsterdam—the list went on and on and on.

Cecilie never wanted to live long-term at one of the Sept-Houses in a distant city, but she had often dreamed of being sent to do a special job to some exotic place, Santa Fe or Singapore or Bahrain. Sept-Fortune had been aptly named. It was not only one of the first tier groups that had pioneered electronic privacy, but it was one of the richest as well.

And the Sept had never hesitated to spend money on itself. The House in Venice had once been owned by a merchant prince. It was tiled in marble, and the walls that were not covered in silk or carved wood had been painted with murals on classical and natural themes. The courtyard garden had once been part of an adjoining property that the Sept had purchased and incorporated when the Venice House had become one of the two training centers. Generations of apprentice girls had perched on the edge of the fountain to do their lessons, careful not to trample the flower beds where Signora Tima cut roses and lilies to put on her desk every morning. A new top floor had been added to the main wing; it had a gym with a swimming pool under a glass canopy that could be closed in winter.

This was where all the apprentice parties were held, when the older girls wanted to invite the brothers from Sept-San Marco or Sept-Lynx. Except for meals and parties, the apprentices and students were relegated to the newer building, incorporated later, where there were no murals or gilding or crystal chandeliers from Murano. Cecilie had been in the Main House ballroom only once, when Flavia got married. The wedding was held in the cathedral, and afterward they took a full regatta decorated with white and gold streamers to the Sept-House, where a Pietà chamber choir provided the music. Cecilie had thought Flavia's wedding was like a fairy tale, and expected her own reception to take place in the same ballroom with the same music and the same piles of sugared pastries on silver trays in the corners of the room. All the food, all the music, the whole reception had been provided by the Sept, and the House chefs had worked for weeks on the menu.

There were two chefs employed in the Sept-House kitchen, as well as several sous-chefs. Dinners were served in the main dining room and always counted a full five courses. The island was too far for anyone to go home at midday, and so everyone, from Signora Tima to the youngest girls in their first-year apprentice jumpers, ate under crystal chandeliers and drank from centuries-old Murano glasses with blue and green dolphin stems.

Sometimes the Sept would purchase blocks of tickets to a play or opera. Every summer there were trips to La Scala, and in the winter they went skiing in the Alps, in a lodge owned by the Sept and with interface capabilities in case someone had to catch up on work.

Upon attaining journeyman rank, a Sept sister was entitled to a month of vacation every year in one of the pleasure lodges— and if she was married or had children the entire family was of course included. Cecilie had often seen vacationing families when she and Julietta went skiing, older Sept sisters from all over the word taking their families on holiday.

Cecilie reminded herself of these things, of her parents' wonder and her sister's jealousy when she was accepted as an apprentice. There had never been any question: she would do what she had to in order to stay. Her parents and Mena had never been to La Scala, had never been skiing, had never really had a holiday.

She told herself this, but she still felt uneasy, out of sorts. She wanted to run, run away forever, so that she wouldn't have to face herself.

A chime sounded a clear C. Cecilie sighed. Zizi had returned. She slipped back into the interface. There was a moment of nausea and then she was sitting at the Sept-Fortune table in the Library, where a small bird with curling feathers that shaded from cobalt to aqua paced on the table. As soon as Zizi saw her he fluttered to her shoulder and preened her mask. Zizi didn't like her masks. He preferred to play with the long strands of her hair. But now she was too old to go into the net face-naked. It would be rude of her to show unmasked the knowledge she had about anyone. And so Zizi worked his small beak on the mask that was not a mask.

"Data," she demanded.

The bird-familiar whistled, then began to speak in the voice she had resampled five times in the past twenty months. Now the whisper was high and squeaky and almost innocent, suiting the familiar's shiny round eyes and eternally smiling beak.

"Data on request one unavailable. Security record in Sept-Fortune, designers Alice Sung and Lydia McElroy out of San Francisco House, installation completed August, final payment . . ."

Cecilie shook her head. She didn't want to know what the Sept had been paid. Signora Tima had made it more difficult, pitting her against designers from a distant House. She had studied with the best in Venice, and attended when several Sept sisters on vacation or on temp assignment had taught seminars. But not these two; and so she wouldn't know their style.

Maybe not so. She smiled. "Access Sung and McElroy's study records," she instructed the familiar, and then left the interface again.

Some people would just go in and try to muscle it out. Valentina would do that, Cecilie thought. Valentina solved problems by being nastier than they were and waiting them out. If a program did not yield to one form of persuasion, it would yield to another.

Muscle was not elegant. Cecilie prided herself on her refinement. Her programs were spare and efficient, her tracers direct and focused. Valentina sometimes got there quicker, but never beautifully.

Perhaps Signora thought she had found something Cecilie couldn't crack, a security system designed by two sisters who had never seen Venice and whose style Cecilie wouldn't know straight off. There was Sept style, of course. Cecilie could immediately recognize which Sept was responsible for any piece of netware by the signatures and flourishes, the combinations of paradigms and the underlying structure, though within any Sept's style there was infinite room for creativity.

The chime came back faster this time. She returned to the interface, and this time Zizi did not try any preening.

"They studied together in San Francisco House, never left," Zizi said, and Cecilie's hopes fell. "But one of their main instructors was Marguerite Michaelazzi." Cecilie wanted to whoop. Now she knew exactly how to approach the problem, where to begin. Unless they had completely revolutionized the entire practice of security design as they had been taught it, if they had been Michaelazzi's protégées they ought to have left a few things Cecilie would recognize.

Marguerite Michaelazzi was one of the greatest designers and teachers of her day, and she had trained Signora Tima and Signora Lucia and Signora Amelia, who had taught Cecilie.

So it wouldn't be so far a stretch, she thought. It should be like trying to follow Signora Tima's markers, which she had been assigned to do last summer. If they followed Michaelazzi's philosophy, as Signora Tima did, then their code certainly was not unbreakable. And there would be familiar patterns, even if only in the underlying structure. *Barrier, password, cipher, verification, identification* the litany went, in ascending order of reliability. She had memorized that her first months in the Sept. And the best way to create any security system was to use a mix of all of them, in ascending order so that a would-be break-in would get trapped at some interior stage and tagged and traced.

Suddenly she was excited, and the guilt and worry that had been pushing her for the past day disappeared. The challenge consumed her. Feeling as if she could do this thing, she wanted to try, to see if her skills were up to matching the best. Cecilie knew she was good, but she didn't know how good. She had never known. Too much had come too easily. The thought of knowing, of trying, of outwitting two of Michaelazzi's students in one afternoon, thrilled her as nothing had since she had met Donato at the San Marco party last month.

Learning to create security systems had given her all the skills necessary to break into one, she realized suddenly. For a moment she felt dizzy. She could do anything with this ability, go anywhere, take anything she desired. No one could stop her.

The knowledge that she had such power—or might have it if she was really as good as she thought—exhilarated her. If she could do this alone, then together the Sept-Fortune sisters could rule the net. Which was the same thing as ruling the world. She felt as if she could see into something larger, as if a pattern were coming together and she was just at the edge of a deeper and more profound understanding. Then it was gone.

She scratched Zizi absently and sent him off to his perch in her home queue. Then she left the Library.

Out the front door and down into the pedwalk, she was alone and so marked as Sept for at least the first few meters until she hit the Mall. The Library had been carefully constructed near the Mall so that Sept sisters and brothers could disappear into crowds easily. The Mall was always crowded. Cecilie had always hated it.

It was ugly. There was no reason for anything to be ugly in the net. Everything was mutable and had been carefully designed, could be redesigned. But the Mall, for all its incarnations (brass and ferns, marble and fountains, neon and brushed aluminum, oatmeal carpeting and amber lights—there had been others, but these were the general cycle Cecilie expected) was always hideously crass. Tasteless, she thought, even though today (in the brass-and-fern motif) it pretended to be genteel and respectable. The shop locations never changed even though the decor cycled. And the shops were boring: all the clothing at knockdown discounts, all the housewares of second quality—or so they were portrayed in the Mall. Once they showed up in Real Life they could even be worse.

Cecilie cringed from the thought, from the cheap sweaters

and towels and garish cosmetics displayed on tables near the doors. There was hardly any security here. In a virtual Mall there was no way to steal. The punch-up on texture wasn't nearly high enough to make any of the merchandise all that appealing anyway.

Not to a Sept sister, at least, who lived Real Life surrounded by silk and flowers, water and music. The Mall was miserable, but it served its purpose. She was one of dozens of customers in the same mask. She made two full circuits, stopping in at the places she found palatable—the florist, the hosiery shop, the candy store (where she almost ordered a box of four truffles) and the stationer's.

On her second time around, as she examined the paper uploads, appreciating the good software that conveyed texture and weight, she bought a sheaf of dyed Japanese rice paper. And when she had finished the transaction she realized that she had created an alibi without meaning to. By making a purchase she had put a marker on her own presence here with a time stamp. That was considered very good evidence in court.

Signora Tima should be pleased with that additional detail. The signora always said that it was the details that mattered most. Now Cecilie understood that the caution had been meant two ways.

She left the Mall through the Commercial Gate. There were twelve gates to the Mall, which was the center of what had been planned as the Main General Interface but was generally just called Mall level. It should have been a garden, Cecilie often thought, or a beautiful cathedral, but the level had been designed by a Houston team. On the Sept Prime level the Library extended into the central zone, but that was the place beyond the restricted doors where she didn't have the keys to go.

The Commercial Gate markings were grey on every level, even those that no one but the Septs knew were there. At the

Commercial Gate menu Cecilie chose the banking icon. The doors slid open before her and she got into the plain cubicle. Doors shut around her. When they opened again she was in the banking sector.

There weren't many people in the banking sector. Mostly, datapackets were shot between icons of various establishments, with a few random kiosks outside for the convenience of the few elderly who preferred to bank in person rather than through a kiosk.

"You can bank at any convenient kiosk in your hometown," the announcement said in welcoming tones. "We can serve you at over ten million locations wherever you work or play."

Cecilie tried not to snicker. For all its programmed friendliness, it was primarily designed to get rid of customers, suggesting that their best interests lay elsewhere. She had heard that line before. She got out of the transport and began to wander through the canyon of dull blank façades. They didn't want her to enter.

Some were better jobs than others. Two really old ones looked like they had been designed when banks had their own program staff and were either too cheap or too hidebound to have it redone right. Sept-Prado's recent work was really impressive, Cecilie thought. She could tell which illusions had been written after the Sept split had taken effect and cornered the market. The images they presented gave the impression of great stability and wealth and made her feel like a little girl with sticky fingers at a grown-up dinner party. She wanted to be anywhere else. Which was exactly the point.

Two kiosks guarded the entry to the street. "The kiosks at the corner are fully equipped to see to any banking need that may arise. They are connected to every financial institution in this area," the announcement told her. Cecilie passed and walked down until she found a doorless structure labeled NORTH

AMERICAN. Definitely Sept-Prado work, and a recent redesign at that. She turned and faced it. Nothing happened.

"I'm looking for information about a loan," she said, and tried to giggle the way Julietta did when she was nervous.

"This is not the correct interface. This is not the correct format. Any banking kiosk in your home city will be happy to assist you." This time the voice was quieter, directed only at her, and emanated from the darkness in front of her.

She tried to giggle again. "But I'm already here, and I paid my access fee. So how come I have to waste my access and go back out and do it again?"

The voice sighed softly. Cecilie was shocked that such a customer-unfriendly response had been included in its repertoire. A window appeared in the dark, a screen and scratch pad under it, and a series of keys on the side. It was not quite a standard interface. Cecilie smiled.

She went through all the loan information she could manage, paging through everything from mortgages to educational enhancement to personal development. She realized that she had lost the first taste of information because she was excited that her ruse had worked. Now she had to keep her mind off that and concentrate on how the data were being accessed and presented to her. It was almost standard, but there were the quirks she had hoped to find.

Every system had its signature. Every institution had its own style. Which words were highlighted and where, and how they jumped from one set to the next, gave her some insight into the collective mind that had become the bank's programming stamp.

"Style counts," Signora Amelia had said in seminar. They had been discussing different signatures and styles, personal and group variations, all the microscopic technicalities that went into every single choice of color, image, words and font. Each of those bits of trivia meant something from a security standpoint, whether it was analyzing customer needs or creating an interface that would suit the client's corporate culture. Such clues were also useful in assessing clients' previous upgrades, and what they were willing to spend.

Now Cecilie understood much more. Even whether the program ended with "quit" or "stop" or "bye" or "exit" told her something. And she could use that knowledge to design or implement or upgrade a security system, as Signora Amelia had taught was the goal in seminar. Or she could use that same information to evaluate the security system in place, who had written it and what the company's needs and goals were. Which would tell her more about how the security was devised—especially if that security system had been written on a Sept-Fortune contract.

Cecilie had gleaned all the information she could from this level. She closed down the window and sauntered back down the street, back to the transport, and this time touched the icon for the Parc.

3

The Parc had the same function as the Mall, only three levels up in hierarchy. There were no crowds here. A few people wandered around the pond admiring how well the swans swam, how they bent their necks back to preen their wings. These people didn't wear generic masks. They had software from the finest shops in . . . Rio? Yes. Definitely Rio. Rich tourists, then.

Rio, New Orleans and Venice had the best maskmakers in the world. Freelance software by non-Sept programmers flourished there in small private ateliers. Maskmaking was the final bastion of the freelancer on the net, unregulated by Sept organization and rules. Cecilie had never thought to wonder before why they, of all the functionaries in the net, had not finally created a formal Sept of their own and joined the Board. Perhaps because the designers didn't have to be in the net at all to concoct their creations.

The freelancers built only custom work that cost a fortune

and would draw every eye in the net. Styles in these mask-design centers were very distinct, and there was no mistaking a Venetian costume (ambiguous and elegant) for something from Rio (very revealing) or New Orleans (historical and thematic). All three cities were major Sept centers with a history of maskmaking, and with the glitter-walkers who could afford the most extravagant styles for their one or two forays a year into their private accounts.

With more careful examination, Cecilie realized that the costumes were not truly top-of-the-line designs from a name Rio studio. They were knockoffs, copies of the ideas that looked perfect from a distance but didn't hold up under scrutiny. The motion, while more fluid than the off-the-shelf standard style Cecilie wore, did not have the rich grace of the really expensive masks. The colors were brilliant, and it wasn't until she looked more carefully that she realized the hues lacked complexity and depth.

Okay, so maybe they weren't tourists. Maybe they were company hackers on a lunch break, showing off their net.knowledge to each other or to some poor management dupe from the upper floors. Cecilie had run into these kind before. The Sept sisters ignored them. They were good enough to access the three main levels, but their jobs generally revolved around databases and company networks and training new hires on whatever slutware packages their companies routinely used.

They looked over, saw Cecilie and didn't acknowledge her. Her generic costume on this level meant that she didn't belong—or that she was Sept and no business of theirs. Which was just as well. Cecilie had no desire to be polite to suits, even if Signora Tima did call it "marketing" and tried to encourage all the apprentices to be helpful to potential clients.

Besides, thinking about it all was just putting off the inevitable. Procrastinating and figuring out amusing little tasks she could justify as research didn't get the job done. Even through the interface she could feel her stomach knot and her knees go weak. She wanted to sit down on one of the benches and breathe hard until it passed.

Only it wouldn't pass. It was guilt and distaste and a childish wish that if she waited long enough it would all go away.

It wasn't going away. It was a wall. Even this sojourn on the third level of the net was a diversion. In order to really do anything she would have to go to the deep level and swim in the datastream itself.

She had practiced on the oceanic level maybe once a week since she had been in Signora Amelia's seminar, but she had never been there entirely on her own. That was Sept territory alone. No other users knew it existed. There were six Sept territory levels, several of which were for maintenance and the rest of which had been built gradually as the Septs slowly took over the various functions that kept the net running. Every level had its own special uses and designs. Signora Amelia had emphasized the oceanic level as particularly useful for both building and testing security systems.

Slowly she waded into the pond. There were other, much more orthodox ways to access the deep level, but she liked the idea of this one. She had never tried it before. Signora Amelia had mentioned it a few times in seminar as an "evasive tactic." At the time she hadn't comprehended exactly what that might mean.

There was no sensation of water as such, but Cecilie could no longer feel her legs. They were immersed in the deep level. She felt as if she were melting—no pain, just a strange sensation of disassociation. Then her head sank beneath the water and the deep-level transfer was complete.

She was a finite point of location in the consciousness that was the infosea. Movement was rapid, fluid, everything in neat packets on a definite course. There were tides here, connected to the currents and eddies that were the direct routes of the datastream itself. Here there were outcroppings and reefs and even the sunken wrecks that marked pre-net sites and libraries.

The oceanic metaphor level was one of the deepest constructs in the net, and it was not wholly human-oriented. This was where the millions of machines that composed the net and the humans that swam in it could interact most directly. Here beneath the surface interfaces, the data structures were more vulnerable, more amenable to intervention. This was where the security shield would be weakest. This was the eternal back door, created by the Septs and maintained by them in secret— a secret easy enough to keep from those others, but important enough to guard zealously. A secret that even if known could not be used without training and practice and knowledge of the paradigms that had formed it.

The Septs had created this level of the metaphor and the Septs guarded it. All their luxury and power and wealth were enticements to keep this expertise private.

Cecilie moved through the medium that seemed to her to glitter like water. But moving there was nothing like swimming, or like moving through any of the other layers of the net. Paths were mutable and currents often diverted and changed. There were only the markers, the lighthouse posts along the way. Each lighthouse was a site, and each site opened into a vast lagoon that had been shaped by artists and by Sept-Prado and by the users themselves left over from the time before.

Signora Amelia had taken the seminar group to the Disney Network lagoon for practice. There the structures were familiars of childhood and yet completely appropriate in the underwater world. Sleeping Beauty's castle looked like it was on the bottom of a giant aquarium, and the Little Mermaid's long red locks floated like scarlet seaweed. Here Sept-Prado had not altered the iconography—there was no need. Everyone understood just what those images represented, and it would have been heresy and an assault on every childhood in the world to transform any of them in even the slightest detail.

Which was not always the case. Most companies had not been designed by the likes of the Disney artists, and experts from Sept-Prado had spent thousands of hours trying to establish a visual base for most of their clients. Cecilie was certain that the Bank of North America would be one of the stodgier and less appealing lagoon sites.

She knew the lighthouse series to get to the banking archipelago, and she was there almost as quickly as she could think through the steps. The datatide swept her along, then broke on the first barrier reef to the entire mass of islands. Each island contained a lagoon, each belonging to a single bank. The barrier reef was only the lightest security, purposely made so that authorized users could enter easily.

The first reef was far simpler than any of the constructs at Disney. There the security had to be invisible so that the site would look as if there was nothing at all hidden. There the reefs were brightly colored and covered with bright fish and seaweed to distract from their function. Sea caverns made in the likeness of classic movie sets hid other project interfaces that were still secret.

Here there was a path through intentionally threatening coral branches and the poisonous tentacles drifting innocuously around the jagged spines. There were colored fishes and flashing electrical eels on their watch patterns. But there was a way through. The barrier reefs were made to be traversed by someone who knew how to look for gaps in the defenses, who understood that to travel too fast would attract attention from the eels and to go too slowly would summon the neon watchers.

Cecilie hung back and watched the reef. She watched how

the rest of the sea flowed around and through it, how the sea images wove together and parted, where the random timing had been done and where a regular watch schedule had been set. And then she saw it, the smooth rock between oversized outcroppings of coral. It looked vicious but it was large enough to admit the watcher fish and packets from the stream.

Here in this medium she didn't have to image her body. She could be one more packet sent on the tide. She retreated to the nearest lighthouse, where she could reconfigure her own exterior read, and then launched into the datastream with the brightly coded red and green and orange packets on their way into the lagoon.

Being passive was hard as she was whisked through the medium and rushed toward the reef. It looked too close, the coral ready to pounce, the rigid spines to tear and grab. The energy pulse shoved her through, diverted her just as she was about to hit a spine and spun her quickly on her side. Disoriented, she was flung down an obstacle course that she couldn't have negotiated on her own. Preset paths and switches diverted her from danger after it already seemed too late.

And then there was silence. The water shimmered pale turquoise-green and everything was full of light. After the turbulent passage through the reef, the lagoon was a paradise of calm.

Cecilie took a moment to finish shaking, as she did after riding the big roller coaster she'd initially hated but felt obliged to try lest Julietta call her a coward. The reef was scarier than any roller coaster Julietta had ever found, and now in the safety of the aftermath she felt the backwash of terror blossom after any reason for it was past.

She had been deposited in a holding site, a central pool with eddies and links to various structures, all piled over each other and shifting position through the lens of the illusion. Several of the constructs went transparent as light touched them, and she could see through five or so at once, as if they were objects made of glass.

Now she had to find the site she wanted among all the strange icons in the lagoon. Not the stolid bank icons that showed up on the kiosk menus and marked the commercial-banking segment on the Mall level of the net, these had been changed into sea myths and images that bore no relationship to their names or functions. She had garnered all she needed about the internal workings of the bank programming on the Commercial level, where the company had a great deal of say in how its image was interpreted.

Here, though, everything was interpreted differently. In fact, Cecilie wondered if the executives and computer departments of the various institutions had any idea of how they appeared here. Most likely not. They properly shouldn't even know this level existed. Even if they did, this was not exactly territory where they were welcome to come, and the back doors by which they could enter this level were carefully safeguarded by Sept security.

She had been only to nonsecured sites on this level before. And while nothing here was safeguarded the way it was in a more public venue, there were still barricades and defenses, the first of them being identification. Whoever had plotted this lagoon had had a vivid imagination.

Looking around, Cecilie could identify the wreck of the *Titanic* and the *Nautilus* and three Spanish ships with great red crosses on their sails. When she looked more closely she could pick out Sinbad's boat and a great white whale cavorting with a great white shark. Each one was a banking icon.

No, whoever had designed this had not only a great imagination but a twisted sense of humor. She wondered if the other lagoons were equally strange, if perhaps one had all the characters from *Alice in Wonderland* and another was full of figures from the Old Testament. It would make as much sense. Which was none. Which was what Sept-Prado needed to do for their own sanity, she supposed, after trying to appease clients with neither imagination nor humor.

But she had to choose something. Vaguely she identified the three Spanish ships. Columbus had sailed to North America. It made as much sense as any other representation on this water-logged menu. She pointed at the ships as if she were reaching out to touch a board.

The focus froze. Everything went two-dee, and then there was a flash of blank green before she found herself facing Bank of North America yet again. The representation had changed to dry land, and this was now an impossibly high skyscraper that belonged in a financial district. It dwarfed her and made her feel that finding what she wanted was going to be impossible. Defeated.

And then Cecilie realized that was the whole point of the image. It was no more a true representation of Real Life than were her own chalk white skin and the glittering ruby tear embedded in her cheek. In fact, as she looked more carefully, she realized that it was the same building she had seen in the commercial sector earlier.

If there was a way in, it would be a back door. Utterly obvious. So obvious that it could even be subtle. Cecilie abandoned the steel façade with its blackout locks and ID ports. Instead she walked around the structure, which seemed to go on forever. She turned two corners with no sight of a breach in defenses. She turned two more and still found no sign of the back door that had to exist. Though there was no guarantee that she was near the back yet anyway. She was starting to tire and become frustrated. She went around a fifth ninety-degree angle, one that was more like sixty degrees, and the seventh corner was more like an S curve. And then she saw it tucked into the curl of the S, and was thankful that at this level no one bothered to write in smell. Because she would have gagged.

There was a dark gap in the faceless building. Dumpsters full of garbage guarded the shadow of a door. They had not been emptied in a very long time. Cecilie noticed that they were over-full and that whoever had created them had bothered with fine detail like tossed cups and candy wrappers in among the piles of shredded paper and coffee grounds.

Cecilie slipped between the dumpsters. Even though she knew there was no support for high-level kinesthetics here, she was sure she could smell the stench and her stomach protested.

She tried the door. It was locked. She smiled. It would have been ridiculous otherwise. Just because Sept security always left a back door didn't mean that they had to make it too easy to get in through it.

She examined the mechanism and could see nothing. Probably passworded. The designers had been of her own Sept. The back door was not only for their personal convenience, but for the Sept as well, in case some other sister was called in a decade after the designers had died. There were a few passwords that were common to the Sept. Now all Cecilie had to do was figure which one the San Francisco team had used.

Not Orff, that was too musical a reference and she didn't think that any other city had quite the musical advantages of Venice. And Nevada was older and too obvious for North America. Then she licked her lips and said, "Men's eyes." It was the password she would have used.

The door didn't budge. Cecilie could have sworn that she had chosen the correct password. There were others, certainly, but she reined in her frustration and thought about it logically. The designers had been from the Sept's San Francisco Headquarters House. The bank was also North American. Cecilie thought about it a moment longer, and then carefully translated the phrase into lightly accented English.

The door opened a crack. Cecilie slipped inside and closed it behind her, hearing it lock shut. She was in. But she was still identifiable as a foreign body in the workings.

She crept down the one dark corridor with her back to the wall. Her hand brushed something soft and she recoiled. There was no one inside, and she touched the soft thing again.

Sung and McElroy did leave themselves an opening. Cecilie pulled on the janitorial overalls over her Carnevale costume. Now she was camouflaged as a mere utility function against the automatic telltales and tracers. She wished she could get Zizi inside to do her datasearch. Zizi would be faster than she, and less noticeable.

Still, it had been almost too easy, she thought. So she knew how Signora Amelia always left access and how Signora Tima told them never ever create a system that a Sept sister couldn't penetrate—in case she were hired on to do additional work, of course. Always keep things in the family. No doubt there were harder ways to go.

At an intersection in the corridor was an in-house information kiosk. Cecilie pulled up a datamap that managed to miss all the interesting sites, but at least it told her where not to look. Figuring out what was missing and what ought to be there might be difficult for some half-trained Company hacker, but for her it was easier than the final exam in the subject two years ago. Signora Tima had taught them what kinds of references should be deleted or layered or embedded elsewhere for internal security. Now that lesson worked well in reverse.

She had three good bets as to where to go. The map showed her where the transport banks were, transports just like the ones on the Mall level only with much more boring icons. She sighed and pressed one that didn't appear on her map. The system didn't question her.

Typical. There was much less security from the inside. The transport opened, not onto a typical library, or even a terminal-access area, but into something like an old-fashioned bank, with a high marble counter and human-seeming tellers behind ornate brass grillwork. The tellers were retrieval familiars, like Zizi but less sophisticated and autonomous. Though Cecilie never had heard of a bank that promoted autonomy.

There was no line. She asked for everything Signora Tima had requested, names of principals and their percentage of voting stock, recent acquisitions and mergers and loans to affiliated companies.

"I'm sorry, I must request your codeword clearance for that data," the teller informed her politely.

Cecilie smiled tightly. Now or never. There were a couple of good guesses left from the stockpile Zizi had brought: names of children, names of pets, names of grandparents of the CEO or board members were all good bets, and Zizi had given her that much. Family names were public record; pet names were registered with the appropriate licensing agencies. She was glad she had built in a subroutine that consistently gathered that data on any inquiry request, whether or not she specified.

So start with the CEO and work down. The first name on his close family list was Alister, the border collie. Without hesitation Cecilie gave the teller the name.

The teller blinked twice, processing much too slowly for Cecilie's liking. And then she was handed a transaction script that would immediately transfer the full complement of data to her personal account. She took the script as if she were bored and walked slowly to the transit box. Just in case she was being observed she punched the mop icon and reappeared right outside the broom closet where she had entered.

Thinking about it, Cecilie nearly laughed. The designers of this system, her own Sept sisters, had been both very obvious and very clever. There was no reason at all for a virtual establishment to have a maintenance service, or a broom closet, or dumpsters or overalls. People who lived in the meat world would never question it—they were much too accustomed to custodial personnel to even see them. Even those who were more conversant with the norms of virtual space wouldn't question the image. They would simply assume that these were appropriate metaphors for the boring but necessary housekeeping subroutines and dismiss them out of hand.

Even Cecilie hadn't found the incongruity striking until she actually touched the mop icon that was found in every building in physical reality. And then she had only realized that the mop and the idea of a broom closet and the overalls she had pulled off and replaced where they had hung were not the usual guise for routine machine functions. Silently, as she slipped out through the back door, Cecilie admired the elegance of the breach.

Maybe that was why she had been sent here in the first place. Signora Tima knew there was an easy way into this system, at least for someone who was careful in her work. That set Cecilie a bit on edge. Maybe the whole thing was a set piece and she hadn't violated any confidentiality and she wasn't guilty of sin and criminally liable to boot. If she had worried herself sick about a fax run she would be very angry.

In fact, she was angry. Angry at Signora Tima for misleading her and angry at herself for not realizing that no one would ever really ask her to violate Sept codes on that level.

She was so angry that she didn't think too carefully as she left the lagoon. From this position the reef was easy to traverse. It was only getting in that was hard.

The anger overcame everything else, even the relief at having made it through something that was much simpler than it ought to be. She hit the first lighthouse marker, familiar from her childhood, without even a quick scan to see if it was occupied. She passed by the chipped red reception desk with full schematics and transfer data spread all over it, and headed directly to the Sept lounge. No one was ever in the marker-point lounges—Cecilie had often wondered who had decided that they must have hard backless benches and scuffed linoleum floors. Someone had gotten carried away with the word "lighthouse."

She heard someone chuckle and she started.

"Very nice. Now, if you'll just hand that script over to me . . ." the stranger said.

She turned briskly. There, standing as far from the splintering benches as possible, was someone in a full Venetian mask. It was a custom job, very expensive and beautifully tasteful. The face was a Renaissance sun and the golden flares twisted and twined in the marker environment. The body of the costume was sky blue shot with gold, shapeless as all good costumes were to hide the body underneath. But Cecilie was certain this was a man, however well concealed. He was not only tall but broad in the shoulders, which Cecilie found amusing. He could have chosen to hide more carefully. Or to deceive her.

Signora Tima! Or one of the other Mistresses of the Sept, who would know where to find her and what she had been after.

She shook her head slowly. "I know who you are," she said, the fury just banked in her tone. "I'll give you what you wanted when I get back, only I'm going to want some answers. Like why did you lie to me and why did you have to make me believe that I was doing something—evil?" She hissed the word.

The figure in front of her did not respond immediately. When he did speak he seemed just the slightest bit confused. "I didn't know you knew what I was after or that you would give it to me," he said. "We've never even met properly. And if you did know what I wanted, I wouldn't believe that you would give me anything anyway."

She was off guard and angry, certain that this was not one of the signore from the Sept-House. From her Sept-House, anyway. Or from her Sept at all, from any of the other Fortune Houses that dotted the globe. There was something not quite— Sept-Fortune in the choice of words, in the precise design of the mask. She did not feel the familiarity that long years of similar training and experience bred in all the members of Sept-Fortune, no matter what their generation or city of residence.

"Tell me who you are," she demanded, sure that now that the game was over it would be a member of some other Sept who had just made senior apprentice. This was an initiation joke, perhaps, but she was already tired of it.

"You don't know who I am," the sun said. "And it wouldn't matter anyway. I just want that script you have in your sleeve and then you can forget you ever saw me."

"This isn't funny," she snapped. "It wasn't funny to begin with and now it's gotten really boring. So why don't you just get back to your own Sept-House and leave me the hell alone, okay?"

Sept-San Marco, she was willing to bet money on it. This person had the same brand of arrogance. Signora Tima often mentioned Sept-San Marco, and not pleasantly.

Even with the impassive mask, the sun managed to look confused. "I'm not from a Sept. I'm not from any Sept. Give me the script or I'll publish the tracer I've got on you, with ID. Even Sept ID. Give me what I want and I'm gone like I was never there."

"Oh? For how long? Until you decide to use the tracer on me again?" Cecilie asked.

"No, that's the deal. You get your records, I get the bank's records, and we're even," the sun explained.

Then Cecilie began to worry.

"You're not from Sept-San Marco?" she asked as a scenario came full-blown to mind. This bank with its easy back door had been set up to be used as a test by all the Septs. One of her Sept brothers had followed along on his test and was gathering his data. From her.

It made sense. At least it made a lot more sense than anything else. That was just the kind of thing she'd have expected from Sept-San Marco anyway.

The sun laughed at that question, too. "No, Cecilie, I am not from any of your precious Septs," he said, slurring his words. "And you don't have any idea who I am. So why don't we just complete this transaction before I turn over my trace records to the authorities and let them deal with you and the Sept both."

"Go ahead," she sneered. "You haven't got a real trace anyway. Anyone who really was Sept would know that I didn't break into a real database so the data is useless and so is your damned trace. So you can just crawl under whatever rock you crawled out from."

The sun began to laugh with surprise and good humor. That startled Cecilie more than the demands and the derision. Even more than her outburst, which had frightened her. As she had said the words she had been aware that his traces would be perfectly good and that intent had nothing to do with breaking security codes. And if the data was only fake, that was the thief's problem, not the court's.

But she had been given too many ultimatums lately, had been forced to do too many things that she hated. And she wasn't going to give it all up because some jerk in fancy dress threatened her. Maybe it wasn't smart, but she wasn't always smart. Sometimes she was just plain mad. This time she was angry at everyone, at her parents and Signora Tima and the Sept and everything she had done for the past day.

Only her parents and Signora Tima and the Sept were not there, and the figure in the sun mask was. Cecilie felt not the least bit of remorse over her outburst, and was even angrier over the laughter.

Finally the sun stopped laughing. "Damn, you're good," he said. "I mean, I knew you were good, but you're totally off the scale. I didn't expect to be that impressed."

Which didn't make any sense at all. Not that Cecilie cared. "I'm not here to impress you, Mr. Smartypants. I'm not sticking around to listen to your patronizing, snooty drivel, either. I have a job to finish and you can just sit on your hands or you can get out of the way. And be real glad we're not in the meat world, because if we were I'd turn your face into mashed potato."

Her hand darted out and plucked the grey trace file from the sun's taunting fingers. Then she began transfer procedure to the next marker.

The sun blocked her path. "No you don't," he said. "That was pretty impressive but I'm not going to let you get away with it."

"You can't let me or not let me do anything," Cecilie snapped at him. She began to weave the connections on the pale green routing map tacked to a dingy wall that had maybe been pale pink. A corner of the map was torn and it was faded across one side. Cecilie didn't even acknowledge these fine details as her fingers touched a series of dark triangles and red lines that looked just like the highway map of the Venato her father kept tucked in the Bible.

The sun pushed between Cecilie and the wall. He was large, bulky enough that he could hold her arms at her sides and prevent her from finishing. That didn't matter, Cecilie thought with satisfaction. She'd created most of the transfer before he even realized what she was doing.

He grabbed her arm as she tried to fade into the protocols

that had appeared as a freight elevator opening in the wall. She struggled but he surrounded her. The doors chimed and tried to close as Cecilie bit his arm. Then she felt embarrassed. That was a fairly minor tactic here, even if it had been effective on that drunk Sept-San Marco apprentice a few months ago.

"Then promise to meet me," he said as he pulled her slowly toward him. "Tomorrow night at the Café Luna. For music. Music that'll completely change your life." And he snatched the datapackets from her as she bolted back to the elevator.

Now the elevator was gone. Only pale pink walls with layers of grime remained smooth in the place escape had been. She was too late and he brandished the data he had taken from her, gloating.

Cecilie couldn't believe that he had actually done that. Twice. Well, if he wasn't Sept there were a few tricks he wouldn't know. She had seen that kind of attitude before and knew that he was trying to take control of the situation.

In his dreams, Cecilie thought. While he was busy with his little victory dance he had given her time to summon her familiar. Zizi appeared through the wall in a flurry of blue feathers. She pointed to the grey trace file and the bank data tucked under the sun's arm.

The familiar was smaller than many, but it still was large enough to be threatening, and its beak was sharp. The bird of paradise did a lazy turn and then dove like a peregrine directly at the sun.

The masked thief dropped down instinctively as Zizi swooped down from the ceiling, and he lost hold of the files for a fraction of a second. That was all the time the familiar needed to pluck the papers delicately from the floor and make off with them.

Cecilie smiled slowly, nastily. "Checkmate," she said. " 'S over."

The sun shook his head. "It's only starting," he said. "You might as well decide to work with me now. The two of us together could run the universe. Who else knows that there's someone else in here, someone running around in your precious secret levels? Or that there may be more wild cards than just me. You. Me. That's it. The Septs don't know."

Well, he hoped the Septs didn't know. He couldn't believe that any organization was sensitive enough, flexible enough to pursue the matter even if Cecilie had reported it.

Cecilie silently cursed that this was not a physical medium. She would have loved to bash his face in, put her fingers though that elegant mask and obliterate it and the sparkling, satisfied eyes behind it. How the hell had he known?

And then another figure appeared. This one wore a human face as a mask, an ancient human face that had been weathered colorless and wrinkled so that all expression was present at once. Cecilie wondered why anyone would choose such a mask with so much else available.

"So that's where you went," the old man said.

The sun darkened visibly and Cecilie realized that the old man was talking to him, not her.

"I was careful," the sun replied. "No one could trace me."

"I traced you," the old man said acerbically. "You should know better. This was very stupid, David. You are not usually stupid, so I will give you another chance. But you have been very very lucky and what will you do when your luck is all gone? What will you do when someday one of your little games doesn't work?"

"What about her?" the sun asked, illuminating Cecilie.

The old man sighed. "I suppose we should bring her along," he said after some hesitation. "We can use decent Sept work. But it was still very dangerous, David. What if she reports us? What if she doesn't believe you? Then what?"

Cecilie listened, amazed. She thought she understood and closed her metaphorical eyes. She would have liked to take off her mask, to see this David without his. Because now she understood that she had been set up.

Maybe the whole thing was a setup and Signora Tima was involved and the whole Sept as well. Only that was too crazy. This was too crazy. Her head spun. At least the data was safe with Zizi.

She should run. No matter what they wanted, it had to be bad for her. Otherwise they could have just issued an invitation, not played all the games.

And yet while Cecilie was frightened and angry, she was too curious to leave. She wanted to know what they wanted. The whole procedure felt faintly like the games that had brought her to the Sept.

"I suppose we should invite her for some sherry," the old man said. "Perhaps you ought to do that and explain it all to both of us. Because I did not authorize you to find anyone else."

The sun sparkled even more radiantly than before. "But this is one we can use, Artos. She's Sept. Sept-Fortune, in fact."

The old man, Artos, seemed to huff indignantly. And then he disappeared.

"Don't worry about him," the sun told her. "He'll really be very pleased when we're in the meat world. But we have to be careful. This place is secure but Artos doesn't believe that anything or anyone is ever secure. So . . . I will contact you. When we should meet. You will come, won't you? To hear the music. Then you'll understand."

Cecilie shook her head. "I'm confused. You don't have anything now and I'm out of here. Why do you think I'd show up just because you asked?"

The sun smiled, an intoxicating smile that she could credit only to the finest maskmakers. "Because you're curious. You won't be able to help it, you'll have to know. It'll make you crazy. But tomorrow night at eleven you'll find me."

"Oh, and how am I going to find you?" she asked. "You're going to be all blazing like you are here? Or are you just going to be this much of a jerk?"

She didn't wait for an answer this time. He didn't try to hold her as she called up the elevator that appeared in the blank wall, but she shouldered him aside hard anyway. To make up for the tension, for the indignities. For all the miseries of the past twenty-four hours.

She was going home now, to the Sept, no longer innocent. She would give Signora Tima the maybe false data and she would destroy the trace Zizi had stolen. And then she would go out and buy clothes and become a senior apprentice.

All her dreams and goals were about to be realized, but Cecilie felt only tired, and dirty, and disillusioned with the whole world.

4

David Gavrilli stretched and opened his eyes. It was late afternoon, and the ceiling shimmered with the reflection of the water in the canal below. The old lady's squint, the Venetians called it. The only place in the world where they had a special word for that particular ripple on the ceiling. David usually thought it charming, but today he didn't notice.

The old man had nearly ruined everything. How Artos could just blunder in like that and pretend to take charge . . . Gavrilli sighed and pressed his palm to his eyes. The old man still thought he was in charge, that he had the great plan and that David was simply his best and brightest tool.

And David knew it was his own fault. He had let the old man believe it, had played impressed with the palazzo and the interface and all the amenities the old man had provided. Though of course they couldn't compare to home. Not that the old man knew that.

And even if he did know, even if he knew David's family

name and the balance in his Swiss account and the full inventory of houses, vineyards, islands, artworks, even then the old man would think that he had given David something very special indeed. Because the old man had brought him to Venice, and to a Venetian there was nothing of greater value. Even the meanest apartment in Venice was worth more in their eyes than the largest and most perfectly appointed town house in Rome. Venetians were snobs.

Sometimes, like right now, he wondered why he bothered playing to the old man. He didn't really need the help, not even the introductions and the bitterness Artos carried. He could do it on his own, and better, too.

He had the Pietà singer who couldn't get enough of his body and paid dearly in music and information. Though what information came out of the Pietà often tended to be fragmentary and useful only when fitted with other data from varied sources. Still, he would have preferred the singer's bed to his own. At least the old man hadn't traced him there. Yet.

But the old man had that nearly forbidden music, and in the end it was the music that kept bringing David back. It was the music that opened his mind and gave him the greater vision, the soaring moments when he realized what could happen if only the Sept system were broken. If anyone could be free to access without all the layers of the kiosks and the Mall separating them from real interface, there would be a revolution. The Septs would die, their stranglehold on the infosea swept away in the datatide.

And there would only be freedom and movement and improvisation like a sweet sexy riff that turned and invented itself again and again, tossed between instruments until it had grown tears and smiles in all the wrong places.

Or so David thought in his optimistic moments. This was not one of them. He could have managed things with the Sept sister, and the old man almost made it fall apart. Even now he had little idea if she would actually show up, if he could get her to listen to the jazz, corrupt her soul so that she would lead him through the levels he couldn't quite comprehend.

He wasn't sure she truly understood them, either. The Septs behaved as if they were the ultimate repository of all knowledge about the net. Their skills and training were legendary. But David Gavrilli would not, could not admit that they might have some edge on him.

Only because he couldn't become one of them. He had been recruited when he was seven, his parents contacted. And he had known what the contact had meant and had lain awake anxious for nights hoping desperately that maybe this time they would see reason.

There was no basis for this hope and his parents reaffirmed all his sureties. "You, an apprentice?" his mother said, her cultured voice sneering at the word. "As if we couldn't buy and sell them fifteen times over." She had sighed. "I suppose they do offer advantages to the middle class, but why should David have to go to a lesser school and spend all his time learning access that he can hire someone to get?"

"And who else would take over the business?" his father had asked.

His father had never had to say any more. For over a hundred years the Gavrillis had headed one of the greatest trade consortiums in the world. David knew from before he could talk that he was already apprentice to his father's position, and his grandmother's before.

It wasn't fair. He had an older sister. But there was something wrong with Serena, something that all the money and the best clinics in the world didn't understand and couldn't change. And so when she was eight and David had been only five she had been sent off to a residential school for other children like her. David remembered only that she didn't speak and sat in the rocker for hours and hours and would sometimes shriek and knock her head against the wall.

He had to make up for her as well as for himself. There were things in life that interested him that had to be put aside. He was expected to be excellent but not to do anything about it. Never to go on. While he had had the raw talent as a skier, he had not been permitted to pursue the serious training that he needed to become an Olympic racer. He had always loved music and his parents thought it appropriate for him to study piano until in his passion he had auditioned at one of the world's greatest conservatories and had won a place. Then he had been placed under lock and key for months to prevent him from taking it.

He had wanted the Sept training more than he had wanted both music and skiing together. They had exiled him from his real life, from everything he wanted and loved. He was the heir of the Gavrillis and that was the end of it.

When he was eighteen and no longer a minor, David Gavrilli had disappeared. There had been a major police effort and his parents had appeared crying on the news, begging the kidnappers to release their son. They would pay happily. Anything.

They never received a ransom demand and the trail was cold. But David still needed the old man for a place to live where he didn't have to pay rent or create a new ID, if nothing else. He had money that couldn't be traced, access that was clean. Better than he should have done as a runaway, he thought angrily.

Because at eighteen he wasn't really a runaway. He was an adult and had some right to his own life and to his inheritance. Which he couldn't touch without revealing where he was. Or at least *that* he was. And he couldn't let his parents know yet, or else he would be dragged back and locked into the country house the way his sister was locked in at her elegant hospital.

The Gavrillis were great merchants, but the Soldanis, his mother's family, were either great artists or crazy. His father blamed his mother for his sister's condition. One thing David had always feared was being put away like Serena, being crazy.

His mother was not crazy at all. She had been a poor girl with a beautiful voice, a singer in one of the great Venetian choirs. One of her brothers had been crazy, she admitted, and taken away when she was twelve. But there were others, two uncles and an aunt, and there had probably been cousins that he had never met.

It was at least a reason people understood for why he had come to Venice. He knew that it was a stupid choice in some ways. Staying hidden here would be harder. His family would look more carefully in a place where they knew he could run to grandparents and cousins. And he pretended that was the reason he had chosen this place over New York or Paris or Vienna.

He could also say that in Venice he could go masked and there would be no questions. Which was true. Most people in Venice masked most of the time. Scholars said that people masked more since the Sept days than in the worst periods of the Carnevale, where nuns would go in their bautas to meet lovers and gamblers would wear long-nosed plague masks so that their creditors couldn't find them. So David Gavrilli could wear the masks he had bought, the wonderful golden sun and the filigree exotic and the white-rose corpse, and never be recognized even by those paid to watch for him.

He told himself that he had come to Venice to escape. Sometimes he almost believed that here he could find family and peace and simply be a real person.

In his heart he knew that was a lie. He had come to Venice for the Septs. If he was only close enough he could get what he craved. He knew this.

David Gavrilli had never gotten what he truly wanted in his entire life. He had been given what everyone else thought he should want, or what they wanted. That was why they could not find him. Why would the heir to the Gavrilli fortune spend his time wandering the narrow lanes of the Sept island in Venice where the overly ornate crumbling grey walls made canyons of the street?

The Septs had their own island in the lagoon. It was not theirs exclusively, but they were the predominant force and there was something in the air that reminded him of the currents in the infosea. The economics that made Venice the center of the Septs were well known to him. He had been trained far more thoroughly in economics than he had ever desired.

There was an old law on the books that the huge old palaces could not be broken into apartments that people could afford to buy. No one could afford the palazzi, and those who owned them could not afford to keep them up. People had moved out to the surrounding countryside, where much of the techno-industry of Europe was located. Venice was nearly abandoned, adrift, far too expensive to be viable, but still dreamed of her glorious past.

The Septs could afford the great palaces easily. They could afford to keep them up, and they needed the space. The city had always been a merchant concern, with little respect for anything but beauty and success. The Septs were very successful and so Venice welcomed them home.

The Septs had been good for Venice, too. They had brought in thousands of people who had lots of money to spend and who could afford services that were rarely used anymore. There was money to be made; artisans and specialists and merchants returned and prospered. The choirs and the traditions of masking, which had died in the harsh light of Reason, were revived.

David Gavrilli had known all those things, but he still had

not been prepared for Serenissima when he first arrived. He had wandered through this area in the mask of the corpse with white roses. The costume and mask were covered with a great veil that floated around him and isolated him from any contact with the city.

Near the Sept-Houses he was a dead thing, and the costume, while being without gender as all good costumes were, still seemed to Gavrilli quite feminine. The features of the mask were delicate and there were the silk roses that covered his hair and were sewn all over the shroud. The flowers all were colors shaded with death, pale cream with yellowed edges, blush pink and some that whispered peach tinged with grey.

He had bought the costume because it was different from anything he had ever seen, and it was sad. Maybe it wasn't a mask at all, he had thought, but his true face while he wandered exiled from the Sept life he knew he should have. Behind his white mask he watched the apprentices come and go from the island in their uniforms. He could tell the different colors and plaids, the grey and blue of Sept-Fortune and the red and black of Sept-Lyon and, above all, he watched the navy blue and green of Sept-San Marco. The boys in their little blazers and ties all trooping together with their schoolbags chattering like pigeons made him want to cry. He should have been there, one of them. Not in the cold of the outside.

He had stood like that for many days, had wandered the streets until the old man had found him watching the steps down to the lagoon water as the last motoscafo's wake left a silver trail to shore. The sunset had turned the water bloodred and the stone steps burning amber. In the distance he could hear the voices of the Pietà singing something clear and tenderly heartbreaking. Palestrina, he thought, remembering the pleasure of his piano lessons as the music had taken shape under his fingers. It had been a long time since he had played.

"Have you ever heard jazz?" the old man had asked him. It was an innocuous question, Gavrilli thought. And the old man certainly seemed harmless enough, a perfunctory eye mask not hiding his age. The old man tossed crumbs from a crumpled bag he held out onto the stone steps. Pigeons fought over the stale bread.

"No," David admitted. "It wasn't permitted at home. My mother was once a singer."

"Ahhhh," the old man had said. "A singer with the Pietà? Is that why you wander here, to hear the music she sang for you when you were small? And you are sad because you have not inherited her talent and feel exiled."

David had nodded, amazed. Not that the old man had it exactly right, but he was closer than anyone had ever come.

The old man sighed again. "We're all exiles here. Only those children have a place forever, and then they feel like exiles among the rest of us. But you still love the music."

David did not respond. Saying that he loved music was not reasonable, any more than saying that he loved to breathe or to eat or to walk out into the sparkling November sunlight.

"You love music but you've never heard jazz," the old man said, and his voice was filled with wonder. "Of course, it isn't entirely legal in this city. It isn't completely forbidden but it isn't exactly approved, either. It lives in that grey area where all of Venice lives. Nothing here is ever clear or simple or exactly what it seems. Everything wears masks."

The old man sighed heavily. David wondered how to edge away without seeming rude. The old man was just some old pensioner who had nothing better to do with his time than to feed pigeons and talk to strangers. While David—David didn't really have anything better to do either. At least not today.

"But there is a private jazz party tonight near the Lido," the old man said, seeming happier. "Here, let me write down the address for you. Do you have a pocket in that costume of yours? Come around ten tonight, before then it's just the social crowd on their way around the parties before they start gambling. The real music people don't arrive until later. And of course no one would play questionable music before questionable hours." The man chuckled at his feeble joke.

"Who are you?" David asked edgily.

The old man smiled. "You can call me Artos. That's enough for the people at the door. Tell them Artos said you were invited and you'll be fine."

A bell started tolling across the lagoon, a large bell that sounded out death and danger at sea. David watched the last of the color fade from the sky. When he looked next to him the old man was gone.

He took a gondola back to the pensione, a small and ragged place where they didn't look too carefully at the forged ID they read into their records. Someplace that had a better monitor or a more current reader would have bounced him, and so he had no choice but the places with cells like a monastery and one shared bath down the hall. A place that accepted kiosk cards or cash, no questions asked.

The first night in the pensione had been an adventure; the second night there was still a tinge of excitement. He was living like "real" people, without all the advantages of the Gavrilli accounts and retainers. By the fifth day he hated the stiffness of the sheets, the smell of mold and disinfectant that seeped through the walls, the sound of the toilet flushing in the early hours of the morning and the rhythmic thumping of the bed against the wall every night when the man next door came in from the bars with a new conquest.

In five nights and six days wandering Venice in a white death mask, he had found nothing at all. He was no closer to the Septs and no closer to his mother's family. Maybe it had been a mistake, he considered. Maybe it was worth his father's stern lecture and his mother's tears to go back home and give up, become the heir the Gavrillis wanted and forget all the sweet dreams of freedom.

He had planned to leave the next day. A week was long enough, especially for David Gavrilli, who had never had to wait so long in his life, who didn't think he could live one more night in the Lysol stench with the constant thumping from the room next door. He was all ready to swallow his pride, so what would one evening with some music and a little human companionship matter?

He had had little to do with others since he had arrived. He knew no one and hadn't cared to know anyone for as long as he'd been in Venice. David was starved for company, for the sounds of casual chatter and a fleeting smile of perfunctory hospitality, and he hadn't realized that that was the problem. He assumed it was his thwarted desires.

Watching the boys in the San Marco uniforms he felt more clearly cut out of them than he ever had surfing the infosea. His fantasies were smashed to shards, all his dreams evaporated like spun sugar in the rain. Only the hard reality of grey stone and silver-green water remained, mocking him and reminding him that he had made a choice. And he had chosen wrong.

He wasn't even sure about going to the party for a while. Lonely and miserable, he could only imagine it would be worse surrounded by beautiful people who all had companions and were sought out and desired. David Gavrilli remembered being popular that way and always assumed it was for his money and never for himself. At least this would be one more thing to do, to prove that position. He would go to the party, he would be ignored and rejected, and then he would always know that whenever people showed an interest in him they really were interested in just one thing.

The more he reassured himself that he would be miserable the more he was certain that he had to go. Finally he steeled himself to take his soap and small towel down the hall to the common shower, which was empty at the beginning of dinner hour. He washed in the tepid water to the sound of old pipes humming. The pensione bath was stained enough that he never felt completely clean.

He didn't even towel his hair dry before returning to his room. There was a small sink and mirror affixed to the wall. He shaved and combed his hair, and then put on the sun costume for the first time.

The blazing sun costume was the first he had bought when he had arrived in Venice, but he had never wanted to wear it before. It was beautiful and bright and it drew attention. The sun mask was gilded and adorned with pearls. The costume that covered his entire body was the pale color of the summer sky. Gloves and shoes that matched were part of the costume, and when he was fully dressed not one millimeter of skin or hair showed. The only part of David Gavrilli that anyone could see was his eyes through the holes in the mask.

He took a water taxi to the address the old man had given him, and was deposited on steps leading from the house to the water. It was the first time he had arrived at a proper Venetian front door.

Inside the house was brilliantly lit. He could hear the laughter and catch phrases of song as he saw elegantly masked people glide behind the windows. For a moment he wanted to go back to his pensione and return home in the morning and call this Venetian adventure a failure.

But this was the last night and the first party, and he'd heard about parties in Venice. He'd heard that the whole city was so old that its decadence was no longer merely dissolute, but had acquired forms and structures and traditions of its own. From the darkness in front of the party-bright house he could believe that.

Then he shook his head. This was just more fantasy. He had found nothing depraved or even deliciously risqué since he had arrived. The masks made everything so alien and unreal that he had to think to remember that, stripped of their exotic disguises, Venetians were exactly like everyone else. And this party was probably like every one he had ever gone to in his life, with the same caviar and the same salmon mousse, the same expensive champagne and the same dull gossip as every other party in the world.

It was ten past ten when he went inside and decided over the course of seven seconds that it was like every other party in the world. Then someone small in a pale green and gold costume came over and took his gloved hand. "The Count says I am to take you upstairs," a female voice told him, her Italian accented just slightly in either English or German. David couldn't be sure quite which.

He followed her obediently through the party rooms and up what once had been a grand staircase but was not in good repair. The stone changed color about halfway up and his guide noticed him look at it.

"That was from the last flood," she told him. "They weren't sure if they could even save this house, the silt was so bad. But we managed." She shrugged lightly. "That was when I first came here and met the Count, digging out all the mud."

She laughed lightly. David suddenly had an image, not of the glamorous foreigner who drifted through dreams, but of a serious architecture student in work clothes with her hair pinned up untidily wading in muck boots through sludge. How often the foreign students had come to help the Venetians reclaim their city one more time. The mud angels, they were called, and someday the lagoon and the Adriatic would have their own and reclaim the city that had encroached for so long. Every time it threatened, and every time the Serenissima recovered again, a little more tawdry and frayed around the edges.

The mud angel led him to an upstairs parlor, done in muted blue and rust silks with large tassels on the ornate chairs. Maybe twenty other people were gathered up here and most of them had already unmasked. Many were young, or at least appeared young. When he looked more closely he realized that their appearance was not the result of good surgery. They each sported imperfections that would have been corrected before grade school in any other city. One man with beautiful dark hair had a nose that was too long, and several of the women had mouths that were not full and overripe. No one in the room seemed to have the cheek implants that had become fashionable over the past few years, and one man had ears that stuck out and hadn't even grown his hair long enough to hide them.

They didn't talk to each other like the partygoers downstairs, but whispered what conversations they had almost furtively and rarely remained with anyone long.

The mud angel removed her mask, and David was disappointed. She was not pretty; at least, she had done nothing to make herself pretty. Her nose was reddened and her hair was limp and pulled back sharply with barrettes.

But then, with the masks, no one would bother much with their appearance, David thought. Which was a great shame. In Rome and Paris and New York, where no one masked, people went to expensive hairdressers and even more expensive surgeons. Everyone was beautiful and everyone worked at it. Here one merely purchased a mask. And when the masks came off they were a collection that mirrored the gates of Hell, all irregular features and less than perfect symmetry in their faces.

He was appalled, and reluctant to remove his sun face at the same time. Without it he was clearly revealed as not Venetian.

His nose had been shaped, his teeth straightened as was only considered decent grooming in the rest of the world. He was nothing at all like anyone else in this room.

He was saved having everyone stare at him when the lights dimmed and he could take a place in the last row. There he removed his mask while no one paid any attention. All their eyes were on the small dais on the far side of the room, where a drum kit and a bass rested.

Four players came out. One of them was the old man who had invited David, and the old man carried a sax. It took David a moment to identify the instrument. Another was a redhead with a scowl that David found enticing. He had never seen anyone approach music angrily before, and it fascinated him.

Then there was only music, music the like of which David had never heard before. It wandered, it re-created itself, it reminded him of Mozart but the structures twisted like Escher prints. His brain felt like it had been wrapped around a Mobius strip. Heaven and Hell were the same place and they were both in this room.

He had no idea how long the music lasted. He was aware of songs changing, tempos that made him want to dance melting into yearning desire or mourning tears. When the music ended and the others got up from their chairs and left, David Gavrilli could not join them. He was stunned. And he was not the same person who had entered.

He did not realize that Artos had come up to him and begun talking at first. Snatches of melody filled his head and he was reluctant to have to come back and listen to mere words.

". . . considered the possibilities of bringing this structure into other parts of the world?"

David blinked. He wasn't sure he understood, or even wanted to understand.

"Jazz is a revolutionary force," the old man said patiently.

"Whatever you want to do in your life, if you listen to it you will find yourself more alive, more able to see different possibilities."

David gulped. "Do you use piano in this?" he asked.

Artos laughed. "Of course. Some of the best is done on piano. So, are you really a player, then?"

David nodded. The music had left him defenseless, and suddenly the whole Gavrilli clan had become immaterial. The Septs—well, there was something useful here too. All of a sudden he wondered why he had to be Sept to experience the full range of access he craved. Why he had to have their approval and training to do whatever he wanted. There was no law that limited him, no particular reason he knew that bound him to choose.

Because there was no choice. He wasn't Sept, couldn't become part of their closed system. His privilege had barred him more than his talent had made their skills accessible. The Septs were like ancient alchemists to him, who would guard their secrets to the grave unless an apprentice took all the correct initiations and passed all the tests.

But subtly, with the new music quivering in his brain, he realized that everything had changed. There were no rules anymore. He could take the motif he had been and reinvent himself like a riff improvised on a theme. His family and the Septs had not given him choices.

So he could hardly refuse when the old man asked, "Would you like to stay and study?"

5

This is beautiful," Signora Tima said after she inspected the data Cecilie had dumped in eyes-only hard copy on her desk. "Better than I could have hoped."

Cecilie said nothing. Signora wouldn't be so pleased with a fake. There was nothing she trusted anymore. Nothing at all made any sense.

Signora hummed in her throat. "You know, Cecilie, I had hoped that you'd test your promotion before the Board meeting. So that by the time they arrive you'll be a full voting member of the Sept. We're on the verge of a new world here. If we can manage to work together we won't have to put up with all the annoying unlicensed dreamboxes and all the kiosk-riders who need their hands held. It's the new age of the net that we have been working for ever since the Septs were merely a handful of a million working groups."

Cecilie gulped. She had heard vague rumors and dreams about a net run only by and for the Septs. Where the outsiders would be kept in their own proscribed places and could be truly denied access to the inner workings. She had always thought it merely fantasy. The net had always been a jumbled anarchy, and while the Septs had made great strides in organizing a coherent whole it was just not possible to keep absolutely everyone confined to the public areas. Or maybe not, she thought. Maybe it really could be done. Certainly it seemed as if Signora Tima believed it, and Signora was usually two steps ahead of the rest of the world.

The Board meeting was just another Board meeting. They happened every two years. The only reason this one was special to Cecilie was that it was scheduled to take place in Venice, and Sept-Fortune would be one of the major hosts. All the great designers and net.ninja would be here. She might even get to meet the sisters who had created the security system she had just breached. The idea made her skin crawl.

She looked down at her hands in her lap, not daring to look into Signora Tima's face. Her breathing was rapid and she felt disoriented. She wanted this interview to end, for the world to turn back to normal. Somehow she could walk out of this room and the past two days would never have happened and nothing would change. Everything would be perfectly reasonable. She hoped.

And she knew that it wasn't possible.

"You have the afternoon off. In fact, I'll credit your account and you can go shopping," the Sept mother said, smiling. "How does that sound?"

"Thank you," Cecilie managed, but she could not force the enthusiasm into her voice that she thought the older woman expected. Even the prospect of shopping did not attract her. She would rather go home and hide in her room, turn on some music and try to forget everything. Again.

Instead she got up and left Signora's office and walked across the loggia. She wandered downstairs to the courtyard and into the back corridors of the house. She could smell the leftover scents of lunch still heavy near the kitchen, but all the noise was gone. Suddenly she realized that she was hungry, that it was late in the afternoon and she hadn't eaten all day.

Well, it was after lunchtime and no one should be there now. She had a right to take an extra slice of cake, a bit of bread, as she had missed the meal. The kitchen doors were not even latched yet.

Cecilie went in and fixed herself a sandwich, a very thin slice of prosciutto on bread with a slab of red tomato and some basil over it all. She wrapped the sandwich in a white napkin and wandered out of the back door wearing only a half mask so she could eat.

She walked down the blind back alley to where it met the street and wandered toward the center of town. In the distance she could hear the deep tolling of a church bell and music carried light on the breeze. Not the Pietà, it wasn't loud enough to be so close by. It had to be one of the other choirs, rehearsing something by Haydn, she thought. Though she only caught snatches of it; she could have been wrong.

Tourists crowded the streets as she came closer to the main square. Tourism was rampant even at this time of year, and the millions of people with their talking guides in their ears and their uniformly ugly shorts made her avoid the central part of the city. Usually she could manage to stay away from their rude inquiries, usually prefaced by a request for a language she might speak but of which she generally preferred to feign ignorance.

She managed to keep to the shadows and drift by the organized groups, the school seminars where all the students were busily trying to avoid their chaperons and the serious art tours where sour-looking elders stared unhappily at various examples of this or that period of architecture while trying to absorb all the data in the talking guide. Though they did stare at a city native in a half mask as if it were remarkable, as if there were not more people on the street in the full white masks of the city than had their faces exposed.

Cecilie managed to stroll and munch, enjoying the tepid warmth of the day and the excitement around her. She finished with her sandwich, wiped her hands one last time, crumpled the napkin and threw it into a trash barrel already half full of cups from a popular ice-cream shop. This was Real Life, here in the taste of a snack and the bright red tour guide's umbrella.

Stealing in past a secure banking system and taking something that she was not even sure was real data receded like a bad dream. Between the polyglot bus groups and the student intellectuals, all with their ice-cream cups and tiny shovel spoons, the past day was simply not believable. There was nothing at all she could touch to bring it back.

She smiled slowly. The worst was over. And she was going shopping. She went down two more short blocks to the maskmakers, thinking that something new for the concert would be nice.

She wasn't supposed to go to the concert. She wasn't supposed to listen to any music that was not approved and programmed. But then, she thought she wasn't supposed to hack through security systems set up by her own Sept, either. She was already on the wrong side of the line. Going a little further didn't matter.

She went to Vincezo's, one of the most famous shops in the city. Not the very best or the biggest, but known for quality work and some originality. Besides, the owner's brother and prime designer was a neighbor and his daughter, Luisia Maria, was Cecile's age. They had grown up together and Luisia had taken Cecilie to the shop many times when they were little girls, and taught her an appreciation for fine design and what to look for in a good mask. Even if she wasn't shopping it would be nice to see Luisia Maria again.

As usual, Luisia Maria was behind the counter looking at her screen when Cecilie walked in.

"Hello," Luisia Maria said before she looked up. "Can I help you with something?"

Cecilie giggled. Luisia Maria had a habit of not paying attention to her surroundings. "Do you speak French?" she asked in that language, in her worst accent.

Luisia Maria began to answer when Cecilie pulled off her mask. Then Luisia Maria joined her laughter.

"Are you looking for something or were you just nearby?" Luisia Maria asked. "We have some new software masks that are experimental but quite beautiful. I think you'd like them, if you want me to bring them up."

Cecilie shook her head. "I'm not looking for software," she said. "And I don't know what I want. I mean, this is my first real grown-up mask. Maybe I'll just look and see if something feels right."

Luisia Maria shrieked. "You mean you graduated? Oh, Cecilie, congratulations. Pick out anything you want. Daddy would want you to have it as a graduation gift. That's so exciting."

"Oh, no," Cecilie demurred. "I mean, I have this new account and got a bonus and I wanted to purchase something like a grown-up. You know."

Luisia looked a little disappointed, but smiled anyway. "Sure. Though you know Daddy'll skin me if he knows I let you pay for your graduation mask. But I know what you mean. I just sold my first design into production."

It was Cecilie's turn to squeal and hug her friend over the counter. "But you only finished your first year at the design institute," she said, amazed. "Your family must be very proud."

Luisia nodded shyly. "They are. But you know, it was because of them and some luck that I made the sale. There are better designers in my class. Just that Uncle Carlo had a sales rep in from Milan and I was there with my portfolio. So it just happened." She colored and hung her head. "Anyway, there are some new things here you haven't seen yet. One or two are mine." She blushed even more furiously.

Cecilie stared at the masks on the wall. There were hundreds in every color and composition. There were gilded masks and the traditional whites with black rings around the eyes. There were the jeweled masks, painted in delicate pale tones and decorated with designs in silver and goldwork, set with precious and paste jewels. There were masks made entirely of pearls and others that were famous character masks.

On another wall she saw the familiar sun and moon masks, and hesitated. If he had been the sun then perhaps she should take the moon. That was a traditional and complementary pairing.

But she didn't want the moon, though there was a pale pretty one in delicate shades of midnight and morning. The one she wanted was on a different wall, all black iridescence with three glittering diamond tears and silver filigree over one eye. The silver ran over into a lace fan at the edge, where it would cover the domino.

Cecilie took it down off the wall as if in a trance. "This one," she said. She hadn't even asked the price.

"And the rest of the costume?" Luisia Maria asked, encouraging. "You could wear this with a plain domino, of course, but we have a high velvet turban and the robe and gloves to match."

Cecilie nodded. She didn't trust herself to speak. She could already see herself in this disguise, silent and powerful behind the shadows. She could even meet the sun-mask for music on his own terms disguised as the Queen of the Night.

Luisia Maria returned, her arms filled with black velvet and
diamond glitter dust, purple satin and black suede and links of
silver filigree. She sorted the pieces on the counter, a turban with
dazzling rhinestone chains dripping over the end into a tassel
that fell over a black velvet shoulder. The heavy sleeves of the
overrobe were held back by bands of purple satin, jacquard ribbons with silver threads picking out the rich pattern, which
matched the underrobe that started at the knees and fell to the
floor. Black suede shoes matched the gloves, both patterned
with sparkling starbursts. Yet for all the jeweling the costume
looked refined, tasteful, almost sober. Perfect for wearing outside of the Carnevale time, impressive for those who understood
the subtleties of Venetian masque and too plain for those who
did not.

"I'll buy it," Cecilie said.

"Don't you want to try it on?" Luisia Maria asked.

Cecilie shook her head. Such costumes were made to be
worn by anyone. They were always large and full, hiding her
female shape as well as her features. What mattered was that it
was beautiful and of a piece.

"Shall I have it sent?" Luisia Maria asked. "Your measure-
ments are still in your profile, we can do the tailoring and have
it ready by . . ." She consulted the readout on her register.
"Wednesday."

"No," Cecilie said. "I'll take it now."

"But you'll need at least three inches off the sleeves and
more on the hem," Luisia Maria protested.

Cecilie smiled, face-naked. "I'll take it now." She replaced
the street mask she had worn as Luisia Maria debited her account and wrapped the costume in tissue and then folded it into
a gilt box. The box went into a red lacquer bag with gold tassels on the handles.

"Is it for a party?" Luisia Maria asked. She had heard about the Sept parties. They all had. Stories filtered through the city like water in the canals.

Cecilie saw the faint wonder in the other young woman's face. As if it was so wonderful to be able to go to parties and see anyone you wished, not to have to marry or have to sleep with the same lover for more than a night. Cecilie knew what Luisia Maria thought, even if all the stories had been exaggerated and twisted to the point that no one in the Septs could recognize them.

Though it was completely ridiculous. Sept sisters married and had children and quarrels with their husbands. They worried about good nutrition and where the children should go to school and whether they should invite their in-laws for a week at the beach.

They didn't have to marry to live well, that part was true. But the romantic rumors of unbridled license at Sept parties, of their orgies and debauched revels that rivaled much earlier days in Serenissima, were more the products of imagination than any reality. Cecilie had giggled with Julietta and Valentina over the image of Signora Tima at such an affair. Or any of the signora-teachers of rank.

She had also been trained to never let outsiders know about Sept life. In the beginning it was just fun. As she grew older and dealt more with the world of RL, she realized just how prudent those precautions were. And so now she merely smiled tightly and shook her head. "No parties," she said. "Just streetwear."

"Have fun," Lusia Maria said sadly.

The walk home was like flying, like surfing in the system, Cecilie thought. Buying a new mask was such a special thing, taking a new face and persona. She walked through the streets with the bag that proclaimed to all that she had not only bought a mask, but that it was from one of the finest shops in town and was a full costume. She was not a tourist with a souvenir, but a native who had selected new streetwear, a new disguise in her hometown.

She peered out the smallish eyes of her plain white mask at the people around her. She wondered whether one of them, face-naked or decently disguised, was the radiant sun she would meet so soon. Thrill ran through her, a sexy small tremor that made her insides as liquid as the infosea. Soon. Soon.

The largest rehearsal hall at the Pietà was prime performance space. The ceiling had been painted in the sixteenth century and the walls were covered in greenish grey silk moire, without the mirrors that were so popular in most of the grand spaces in the city. Mirrors were terrible for the music and so there were none in any of the public spaces at the Pietà. Performers had to make do with the dressing rooms and students were reduced to using the washrooms.

The second choir was standing in its place after rehearsal. It had been a new piece and it hadn't gone well. Lina was tired and wanted to sit down. It wasn't really their fault the new work was so ragged. They had only been given the sheet music two days ago and there had hardly been any time to study it. Though, to be honest, in the few hours she had possibly had free she had been too distracted by the coming jazz concert to concentrate on learning new music.

She was ready for the tiresome tirade that Maestro always let loose when they were less than perfect. All she wanted was for it to be over so that she could sit down. Her legs ached, her back was tired and her shoulders were tense. That was not good for the sound, either, and she knew it, but the rehearsal had had a very unpleasant feel to it all along.

"This piece is important," Maestro ranted in his usual voice. "We are performing it on a historic occasion. It has been especially selected to aid the work that we are facilitating and you should be thrilled that you are going to be involved. The second choir, you aren't even fully graduated yet. And still, we have been employed to keep constant music and the Pietà has never let the Septs down."

"What historic occasion?" Sean asked. Sean was never afraid to interrupt Maestro with a question, a habit that had not endeared him to the upper choirs. So he was still stuck with them when he should have been promoted long since. Which only served to make him more obnoxious.

Lina stifled a yawn. She thought Sean had to be dense not to realize that he was ruining his own chances. With his voice and musical expertise he should have been a soloist in the first choir by now, and not a mere member of the second, but he had never mastered the Italian proprieties. And the more adaptation would help him, the more stubbornly Sean clung to his abrasive ways. Lina agreed with everyone else that Sean had a death wish. Or at least he had no ambition in the Pietà.

Which was odd. If he hated it so much he would have no trouble, with his excellent skills, in finding a much better position in one of the other choirs in town. Lina wished he would go. At very least she wished that he would shut up when she wanted to be dismissed, sit down, and not be subjected to yet another one of Maestro's lectures.

But Maestro did not start yelling immediately, telling Sean that if he valued his music, if he honored his training in the most necessary of the arts, he would learn to behave and not question every decision made by the Maestri of the Pietà Academy. Instead, Maestro put down his baton and motioned them all to sit. Lina was so grateful and surprised that she forgot to curse Sean's lack of manners.

Maestro sighed heavily. "We have a great commission from the Septs. All the Septs. They are having a meeting here in Venice, representatives from all the Houses all over the world.

And the reason they chose Venice for this historic meeting was because of the Pietà, because we are here and they need our help. We all know the Septs have fought blood feuds for generations. They have fought in the streets, made life difficult for us all. And this has been the case in every city in the world where there is more than one Sept-House."

Lina blinked. Maestro was being operatic. There had been no fighting in the streets between the Septs for as long as she could remember, and she had the impression that whatever differences they had ever had were not solved with fisticuffs. But it did suit the notion of history and the city to think of these as great feuds that would lead to such operas as *Romeo and Julietta*. According to the orthodoxy taught at the Pietà Academy, a little blood shed so that one could have such sublime music was a very good trade.

"But the Septs wish to negotiate a truce," Maestro went on. "They wish to reconcile their differences. This can only have a beneficial effect on all the world. And we of the Pietà are the force that shall make that happen. With the correct music we will be able to keep the peace during this meeting. We will set their minds at ease and foster harmony and even feelings of brotherhood among them. If the Septs are able to come to agreement for the whole world, it will be because our music has brought them the inner peace they need to effect the outer.

"Always we have held and taught that our highest responsibility was to keep the minds of the people sharp and their work focused. We have never attempted to hold a truce between warring factions. It is a new opportunity for the Pietà, a new goal.

"This music is new because it has been chosen with this new purpose in mind. When you rehearse, think of how you are supporting the good of all the world."

6

He had already decided not to talk about any plan before the music had done its work. She was Sept and her whole mind-set was ordered by the regularity of Mozart, the calm of Palestrina. This was only the first crack in the armor of a lifetime. This was her first jazz.

So David Gavrilli let the energized asymmetry wash his being clean, rearrange his thought patterns to something more spontaneous. Maybe something restless like the flutter of the music against the restraints of form. He had felt this recklessness before, that first time he had heard real jazz and fallen from grace in Artos's upstairs salon.

That felt like an aeon ago. He had been a different person in a different life then. He had not known how to really feel alive, not the sparkling alive that mingled danger and freedom and sex. The feeling that was greater than ideology alone—that feeling was his reason for his plan, his vision.

Because after he had heard that first breath of new music,

he had experienced a subtle alteration of his perceptions. Paradigms slid and shifted. Nothing was what it had been. Not even his desires.

He no longer wanted to be in any Sept. As he had left that house on the canal, he realized that he was unutterably free. He no longer had any past because he had no ambition. In that instant when the music had changed his soul he realized that all the structures he had lived by were mutable. The Septs, the old music, even the Gavrilli family thought they were ancient and represented some kind of absolute truth about the world, or themselves. That perception had been a lie.

At first David had seethed. He had been betrayed. Nothing he believed had been real and they must have all known it all along. That all the solidity and structure was merely another illusion laid over the honest complexity of reality.

He had not returned to the pensione that night. The next morning he settled the bill and moved in with the old man and started to learn to play jazz.

In the first year of his study he realized that he had not been willingly lied to by everyone around him before he had come to Venice. No, everyone he had known in that other Gavrilli life had been lying to themselves. They had believed all that claptrap about structure and reality, orderly thought and logical relevance. Maybe they believed it because they needed to believe, maybe because they weren't creative enough to see past whatever they were given. Garbage in, garbage out.

David Gavrilli lost the immediate sense of rage that had motivated him at first. It felt like a loss when he let it go. Without the anger he seemed to have no purpose.

And the music he played had no real purpose. It was not like the music of the choirs that performed approved pieces to increase associative intelligence, it was not to calm and soothe, to make complacent and comfortable and sometimes to pierce through with the sheer beauty of it all. There was more hurting than anger in the music, and more longing than he had left.

Though he understood the longing, understood the scratch-dirty pain in the blues. The hole inside him that had been full of rage and desire had gradually become full of hope. Somehow he was going to break the stranglehold on everyone's mind. He would tear down the Septs to their roots and root access.

The vision was his lover and he belonged to it utterly. He guarded his vision as merchants had once guarded their daughters.

He was not the only one the old man had recruited, had brought to the palazzo. He rarely saw the others. Most masked when outside their own rooms, and all whispered down the halls at odd hours, trying to avoid contact. David didn't care. Real life was to be avoided. The only life he wanted was in his vision. Nothing else mattered.

After almost a year the old man pronounced himself pleased with David's music and gave him the one reward that David had never considered. In the year that he had spent all his time with music and imagination, he had missed life in the infosea. But there had been so much to learn.

Now Artos brought David to a dreambox like the one he had used at home. Not quite as inviting, to be sure, but the interface was state-of-the-art even if the amenities were lacking.

David enjoyed that. He found that, after a year away from the dreambox and living for music, he saw everything differently. He entered through the Mall, which was the way he had always gone, the way the kiosk connections were linked, the way everyone always went. Only most people never went beyond the Mall level.

Now he saw the concourse differently. He was in one of the brass-marble-palm-tree decor phases, but he could perceive the faintest shadows of the other possible realities that were equally part of the program, merely incipient in the now. Suddenly David wondered if all the possibilities were present all the time, and if it depended more on the individual and the interface mechanics which rendition of the place one encountered.

The other people there seemed less substantial than he remembered. At least most of them did. A few gave the impression of weight, of tangible flesh, though of course there was no flesh at all.

At first he thought these were the ones who had been to the better maskmakers. The higher-priced software did give off a more realistic appearance as well as finer design. But then he stopped and really studied the costumes and masks of the more concrete participants, and many of the designs were merely second rate. The software might be better but without elegance and artistic superiority, David was not about to accept that these were merely the products of a better shop. No, an atelier that produced such fine detail in the Mall would take care that there was some reason to bother with the detail. They honored the truth that function was beauty.

The next two times he entered the Mall he noticed the same thing and started to follow the individuals who had impressed him. They all came from or went to a place just outside the Mall. A library.

Then he knew they had to be Sept. There were places they could go that he could not, and he had heard about the Sept center on the Mall level. So much else he had learned had been false that he could not honestly believe he had cracked their mystery until he walked up the impressive steps past the carved griffins and through the front door.

He was not barred. Maybe they thought it wasn't necessary. He found the reading rooms and began to explore, though he watched the solid-looking Sept members at their assigned tables. There were animals and legendary things that came in and out and reported to their owners. Once he saw a cartoon creature; another time he saw something from a famous picture. He watched the interactions and saw what they had brought to read, and saw that he was ignored.

Maybe it was just that everyone was ignored as a matter of course. Or maybe the fact that he could get in here meant that he was free to use what he could, to explore as he might.

Being raised as a Gavrilli meant that David was accustomed to privilege. He was used to doing as he liked, getting what he wanted, and so he didn't hesitate to take as much advantage of the library as he could.

There were things there that he was sure most Sept members didn't access, most of it data about the net itself. And so David learned off the early design specs for the datasea and how to surf the currents and ride the floeroads. He saw how once upon a time the whole was a chaotic hodgepodge where things didn't always fit or work. Reading more about the process of design and when the Septs came along and began taking over routine work and keeping the place tidy, he realized that the difference between the anarchist net and the organized one was much more a function of philosophy than technology.

This knowledge made him sad and angry and a little afraid. He began to read more, to access the vast history stored in this library's memory and storing it in his own. He was shocked to realize that the Sept system was barely a hundred years old. In that time they had risen from specialty working groups in a vast array of programmers to the only people with the training to create and dominate all of virtual life. Which meant all of life as he knew it.

He began to wonder if he were paranoid, seeing an intricate conspiracy where none existed. He could not deny the information he had retrieved, though. From short histories and Sept school texts he had gone into the sets of personal memoirs and to original source code. Everything corroborated his growing distrust of the entire net.

From there he went further, studying the Sept manuals on the whole of the net as they had reconfigured it in the first decade of their power. They had created layers and layers of levels that only they had the knowledge to access. Only now he had that knowledge, too.

He practiced in each of the stages as he discovered it, learning to swim in the oceanic tides of the infosea, discovering how to navigate the subbasement, where things sometimes grew on their own. He was discreet in his exploration, always afraid that some Sept brother or sister would come upon him and know he didn't belong. He had no idea what they would do to him, and he suspected that they might be willing to kill.

For months on end David didn't see the old man. He spent all his time in the dreambox and the library, where he didn't see any of the others, the wraith creatures who hid behind draperies and whispered at the table. He could believe he was alone in the old, old building sinking into the canal as the water crept through the stone supports. He was alone and he was obsessed and he was untouchable. No one ever found him.

But he couldn't do it all alone. That had been the final blow and the most painful. He had not yet paid back the old man in full, though he had every intention of doing so.

Soon. When the Septs were broken. When jazz was free. When he took control.

Once he had thought that to be Gavrilli meant to have power. Wealth was power, he had been taught, and authority. Trade and deficit and ownership were all power. Compared with what he had now, the power of the Gavrillis was a paltry thing. He looked back with amazement that he had ever considered it significant.

Now he was a god. He could create and destroy in the infosea, he could ride invisible and omniscient over the tides. He made music that shattered the structures of the mind and he embodied levels of reality beyond anything the Gavrillis could ever imagine.

He called up the image from the Academy in Florence, the white marble with the settled face created by Michelangelo, and then decided that he liked the Donatello David better.

"The Septs have always had power," the old man said one morning when he finally insisted that David join him for breakfast. "But they have always had the competition among them that has let power slip down the cracks like canal water. Now they know that and they are resolved to seal these the way we restore the ancient places. To make them watertight so that no one may enter. So that no notes can bore into their minds and restructure the whole."

After he had acknowledged his own power, the old man had returned with a full retinue of wan young followers. Most of them knew jazz but didn't play. Most, David suspected, didn't have the discipline to practice for hours at a time. Their languid soft hands were too weak for the keyboard, their skin too delicate for the strings, their palms never callused by a drumstick. And yet the old man expected David to accept him, to accept them.

While David was confused, he decided to play along. He wasn't sure yet if the old man and the wraiths could be useful to him, and the Gavrillis trained him never to pass up anything that might be useful. Which was how Great-Grandfather Vittorio had taken a reasonable inheritance in Roman real estate and turned it into a frightening fortune that spanned the globe and included foodstuffs and pharmaceuticals along with electronics and transportation and even textiles. Great-Grandfather Vittorio had never said no casually, never turned away an opportunity, never assumed that something was worthless merely because it was flawed. He bought it and turned it into what it should have been all along.

David had been taught these things. He knew that he had more of his great-grandfather in him than his green-hazel eyes and his heavy dark hair. Sometimes he had looked at his father, a pallid manager who wanted only to conserve wealth, and his mother, who had been a soloist at the Pietà at the age of twenty-two but had been too frightened to leave the compound since David had been small. They appalled him. Now he remembered who and what he was, and so he listened to Artos and played along carefully because the old man could be useful. In just what way David had not yet decided.

They were out to dinner at one of David's favorite places, where he could get pasta with spicy peanut sauce and ginger ice cream. It was one of the few cuisines that tempted David to eat at all. The old man kept saying he was too thin and should eat, eat more, eat healthful food. David was always too busy to bother.

"The Septs have been planning a meeting," the old man continued. "The kiosks are not so free anymore. And now the Septs want to take them out of the jurisdiction of the city and put them directly under themselves." The old man sighed heavily. "The one thing that we could always rely on was that the Septs hated each other. They competed against each other, this one in that market, the other in this city. All of them never trusting the others. I remember that when I was young. But now it's all different. And I hear that they are going to meet in some Grand Council and find a way to forge a monopoly. If they don't kill each other then they will succeed, too."

David smiled. "Maybe we should have someone poison the paté," he suggested.

The old man shook his head sadly. "I have considered it. Inelegant, and fairly out of date. Also much too easy to trace."

David was surprised. He had not thought that elegance in the classical manner mattered so much to Artos. But then, of course, he was a Venetian. David, as a Gavrilli, was much more concerned about what would work rather than aesthetics.

"No, I think it would be best if we were more subtle and provoked some dissension," the old man went on. "They have never been very happy to trust each other, but in recent years there have been too many mergers, too many marriages, too many parties. And if we could simply make sure that they split, perhaps into several major camps instead of splintering entirely, we would still be safe. Open. And they couldn't fix prices and access and take over the kiosk trade and do all the other things they want to do."

The old man lifted his glass and looked through the garnet Chianti as if he could read the future in the wine. "And they want to kill the jazz. That is the worst of it, and that is a thing they will all agree on. They will mandate music so that we all think like them forever."

David put his fork down on the pink tablecloth. He sipped his wine while he thought. His head reeled. Here was opportunity. The Septs' original function had been to keep and work in the system, the same way the roads were maintained and the parks replanted with impatiens every year. They could not be permitted to stop the music, they could not limit thought and being. The very image was beyond what David could bear. Suddenly his vision, his desire, grew and became focused for the first time.

He had not imagined the system without the Septs keeping things organized, keeping the postal records. How else could someone be punished, without a Postmaster or SysAdmin to revoke privileges in the case of misuse? Once upon a time there had been millions of local sites, but the Septs had been so much more efficient at the organization. And no one wanted to bother with things like "proper usage" and "harassment" anymore. Those, David was convinced, were leftover from the early days, when there had been no full interactive and only a few of the elite had access. It had been a different world, where people cared about things that did not concern him, like commercialism and etiquette. As if the system could be made completely profit-free or polite. Better not to pretend to try.

But no one pretended that it was either profit-free or polite anymore. The Septs lived off it and lived very well, too.

But then, the Gavrillis had made billions off riskier gambles. The Gavrillis—and himself in particular, David was convinced— were much better suited to running something as stunningly huge as a few billion cybernetic lives. They had experience running everything else.

The old man waved the waiter away. No second cup of coffee, no dessert to interrupt their privacy. "So. You're meeting the Sept sister. You got the data from her, didn't you? Was it useful? Was there anything that we can use? You took a terrible risk there, you could have exposed us, destroyed us. And maybe she still will. Because once she knows that we exist and what we are she won't have any choice and neither will they. And we can't fight all the Septs together head-on. This would be just the thing to create the unity that we have to break up.

"You were stupid, David. You are usually better than this. Now we're all in danger and maybe the whole world is too. Maybe we'll all be owned by the Septs by the time this is over. That's their goal. Or are you an impostor, a spy sent into my organization to destroy me? To destroy all the freedom we have left?"

He closed his eyes, not with fatigue but looking backward into a deep past where David could not follow. "We must destroy them before they change the music forever. While the world is still alive and open, while the window remains. Otherwise we will find that we can do nothing but watch as the world re-forms around us and we are caught in the change. Look at the Septs, at the access. How many identities have you created? Isn't it getting harder to establish each one? As if the system it-self were fighting your anonymity, your mask. Should only the Septs have the right to mask? The mask is our mark as civilized people. It renders us all equal, it gives us choice and fluidity. It even eliminates discrimination—who can tell behind the mask who is old and who is ugly? The mask is what has made us great. And the Septs are making it harder and harder to mask. Some-day they will strip the masks away entirely and we'll all be left with face-naked IDs."

David heard and didn't hear. He was too busy planning. He needed to see the Sept-Fortune apprentice and was terrified that she wouldn't show up.

He hadn't misjudged her, he was certain of it. There were moments, when he had found her, that he had been worried, but it never occurred to him that she might betray him now. Not when she was crucial to his plans.

He had first observed her when they were fishing in the bit-stream, thought-lines cast down into the rapidly running flow that glowed with dizzying thread striations. Catching the cor-rect thread and tracing it back to the dry land, perhaps all the way back to the Library itself, was something that took great patience and training and talent. Snagging a Sept sister without her knowledge had been even harder.

David tried to cast down a thought-line into the stream. He used one of the Sept rods, a simple thing patterned on a simpler time. He drew back the long line and threw it with all his strength into the bright water. He came up empty. He cast again and a second time nothing bit. Then he wondered what was wrong and he realized that he had forgotten to bait his line. He considered for a moment, and then he cast once more, this time impaling an image of himself through the shiny hook.

The catch was firm. He felt as if someone had grabbed his head and wrenched him into some other level of existence. His awareness quickly flushed from the stream and into the infosea, where he saw/heard/knew his own diffusion and inconsequence.

In this place he was nothing at all. Frustration turned to anger quickly. He was young and strong and he should be able to affect things around himself, but the information that was the matrix of the sea was liquid, infinitely adjustable. It merely eddied around him and created new paths and microcurrents in the limitless array.

And then he was lost. He felt as diffused as the reflection of himself in the matrix. He was in the mix, part of the entire sea, and he lost coherent thought, for how long he could not say. When he had come out of it he was no longer in the net, but in his bed in the palazzo with late-afternoon sun resting on three dark irises in a jar. Outside the open window he could hear the measured strains of Haydn sung by one of the off-island choirs. The music and the flowers, the balance of atmosphere after the insanity of the datatide, calmed him. The terror and the anger seemed far away, locked where he could observe them without being touched. The calm had been her aura, her touch.

This state had remained constant for two days. Every morning he was wakened to songs by Mozart sung by choristers on their stately way to the workstations and palazzos of the Septs, their song setting the entire population for a productive, orderly day.

David did not enter the Sept levels for two days. He spent his time quietly, using the normal channel feeds and dutifully following major threads. He wore his own ID, his own face unmasked as he would be ashamed to walk in the streets. For two days this equilibrium held intact. Then he heard someone playing jazz in the dark hours just before dawn.

He didn't know who was playing, or even what piece it was, and that surprised him. He thought he knew the literature whole, was fluent in the variations. Only outside his window, open to admit the spring breeze, he heard an instrument he could not identify playing music that was so sad and sweet that he wanted to cry. He felt it inside himself, this music like nothing any of the choirs ever sang, any work group ever played during working time.

The low, sonorous sound wandered and wailed, it curled around itself in twisted loops that no program could even repeat, and then it drifted away like smoke from a cigarette.

He tried to follow it. His thoughts coiled and undulated with some pattern that never followed a datatide. It was as if some part of his brain that had never been stimulated before had been turned on and he could *see* things in formations that had never existed before. Or rather, he could now perceive things that had always been there under the layers of order and sanity that seemed to dictate the infosea. Now he could see that they were only the skim-layers of organization.

Inside the sea he had been aware of something that had been built on the sensuous curves of this new music. It was regulated but free, utterly beyond the direction of the Septs and the users. It was even beyond the old man.

This was a power he couldn't identify, and yet he knew that it was this power that had linked him to the Sept sister. This is how they had been found, found each other. She had been something else moving, fluid and free of Haydn and Brahms. She had known his soul and had recognized him, or so he decided in this delicious moment of heady command.

The Sept sister would come. She had to, he knew it with something like despair. The music would convince her and his evidence would show her that they had been born to rule the world together.

The old man didn't understand, but he was useful. His wraithlike followers were useful, too. Once David got Artos to give him the details so he would know where and how they got their information and where they were placed, David would be able to use them the way Artos couldn't begin to imagine.

He would do something good for the old man someday, David decided. Once this was all done, he would make sure Artos had music and masks and all the parties he could want. David was vaguely grateful for the time he had had to explore, but now it was time for him to act, time to leave the old man behind.

Artos stood up and adjusted his mask. "I hope for your sake she comes," he said. Then the old man was gone and David was alone with his hopes and fears.

It was early still, too early to go to the Luna. But David did not want to stay here and think about what the old man had said. He wanted only to be ready when she arrived, to create his new and impossible world. So he got up and checked his mask, then turned on the little power switch to make the sun blaze and sparkle.

He found that Artos had cleared the bill, so he left a tip, a large tip because no one had interfered and the food had been good. Then he went to Café Luna on foot, hoping that the walking time would eat up the early hour and his restless energy.

Outside, the city was far too friendly. Tour groups were leaving the large restaurants, and groups of students moved through the streets. It was crowded and warm and everyone looked at his magnificent mask.

Someday, David thought, *someday they will look at me because I am me, because I am the owner of the world, because I broke the Septs. Someday they will look at me.*

He didn't realize that when he thought that he had imagined

his parents and the old man, not the tourists and the throng in the street. He didn't think about his family on his walk to the Café Luna to get lost among the crowds.

Sean paced around his living room biting his lip. He had failed again. He couldn't keep still about any of it, and now he was going to fail David as well. He walked from the oversized draped windows to the front door without seeing any of it.

Like everything else, he hated the apartment. It had come to symbolize all the other failures. He was old enough to move out of the student dormitories, but did not rank high enough in the choir to be offered one of the beautiful apartments the Pietà owned and kept for their stars. Sean had been in one of those apartments once and remembered the antique moldings on the ceiling and the parquet floors. He would never live in a place like that, just as nothing else good would ever happen to him.

And he could never go home.

Sean had come to the Pietà late, at fifteen. Males were not permitted to audition until they had attained their adult voices, for obvious reasons, but most who had the voice clamored for admission as soon as they could possibly be accepted.

Not so Sean Douglas. He had been forced, sent away, exiled. His family had cut off all communication, not because they weren't proud of him but because they didn't want the authorities to trace him. Sean would still be arrested and imprisoned if he were found. The leaders he had respected had convinced him that the Pietà was safer than a convent and far more acceptable—at least for someone with a voice like Sean's.

When he was agitated he remembered everything he had left behind, only over time the memories had become softer and more alluring. He remembered the warmth of singing with his father and uncle and his uncle's girlfriend, who had a voice like an angel. He didn't remember all the fights with his father and all the times his uncle had called him a disgrace to the movement and an uncontrolled child and not a disciplined freedom fighter at all.

Mostly there was just the memory of the music, and of Michael Brennan. Not of Michael's funeral, at least. He had not been permitted to go. The authorities would be looking there, his comrades told him. The authorities didn't frighten him. Mrs. Brennan did. She had gone over to his parents' the night Michael had died and cursed him and dug her nails into his throat. She had threatened to turn him over herself, had said that he was responsible. She had cursed and screamed, and then in a low voice said that he had killed Michael, had led him to the movement and then lured him to the bomb site.

Sean had said nothing. He had stood there with tears running down his face knowing that it didn't matter who had done what, or who had led where.

Mrs. Brennan would never believe that it had been Michael who had turned their anger into something more organized. Michael had been the one who had contacted the underground and had brought Sean into the cell to swear his life on a Bible and a gun. The bomb had been Michael's idea, too, though they had flipped a coin to see who would deliver it.

But then, Sean would have done anything Michael wanted. It was his greatest weakness and he knew it and he dared tell no one. Especially Michael. Michael would have lost all respect for him if he'd admitted that he didn't really want to build bombs in the basement of the old firehouse. Michael needed him. And Sean had been very good at building things. Once he had wanted to be an engineer.

Sean knew he was wallowing, letting all the past hurts build the present one. The present one was bad enough. He had not gotten on to the choir that was going to sing for the Board.

David needed him at that meeting, needed the information as it was being discussed.

David needed him the way Michael had. And David loved him more than Michael ever had, though Sean felt guilty even thinking it. Michael was dead and had therefore become perfect. And Michael was part of home, part of all the careful, comfortable memories and the songs he sang when he was alone.

They were old songs of an old country where music was revered far more than it was here. At home people understood that music was not a scientific tool to create patterns of thought, but the center of joy and strength. There music mattered for itself and not only for what it could do.

Being here at the Pietà not only betrayed Michael and his old comrades, it betrayed music as well. The music here was never pure, never about expression and feeling. It was always about work, about productivity, and so Sean found it hollow.

The way he was hollow, the way even his rage and his insatiable insolence was at the core meaningless sham. In the end, he served nothing and believed nothing. Or so he told himself while he paced, waiting for David.

Maybe David would stay tonight. Sean had planned dinner, something simple with fish and potatoes because he had never learned to cook in the complex styles of the Continent. But then, maybe David wouldn't stay. He would probably be disappointed in Sean, and more concerned with the Board meeting than the dinner and Sean's hopes.

Sean thought that only fair. He had failed again and David should make him pay for the mistake.

So he paced, wondering how he was going to tell David the bad news. It scared him. He imagined that David would get angry and leave immediately, not even stay for dinner. Then he would never see David again, and would not ever really feel alive again.

He heard the footsteps on the stairs first. It was an old building and the lift was unreliable so David always took the stairs. Sean tensed, moved to the door and then back to the middle of the room, uncertain.

David knocked, ignoring the perfectly good bell, and Sean had to go open the door. He had barely closed it behind his visitor when he blurted out the bad news. Bad news never waits.

"I wasn't chosen," Sean said miserably. "I'm not in the group to go to the Board meeting and I won't be able to change that. Maybe I can find someone who would be willing to report on it but no one else has any notion of what you need. I'm sorry. I guess you'll have to find someone better."

He stood trembling in the middle of the room. David came over and put his arms around Sean. "It's not a problem," he said softly. "We'll figure things out. Now, what is it that smells so good?"

7

Cecilie stood in front of her mirror adjusting the new mask. She had taped up the sleeves so that they fell to the midpoint of her very elegant gloves. And she had rewrapped the headpiece three times, making sure every strand of hair was tucked under the black velvet cap. Really, this costume had been a very sensible purchase. It would do her well when the Board arrived, representatives of all the Septs from all over the world. Major Septs sent people from at least every continent, and every minor Sept was invited as well.

Most of them would have some kind of mask. If nothing else, a souvenir picked up from one the cities where identity was considered a very private matter. So few cities in Real Life respected private business. Unlike the net they were all used to, where identity was very private indeed, people in too many places thought that there was something subversive in masking. Or so Cecilie had heard, though her only real experiences out of Venice were ski trips and beach excursions.

Here the Board of the Septs could walk unknown through the streets. That made security easier, which reduced cost, among other things. Cecilie remembered Signora Angelina saying that over dinner the other day. Signora Angelina was in charge of housing and security for Sept-Fortune, and they would host several sisters from other Septs that did not have Houses in Venice. Smaller Septs aligned with their own. Signora Angelina had been scarce recently, much too busy with her duties for the Board to be concerned with training mere girls.

In this mask and outfit Cecilie didn't look like a girl at all. Behind the black and purple mask and wrapped velvet cap she could imagine a senior Sept sister who was respectfully called Signora Cecilie and had a two-floor corner apartment in the House with double-height windows and a fireplace that had been restored to working order. She imagined that she was getting ready to go to the Board meeting herself, instead of some underground weird concert that she regretted agreeing to hear.

What use did she have for music that could hurt her? That couldn't make her organized and smart the way the Pietà always did. And yet, she had heard enough about jazz that it intrigued her.

"Dinner," her mother called from the kitchen.

Cecilie placed the mask over her face and fixed the eye holes so that she could see easily. "I'm going out, Mama," she called.

Her mother came to the door. "Now? Why didn't you tell me? And that costume looks very expensive," her mother said, tugging lightly at the shoulders and straightening a seam.

"I'm invited out to dinner and to a concert," Cecilie said, aware that her cheeks were warm and glad of the mask that hid them. "It's a celebration. I thought I told you."

Her mother shook her head and sighed. "I suppose now that you're a senior apprentice I can't tell you anything," her mother said. "But be careful, you know, don't go anywhere near that group that hangs down at the Luna. And be home by midnight, or at least call. Do you have money for a taxi?"

Cecilie obediently showed her transport card.

"Now, I want you to take a taxi if you're out late. Don't let some stranger drive you. And remember, you still have to go in tomorrow."

"Thank you, Mama," Cecilie said, and kissed her mother on both cheeks through the mask. Then she fled out of the apartment and down the stairs before her mother could think of something else to check or another stricture to add.

She was early. And she had lied to her mother, just like she had lied yesterday and this morning. It was becoming too easy, but at least this lie was harmless. She had really only been invited to coffee and whatever before the music started. It was still early and she could have pretended to eat and make conversation at home. But she was too excited to eat and it would have been very hard to sit at the table and not say anything at all. Not that her parents would understand it. Or maybe they would and that would be even worse, Cecilie thought.

Cecilie arrived at the Luna just as the door opened. The chairs were still mostly empty and carefully grouped around the tables. A bored man in a black velvet half mask asked for her ticket. Cecilie was flustered. She had been invited, she hadn't thought about a ticket. The concerts she went to didn't require them. The choirs were paid by the Septs to sing; Cecilie had never had to think about it before.

Now she didn't know what to do. She didn't have a ticket. Gingerly she held out a kiosk card but the man waved it away. "We're sold out," he said. "You don't have a ticket you're out of luck."

Cecilie blinked behind her mask. "But I have a ticket," she said, hoping it was true. "I was invited and someone will be coming to meet me. Someone in a sun mask. He has the tickets."

The ticket taker looked unimpressed. "Don't care what kind of costume anyone wears and I don't care when they show up, either. Only you got to have a ticket to get in. Besides, it's way too early. Nobody'll be here for an hour or more anyway. Why don't you go around the corner and get a smoke or a coffee?"

The last was said kindly, but made Cecilie no happier. She turned down the street. On the corner were two young women, about her own age. They looked nothing like the apprentices and students she knew. These girls had their hair elaborately done so it fell all over their faces and shoulders. They wore no costumes or masks, even half masks, but their makeup could possibly qualify. Painted turquoise eyes were all Cecilie could see under the streetlight.

She walked near them and they seemed to fade into the shadow, three steps from the puddle of brightness in the street. Only the glow from the tips of their cigarettes illuminated their faces, and the orange embers were reflected in their eyes. Weird and scary, Cecilie thought, and she realized it would make a great disguise. Have everyone terrified.

She asked the girls where the nearest coffee bar was. The two of them stared at her as if she'd spoken Finnish. She asked again.

"What the hell is someone like you doing here?" one of the girls spat.

The other put a hand on her friend's shoulder. "The show at the Luna. You know they come down. So what? Old man Cecchi could use the business." She turned to Cecilie and spoke very slowly, as if to a tourist. "Turn left at the end of the block and go halfway down. There's a streetlight out front. They have good sandwiches. But they'll close soon."

Cecilie was glad that she didn't have to smile behind the mask. "Thank you," she said, and made off, worried that the girls might follow her and try to steal her cardcase or her mask. Or just try to scare her for fun.

She was relieved when she found the sandwich shop. For all the food was old and stale-looking, she was hungry now and she wanted to eat. They were only going to throw it away now, she thought. And then she saw the counterman take a tray with the leftover sandwiches, turn out the lights and lock the doors behind him. He took the tray down to the corner where two old drunks waited on a bench. He gave them each a sandwich and walked into the dark.

Cecilie could think of nothing else to do. She walked around the block and returned to Café Luna, which looked no more inviting now than it had earlier. Only it was darker and the girls had left, glowing cigarette butts lying in the gutter the only testament to their passing.

Cecilie decided that she would go home. It was her own fault that she was early, but she had had enough. She wanted to be out of this hostile district, she wanted to be back in the comfortable place where she belonged. There the world was familiar and predictable, and Cecilie 8 Sept-Fortune had a position and respect. She never wanted to see this place again. She wanted to go back home and watch a few programs with her parents and heat up whatever was left over from dinner. Her mother had been making chicken, she remembered.

But that would be too embarrassing. Her parents thought she was out with friends at a concert. She couldn't go home and admit that she had gone to Café Luna and been stood up by her date.

She could go to the Sept-House. The residents would still be there and there would be leftovers in the kitchen put away as neatly as her mama's.

As she turned to leave she saw him down the block. The sun

mask was almost as vibrant as she remembered it, and he walked with the same arrogant grace that had marked him in the datasea.

She could go on, walk right past him. Her mask and costume hid everything, and he had never seen this outfit before. He would not recognize her and she would be gone.

Instead she walked up to the blazing sun. "I didn't have a ticket so they wouldn't let me in," she said firmly. "I would have thought you would have left a record for the door."

The sun laughed. "No, they do it the old-fashioned way. Tickets and all. On paper, no less."

He pulled out two pieces of pale green paper printed with the date and the logo of Café Luna. Cecilie fingered the ticket and cringed. The paper was cheap and stiff to the touch, nothing like the heavy creamy invitations that the Pietà sent out for their very exclusive performances.

Cecilie handed her ticket to the bored man, who deigned to smile at her this time. She was glad of the mask that shielded her expression, because she wished she had passed the sun on the street and gone on back home. She could have told her mother that she was stood up and her father would have threatened to tear off the man's ears who would do that to his baby. Then Mama would slice off large pieces of *torta del nonna* and they would sit together in the kitchen. Instead she was here.

Once her eyes adjusted to the gloom she realized that the place was not quite so unsavory as she had first imagined. The grey streaks on the walls were paint and there were abstract oils that had some sense of music hung unframed against the subtly multihued glaze.

"Would you like something to eat?" David asked.

Cecilie was flustered. She was hungry but she didn't want to remove her mask. She shook her head.

"Some wine, then?" he asked, and without waiting for her answer ordered.

The wine was served with narrow straws that fit through the mouth opening of the mask. Some masks didn't have any opening at all, but Cecilie was glad that this one did. While the wine wouldn't satisfy her hunger, it was at least something. She sipped it greedily though it was cheap and tasted raw.

"Why did you want me to come here?" she asked bluntly.

David waited for a moment, not sure how much he wanted to answer. "I wanted you to hear this music, that's all," he said.

Cecilie made a dismissive noise. "You want something else," she insisted. "You're too good and you're not Sept. I know that, I looked and it seems you don't exist at all. Someone with a wild talent good enough to access Sept levels should have left some trace of training or been on some Sept's recruitment list. I backtracked recruitment lists and notes for the past thirty years and I couldn't find a single individual whose follow-ups fit your pattern. I think you want more internal Sept data that you haven't been able to get hold of on your own and I don't know why you think I'm the one to use to get it."

David was taken aback. He knew that she had to be intelligent, had to have ability to see patterns and recognize what was beyond. But he had not expected that ability to be used against him. Still, she had also given him an opening that he was not about to waste.

"No," he said. "You're right, I do need help from someone who's Sept. I don't have the training. But because I don't have the training I also have more flexibility. I'm able to do things that you can't because I never learned to do anything the right way. Sometimes my way is weird, but I can get different results than you. And because of that we'd have more strengths. You with your training, you could access much more with me in ways that your Sept could never follow. And I could learn more too. The thing is, because I don't follow any of the prescribed routes and routines I see things from a different angle, and I tell you that this Board meeting is dangerous to all of us. I watched you, looked up your traces. You strike me as a very honorable person who would be willing to discover the truth."

Behind her mask, Cecilie was glad to know that he couldn't see her fear and anger and her sense of betrayal, all called up by his allegations and her own much too recent experience. He had put her off balance by mentioning a thing that was never discussed in the House, not in front of junior apprentices. "What do you mean?" she asked very softly.

David shook his head. "What happens when all the Septs get together?" he asked his voice shaded only slightly by bitterness. "You're going to take over everything. Because you can. Whatever we do in the world, that doesn't change. Someone always wants power, someone is always ready to push everyone else around."

Cecilie sat like she was made of stone. The words didn't make sense. "How do you know about the meeting?" she asked.

"I told you," David replied. "I can get things you can't. In ways you can't."

Cecilie stood up. In her costume she looked dark and menacing and magnificent. The tips of her gloved fingers rested lightly on the table. "This is enough," she said softly. "You want to destroy us, destroy everything. I should place a marker on you and have you banned, so that you can't even get to the Mall from a kiosk. You're a terrorist. Are you from the Red Army Faction?"

David laughed aloud. "The Red Army Faction? Those idiots who keep threatening to blow up artwork and kidnap rich kids off the streets? Them? All they want is a cheap way to live without work."

Suddenly he wondered how much she really knew. It was one thing to talk about the Septs and their power with the old man and his minions. It was one thing to see them floating through their library or ignoring the displays in the Mall. It was quite another to be seated opposite one of them drinking wine as if she were just a real person made of flesh and not at all the monster the old man would have her be.

Suddenly David wondered if he might have been wrong. If maybe the Septs were honorable and their power in their own realm would be good for everyone. Just like the Gavrillis.

The café was full now. There were people standing in the back near the bar three deep at least, and every chair was occupied. People in the far corner had begun chanting, "Luna, Luna," trying to hurry the show.

David looked around quickly. "Will you excuse me for a moment?" Then he disappeared.

8

David Gavrilli left Cecilie alone while the lights went dim and the band walked onstage. It was a small stage and the musicians were unmasked, which Cecilie thought was utterly daring. But then, this was jazz. This was the edge of the underworld.

The band consisted of three men and two women. They ranged from a sax player who was old enough to be her grandfather to a young girl—not more than sixteen, Cecilie thought—skinny and pale, who played the bass. The drummer and the keyboard player looked more like her image of what underground musicians should be—both were young enough to believe in immortality and old enough to understand the pain in the music.

Cecilie stared at them and thought they were both attractive in very different ways. She didn't often get to see young men unmasked, at least not of her own class and kind. Already this show was vastly different from a Pietà concert, and not a single note had been played.

The band did not enter formally. They took sips of water on-stage and checked the tuning of their instruments, strapped things on, clipped microphones to clothing or jewelry. Then, with no warning at all, the lights went out and the music began.

Music overwhelmed her. It was like nothing she had ever heard before and it drove her body and made her hurt inside. The relentless drumming made her want to swing her hips. The rhythm pumped wildly in her veins. It was the power of blood and of sex twined together. Guitar and keyboard harmonies made her want to soar. And the sax, sweet and low, longing and enticing, seduced her and made her want to cry.

Cecilie could not help but respond to this music. The power was greater than her body, the drive was worth her soul. She did not remember getting up or drifting to the middle of the room. She had never danced before, not the way she danced to jazz. It filled her and commanded her, told her how to move. She was transformed into something exotic and rare.

She held her heavy robe in her hand, satisfied by the way it twirled around her legs. Her gloved hands gestured in the colored lights, now changing from amber to blue to red and back again. She forgot her mask in the frenzy of the moment.

Then the music died and Cecilie realized that she was alone gyrating in the small space before her seat. Everyone else was settled as if it were a Pietà concert, and their applause was restrained and polite.

She felt like an idiot and immediately dropped into her chair. Her companion the sun had not returned, and she wondered if he had simply dumped her here while he went on to do something else. Maybe he had lured her here to use her ID to access Sept secrets.

Cecilie laughed at her own highly developed paranoia. For all the man in the sun mask was good, he wasn't that good, and he had been here with her only a few minutes ago. Probably he was in the washroom. Maybe there was a line, or it was hard for him to walk through the crowd. Maybe he was trying to get some more of the harsh wine from the bar, but the crowd at the bar was deep and demanding, and it would take a while. Perhaps all three.

The next piece was slower, not as demanding on her body but making more inroads into her mind. There was a fluidity to it that reminded her instinctively of the dataflow. The underlying structure that was too complex to immediately analyze, chaotic in form and yet a medium of organization more powerful than something tidy and human-scale, resonated with familiarity expressed in a different and startling manner.

Music and the net fused and she could see the whole workings of the infosea as she listened to the music that was both too raw and too improvisational to fit into any schema she had ever known. Nothing, not all the imposition of order from Bach to morning, had changed the organic nature of the net. It was alive, alive the way this music was, creating itself from itself. Cecilie was enraptured. The vision was complete and she felt as if she understood the entire world.

And then the music stopped, the performers left their instruments and the audience broke into applause that was no longer restrained. Some held handlights and flickers in the dark, so it looked like a sky full of stars. Cecilie didn't join in. She was still too shattered by the experience. The profundity of her new knowledge threatened to overwhelm her entirely.

"What did you think?" he asked.

She blinked a few times and looked. It was the keyboardist in the band, still indecently unmasked before her. He wore a towel over his shoulders and his thin shirt was soaked with sweat.

"So, are you glad you came?" he asked.

The voice was familiar. Cecilie couldn't place it at first. She knew only that she had to struggle back from her newfound understanding to use language at all.

"It was—everything," she said, wishing she had a better word. A better way to explain. "It told me things so that I can see everything and how it works. And it doesn't work the way I thought. The way I was taught."

She didn't hear the wonder in her own voice. The keyboardist sat down in the chair he had occupied earlier and sipped at his wine. Then she remembered the voice. The sun. This musician had been the sun that had brought her here.

No wonder he was able to function in the various layers of the net so very well, even without a Sept background. The music explained it all, the music echoed the structures he would need. And so the music had taught him to navigate just as the constant background of Mozart in the Sept-House was to teach them all to think. She hadn't realized that she had reasoned part of this aloud until he replied.

"That's the point," he said gently. "Why don't they want you to have this music? Why do the Septs want to keep us from understanding order? Why would they keep you from being able to really see the dataflow the way you need to? And you're one of their own, a golden girl with a brilliant career before you. I saw your records. I know it's true."

"Who are you?" she asked, her voice soft and dreamy.

That was when he realized that he had never given her his name. Silence was an old habit from the early days with the old man. Never tell anyone anything—ever. That was the way he lived in his first days in Venice before meeting his mentor, and the old man had insisted that become a way of life.

"You can call me David," he answered.

"David? A little obvious, aren't you?"

It took him a moment to understand the reference, and then he laughed. Oh, he had chosen right, she was smart and strong and not afraid to see. And she was not afraid of irony, either.

"No, it's my given name," he said. "Sorry to disappoint you."

She shrugged. "That doesn't diminish the metaphor, even if it's true. Not that it matters. Names and faces don't matter, not really. We only pretend they mean something. In the end they are all mutable. Everything is changeable. So you give away your name and you give away nothing at all. The metaphor is more important than the information."

He smiled. "Well, if that's so, why haven't you unmasked. I still haven't seen your face, Cecilie 8 Sept-Fortune. And if it's so insignificant, I don't know why you kept masked while you danced. You dance very well, you know."

Cecilie felt herself blush and was grateful for the face over her own.

"Look, they want to kick us out of here. Would you like to go somewhere for a coffee?" David asked.

Cecilie hesitated. It was already late. Her parents would worry. But she had told them she'd be late and she was an adult with her own accounts now and she should stay out if she wanted to. She might even move out in a few months, though she thought that would horrify her mother and maybe wasn't such a good idea anyway.

"There's a place I know nearby," David said. "It's just neighborhood, but they know the crowd here and stay open late. They have wonderful pastry."

Hunger decided for her. "Do they have sandwiches?" she asked, aware only that she wanted something very soon. The wine had made her light-headed and her stomach felt uneasy.

"If they have any left," David said. "Come on, I could use something myself. Playing is hard work."

She stood up uneasily and followed him the few blocks to the coffee bar, a different place from the one that had closed earlier. This was nicer than that place. It would have been typical in her neighborhood, or near a Sept-House, small with a few tables and chairs, most people taking their coffee in white porcelain cups standing at the counter. A few wilted sandwiches were shoved aside in the glass case that proudly displayed slices of cake and various pastries and piles of chocolates.

Cecilie sat heavily in one of the chairs. David went to the counter and got two espressos, a sandwich and two elegant-looking stuffed tarts. He brought it all over on a tray.

"Well?" he asked.

Cecilie looked at the sandwich. It had not been tempting at lunch, when it had been made. Now the salami and ham were glazed by cheese, and the lettuce was brown around the edges. She thought it looked delicious. She was sure she had never eaten a sandwich so good.

But to eat meant taking off her mask.

There was no place to unmask here, no screens like there were in the elegant places to keep matters of identity private. If she showed her face here she showed it to everyone, immediately.

It was undignified. It was unrefined. It was bad manners. One did not remove a mask in front of an entire roomful of people. It wasn't done.

But in this place no one was masked. The people around her did not speak in an educated manner. Most of them looked like they couldn't afford a mask at all. There were night workers and people in city coveralls, girls who wore too much makeup and were too young, smoking and trying to look sophisticated. There were their dates, young men with predatory eyes and rough manners.

These were not the kind of people that Cecilie understood.

She was an outsider here, clearly marked. People looked at her out of the corners of their eyes, always glancing away quickly.

David did not look like he belonged in the crowd, but something about him seemed to melt into the background. He had looked that way at the club, too, and Cecilie could easily imagine him at a Sept party or as a guest at a family wedding.

He was casually handsome, as everyone from moderately middle-class families upward was. His hair was dark and long, thick and wavy, like that of most of the boys in the room. His eyes were unusual, bright green behind dark lashes, but they were not what made him so different from the others around them. It was how expression marched across his features. If anyone needed a mask, it was this David.

Yet the animation on his face made him more than simply interesting, or even compelling. It made him seem more alive. Cecilie could not remember when she had seen anyone who had such enthusiasm, such excitement, such soulful dedication painted right out in the open for anyone to see.

And then she saw the sandwich again and felt the hunger in her and the decision was made.

At least there was a restroom where she could unmask with some semblance of seemly privacy. She took off the headdress as well, and combed her fingers through her wild hair. It looked a mess, all tangled curls that she couldn't possibly force to order.

She sighed. She had no comb. And the headdress without the mask was silly. She put the mask into the headpiece and returned to the dining room, where David had not waited to start on his tart.

She dove into the sandwich without saying anything. She didn't even look at him until the meat was gone, every crumb of it. Only then she deigned to take a tart filled with sweet cheese and the espresso. The coffee was already cooling.

"So are you willing to talk now?" David asked.

"Me?" Cecilie asked. "You. You're the one who tried to steal my data. What did you want that banking info for anyway? And then you talk to me about some Sept meeting and you think I have to explain anything to you? You're out of your mind."

She watched the expression on his face change from smug to astonished, and she got great satisfaction from it.

"I don't have to explain anything to you," he said, anger turning his cheeks dark. "You're here because I asked you, because you wanted to hear the music. Okay, so trade. Talk. Or don't. You're not high enough in the Sept to tell me what's on the agenda for the meeting anyway. I probably know more about it than you do."

That was more than Cecilie could handle. She stood and slapped him across the face.

The entire room froze. Everyone stared at them, and then the night workers and the rough boys and their hard girls broke out into applause. Cecilie smiled.

And David smiled back at her. "Sorry," he said, making a dismissive gesture. "I couldn't help trying."

"You should forgive him," one of the women with close cropped hair in a city coverall said.

"Now, wait a minute," one of the girls with too much make-up replied. "Maybe you should butt out, Nunzia. Not everybody in the entire city needs the benefit of your opinions on everything in the world."

Nunzia finished her coffee, left the cup on the counter and walked over to the seated group. "Yeah, right, Concetta. Maybe your mother doesn't need to know where you are right now and why you never can quite wake up in the morning to get to a job. How many have you had recently?"

Cecilie giggled and covered her mouth with a napkin. David put his finger over his lips and shook his head slightly.

"I don't need a job," Concetta replied haughtily. "Renzo just bought me this." She held up her hand. Glitter circled her wrist.

"Very pretty, Concetta. But how is it going to help with the rent? Or are you going to sell it?" Nunzia asked.

Concetta stood up and balled her hands into fists. "My rent isn't your business, you got that? Or are you going to get out of here now? My mother says she thinks you're a witch. Renzo can take care of me." But just in case, Concetta made the sign against the evil eye.

"Come on, Concetta," the counterman said, breaking between them. "Sit down. Nunzia has finished her coffee and has to go to work anyway. So why don't you just relax and have an ice cream and forget it, okay? Nunzia, you come back after your shift you get a cappuccino on the house. Concetta, you can have an ice cream now. Everyone happy?"

Nunzia gave Concetta a withering look and left the establishment. Renzo waved a hand. "Ice cream for everyone," he announced.

Cecilie looked at David. "What was that?" she asked.

"Neighborhood politics," he told her. "We play down here sometimes, and I come down to the Luna for other music too. Those two are always at it. And Nunzia does have a reputation."

"As a witch?" Cecilie demanded, incredulous.

David shrugged. "Some people think so. Nunzia can curse with the best of them, and if you get her in a good mood she'll read your palm."

"Has she read your palm?"

David blushed. "Well, I couldn't exactly get out of it. Everyone was doing it. Anyway, what she said could have applied to anyone, it didn't make any sense at all."

"What did she say?" Cecilie asked.

"I don't remember," David replied. "Something about my family and how I was going to have a long and interesting life. Junk like that."

"So what is it you want? You want me to spy on the Board meeting for you, was that on the program?" she asked.

David started for a moment. He hadn't expected this. After all, he was supposed to be the questioner here. "Why do you care?" he sneered. "After all, you're Sept. You're one of them. I was an idiot to ask you to come out tonight. You haven't even figured out that this could have been a date."

Cecilie stood up. "If I had known that was what you were thinking I would never have come." She stalked out of the café and let the glass door swing shut behind her.

David sighed with exasperation and let her walk. He had tried, and he was tired. Besides, she had heard the music. That would do something inside a Sept head. It had to.

What a waste of time if she wouldn't help him. He'd used the line about the date but it had just been an immediate attack. If he had a date it would have been with Sean, drinking their espressos and companionably discussing music. Sean might even have some tasty bit of gossip from the Pietà or someone who had attended a concert.

Strange how people ignored musicians, talked in front of them as if they were walls.

It was not only for Sean's possible information that David wanted to see him, and recognizing that fact made David uneasy. There was something in the iconoclast singer that touched David as very few people touched him. Most people he used, but then there were the ones like Sean, who brought out something more, who invaded his plans and dreams and became entwined with his desires.

People who made him feel this way frightened David, though he wasn't sure if he was frightened of them or of his reaction to them. Sean . . . one of these days he was going to have to make a decision about Sean. He would have to acknowledge his feelings to the singer, or he would have to run away.

He had always run before and it was his instinct to do so now. But he didn't like to think of a future where he wouldn't ever see Sean again. Or, worse, see him in a performance, angry at David and unreachable.

Still, David knew that Sean and several others from the Pietà had been in the audience. Sean had told him and David had made sure that Sean had a free ticket. Now he regretted spending the after-performance time with someone who was his adversary rather than his lover.

He got up slowly, tipping the counterman almost absentmindedly. *An interesting adversary,* he thought. *Black velvet. Not a bad choice for an intrigue—if that was what she'd had in mind.* But the cap had hidden her hair. He hadn't imagined her with the red hair that had always been considered desirable in Venice.

Still, she hadn't exactly fallen into his arms. He would have to annoy her again soon. The thought pleased him and he forgot he was face-naked on the street, so he smiled for all the world to see.

"What did you think of the concert?" Sean asked casually as they took their seats at lunch. He had not seen Lina for several days. They were in different groups rehearsing different pieces. He had been frustrated because he had been quite certain that she had been deeply struck and he wanted to know all the particulars. Besides that, he wanted to make certain that she saw him as a friend, someone to turn to, to gossip with, to tell secrets to.

He knew he was doing it because he could use her. She was in the group that was being sent to the meeting, to keep the harmony of the Septs while they negotiated among themselves. She was going and he was learning music to sing at several private recitals that had no political importance whatever.

Sean didn't like that. He didn't like it for himself, but more important he didn't like it for David. David needed him and he'd let David down. He'd sworn that he wouldn't do that, and it hurt more than any other thing he had or hadn't done. David was more important than any of them, Sean thought bitterly. David understood.

Although he had never said anything, Sean was certain that David thought that Sean was important and mattered and that meant more than everything else together. Sean let his mind linger on the sensual memory for just a moment and then turned his attention away. No time for that now. He had to get Lina, get to Lina. She would help him, and more important help David. Without her knowledge, if it had to be that way.

Of all the singers in the group going to the Sept meeting she was the most likely to help. He'd studied them carefully enough. Lina had gone to the jazz concert, had liked it. That alone made her vulnerable.

She was also isolated, not part of any of the cliques or pairs that were common among the singers. In fact, she was very much like him—a loner, a dreamer, someone who didn't have the ordinary ambitions. And so she might be better suited to the purpose than he had thought.

"The jazz concert?" Lina replied. "I'm not sure. The music was wonderful—so fluid. But I also found it very disturbing."

"You liked it though?" Sean pushed. "Even if it was disturbing."

Lina nodded. "Yes. But then, some disturbing things have their own kind of beauty. A kind of glory in ugliness, perhaps, though I'm not sure if I could think of a musical example right off."

Sean tried not to smile. "Would you like to come meet some of the players?" he asked, carefully casual.

Lina shrugged. "It's the music, not the players, that counts.

Besides, my schedule is insane for the next few weeks. You know, we have to do the meeting music on top of regular repertoire? I won't even have time to have my nails done."

Sean glanced down. Her nails, painted sky blue with gold patterns, were perfect. He shrugged. "Have it your way. I thought you might like to meet some of the people I know. They're having a party next week and you'd be welcome. Besides, I think you'd like them. I think you'd like their ideas."

"Ideas on what?" Lina asked.

"All kinds of things," Sean said, and his eyes lit up. "Not just music. Everything. The way the world works. Why we wear masks. Why some people have all the power and why we have none and what we can do about it. What we can do about the Septs."

Lina looked confused. "What do you mean? We have a lot of power. Nothing would work right without us. And what's wrong with the Septs? They do their job, we do ours, the world works. I don't see a problem."

Suddenly Sean was angry. "Oh, right, we do our job and they do theirs and it's all very nice. And everyone is happy. Well, everyone is *not* happy. Everyone is being deluded because the Septs are taking over more and more of our lives and we don't even notice. We don't bother. When you entered the Pietà there weren't Sept liaisons, right? And there weren't Sept set lists of what was appropriate to play and what wasn't. Remember? Remember how we used to sing things from that weird modern thing? And the operas. We only do approved operas now. First we stopped doing the one-acts because they weren't important enough. And then we stopped doing some of Wagner because we couldn't afford to mount the productions. And two years later, remember, how Sept-San Marco stepped in and underwrote a whole Mozart season?"

Lina was listening very carefully. His memory for dates and

the progression of events impressed her. The past was a cloud of isolated events to Lina, and the only thing that linked them together was the music. Listening to Sean's short summary of events she recalled clearly, the general pattern organized and became whole to her. Things that before had no connection or had not mattered suddenly fell into perspective and she saw into a conspiracy as thick as the plot of an opera. That made it all the more suspect, as operas were invariably absurd. By definition, anything that was like an opera must be completely fantastic.

Lina wanted to toss off her new perception. She wanted the past to become safely distant and indistinct again, and she wanted Sean to laugh and tell her it was a stupid joke. It wasn't a joke though, and she couldn't ignore her own direct experience.

She said nothing for a while, thinking. Then she spoke cautiously. "Yes. When I think about it, yes, the repertoire is more restricted than it was when I entered. And I remember going to places like the Luna when we were very young. There were maybe four or five music clubs in the city and they played everything. I remember this one concert with this old man playing a saxophone."

Sean nodded vigorously. "That's it. Exactly. There's less music and it's all approved. Traditional. And think about shopping, about going to the Mall. You can't go anywhere outside the Mall level without proper credentials. You can't go look up some weird old concert that the Septs have decided isn't on the play list."

Lina studied him thoughtfully. "Have you tried this?" she asked. "Have you tried to go out of the Mall and call up what was recorded? Or is it only that we don't, that we've been so involved in perfecting one phrase at a time that we don't have the energy to listen to music that doesn't really speak to our current needs? Is it that? Because I wonder if it's really that the world is less free or that we are just letting things slide."

"Not me, I haven't tried," Sean said. "But I can introduce you to someone who has. Someone who can go anyplace. You can ask him."

Lina nodded and gathered up her music. "I'll talk to you to-morrow," she said, and left. She needed to think for a while before embarking on one of Sean's schemes. He always had ideas, plans, grandiose dreams and paranoid theories. Lina wasn't sure if this was just one more of Sean's leftover illusions, or if this time he'd been led into something more substantial.

Sean was about half on most of the time, Lina thought. He seemed to always need to rebel, to be different, to assert himself in the worst possible way at the most hideous times. But she was also aware that life at the Pietà was sometimes too comfortable. It was easy to forget that there was an outside world that could be cold and hard. That out there people could go hungry and people had to scrape to find work and sometimes people couldn't afford to live. In the Pietà she had escaped everything, and she knew it.

In that, at least, she was more aware than most of the singers. She did know there was an outside and she remembered it very well. Even the younger students who were local, who didn't board at the school, were wrapped in the ease that was the Pietà. Their parents were given a stipend, their lives were completely regulated. And they were the minority anyway. Like most of the Pietà singers, she had come from far away to audition and then became a boarding student.

Music was all of life here. Nothing else mattered. It was a very beautiful way to live, a perfect dedication to the ideal of music alone. That had appealed to her for a long time.

Only in the past few years Lina had thought that maybe living for music alone wasn't enough. She had been uncomfortable with those thoughts and hid them away. Music should be enough. Music should be everything.

It wasn't. Cracks had appeared in Lina's consciousness and she had become aware of the streets and canals they traveled. She looked into the high windows and wondered what kinds of lives were lived behind the glass and curtains that fluttered over the water. She looked at the people on the Lido and tried to imagine their concerns, to create whole histories for them.

At first she said it was for her opera work. That she wanted to do more operatic roles and she had to learn to act as well as sing. Only she hadn't gotten the roles and she hadn't gotten out of the habit of studying the life around her, either. Instead her new perceptions had only made her melancholy.

The others thought she had become quieter because she was miserable, having missed out on the La Scala season when Maestro had hinted that she would make her debut. She was not miserable. Strangely, she didn't really care all that much. Lina had never been competitive that way, though it was a way of life at the Pietà. Somehow she had never quite worried enough about her roles. She had spent so much time trying to be a pure acolyte of her art that she no longer thought in terms of her advancement alone.

Lina turned inward and began to live all the lives she invented in her head. She had had no lovers since the disastrous casting, as if her failure were contagious. She was singular, isolated, much like Sean the loudmouth rebel, who couldn't keep himself away from trouble. Not even for the chance to serve music the better through one of the most beautiful voices in the choir could he manage to control himself.

Lina had a great deal to think about. No matter how many conditions she put on it, there was always the fact that going out was to maybe touch something again. Staying in the Pietà was safe and nothing could break through the layers of defense here. Nothing except music alone could make Lina feel anything at all.

She thought that Sean was just the opposite of her. Sean's problem was that he did feel, that he didn't fall under the spell of comfort and ease, of emotional distance from anything that was alive.

Alive. And then Lina looked down at her hands, her white fingers that lay limp on the new folio, ghostly and anemic and the next thing to dead on the vibrant blue leather. They looked as if they had been carved in marble, cold and icy and not at all alive. She felt like she had been carved of marble, the pristine angel on a mortuary monument who never saw beyond the cemetery walls.

Suddenly it didn't matter what Sean wanted anymore. It didn't even matter if he was wrong, if there was no conspiracy, if she was half crazy to even think of going to some weird jazz party. Anguish engulfed her as she realized that she didn't feel anything anymore, that she hadn't felt anything since the summer of La Scala.

It wasn't being passed over for the opera that had made her feel dead. It was that the music she had rehearsed and sung, the roles she had acted, had made her feel so much more alive than anything else she had attempted. Lina moved through her life like a sleepwalker, but when she lived Mimi's life her whole being resonated with the passions and pain Mimi experienced.

Lina knew that was the real reason she had not been selected. She was only a ghost unless she took on the more substantial flesh of a fictional character. She would not be the singer she wanted to be, could be, until she became real, until she felt things deeper than the stupor of the Pietà. Until she lived.

So the decision was made. Not because Lina thought it was the right thing, but because she knew it was the only way she could save herself from fading away until there was nothing left at all. She had to act somehow, had to touch that world she had rejected when she had been accepted as a student.

She had to touch the world that had hurt her and scarred her and that she had sworn would never hurt her again. She had to go back out into it or she would end up a ghost in Santa Clara's Hospital for the Insane. She had already been dead too long, living in a tomb of cold music.

That was the center of her fear. Maestro had tried to understand what was happening to her singing. Her voice was still glorious, but there was nothing behind it, he had told her. She had to express something more than precision with the notes, he said, before she could play the passions of opera.

Her mind was made up in the next hour while the reflections of the canal shimmered across the ceiling. She did not tell Sean, though, not right away. For a little while she held hope and fear together while she watched the light ripple across the painted Baroque sky, and she was afraid that the painted sky told the truth, a patch of clear serene blue surrounded by a tumult of clouds. Some of the clouds were amber and rose like sunset. Others were grey like an oncoming storm or like the water in the canal in the early morning.

That grey was like her soul, like her music. Like her life. All around the promise of a moment of clear and a moment of glory.

9

The Mall was in the white marble phase that was Cecilie's favorite. She loved the soaring pale columns, the hard shiny floor, the glossy green leaves of potted plants in contrast to all the pristine white. Julietta and Valentina were waving her over to the newest shoe store in the same way they had dragged her to the sweater shop and the place that sold bad imitations of designer clothes.

The girls went unmasked here today, trying to look like ordinary shoppers. Her mother had not been pleased. "You can't shop in the Mall," her mother had said for the fiftieth time over breakfast. "You can't try something on virtually. What if it isn't flattering? Everything looks flattering when it can adjust to any illusion. To your illusion."

"So we'll just get shoes and accessories," Cecilie had replied, stirring her coffee more than sipping it.

"Shoes. How can you buy shoes that you don't try on your

real feet? How do you know they're comfortable, that you can walk in them?"

Cecilie shrugged.

"I really think you girls should go to the real shops," her mother continued on. "You need to get out and walk in the fresh air and the sunshine. You all spend too much time indoors, with computers, not living life. One day you'll be old suddenly and you'll wonder where all that life went while you were underground."

"It's not underground," Cecilie said. "We're never underground. And there's a nice courtyard in the Sept-House, you've been there. We eat dinner outside in the summer."

Cecilie didn't want to argue any more. Mostly because she was afraid that her mother was right. Her mother's clothes always looked perfectly elegant, more flattering and pulled-together than those worn by most of the people on the street and much more so than those worn by any Sept sister Cecilie had ever seen. Cecilie suspected that it came from shopping in the physical world. Cecilie also thought that she might follow her mother's example, but quietly.

The whole point of getting together was for the newly promoted members of Sept-Fortune to get away from supervision for a while anyway, and to be able to present their new status with their sisters before the Board meeting. Shopping was something everyone, even Signora Tima, understood.

Cecilie had to get away from everyone, from the Sept and her parents and especially from her thoughts of the jazz night. She had to forget David and what he had told her. Looking for the Septs taking power meant that she saw signs of it everywhere, and that made her afraid.

He had known too much and that made her suspicious, but he was right that there was something wrong. She had known there were things wrong ever since Signora Tima had told her what was required for her promotion. Nothing had felt right since.

She had not slept well. Late at night when everyone in the whole city, in all the world, was asleep, Cecilie had wandered barefoot through her parents' apartment. She opened the fridge and stared blankly at fruit salad and a scrap of ham and half a cheese, none of which appealed. The light spilled into the kitchen, making shadows more pronounced, which Cecilie found disturbing. She closed the fridge and opened the shutters over the water. Resting on her elbows, she looked down and listened to the lapping of the canal against the stone in the dark.

In the dark it was worse. In the dead of the night she knew that she had done something terrible and she cried and wished she were a better believer so that confession could clear her soul. The gentle sound of the water was ominous, telling her again and again that there was no escape.

Two entire days had passed since the jazz concert and she had taken no paid work and billed no hours. Instead, she daydreamed, and when she got sick of that she went back through the data she had given over to Signora Tima. On the surface of it, there was nothing terrible. Besides the fact that they were not entitled to it, there was nothing that accused anyone of any crime, nothing that screamed theft or blackmail.

So she looked further. She had been trained to search, to follow threads, to touch leads and make them yield to more leads. Now it surprised her that the skills she had learned to track an intruder or follow corporate ratings could be used against a client's interest so easily. Like the rest of her training, the data compilation and search class that she had taken for three years was two-faced, the threat hidden in the banal. No wonder Signora Sophia insisted they learn for themselves and not contract out to Sept-Bianchi, which specialized in data search and retrieval.

After three years of study, putting together the files she needed was far too easy. She looked at the names in the documents, names that meant nothing to her at all. Lawrence Phillips. Elizabeth Jamison. Arthur McNeil. Vincenzo Gavrilli. Dunya Marikoff.

Just names, and money, and the places money traveled. She had tried it against a template and everything seemed in order. So she started with the names again, looked up biographies, looked to where they linked through the homepages of a hundred corporations and ten million business threads.

One by one she noticed that there were things in common, things that she could not have known without the intense training in search methodology. Two of the principals were dead, their estates in probate and not quite settled. Estates as large as these would be hard to settle, that was no surprise. The surprise was that in both cases, one of the trustees was a Sept sister.

Nothing looked suspicious immediately. Both Sept sisters were blood relations to the deceased. Still, Cecilie desperately wanted to find no connection at all to any of the Septs or the Board or anything that could confirm David's wild theory.

She called Zizi. The bird appeared through the window trailing long turquoise plumage. She thought about changing the color again, and then realized that she didn't have the time. There was not even the time to think about such things. She gave Zizi the names with instructions to pull any mentions of them or their families, paying special attention to any Sept connections.

The bird squawked once and flew around her head once, then headed for the door. Now there was nothing to do but wait and think, so Cecilie decided to shop instead. Anything was better than sitting around wondering when she would get the piece she needed to make sense of the whole thing.

So she met Julietta and Valentina and the three of them went through the white marble Mall, but Cecilie couldn't concentrate on shopping. When she found sweaters on sale she couldn't decide between the deep green and the pale gold and finally just let it drop. Julietta bought two skirts, simple wool but very nicely cut, if the illusion of the Mall could be trusted.

"Cecilie, you haven't bought anything," Valentina pointed out. "And you really need to. You can't wear uniforms once the meetings start and you don't really have anything else."

Valentina was right. She and Julietta had each made sensible purchases, things that they could use daily as full Sept sisters. They didn't have to carry bags. Everything would be sent immediately and most should be waiting when they left their dreamboxes.

Nothing in the Mall appealed to Cecilie. Her mind kept wandering back to the list of names, and she kept wondering if Zizi had found anything. Maybe the necessary detail was waiting in her queue now. She almost itched to get back to the Library, to see what was hanging from Zizi's beak as the bird paced up and down in front of her place at the table.

"Come over here, Cecilie," Valentina called. "I think you might like this dress."

Cecilie sighed and turned back to the store where Valentina was pawing through the racks. She was just not in the mood to shop, that was all, she realized. But Valentina wouldn't be put off. "And look at this jacket." Valentina held it up and motioned Cecilie in.

The jacket really would look good on her, Cecilie thought. And it probably cost too much, or the fabric wasn't good. You could never tell about the true quality of fabric in the Mall. Her mother would think it was too trendy and tell her not to buy things that would look dated in a year.

"Classic, that's what you need," her mother always told her

when they went shopping. "A few pieces of the best quality are much better than a million choices of trash that have to be replaced in six months."

While Cecilie knew that her mother was right, she still thought that the jacket would look good on her. If it wasn't too expensive she would try it on. The color was even nice, a rich olive that none of the others could wear. Maybe her luck was turning.

She went in. Just as she reached to take the jacket from Valentina's hand everything in the shop seemed to ripple just slightly, as if the whole program had been refocused in an adjustment. Only there was more than that. Cecilie felt vaguely ill. And the jacket, which had been a deep, vibrant shade, was now just a bit drab.

In fact, everything was just slightly askew. Cecilie felt as if she were peering through a distorted lens. She moved to one of the mirrors in the store and looked at her reflection. The image that stared back at her was altered slightly, changed, not the careful projection she had spent months creating.

Not that the duplicate was so terribly different. Her hair was still red and it tangled down her back, her eyes were still wide set and her dress was still ecru gauze. But the face that was almost but not quite her face had a softer expression and freckles and her fingernails were freshly polished a pale peach her mother would vigorously approve.

She looked down at her hands. The polish was there, not even chipped. Cecilie could not remember when she had ever worn nail polish that hadn't chipped or smeared by the time it had dried. It was so unlike her she had never thought to write it into her appearance program, though there was no reason why not. Why couldn't she have perfect nails all the time here, even if not in the meat world?

In fact, she should have written this into the program. It would take hardly any work and she could have something that she had despaired of in Real Life.

She was wondering it all so deeply that suddenly it struck her to wonder why it had happened in the first place. She hadn't written it into the program and it shouldn't be interpreted that way in the Mall. She stopped staring at her hands and started to look around. The store was not different that she could tell. The jacket was back to the original color. Valentina and Julietta looked like themselves perfectly—better made up than usual, Cecilie thought.

Then she looked at their hands. They also wore perfect and understated pale nail polish that was nothing like the dark reds and purples they had discovered when they were fourteen. Valentina and Julietta still wore the shades that Cecilie's mother would not tolerate in her home.

The others didn't seem to notice the change. Cecilie wondered if she was losing her mind, seeing things that were completely irrelevant and letting them disturb her. It was all just so stupid. She should forget it.

She purchased the jacket.

"Is that all you're getting today?" Julietta asked. "It's almost dinnertime, and if I'm late my mother is going to kill me. Besides, I really want to try this stuff on in Real Life, you know?"

Cecilie nodded, distracted. Her friends took their leave, but Cecilie dawdled behind, looking at all the details about the Mall she had never quite noticed before. The marble had given way to the Victorian rendition but the underlying structure was still the same. The pillars and fountains remained in position, only their style altered at each cycle shift.

She wandered to the lower court, where there were seating areas for those who felt tired after parting with their money. In the Victorian version, the chairs were all upholstered wingbacks and there were potted palms and hothouse flowers and low wooden tables full of silver and crystal illusions. She preferred the marble look; the Victorian was too fussy for her taste.

Still she sat down and hoped to quiet the churning inside her. Something had passed through, something had touched her and made her queasy. And changed her nails. No one else noticed, or at least no one else indicated that the whole fabric of the interface had come unglued.

She thought of this effect as "the anomaly." She had encountered it three times before, and it always left her feeling vaguely ill. Perhaps the rippling movement of color at the moment of appearance made her motion sick, as she had been every summer sailing on the lake. Only there was something beyond the motion-sick feeling, another feeling that was more like after having eaten something bad and wanting to throw up and not being able to. That felt more like it to her.

Resolving the description did not make her feel any better, though. She didn't understand it. There was no way something could move through her environment and change her personal-appearance projection permanently. Though she didn't know if it counted as permanent if she got out and came back.

If she got out and took out all her code and saw if there had been an inclusion. A virus, maybe? But a virus that painted her nails and did nothing else was so silly she had to laugh. How her mother would approve of such a virus, would try to get it replicated in the real world.

"A virus for perfect nails, you could make a fortune," her mother would say. Though her mother always had perfectly groomed nails. The manicurist only had to shape a little and change the color. Cecilie didn't know how she managed, or if it was just something about being a real grown-up. Signora Tima had perfect nails, too. Though Signora Angelina bit hers, which profoundly reassured Cecilie.

She wondered how many other little things she had never noticed had been mildly changed. Made more perfect perhaps—or less. She had no basis for comparison.

"What happened when it hit you?"

The voice startled her and her head jerked up from contemplation. The blazing sun stood in front of her. David, she thought. He seemed much more manageable as David.

She was more surprised that she accepted his presence so easily. Perhaps the anomaly had put her beyond shock for a while. It was certainly much more startling than the presence of a would-be net.ninja in the Mall.

"Why should it affect such stupid things?" she wondered aloud.

"Stupid?" David asked suddenly. "Like what?"

She held out her hands. "My nails," she said. "They're never this nice, not even here. And they didn't change back the way the colors did."

The sun stared down at her hands. "It never changed anything before," he said.

Cecilie shrugged. "That you noticed, you mean. We really don't know. Maybe it's been changing things all along, only they aren't things that mean anything to us. So we don't see it is all. Maybe the whole world is different than it was and we just haven't paid attention."

"So now are you convinced?" he asked.

She blinked. "Convinced about what? That there's something here I don't understand? You wouldn't believe how much there is here I don't understand. Stuff that no one understands. We built it but we can't control it."

"That we have to find out who is creating this anomaly, and do something about it," David said, hissing through his anger.

Cecilie began to giggle. "Do what? Arrest it? I mean, we don't have any authority. No one has the authority to throw something or someone out of here anyway. If they did, you'd have been the first to go. So what do you think we should do? Play kid detectives and report to our elders? And what are they going to do? What's the point?"

"Oh," David said slowly. "I made a mistake. I thought you might care. That you might have figured out that it had to be one of the Septs trying to take over, maybe one of several attempts that haven't quite worked. But I was wrong. You're just like all the others."

He turned as if to leave. Cecilie grabbed him by the arm and he turned back. "I do so care," she protested. "But you don't make any sense and all you want to do is blame things on the Septs anyway, just to get back for your own bitterness. I mean, think of how you've treated me. First you try to steal data off me, then you take me to a concert and now you want to track down this anomaly. And everything is the Sept's fault which makes it my fault, and somehow you expect me to make it all up to you. You're completely paranoid."

David looked at her, stunned. "I didn't realize that you thought of me like that."

Cecilie threw up her hands. "I don't believe you! I mean, you go looking for an apprentice to use to confirm all your paranoid illusions, and then when they figure out what you're up to you're surprised. You need a good therapist and I'm not qualified. I wish you would leave me alone."

"Really?" David asked.

"Really," Cecilie repeated. "Really, really, really."

The sun disappeared back through the wingback chairs, through an exit to the side of the roaring fireplace. Cecilie waited until she was sure he was good and gone, and then left herself. Only she went out one of the upper doors onto the street that led to the Library.

When she got to her table, Zizi was perched on the back of

her usual chair, preening. He seemed very pleased with himself.

"What did you get?" she demanded.

"Why the boy wants the data," Zizi replied, hopping from one foot to the other in excitement. "I found out, I found out."

"What?" Cecilie asked, wanting to throttle her familiar. Even though she had created his personality. Maybe she should alter the program to make him just a bit more compliant.

"In the folder, on the table," Zizi said.

There was a neatly placed folder in front of her chair. She opened it and turned the pages quickly. The picture leaped out at her first. She had seen this face before, very recently. She recognized David in the folder as the sun, the musician, the person who'd been making her furious without fail ever since her promotion test. What did he have to do with . . . She picked it up and read only his last name. All was made clear.

Gavrilli. No wonder he wanted to know. David Gavrilli was listed as one of the principals of the bank, the heir of Vincenzo Gavrilli. He was too young to actually function in any capacity in the bank, Cecilie thought. She tried to remember her classes in ownership and inheritance and legal matters, which protected her clients and kept her in Sept-range fees. The rich often purchased things and put them in the names of children. It split up the fortune.

Indeed, she had even known of cases where the children were expected to behave like owners and make decisions. The very rich had their own apprenticeship system; Cecilie could appreciate that.

But she was stunned that the musician in the sun costume turned out to be—one of them. He wasn't what she thought they would be like. He wasn't a snob, wasn't aloof, even if he was arrogant and cocksure.

He was still one of the principals of a bank where administrative trusts were slipping into the hands of the Sept. No wonder he'd been watching her, watching the Sept, anxious to make inroads. Cecilie whistled between her teeth. This was one where she needed to be very careful. He wanted to use her, and she trusted him less and less. He was completely crazy, Cecilie decided, but that didn't mean he was less intelligent or less dangerous.

Then she came to the full report on the principals, and she was shocked again. Not only was he a principal, but David Gavrilli had disappeared—presumably kidnapped, according to the police report—three years ago. Though the police and the family assumed he had been killed, there were years to go before he was declared legally dead and his fortune went back to the family coffers to be distributed again.

He had disappeared three years ago. He had been here in Venice for a while. Maybe he had been here the whole time, though how he had managed to remain anonymous for so long was beyond Cecilie's imagination. The entire system, both Real Life and in the net, worked on series of identity proofs. The kiosks verified financial status before the meter turned, the banks filed retinal scans and voice recognition patterns. Bluepaper documents were needed to get the universal account transfer cards that permitted access to kiosks, accounts, shops and apartments. Without that card he couldn't have held a job or checked into a hotel or rented an apartment.

There was more going on than she understood, and Cecilie realized that she was lost. The pieces were adding up to something much bigger than she had expected. Bigger, and more subtle.

She smiled. At least now she had more on him than he had on her. What she had was useful and could be sold. His family had never rescinded the offer of a reward if he was located, dead or alive. That was included in the file, too.

She wondered idly how much he'd be willing to pay or do

to keep his whereabouts secret. Cecilie had no doubt that his disappearance was his own doing. Or perhaps the original situation was not, but he was obviously free to come and go and he had not returned. She wondered if he really was crazy and his family was going to commit him very quietly to some elegant spa with the finest psychiatrists and therapeutic genetic restructuring that money could buy. Running away from that fate was something that made sense, which was the only comprehensible thing she could conclude about David Gavrilli.

Cecilie thought about that very generous reward. She was fairly certain that David alone couldn't match it. She wondered how nervous it would make him, to let him know that she had the power to return him to the asylum he had fled.

Until now, he had had the power. Cecilie felt the shift as the whole puzzle changed shape yet again. Now, even though he didn't know it, she had taken over.

Information was both wealth and power. The Septs built their Houses on this. They had already taken over the world, only the world didn't know it yet. Soon, very soon, the world would know. Once the Septs met and divided their territories, then everyone would know where the real power in the world was.

Families like the Gavrillis were obsolete, living out of a privilege hundreds of years old. They had lived past the time of their natural death and their power was only a memory, but they hadn't recognized that yet.

Cecilie knew this, but it felt so different, so strong, so good, to hold someone like David Gavrilli in her grasp. Information was power, and even the most junior senior apprentice in Sept-Fortune had more data at her command than the scion of the wealthiest and most influential family in the world. And the data had delivered him.

No wonder David Gavrilli hated the Septs so deeply. No

wonder he thought there was a plot to wrest control from the old bastions of command. Perhaps he was not so much crazy as threatened and afraid, Cecilie thought. Perhaps he was jealous and bitter as well, knowing that he had had the talent to join the new elite but was tied by allegiance to the old.

Oh, yes, Cecilie had him precisely. Now she only had to decide how to best use her newfound cognizance, her new experience of dominion.

Cecilie Sept-Fortune didn't know she was crying.

10

Once upon a time, the courtesans of Venice would sit out on their balconies with their long hair soaked in lemon juice and then spread over broad straw brims to lighten it. Once upon a time they would rise at noon or later and spend the night in gambling parties. There were stories about a convent rumored to be a brothel on one of the islands in the lagoon, where the young nuns were offered as whores and their babies killed.

Venice had been many things, David Gavrilli knew, but none of them had been respectable. Although the day was overcast, grey clouds over grey water, the whole city enveloped in a charcoal wash, he had gone to Murano. Among the tourists trooping through the glassworks and the shops he could lose himself. They went unmasked, groups from Japan and Germany with their ever-present cameras, guides with red furled umbrellas, schoolchildren trooping along, glad to be doing anything but their assigned studies.

On a grey day he loved to watch the furnaces, the hot open

fires for melting the glass and the burly men in undershirts that swung the long lead pipes like reeds. He watched now with a group speaking some language he couldn't identify. He didn't care about the guide's description, he could fill in the words himself. Instead he found himself mesmerized by the fire, by the rhythmic swaying of the pipes, by the thick arms of the glassblowers. Above all he was entranced by the red molten glow on the end of the pipes that arced in the darkness as it took shape. This was magic he could watch forever, animals and colored flowers with leaves all veined taking shape at the end of the leaden pipe in the dark.

It looked like Hell, like all the classical descriptions, like all the paintings in the Roman churches. Dante had written about the dark and the fires. But in Hell they did not create things of such beauty, they did not laugh and blow and take such care with the exact hues of the colors.

The old colors, David knew, were poisons. He had taken the tour when he had first arrived and still was fascinated. Arsenic made green, for one, the rich emerald that had been produced on Murano for centuries before cheaper substitutes were found and glassblowing was no longer a cloistered priesthood. Poisons, and prisoners. The masters of Murano were accorded the respect of aristocracy and had more wealth than many, but were not permitted to leave Venice. Ever. Lest they take their secrets with them. They stayed on Murano and married into each other's families so many times that the family trees rivaled any in Europe for complexity. Their glasswork was no longer their monopoly and their art was old, but they still reigned among the great artists in the world.

David had seen some of the newer glass from Prague, where artists worked in modern designs. Once he had thought to go there, but had never managed it. Always there was so much to do, so much work to accomplish before he could rest.

Today, watching the glass become the traditional dolphin stems for wine goblets, David wondered why he hadn't gone back home. He had the power, surely, but the desire was gone. The thought was as foreign as Prague. Home was the palazzo off the Grand Canal were the silk moire was rotting off the walls and the masked still gathered for music and games the way they had before the time of Napoleon.

Here in Murano he was an alien, looking into a world that he could never really understand. The glass masters were true priests of their art. That made him think of Sean and the Pietà, dedicated to the bone. There was nothing else for the glassblowers, or for the singers of the great choirs. Compared to them he was a dilettante, with nothing to lose. Greatness in art, be it music or the net, was not suitable for the heir to unimaginable wealth. Mastery was reserved for those who had been given nothing beyond a particular aptitude and the single-mindedness to follow wherever it led.

David felt more estranged than ever, a ghost walking through the world. He wished he had his white corpse mask and the costume of the shroud with the dead roses.

He rode home in a speedboat as the sun set over the water. It was silent as a dream and more ephemeral. He got off at the stone platform that was hundreds of years old, the stairs down to the water eroded by millions of feet. He thought he saw a flicker of movement under the archway that decorated the portico of the house. Only a trick of the light, he thought. The light in Venice was famous like her whores, their beauty the result of desire and mirage.

Then the movement came again and he was sure he had seen something. It touched the world around him like the anomaly let free of the net. He walked over and ducked under the archway to investigate.

At first he thought it was garbage that had been dumped.

The shape was vaguely human and he considered that it could be one of the needle kids curled up for the night. It had happened before. He grabbed at what he saw was a wrist and began to pull, hoping that the indigent would get the message and leave without altercation.

Then he realized that the skin was cold—colder than the water, as cold as the grave. He didn't hear himself shriek and pull away, run out from under the stonework and puke into the canal.

He got his breathing under control. His stomach threatened to heave again but there was nothing left in it. David shivered and shook as he squatted hugging himself on the landing. He had never seen anyone dead before, had never touched a body before.

He should call the police or an ambulance, he thought. But maybe he should see if he knew who it was first. It was the old man's palazzo and Artos would want to know.

David didn't want to know. He only wanted to get out of there, get into the warm light of familiar rooms and call someone whose job was to make unpleasantness go away. That was what he did in the end. He didn't want to go back to the corpse by the water, didn't want to see that it had once been human. Instead he did the easy thing and called the police. Someone dead, he said, under the archway. He didn't know any more and didn't want to.

So when the police arrived he was surprised when he was summoned back outside under the floodlights. "Have you ever seen this person before?" a weary police sergeant asked him.

David glanced down and his eyes went wide. He had truly not expected to know who the body belonged to. He certainly was not prepared for this.

Lying mostly covered in plastic was Artos, a small burn hole between his eyes.

Artos had been murdered. Who would kill the old man? David wondered feebly. He trembled, confused both by the idea that Artos was gone and by the very fact of death itself. Artos looked like Artos—and didn't. The features were the same but his skin didn't look real and there was nothing familiar about him. There was no presence there at all.

"Are you a relative?" one of the police asked.

David shook his head, still dazed. "I played music with him," he answered.

"We can spend some time here asking questions. You could help us. In any event you'll have to give us a statement on how you found him," the officer said.

David shrugged. He didn't understand any of it. "Was it the Red Army Faction?" he asked vaguely.

"We don't know yet," the detective answered gently. "We don't know anything yet. Why don't you tell us again exactly how you found him and what you saw?"

So David went through it again, only this time he had come back to his senses just enough to be afraid. Maybe the anomaly had killed the old man. He didn't understand how the thing could get free of the net. Perhaps it had some grudge against Artos, or maybe against jazz.

Most likely the Septs killed him. The old man knew about the meeting. But then, so did David, and David was far more suspicious. He had been the one talking against them, he had been the one who had told far too much to Cecilie.

Cecilie. Damn her. She probably went and told her superiors. She thought that her Sept was unassailable, perfect, and that her signoras were the next thing to God and the Madonna.

Only if it had been Cecilie, why had they killed the old man? Why hadn't they killed him?

David pondered this question as he gave yet another statement to yet another detective, this one younger than the rest. A detective in training, David thought grimly. At least he still could think.

He had given them the library of the old man's palazzo. It had chairs and two desks and another writing table, so David thought it was more suitable for detectives than the ballroom or the parlor. Now the whole house was sealed and David was outside wondering where to go. He hadn't told them that he had lived here on the third floor for years and that most of his belongings were there.

Now his things would be searched, and he was grateful that the old man had made him get rid of his Gavrilli IDs and anything that could link him either to his family or to Rome. Artos had burned his picture disk and his family records the third month he had been in residence. They had made a ceremony out of it, tossing it into the fire and then the ashes into the canal. David had missed those mementos of home. Now he was glad that Artos had insisted, had divested him of any past. Now there was nothing at all to link him to the things in his room in the house, and nothing to link any of them to the Gavrillis.

Only he had to find a place to go. He had his kiosk key around his wrist like almost everyone else in the city. A few of the girls had taken to wearing them on ankle bracelets or on fine chains around their waists, but on Artos's advice David had accepted the common fashion of wearing the brightly colored laminated card on a heavy chain next to his watch.

He could get money from a kiosk and go back to the pensions, where they weren't particular about his identification. Then he thought about the Septs and decided he didn't want to risk it. Anything that went through a kiosk could be traced. It might be time-consuming and it might be difficult, but that was what brought large contracts into the Septs.

Instead, David stepped into a cheap mask shop and bought a plain white plastic mask that looked worn already. He paid in cash. He had a little more cash on him, enough to take a taxi certainly. Instead he walked the streets and bridges in the dark, the streetlights reflecting off the water.

From the distance he could hear the music. A rehearsal, probably, and most likely a student group. But the singers were still Pietà and their voices were pure and liquid.

David waited until the music ended and then he went not to the bronze oversized Pietà door itself, but to the residence down the street. Unlike the Pietà's main building, this building had no reliefs cast on the door, no painted balcony with pierced work around the second floor and no impressive bank of stairs to the street.

Still, the place had charm, a very sweet courtyard inside and truly exceptional tiles in the halls. He rang the bell for an apartment on a middle floor, an apartment made from a carved-up house that had once belonged to a rich merchant. The Pietà owned several such buildings in the neighborhood and leased them to members of the choir and the staff. They were free to live where they liked, but the official residences were convenient, inviting and subsidized. David waited with his hands in his pockets, hoping. It was always possible no one was home. Rehearsals often ran late and performances happened at any hour.

He rang again and this time an irate voice came through the speaker. "No sales," the voice snarled.

David smiled. "Sean? It's David. Can I come up?"

He was answered with a bell to signal that the security door was unlatched. David climbed three flights of winding stairs. The lift was almost as old as the stairs and no one used it.

Sean was waiting outside his door when David made it to the landing. "Come in, I just got in from rehearsal, it's wonderful to see you," Sean said all in a rush. "Can I get you anything? Come in, take off your coat, your mask."

David waited until he was inside the door to remove the

flimsy mask. "Artos has been murdered," David told Sean. "Can I stay with you for a few days, until things calm down?"

Sean's eyes grew large. "Can you stay? David, I would like you to stay your whole life, not just a few days. You know you are always welcome here. But come in, you haven't had supper yet, have you? I was making chicken."

David almost declined before he realized that he was hungry. The chicken smelled good, even if Sean was a terrible cook. And David could not offer to go out. He didn't want to unmask and he couldn't afford to eat in privacy, not unless he went to a kiosk.

"You said Artos was killed?" Sean asked, bringing two glasses of wine from the tiny kitchen. "What happened? Who did it? Why?"

David shook his head. "If I could answer any of those questions I wouldn't have to beg on your doorstep," he said. "I'm scared, Sean. I'm scared and I don't want anyone to know where I am. Thank God I have some clothes here."

Sean nodded solemnly. "You are always welcome to show up on my doorstep, David," he said. "Even though the news is bad, I'm grateful if it brought you to me. Even for only a few days."

"I'm sorry," David said, but Sean cut him off. "Don't be. I'm happy I can help. I'm happy if I can be with you. Even on your terms."

David closed his eyes. He had had too much emotion today already to handle Sean as well. Especially whenever his mind turned to the body, to grabbing a stone-cold bony wrist and flesh that felt soft and fake and icy cold. Death was a new experience; he had managed to miss that before.

Now death clung to him like fear. The glass of wine, the pictures on the wall were all less real than the memory of the dead man.

David did not think about vengeance. He thought about who would have killed his mentor, his benefactor, and he could think of no one but the Septs. Only, even as full of hate of them as he was, David had never heard of the Septs killing anyone. Ever.

"There's one more thing," David said when Sean returned with a spoon of sauce. "I need access to a dreambox. Tonight. A private one where I don't need an ID to get in."

Sean looked at him and the spoon froze halfway to his mouth. "Tonight? No ID? I don't know if I can," Sean said, trying to think desperately.

The Pietà did not have dreamboxes. Those belonged to the Septs, to the wealthy or to the net.walkers. Normal people used kiosks and commercial servers.

But being in the Pietà, Sean did know a few of the powerful and wealthy. A few had been patrons. An even more select few had become friends.

Mentally Sean went through his list, biting his lip. "I don't know," he repeated. "Let me see what I can do."

David gazed into his eyes, remembering more pleasant evenings. "It would mean a lot to me," he said, his voice low and full of promise.

Sean bit his lip harder. "Let me see," he said, but already David knew that he had won. Sean would manage something. Sean always did.

"When there is no reasonable alternative, the unreasonable becomes likely." Cecilie chanted the line like a mantra, because nothing made sense again.

She had gone in search of David. She wanted to corner him, maybe threaten him a little with his family and the reward. Not just for the money, but because Cecilie was furious at him and she wanted to get her own back. She was Sept. She was better than him, had to be better at least in data searches and information acquisition.

That was what galled her most of all. David had traced her, knew what she was carrying and knew it was important. She should have known that and she should have been ready. She had been so very innocent then.

Cecilie was alone in the Sept-House. Well, not entirely alone in the building. There were the sisters in their apartments with their families and there was the night staff supervising the housekeeping. But the working sectors of the House were abandoned and the lights shut off or way too bright.

Cecilie was dressed in a pale green party dress. Her hair spilled in artfully tousled curls over her shoulders and her makeup was both fashionable and extreme. Julietta had done it just after dinner, over Cecilie's protests.

"The party's at nine, which means we can't arrive before nine-thirty," Valentina chattered. "But why didn't you bring a dress, Cecilie? Your mother knows about the party, and I've heard that the Sept-Sorian-House is the oldest and the most beautiful on the island. I wonder how they managed, they're not even really an Italian Sept, let alone Venetian."

Cecilie wished that Valentina would just shut up. She knew as much about the Sept-Sorian-House as Tina did, but managed not to say that they had the building because no one would dare challenge Sept-Sorian in anything they wanted. There were rumors and stories about Sept-Sorian. They were dangerous. And Valentina didn't know anything—Sept-Sorian was the first of the great Venetian Septs. In fact, much of their organization had been established before the net was ever a dream.

She had been vaguely interested in going, but only vaguely. She had heard enough whispers about Sept-Sorian that she felt uncomfortable at the idea of entering their House, even for a gala event. Signora Tima had intimated that they were rivals with Sept-Fortune in some way, and in others that they could not be trusted. Cecilie's interest in the party waned rapidly as Tina and Julietta went on with their enthusiasm.

"It's our very first party as full sisters," Julietta reminded her. "And it's going to be very elegant and formal, you know. Because of the Board meeting. You have to wear makeup and make a big splash. No more boys."

"They aren't going to be here for days," Cecilie stated flatly.

Valentina shrugged. "Maybe not here. But the invitation said that it was to begin the round of festivities for the meetings. So that means there'll be some serious foreign Sept brothers there. I love foreign accents. I wonder if there'll be any Americans? I could practice my English."

"Oh, you always want to practice English," Julietta said. "And German and Russian and Japanese and you're rotten in all of them."

Valentina eyed Julietta steadily. "But they always like to help me out," she said. "And then they talk to me half the night and then, well, if they're cute . . . Besides, do you think I plan to stay here forever? I've already applied for an opening in the Sydney House and I've heard that there'll be an opening in Seoul in the fall. I'm going to get out of here and see the world before I'm too old to really live." She lifted her shoulders elegantly and wrinkled her nose.

Julietta tittered, and suddenly Cecilie realized that Julietta always tittered. Tina wasn't interested in anything except money and how much things cost and how many foreign Sept brothers she could attract. Between them, they had bullied Cecilie into a dress they had begged off an older Sept sister with an apartment and a date and no reason to go to this party. They had chosen this sister particularly because she was also a redhead, and they were right. Her dress looked magnificent on Cecilie.

The more they dressed her like a doll, the less Cecilie wanted to go. She had been to enough Sept parties. She was sick of seeing the senior apprentices and journeymen eyeing each other like meat in the butcher shop, going over considerations of Sept alliance and specialty and future incomes and housing allotments and vacation properties in their heads.

Sept-Sorian was very good for that. With such an elegant house the brothers often had long waits for apartments, if they could get them at all. Though the house was large, the apartments for the signori were proportionately huge. Younger brothers preferred to marry Sept sisters with good prospects for living space while they waited their turn for one of the coveted apartments.

"I hear that most of their brothers *rent* apartments," Julietta said, pulling Cecilie's hair into a clip and spraying it in place. "The waiting list is so long that the younger ones will have four or five to an apartment to split the rent, and they have to commute."

"What about their parents?" Valentina asked, awed that Julietta knew so much about the hosts of the evening.

"Oh, they don't recruit here at all," Julietta said. "There may be one or two who have families here, but mostly they have only full members who come here for assignment. I think their training program is in Sweden or Denmark or something," she said.

"Uppsala," Cecilie said. "And Shanghai, Buenos Aries and Tokyo."

"Ugh," Julietta said. "Four training houses? Sounds terribly impersonal, like they're overrecruiting or something."

Valentina shook her head at Julietta. "Sorian combined with Sept-Sakura two years ago. You remember the fireworks that caused. There, Cecile. Take a look. You are so beautiful that I'm jealous."

And Cecilie was surprised, because she really was as pretty

as Julietta for once. The green dress made her skin look creamy
and the hairstyle made her look much more grown-up. She
hardly recognized herself in the mirror.

"Well, come on," Valentina said. "We're going to be fash-
ionably late now anyway. I don't want to arrive after all the
music's over."

Cecilie got up from the chair, and then sank back down. She
didn't want to go. She could see it all already and it was awful.
Tina searching for someone rich to flatter her and Julietta surrounded by lots of men all evening just to show off. Cecilie felt
sick to her stomach.

"Well, come on," Tina said again.

Cecilie shook her head. "I don't feel so good," she said. It
wasn't a lie. "You go on. I'll rest for a bit. Maybe my stomach
will settle down."

"You aren't getting a flu, are you?" Julietta demanded. "Because I really don't want to get sick and it isn't flu season."

"No, I'm not getting the flu," Cecilie said. "I just don't feel
good. I've got cramps. Why don't you both go and I'll take
something and call a taxi when I feel better? Okay?"

They looked at her and at each other. "Are you sure you'll
be all right alone?" Tina asked. "Are you sure you don't want
us to stay with you?"

"No, silly, I'll be fine in a while. I just need to rest, okay? I
would feel awful if you missed the fun, really."

Julietta and Tina indulged in a few more rounds of perfunctory protests before they disappeared. Cecilie sighed when
they were gone, happy to finally be alone. The silence of their
absence was bliss. Cecilie lay on the lounge sofa in the half-light
for a long time enjoying the hushed abandonment. It was so
pleasant when those two were gone, she realized.

Then she admitted to herself that she never really had liked
Julietta or Valentina. They were silly and vacuous, even if they

were smart. Monkeys could be smart. But her classmates managed to be smart on the net and oblivious of everything except clothes and boys everywhere else. She couldn't understand it.

That was not so important. What was important was that she was alone and here while everyone else was at the party. She had no intention of going to the party, no desire to call a cab. No, she was going to stay right here and she was going to find David and she was going to tell him just what she could do to him. And she could almost taste that nice big reward.

She didn't bother to take off her dress before she lay down in the dreambox. The Library was deserted. One or two forlorn familiars waited for their owners and a clock ticked loudly. Cecilie wondered who had thought up that detail, which for the first time struck her as mildly unpleasant.

She left the Library immediately and headed toward the Mall. It was in neon phase again, light reflecting off brushed aluminum to make a dizzying display. Whoever had done this was not only good, but was obsessed with detail. None of the other Mallscapes had so many light effects, each worked out and sculpted before it had been created out of the whole cloth of the net. She had heard that each of the Mallscapes had been a journeyman's Masterpiece for Sept-Prado.

The Mall was quiet for the Mall. Most of the shoppers here were from the other side of the world, where it was daylight and not time for parties or dates or watching kids in school theatricals. The Mall never closed, but it was quiet by Cecilie's usual standards. There were few people in the aisles and almost none in the shops.

She should go to another level, Cecilie thought. Another place where she could truly affect life in the vast multidimensional city that was the net. The Mall was the center but there were businesses and classrooms, parties and porn, people who sailed through and people who stayed fixed.

She was restless and didn't want to go to any of the places she knew. She didn't want to go to the fashion talks and the diet groups. She didn't want to hang out with the lonely and the bored. She had done that for so long.

Suddenly Cecilie realized that she didn't know where she wanted to go for herself. Most of the places she had frequented were places important to Julietta and Valentina, or to other Sept sisters they had met at parties or meetings or joint classes. There were Sept talk groups and Sept flirt groups and Cecilie realized that she had been tired of them all for a very long time.

She wanted something different, something new. Something that would lead her to David and the anomaly both.

She thought about it but no inspiration came. So she sat down by the fountain that was all a spray of glitter in this version, on a chair that was striking but not really comfortable here, and pondered. Faced with all the possibilities in the world and knowing what she didn't want, she couldn't figure out what she did want. But she knew she didn't want to stay here.

She went back to the Library via the underground route, a two-minute meander following discreet grey signs. The underground was still part of the Mall level, and anyone who knew how to use it was welcome to traverse the shortcuts and avoid the tempting displays of goods in the main Mall. The Library entrance down here was very discreet, the door stenciled with AUTHORIZED PERSONNEL ONLY over a bare metal aperture.

This approach brought her not to the main reading room but to the unfrequented passageways in the undercroft of the structure. In Real Life they would have been full of dust and cobwebs. Here they were merely abandoned, forgotten, written into the code by someone ages ago who had wanted an easy way to get from place A to place B and C without being too obvious. It had probably been left intact because it was too much bother to rip it out.

Besides, the younger apprentices all learned their way around the labyrinth beneath the Library on their own. It was invaluable training for later work in finding alternate routings and keeping well away from the main corridors. The passageways had been fun when she had been a junior girl. There were even ghost stories the girls in Sept-Fortune told about them. Cecilie had enjoyed telling stories for the younger students about Signora Blanca.

Signora Blanca had been a young and beautiful member of Sept-Fortune in an earlier time. Perhaps Signora Tima had known her; no one knew. But Blanca had been talented and brilliant and ambitious and had spent all her free time in extra work. Her fees were astronomical, because she was so fast on her jobs, and her account was the largest in the Sept.

Even though Blanca had been beautiful, she had never bothered with parties. She always said that she would find her true soulmate where her soul would fly, and where else would it fly but the net? The Sept sisters had all thought her a little strange and very romantic and left her to her ways.

After several years, Blanca had found her perfect soulmate. He was from some foreign Sept that didn't even have a House in Venice, but Blanca didn't care. They had their own life together, she insisted. They met down in these very passageways that were part of the Library but below it. He wandered here, pondering questions that Blanca had never heard before.

Finally he had asked Blanca if she would come to live with him, in a place that was familiar to her and yet was not Venice. Of course Blanca agreed. Her Sept sisters were quite put out not to be invited to the wedding, but they helped her pack her ivory lace gown and her trousseau for the journey to who knew where. Because the husband of Blanca's dreams had told her that they would meet one more time in the passages when he would tell her where to go. She wore her ivory lace wedding dress into the dreambox to meet him. She had never come out.

The younger apprentices knew that Blanca and her husband were flatlined and lived in these places that were forgotten. When she had been fourteen, Cecilie thought she had caught a glimpse of Blanca in her wedding dress turning a corner in the passageway. Now she thought it obvious that the legend was just a silly story for children, and Cecilie was certain that every Sept had its own version of the legend.

Still, it had been ages since Cecilie had bothered with this segment of the Library, and being down here again brought the story to mind. No matter that it was legend and that she knew there were no real ghosts in the machines; it still made her feel a delightful tremor of fear as she found herself alone in the tunnel. At least the lights were bright, as they wouldn't be in Real Life, and there was no smell.

Cecilie wandered through the maze. She wondered if David knew it existed, if he knew his way around here. There were odd turnings and a lot of doors that made it look like there was a whole second universe down here. In fact, it was abandoned. When she had been an apprentice they had picked a lot of the doors and found only blank static beyond. A few had been decked out gloriously. Cecilie remembered one in particular that had been done as a dragon's hoard with a sleeping dragon breathing gently, its iridescent scales looking as alive and real as anything outside. There had also been the room of the Arabian Nights and another that had held a masked ball every time they found the right door. Many of the girls assumed that this was where Blanca met her beau and that all the fantasy characters behind the doors were flatlines who had come here to live forever in dreams.

Cecilie didn't realize that she was smiling. She closed her eyes and raised an arm and pointed randomly the way they had when they were girls. Whatever door she pointed at . . .

The third one down on the right. They were all the same from the outside. It was probably just going to be static, she thought, but she might as well see if her skills were still up. She didn't have anything better to do.

She touched the door and was asked for a password. "Open sesame," she said. Whoever had designed this place had had a sense of humor and respect for tradition. "Open sesame" often worked on Library locks as a backdoor password. And it worked on this one. Which it should, since there was nothing here to be guarding at all.

When the door opened there was no static, but there was nothing she recognized, either. This was not one of the fantasy rooms she had discovered when she was a youngster. This was something—different.

She looked at it for a long time before stepping over the threshold. At first it seemed to be absolute chaos, colors and movement and sound that traveled and looped in on itself to make spaces and n-dimensional mobiles that threatened to absorb her and take her through into some other realm. It was not even the stuff of nightmares. It was more disjointed than that and not so personalized. It merely was, in itself and apart from any human expression she had ever known.

Color and sound rippled through it and Cecilie almost perceived pattern before it fell back into disarray. Like looking through a kaleidoscope for a moment, she thought, before all the pieces fall apart. Yet in that one moment there was something familiar and entirely alien at the same time.

Alien. That was the word. She gasped and sucked her breath in sharply. The anomaly. It belonged here, she thought. Or something like here.

The anomaly was alien. It was alien thought touching human construct, interacting, learning, going its way. Which was why it changed things as it learned and yet never could either fit in or be wholly invisible. It followed no rules, no form of structure, that humans could imagine. It did not belong to any human thought at all.

If it were human in origin or thought, Cecilie realized, there would be some thread of logic she would recognize. Even if this were an emerging being formed by the net itself, it would have to follow the laws of human organization that had laid down its core structures. She might not understand Chinese or Turkish, but she could recognize human language. She could tell it from plain noise.

This had no structure that she could discern, and she had been trained to recognize and analyze structures from the first. She knew that there must be some form of organization in this mess. There had been that momentary glimmer. Now the contact and probably the possibility of contact were gone.

Aliens in the Library, in the net. It was open to all. Why couldn't they have tapped in? But from so far away—the idea made her shiver. So far away.

She closed the door behind her and stood in the faux stone corridor again. She closed her eyes, raised her arm and whirled, this time actually stumbling in the direction opposite to the door she had opened.

The new choice looked much like the old, only with a number stenciled in blue on the side of it. She didn't remember seeing any numbers before, but then she had been young and hadn't paid attention to detail all the time. Maybe it had been here all along.

She tried "Open sesame" on this door and it wouldn't budge. She tried again but he door remained firmly locked against her. There were a few other common Library passwords. She racked her brain to think of them. Some were very old and some were Sept specific. "Jason," she said. "Dilbert. Cat in the hat."

Still nothing. That was even stranger. In frustration she put her hands to the surface and pushed.

It gave. This room was as alien as the other, swirling and weird and completely without human presence or precedence. Dimension opened and closed as the entire thing mutated. She didn't know what it was, only that it nauseated her. She lost her sense of direction and her balance at the same time. Something about the movement and the sound together were disorienting, and she groped for the door with her eyes closed.

The walls felt smooth all around. The noise alone was enough to make her gag, and she screamed to drown it out. Her voice was swallowed by the roaring tumult so that she couldn't even hear her own contribution to the din.

Cecilie panicked. She was sure there was no way out, no rest, nothing beyond the next moment of misery. She screamed again, clamped her hands over her ears, and rushed headlong straight ahead of her.

Then she was in the corridor again and it was quiet. She opened her eyes warily, but there was only the quiet faux stone and the endless doors. She lowered her hands from her ears. Whatever lurked behind the door was well shielded.

Here it was safe, it was sane. She could hear her own thoughts again. She could think. Thinking had been impossible in the confusion of alien images. She slumped in the hallway and leaned back on the cool smoothness of the beautifully textured program as her mind cleared.

She would never have gone to the trouble to create such a rich sensorium, as the original programmers of the Library had. She wouldn't be given the time for the project. Newer construction was more sketched in, and never included the delicate touches of temperature perception and tactile stimulation of the original archives.

The builders of those had created them for love. They had competed to produce the best architecture, the most perfect semblance of Real Life. Old places in the net were real places. Even the sea was utterly realized, reproduced and created in perfect metaphor in an outmoded aesthetic.

Nothing that existed in the net had to look or feel like anything outside. But no one bothered anymore to make things solid and strong, and so there was no psychic comfort. There was no privacy either, and no grounding. The abstract structures and ideological architectures that Cecilie had been trained to produce might be more honest in the environment, but they felt much less sincere to living flesh. Sometimes members of Sept-Prado would produce something this finely detailed for a client who was willing to spend the extra for it. These days not many people wanted to pay for the massive number of fine details such a production required. Sept-Prado was not inexpensive.

Cecilie was grateful for the rich layers of embedded programming around her, for the solidity that supported her and made her feel safe. The metaphor was substantial enough to make her believe that whatever was on the other side of that door would stay on the other side of that door, that she could walk away and forget this archive existed.

It wasn't until she thought that that she realized precisely what the thing had been. The thing itself was not the alien. It was the alien's archive.

The more she thought about it the more she knew she was right. The images and colors that had assaulted her, completely without any order she could observe, had been so disconcerting because they had been both familiar and jumbled. The more she tried to think of what she had actually seen, broken down and frozen rather than flung randomly through other images equally absurd, the more they were all memories of things that were frighteningly mundane.

She remembered a whale. Plates from a popular women's fashion disk had swum through markings that she recognized as differential equations, but written in the kindergarten colors of the crayon box in a hand that was unfamiliar with the notation.

Everything had been stripped from its context.

Or rather, it had all been isolated from *her* context.

Suddenly she had an image of the anomalies as alien librarians in camouflage. When the anomaly moved through the net it was collecting things for the cache. Cecilie wondered if her bitten nails were stored somewhere in the bedlam that lay behind the doors.

That immediately brought to her mind Signora Fascista, which had not been her real name but was how all the girls thought of her. She had been ancient, her wispy white hair pulled back severely, her back ramrod straight. Ella Fascista had been the head archivist for Sept-Fortune since well before Cecilie had been born. She had never married, to the girls' knowledge, and three years ago she had had a dinner party and retired to the Sept's Hawaii resort.

The girls would have none of it, though. They speculated that she had really gone to turn the resort into one of the great secret archives that none of the other Septs could access. Ella Fascista would never retire, not until she was dead. And even then, she would probably go flatline in the archive.

Cecilie suddenly wondered if the anomaly had not been alien at all, but a ghost of Signora Fascista. Then she covered her face with her hands. That was ridiculous. Anyone would think she was a baby, thinking things like that.

Besides, Ella Fascista would never ever have permitted anything to look like the jumble of information behind the door. Ella Fascista loved order. She had no higher god than the Catalog, no greater good than to assign categories and files to every entry. No one, not in the whole history of the world, had worshipped organization the way Signora Fascista had.

She had really been very kind, Cecilie realized suddenly as she recalled the years of classes and tutorials under the elderly archivist. She hadn't deserved the nasty sobriquet at all, except for her passion for structure in every aspect of life. The old woman—her name had been Signora Margherita, Cecilie recalled—had always smiled at her classes and seemed to enjoy teaching them how to navigate through the various repositories and sites throughout the net. Before the three years of intensive search training, the librarian had already taught them to find information of every sort, and where to find out where to locate data.

She had sent them on "treasure hunts," as she had called them, asking for such esoteric tidbits as debates on Finnish elections before the establishment of the Eurostate or recipes for squash cakes made without butter. Cecilie had enjoyed the "treasure hunts." They had been a wonderful game. It wasn't until much later that she realized how much she had learned from the archivist, who was no longer there to receive any thanks or gratitude.

But if Signora Margherita (it seemed wrong and cruel to even think of her by the name the young girls had used) had been an alien with access to the net, she would be gathering information and categorizing it. She would be trying to make sense of what she found, and finding associations. No, she wouldn't have merely been trying, she would have made some sort of sense of it. Her juniors would be on constant treasure hunts to gather data that she would then assemble this way and that until something fit. She was patient and she would try every permutation until things fell into some sort of rational configuration.

The aliens must be trying to sort out their collection. Just because it didn't make sense to Cecilie didn't mean that the categories being tried didn't make sense to an alien. Cecilie pondered the idea, and the more she thought about it the more she was sure it was true.

These were aliens—true aliens from another solar system. Humanity had achieved first contact and didn't even know.

All the stories and shows she'd seen suddenly seemed naive and laughable. Of course this is what they would do. Information above all, wasn't that what every Sept sister knew as the universal exchange? She herself had been trained to collect data before making a presence known. That was the only intelligent way to go about it, especially when the data were so outlandish and incomprehensible.

Perhaps they were so far away that it would be impossible to travel. Perhaps then the anomaly, the collectors, were bots running sweeps through the net, downloading whatever they had been programmed to think was important. Then they sent everything back home—wherever that was.

The more Cecilie thought about it, the more she knew that she had discovered the truth. In fact, by the time she traversed the undercroft to emerge into the main reading room of the Library the whole notion seemed quite normal. Of course there were aliens on the net. Where else would they be?

She sat in her normal seat and called for Zizi. The bird of paradise arrived in a flutter of turquoise feathers and with a shrill cry. Cecilie wondered if she ought to redo the familiar's voice yet again. The cry was perfectly authentic and wonderfully birdlike, but it was also obnoxious in the Library quiet. Perhaps she should just edit it down a bit.

Zizi landed on her shoulder and settled down to preen. Cecilie sighed. "Not now," she told the familiar. "I want you to run a term-check on outgoing signals. You're looking for coherent pattern directed at some astronomical location. Find the location. There should be a higher percentage of flow to one than to any other, or compared to what is lost in background."

Zizi looked up from his feathers. "That is difficult. It will take time."

"Just do it," Cecilie said, wondering where the familiar had picked up the idea that he could contradict his creator.

Zizi sighed, ruffled his feathers, and took off. Cecilie wondered if she should build another familiar on a more obedient template. A dog, perhaps, or a mythical creature for which someone else had written the template ages ago, so she wouldn't be responsible if it went off with its own quirks like Zizi. Signora Angelina had warned her she'd have much more trouble creating her own template for the bird of paradise. Cecilie wished she'd listened.

Now she was both exhausted and excited at the same time. She couldn't sleep, but she also was too tired to do anything more useful. Probably it was time to get out of the dreambox. She accessed the clock with a thought, and the time showed up in red digits floating above the oak slab table. It was early, and she could still catch a cab and go to the party. But the idea of going to that party, where she knew few enough people and not one who'd care about her discovery, made her even more tired. Maybe she'd just go home.

In the middle of her considering her options she heard footsteps through the reading room. She glanced up, wondering who else was ditching the party and working instead.

Damn if it wasn't David Gavrilli in the sun mask stalking through the reading room, where he didn't belong.

Anger banished her exhaustion. She got up from her place and confronted him in the middle of the room in front of the fireplace. Here their footsteps were muffled by a red Oriental rug that somehow set off his cobalt blue costume. The blazing golden sun mask seemed softened and made richer by the brass and golden wood that surrounded them.

This infuriated Cecilie even more. Bad enough he should have the audacity to come in here, and in that gaudy, attention-gathering costume, no less. But for her own environment to lend dignity and grace to what she considered show and arrogance compounded her disapproval.

"What are you doing here?" she hissed.

David looked at her, but the mask he wore revealed no expression. "I come here sometimes," he said, his voice completely neutral to her perception. "Tonight I came to find you."

"You're always finding me," Cecilie replied. "And you know something, you shouldn't be so glad. Because I have something to tell you, David Gavrilli. Yes, I know who you are and how much you are worth to your family and how to let them know that you're safe and sound and wasting time playing at being a net.walker in Venice. I'm sure they'd be happy to have the information."

The sun flickered, and Cecilie thought that the gold glittered a little less.

"But you can't," David protested. "Not when we're so close."

There were things she disliked about the virtual community. Right now what bothered her was that if she hit him, it wouldn't do a thing. Her hand would just pass right through him and he wouldn't notice anything at all uncomfortable, and she would have given herself away.

"Look, I don't know why you're bothering me," she said. "I'll give you one more chance, because right now I've got better things on my mind than some spoiled rich kid who thinks this is just one more amusing playground. I probably should have my head examined, but I'm too tired to bother dealing with you now. Get out of here, stay away from me, and I won't tell your family where you are. Though I have every reason in the world to do it. It would sure make my reputation and my rates would go way beyond journeyman. So I'm taking a financial loss on this. Go away."

David stood stark still. "But that isn't why I came. I need your help. The old man is dead. Murdered."

"You need the police," Cecilie replied. "Or a priest. There's nothing I can do about that at all."

"You're expert in investigation, in tracking down information. You found out about me and no one else has ever done that."

Or ever told you, Cecilie thought. Privately, she thought that the old man must have known all along and had his own reasons for keeping silent. Maybe he was waiting for the right time. Maybe he just didn't need the money.

"I can pay your fees," the sun told her.

Cecilie resisted the impulse to make an impolite noise. "Do you mean you're proposing a formal contract for a search?" she asked.

"If that's the only way to do it," he said. "If you got me, you're good. Then you'll be able to tell who killed Artos."

"Why do you care?" she asked, finally. She couldn't believe that David Gavrilli cared about anything very much. Then she understood his reasoning and she groaned. "To save yourself, you mean. They think you did it."

The sun merely nodded.

"Oh, this is great, this is just wonderful," she muttered. "Cecilie Sept-Fortune, private eye. I've always wanted to do that as much as I've wanted to become a, a, a lion tamer."

"The contract will be for the same amount as you would get from my family for locating me," he said softly.

Cecilie could well believe it. Kill two birds, as her father would say. Pay her off and clear himself at the same time.

Of course, nothing prevented her from turning her documentation over to his family after the contract was executed. The realization filled her with both dread and glee—and absolute horror at herself. A few months ago she would never have considered it. The idea of turning in a client was beyond belief.

Now she was becoming someone she didn't recognize, and she felt filthy. One little job, one graduation exercise, and already matters of principle and conscience eluded her. After all, she really was thinking of accepting Gavrilli's offer. Greed was all tangled up with ambition and she couldn't separate the two. They were very ugly and Cecilie could not look at them and recognize herself.

Also, she insisted stubbornly, he could be innocent. At least of murder, or at least of this murder.

As she considered, she came to the conclusion that he probably was innocent. The idea did not appeal to her. She liked it better when she thought she could trap him in his oh-too-clever machinations. She did not like Gavrilli at all, and she would much rather see him tried for murder than clear him.

Down deep something else said that she had to try. That because she despised him she had all the more reason to do the job. The vestiges of ideals that had retreated, wounded and bleeding, at her graduation, proved that they were far from dead.

"Draw the contract," she heard herself say. "We'll file it with the Sept as an exclusive. That's sometimes hard to get for someone as inexperienced as me."

"You'll do it, then?" he asked, incredulous.

Cecilie had the urge to say no and walk. Instead she just sighed. "I just said I would, didn't I? I'm not going to repeat things because you don't get it. Anyway, when you send in the voucher and authorization for my services, include a confidential packet with as much information about the old man as you can possibly find or remember. I need a few places to at least start a search. I suppose I don't have to explain to you how to do a confidential."

"I think I can manage," David replied. Then he walked away, and Cecilie was glad to see him go.

11

They were arriving. From every corner of the world, from every House and Sept, the members of the Sept Board and their associates, their entourages and their advisors and seniors, were descending upon Venice. It was not the first Board meeting convened here, but it was certainly the most historic.

Sept-Fortune was full. There were Sept sisters, from both Sept-Fortune and associated Septs, lingering in the halls, sitting on the benches in the garden and wandering through the loggia of the palazzo. Parlors that had been closed off were cleaned and aired. The game room was constantly full of Sept sisters playing backgammon and cards. Even the ballroom had been opened and set up with desks and microlinks so that their guests could have workspace and check email, though there wasn't room for anything more than text display.

Dinner was served twice a night, the signore eating with the Board members and the journeymen and below eating later, a hodgepodge of what had been left over from the elegant dinner and something plain and nourishing to make up for any shortages.

Cecilie didn't eat at the House. She could get home before the second serving and eat with her parents. They preferred that, anyway, and she would rather go home than stay in the too-crowded palazzo.

Besides, she had a contract to fulfill and she had begun the job already. In spite of the constant chatter and hushed expectation of what the Board would do and the great changes that were happening in the world, Cecilie tried to concentrate on work. After her conversation with David, though, she couldn't help but hear the Board chatter in a very different light. It was much easier to pay attention to the task at hand than to listen to the bits of gossip flying around the House and wonder if the Board really did mean to take over the world.

So far she had just run the basic credit checks and deed accounts for David's mentor. The old man had checked out as expected, well-to-do but not in the same class as a family like the Gavrillis. He had inherited the palazzo and it was only partially restored. The remaining work would cost more than he had in reserves, which was about the situation of most of the ancient grand houses that had been inherited. Left to decay for lack of funds, they were part of the reason that Venice was crumbling as well as drowning. A few very wealthy outsiders had purchased and restored those that hadn't been acquired by the Septs at the end of the last century when the Sept system first became powerful.

Cecilie had been ready to go home after spending all day running down dull accounts. She had her mask in one hand and her fare card in the other. Still, she hesitated. She disliked traversing the long corridors of the ground floor before she could get outside. Usually the hallways were pleasantly silent as she passed public rooms normally reserved for wedding receptions and musical soirees. In normal times the only people in the main passageway were the very youngest apprentices, who often used the space to run races or play soccer. Cecilie remembered when she and Julietta were seriously punished for roller-skating down the long, narrow hall.

Everything was different with the Board members in town. All the doors were thrown open and there was traffic passing through all the time. The blended conversations of a hundred whispers became a hushed roar. Cecilie couldn't help but stare at the senior sisters, dressed in a million colors of finery she had not imagined. Some wore variations and modernizations of national dress, and she spotted a glorious shell-pink kimono worn as a jacket over charcoal slacks and blouse. One of the sisters wore an elegant African gown in vibrant shades of yellow that somehow managed to look regal without detracting from the sister's delicate beauty.

Cecilie was amazed. For all she had been trained in a great urban House and had gone skiing in Saint Moritz and swimming on the Costa del Sol, for all the sophistication and elegance Cecilie had lived with all her life, she realized that there were many ways in which she was very provincial. It made her feel abashed and very young.

Out of nowhere a sister in a designer suit laid a hand on Cecilie's shoulder. "Do you play bridge?" she asked in very poor Italian.

Cecilie did play bridge. It had been one of the required skills in training, along with backgammon, tennis, and tea. She nodded and murmured in the affirmative even though she didn't want to stay. For all the various forms of etiquette she had been taught, Cecilie didn't quite know how to say no to a sister so senior that she was either a Board member or the assistant to one. So Cecilie was whisked inside the game room, seated on a delicately gilded chair and dealt a hand.

"What they're doing with the banks is absurd," the sister who had recruited Cecilie said. "We only own fifty-two, at least outright in our Sept. Most of our capital is tied up in real estate and that's not as liquid as the San Marco portfolios."

"But Leah, didn't Fumiko buy in to the portfolio project?" asked Cecilie's partner. "The yield overall has been twenty-seven percent. If we liquidate those together with San Marco, we still retain our real estate but we can go in on equal shares with the others."

"Which will leave us cash-poor," a sister with iron grey hair said firmly. "We can't afford that, we'll end up with no flexibility. That's the basic problem with the proposal as it's stated now. We have to reevaluate the relative financial power of each of the Septs individually before trying to create a consolidated entity."

"Maybe we can't do it," Leah said in her atrocious accent. "Maybe we've been too conservative all along, buying land and buildings and not cashing in on the more volatile markets."

The sister with the grey hair shook her head, took a trick, and said, "Not at all. Look at the Septs that haven't invested for the long haul. They're the ones in trouble and I'll bet you more than this game that they're the leaders in the whole consolidation movement. They've got to cover their own asses."

"You mean Sept-Sorian again," Cecilie's partner said before she bid. "It isn't that they don't have the resources, but that they're turning into the bullyboys of the movement. Otherwise I can see the advantages, but I wouldn't trust Sept-Sorian to offer a glass of wine without expecting to get some benefit in return."

"But what does that have to do with the Board meeting?" Cecilie asked. It wasn't until the others looked at her that she realized she had spoken aloud.

The woman with the grey hair sighed. "They don't teach you much about economics, do they?" she said.

"Signora Angelina taught a great deal about economics," Cecilie said, defending her education.

The grey-haired woman shook her head. "Angelina knows a lot about how to do money traces, and what certain economic factors can indicate, but she doesn't teach the girls about how the Septs operate financially. How do you think we have the power we have?"

"Because we can get any information anyone needs." Cecilie recited her first-year lesson by rote. "And we can set up any kind of security system. Because we are experts in searches, security and information we command a very high price. Each Sept sister tithes both to the Sept as a whole and to her own House of residence, but our commissions are generally high enough that even subtracting both those donations leaves the individual able to afford just about anything she could desire. And most of what she cannot afford outright, the Sept already owns."

Leah shook her head. "That's for little girls. Now, how do you think that we have created the power base we have and maintain the lifestyle we offer our sisters? Your tithe to the House pays for the House expenses. The House itself is owned outright by the Sept. Your tithes to the Sept all together go to create the working capital that we invest. So as a group our wealth grows and we can afford to live off the interest of our investments and keep our endowment intact. But by investing what amounts to a fairly substantial sum over decades, we have accumulated larger and larger reserves.

"Only they're not simply reserves or investments or capital. As we have more we are in the position of owning more of the manufacturing of the technology we use. The Septs control how many dreamboxes are built and how many kiosks are placed. How many text interfaces there are and where they are available and at what price. We control our technology, and more and more banks and other companies. Our own Sept owns more real estate than any other single institution in the Eurostate. What does that tell you?"

Cecilie felt their eyes on her ice cold. These women knew something, had some idea that she suddenly suspected was very foreign to her. "That we're powerful," Cecilie said slowly. "But even without all that wealth we'd be powerful, because we have access to information."

Leah shook her head. "No, that's backward. You see, access to information has given us access to wealth, and between the two we've managed to take more power than anyone realized. Of course, part of that is because we're separated into different Septs. We work together when we can, but essentially none of the Septs consult each other before making any decisions. Some of the original hacker anarchy still remains. Sept-Sorian wants to change all that, and while they have the seeds of a good idea, they aren't the ones who should be leading it. So if we don't manage to consolidate our power it's because we don't trust Sept-Sorian or each other, not because we don't have the base to organize and coordinate to regulate the cyberverse."

Cecilie swallowed hard. "You mean we're taking over the world?"

All three of the sisters laughed together. "No, little one," Cecilie's partner said softly. "We already have taken over the world. Now we just have to figure out how not to squabble over the profits. Sept-Sorian just wants to be in charge of everything, and several of the other Septs want to follow Sept-Fortune's plan instead. They really don't teach you girls the important end of the politics, do they?"

"The important politics," Cecilie echoed, half hoping and half afraid.

Her bridge partner laughed again. "Well, important to us, at least," she said lightly. "I believe it was Sonja's deal."

Cecilie could hardly keep her eyes on her cards, and she bid two hands very badly. Finally the woman who'd been her partner sighed. "I guess we're keeping you out too late," she said.

Cecilie put down her cards, thanked them and left the table shamefaced. She didn't know if it bothered her more that she had played so badly or that she had learned something more that supported David's wild allegations.

Maybe they weren't so wild. The sisters she had played with had agreed so easily that she couldn't doubt their sincerity. It seemed the real problem was not whether the Septs were going to rule the world, but how they were going to organize themselves. Sept-Sorian versus Sept-Fortune was no surprise. The two groups had feuded since the beginning, and probably before.

Now she wondered if, as a Sept sister, she had any ethics left at all. She wasn't sure if she could bear to find more evidence that the Sept she had regarded as her home and family was involved in a megalomaniacal battle with others of its own kind. She was disgusted with what she had heard but she couldn't discount it. Nor did she have any idea of what she should do.

It made her think of David. Arrogant rich brat that he was, he still had had the guts to leave, to go off and do what he believed in without his family's approval—and without the comfort of their support. She despised him, but she couldn't help but think that part of what she hated in him was that he showed her her own weakness.

The opening of the Sept Board meeting was a civic event. David watched from Sean's tiny balcony wearing one of Sean's plain white masks. The sun was too conspicuous here, with the whole Board of the Septs marching below in stately style.

Though he was not a Venetian, it offended David to see them greeted so formally, handed the keys to the city, feted and treated with deference. That was more than the Serenissima owed them. Or owed anybody. Streets festooned with banners and hangings decorating balconies made it look like Carnevale, though that was months past.

Serenissima was above them. They should be honored that they were permitted to meet in Venice and not the other way around. David suddenly realized what he was thinking and chuckled to himself. Artos had implanted in him a deep love for the city, and he had become Venetian to the core. His Roman family would be horrified. But he could no longer imagine walking on the streets with his face naked to the world or eating bland Roman cuisine ever again.

The parade was passing by. He checked to make sure that no flesh showed, that his costume concealed his age and gender absolutely before he ran down the stairs to join the crowd in the street. He followed, lost in the throng, as they made their way through the old streets to the Board Hall, where the actual meetings would take place.

On the steps a Pietà choir greeted them with Mozart, something from *The Magic Flute*. David had always loved that opera, and it seemed somehow appropriate to him for his own personal trials. He scanned the singers, almost recognizable in their soft cloth half masks, even though he knew none of them was Sean.

David glanced back over the masked crowd. He wondered if Cecilie was here, and he hoped not. He hoped she was in her dreambox doing exactly what he had hired her to do. Once he was free of any suspicion he could move out of Sean's tiny apartment, which felt like a cage. He could resume his usual routines and contact his friends.

More than freedom, he wanted to practice again. In the apartment that had been carved out of the old house in the ghetto, the walls were too thin for him to play jazz. He spent hours a day working on the approved literature, mainly to keep his hands in practice, but the desire to improvise came over him like lust. And there was nothing he could do. He knew he should be glad that he had a place to stay at all.

Now the Board members filed in one at a time, parading the length of the stone porch to display their costumes. There were images that no one had seen, things that had been commissioned by the finest maskmakers months ago and were now shown in public for the first time. There was one costume of a Hindu god that David longed for, and another all made from iridescent feathers. Next year a few of these would be reproduced in the most exclusive maskmakers' shops for wealthy fashionmongers. But until the end of the meetings, the Board members would be the only ones in the city in such extravagant costumes.

Idly, David wondered if anyone thought about what good targets that made them. And they were supposed to be such great experts on security and all. He could just see them picked out in this mob as Artos had been.

He felt a strange twinge inside, something he hadn't felt when he had found the body or gone into the dreambox looking for Cecilie. He didn't recognize the feeling until it had passed, and then he realized that it had been grief. He missed Artos, missed the music and the acerbic comments that had been about the Septs and the Pietà and everyone in Venice twice as often as they'd been about him. He missed Artos. And he realized with a pang that Artos had cared about him. It was not a thing the old man would admit.

The whole of the Board was inside now. The speeches were done and the choristers in their sky blue robes were entering the building like a religious procession. The crowd was dispersing. David noted the time and turned immediately.

He had an appointment and he did not want to be late—nor did he want to appear in this common costume. If he ran, if

everything was laid out and ready the way he thought he had
arranged things, if he could catch a taxi, he might just make it
nearly on time.

"I trust I haven't kept you waiting long," David Gavrilli said as
he sat in the red leather chair. He crossed his legs, now clad in
appropriately somber charcoal. The suit was one that Artos
had selected, more stylish than the norm back home. His shirt
was white silk and the cloth half mask over his eyes was black.
It was appropriate for mourning.

There were five other people present. One was Artos's
lawyer, a woman David had met on several occasions. She was
not only a very good lawyer, but she had an admirable figure
and dressed with just the right balance of taste and panache. He
had never seen her unmasked, so he had no idea what her face
looked like, and she was decently masked now in the same
black cloth half mask that was always appropriate for serious
business dealings. Only her mask, with her usual flair, had a subtle black-on-black design embroidered across the entire surface.
David wasn't sure whether this was for the sake of fashion
alone, or to display wealth on an article of clothing that was
ubiquitous and generally cut across class boundaries.

She was seated not behind a desk, but behind an antique inlaid table that had no text reader or minilink, or even a mail
folder. The table, as always, was perfectly bare, showing off the
intricate marquetry of a lost century.

The three other people in the room were masked as he was,
but even without faces he was certain they were strangers. One
man was tall and lanky and somehow managed to recline in his
armchair in a way that suggested boredom. The woman looked
shapeless under a sack parading as a dress. She looked uncomfortable, as if the mask or the dress was unaccustomed for her.

She shifted and pulled at her skirts every few minutes. David wondered what she usually wore.

The third man wore the same mask, but his black garments were casual and seemed to fit him in a way that suggested this was his normal garb. His hair was cut very close to his skull, and he had a beard. David was certain he was a musician, though he couldn't place the two others.

The fifth, the unmasked man who stood in the back near the door, was clearly a policeman. They were watching him. David knew they would be here, and he had thought seriously about not coming. But he knew that the police, being simple, would take that as an admission of guilt. So long as they were not going to arrest him immediately he was fairly certain that he could fade back into the city again.

So long as they were not going to arrest him. Suddenly David wondered if this had been a good idea. Perhaps he shouldn't have come at all, the way Sean had pleaded with him. Sean had always been in trouble and always assumed the worst so David hadn't listened. Now he wished he had—sometimes Sean was right.

Still, he believed he had no choice. He couldn't ignore Artos's last summons. Nor could he pretend that he wasn't desperately curious as to who these people were and what the will contained. Besides, he was absolutely and utterly certain that no one would ever arrest him.

He was not guilty.

And he was David Gavrilli. Suddenly David realized that he was ready to admit to that, to use his family if he needed them. No police force was stupid enough to try to pin a murder on him. What were they going to say, that he had killed the old man for his money? David could buy and sell him ten times and not notice it.

Besides which, no one knew what was in the old man's will.
It had been his great secret. David didn't really care so much for
possessions—he had plenty of them if he desired—but he
wanted to know why the old man had been so utterly delighted
in keeping his will undisclosed.

Slowly the lawyer brought out a red leather folio matching
the upholstery in the room. She placed it in the exact center of
the desk and opened it as ceremoniously as the Board meeting
had been opened by the city, and with a good deal more decorum.

"The will of Arturo Carlo Camerillo," the lawyer said. "You
have been called here so that we can read his will, which was
never filed with any service or accessible anywhere except in
these offices. This was a strictly paper-secure document that was
handwritten on photosensitive paper. When I withdraw the will
from the protective envelope it should be dark blue. It will
whiten within seconds of exposure to any light."

David tried not to sigh. There was no need for the explanation; everyone knew about security paper. When he was little
he didn't even know there was paper that didn't have to be
sealed in a treated envelope so it would change color at any sign
of tampering. For all the security systems in the net, old-
fashioned paper was still the best way to keep a secret. His parents' chef had used it for dinner menus.

The lawyer withdrew the document. It was still the deep blue
that indicated it had remained sealed since it was written. In less
than a second it had already begun to fade. By the time the
lawyer had drawn it into her hands ceremoniously it was pale
enough to read.

David didn't even bother listening to the familiar opening.
When had he written his first will? When he was ten? Twelve?
He remembered the writing clearly enough. He and his cousin
Matteo had filched the paper from the kitchen and had spent

the entire day figuring out who in the family deserved which games and books and each of their treasures. He had been most concerned about his music, David remembered suddenly. He had spent so much time worrying who should get his collection of download concerts and archival studio recordings of great keyboard artists.

But now the lawyer was getting to the good parts and David paid attention. "To the Holy Innocents School, all of my musical instruments, recordings, and twenty billion lire for scholarships and improvements in their musical program. Also to the Holy Innocents, my property in Padua adjoining the school grounds, including the house, with the provision that the current tenants are to remain until their death." The woman in the shapeless sack sat up straighter. She must be one of the sisters that ran the charity school.

David had heard of the school. Who had not? They were perpetually in need, a favorite recipient of the proceeds of fundraising balls and society parties. Holy Innocents was one of the best shelters for unwed mothers, the only one David knew of where there were never any rumors that the most attractive and brightest charges were sold to flesh-merchants on their way to South America or Asia.

Still, even for a fashionable charity, the old man's bequest had been far more than generous.

"To Sept-Sorian I leave my paintings and the collection of Murano glass."

David blinked. What had Artos to do with Sept-Sorian? The old man had hated the Septs. And the bequest was small and personal, nothing that would matter to the Sept either way. As if a Sept as powerful and rich as Sorian needed more Murano glass or a few second-rate Romantic paintings.

Unless there was something in them. Or . . . David had to try very hard not to smile. It would be way too easy for him to set up the bequest before it was delivered, to make sure that every painting carried an eavesdropper discreetly daubed onto the back of the canvas. That must have been what the old man had meant, David thought, because otherwise it made no sense whatsoever.

But the Sept brother there to listen to the reading and accept what had been given seemed honestly pleased as well as gracious.

"To Gabriel DiNunnzio, proprietor of the Café Luna, the sum of fifty million lire."

The man dressed all in black blinked and shifted his weight. What showed of his face went bright red. "He didn't need to do that," DiNunnzio said.

The lawyer shrugged. "He didn't need to do any of it," she reminded them all. "He did as he wished, and so you are to accept it as simply his wishes."

"But he didn't have that kind of money," DiNunnzio said, a wondering question in his tone. "He worked for me. Played regular gigs, got the band in."

"I assure you, he did indeed have the money," the lawyer said, her patience wearing thin. She didn't normally deal with people of DiNunnzio's class, and in fact had argued quite vehemently against even this modest legacy. But every time she had argued the old man had increased the amount until she had just stopped short and written it in as he wanted.

"And to my dear protégé David Fillipo, also known as David Gavrilli, my house, where he has lived for the past three years, on the condition that he will remain there and will finish the restorations."

David wanted to bolt immediately. He had never thought for a moment that the old man would use his true name. Artos had certainly known it; no surprise there. But David certainly hadn't expected it in a public document. The old man had turned him over, had ruined him!

And yet, none of the others in the quiet office even turned in his direction. Maybe they didn't know. Maybe they had simply been well trained. He would believe that of the nun and the Sept brother. DiNunnzio had probably never even heard of the Gavrillis. If he had, he would never believe that one of the *real* Gavrillis had played for low wages in his club on a regular basis.

The lawyer was wrapping up, discussing her own position as executor of the estate and how long it would take before they could actually take possession. The Sept brother and the nun discussed how much the taxes would be and whether the estate could pay them. DiNunnzio stood there looking stunned. David wanted to shut them up, to tell them all about how long it would take and how the taxes would work and all the things he had been relentlessly drilled in when he would much rather have been playing the piano or wandering through the net.

Instead he rose and, without a word to any of them, went to the door.

The policeman was more discreet than he had expected and waited until he was alone in the hallway to approach. "You were instructed not to leave the city," the detective said reproachfully.

"I haven't left," David replied.

"We've been looking for you," the officer stated.

David shrugged. "If you must know, I've been spending time with a lover. I was upset by the old man's death, finding him that way. I didn't want to be alone."

The detective cleared his throat carefully. "And who is this lover? May we have an address in case we need to contact you?"

David was ready to give it and then realized that he could be putting Sean in danger. Sean was already volatile, unpredictable, and had been in trouble all of his life. The last thing he needed was a visit from the police. He could go off at them, David thought. For no reason, or any reason, because he always expected the worst. He still was worried that the charges that had forced him to leave home so long ago would catch up with him, and that he would be arrested and turned over to a tribunal.

Nor was his fear ungrounded. David had not taken Sean's fears seriously until he realized the extent of the situation. Now he knew better than he would like that Sean would go to jail for the rest of his life. Before the days of United Europe, Sean would have hanged if he'd been found, and David wondered if that was not the more compassionate sentence.

David shrugged. "That won't be necessary. I'll be back at the old man's palazzo, now that I have the right to be there."

The detective raised one eyebrow. "We'll be keeping tabs on you."

David shook his head and smiled slightly. "I assumed nothing different," he replied. "Only don't waste too much time. Because I didn't kill Artos Camerillo and I would like the person who did caught. Frankly, I am somewhat concerned that I might be in danger."

The detective looked puzzled. "Oh, really. Because of your association with Mr. Camerillo? Why do you think that's dangerous?"

"Because someone killed him," David said. Then he let the anger pass through and thought more clearly. He had always had an aversion to aiding the police, and Sean would think him a traitor for even talking to one of them. But the police should be on his side this time. That was a hard thing to remember, harder when they didn't quite acknowledge or believe it themselves.

"We played jazz at the Luna," David said softly, honestly trying to be helpful. "There are a lot of people here who think that's subversive or worse. The old man was dedicated to nonapproved music. He taught me how to play and I owe him. And I'm going to keep jazz alive here even if it's only this side of legal and the Pietà and the Septs would do whatever they can to close us down. That's what I think. That the Pietà or the Septs wanted jazz dead in Venice so that we would only hear approved music and think approved thoughts."

The detective shook his head. "You really believe this is all about music? What about money, about the land or the palazzo?"

David forced a smile. "I don't think the nuns of Holy Innocents commit murder for bequests they don't know they're getting. As for the palazzo, well, you heard my name. Do you honestly think I would bother? Besides, it will cost more to restore than the thing is worth."

"You mean you really are one of the Gavrillis?" the policeman asked, disbelieving.

"It doesn't really matter," David said softly. "But yes, I am."

The detective scratched his head. "You know, when I read the report I thought it was pretty clear. I was surprised that you weren't arrested on the spot. But now, I'm not so sure. I think we need to look into more of this. But don't let that make you cocky. You're still our number-one suspect. And you're not going to disappear."

David shook his head. The detective smiled grimly. "Oh, no, not that easy, Mr. Gavrilli. Put out your hand."

David felt like he couldn't breathe. Better to get cut down than have one of those bracelets . . . Obediently he held out his arm. He had done nothing at all wrong and there was no reason to be afraid. Only there was an ominous note in the *snick* as the lock hit home and activated.

It looked like a plain steel bracelet, no different than hundreds on sale at jewelry stores all over the city. Only inside this one was a homing beacon. He couldn't escape—and he couldn't take it off. Any tampering with the circuit would bring the authorities faster than he could run and was grounds for immediate incarceration. No matter how innocent he was.

All of Truth could be expressed in mathematical ideas. Music was both Beauty and Truth at the same time, creating the patterns and fulfilling them in a single gesture. Music was the manifestation of mathematics, its reflection and its expression all together.

And yet, somehow, this concert was not working. This was not the usual Pietà performance, keeping the order of the universe in line. Lina felt it. Her own voice, while behaving reasonably, was not consuming her mind. The music was in her head and it was contained. It wasn't surging through the room, through the people listening, who needed the extra strength and clarity the music could give.

They were in the main salon of the Palazzo Sept, the gathering hall for the Board. The concert was part of the Board meeting. Pietà members were contracted to stay in the hall the entire time the Board was engaged and sing. Day and night, mealtimes and worktimes, they sang exactly the pieces the Maestro had selected. There were very few that Maestro thought would truly create the right frame of mind for this meeting, so seventy-three minutes of music were repeated over and over and over again.

Lina hated Board duty already, and it was only the second day. She got tired of the same music and wondered why the Board members didn't protest. But perhaps they were used to things that merely did them good and added nothing to the aesthetic experience.

Still, in Lina's experience there was a feeling of unity underlying the music. The Board might disagree, surely; often they did. But in the past there had always been a harmony of vision, a fluidity between the musicians and the Sept members, a silent acknowledgment that together they were responsible for the system. Together they were responsible for the continuation of life, of civilization, of all the things that made life worthwhile. Together they were the embodiment of evolution, that humanity had come to this, and alone.

Today there was no together. The notes were discrete and did not merge into the whole. The Board members were distant from the music and from each other.

Lina saw it, heard snatches of what they said during her break rotations sitting in the buffet room across from the salon. Members of the Pietà were always treated well. In their own way they were the equal of any Sept members, and in the buffet room members of the Board and the choir mingled freely. It was a common pairing, even, musician and net.ninja, couples that were endlessly pictured in the gossip groups but never consented to interview.

It was no surprise to Lina when he came over. Sept-Barbara was one of the smaller foreign Septs that didn't have a House in Venice. Like many similar Septs, it was sponsored by one of the major Venetian Houses. In this brother's case it was likely Sept-San Marco or Sept-Sorian. Lina had seen him talking to brothers wearing those Sept badges. No matter. He was attractive enough, Lina thought, a little pale but there was a kind of icy determination in crystal blue eyes. Lina found herself strangely intrigued. She had seen very few people with such extreme coloring.

He sat down next to her and inspected her plate. "The salmon mousse is good," he said. "Much better than I thought." Then he made a face. "Much better than this session is going."

"Oh?" Lina asked, only half politely.

He gave her a look that said she knew exactly what was going on. She smiled enigmatically and nibbled her salmon on crusty bread and sipped espresso.

"You know, it's like the music," he said between bites of salmon mousse on cucumber and slices of cheese melted on tomato and bread. "Only this time there's something wrong there. They don't listen to us, you know. The outland Septs could disappear for all they care. They have already made all the decisions and we have to go along without knowing any of the details. We can't even get discussion going on what will happen to the small Septs. Are we expected to affiliate with one of the larger organizations, and be absorbed by it? We like to think that having our own identity is a useful thing both for our clients and for the whole net."

Lina said nothing. She was bored already. Strange looks weren't enough to make up for the dull little inanities of the Board and the insecurities of those who were permanently angry that they were not at the center.

"And you know, the net began as an anarchy," the pale man said. "The whole idea of any group gaining too much power is absurd. Sometimes the larger Septs become drunk with their power and they forget where they came from. Where we all came from. My hosts more than any."

Lina had little tolerance for complaints. But the pale man had stopped complaining, and his tone at least was half amused by the entire thing, rather than angry. She could respect that. She could respect it and still want to get away, not have to listen to chitchat during a buffet break.

"But that's not the only problem," the stranger said, speaking more as if she were a Sept sister herself and not a singer who had never been in the net in her life. "There's also this idea of restricting access by 'unauthorized' users. What's that supposed to mean, 'unauthorized'? How would we get our apprentices if we didn't spot youngsters with talent? And they certainly can't think that we're going to take over all the drudgework of the kiosks. That's crazy."

Lina smiled by rote. "I'm sure no one wants to get rid of the kiosks. Probably a lot of what you're hearing is a problem in translation. It might be better if everyone was more careful about what they said and how they said it. We have more arguments over misunderstanding where people agree than where there really is a difference." Cliché advice, but true enough, and Lina was rapidly becoming bored. Maestro and three other Pietà singers had entered the room and Lina wanted to join them. She started to get up and felt a gentle hand on her wrist.

"Please, no," he said. "Please. You seem to be a decent person, I feel like I can trust you. You're a singer, you're not on the net, it can't hurt you. Even if it is death itself, you're immune. You singers, you keep the world in order. The rest of us can only be grateful."

"I'm only a singer," she said, trying to bring the conversation to an end. This Board member made her acutely uncomfortable. "I don't dabble in the politics of the Septs, I don't know a thing about the net. But I do know that one cannot always keep perfect order and perfect time. Then we would be purely something inhuman ourselves. Even the music, sometimes it changes. Sometimes it's Stravinsky, sometimes it's jazz."

The pale man's eyes went wide, as if the mention of Stravinsky and jazz was enough to threaten his existence. Maybe it was, but Lina didn't want to know about it. She smiled tightly and started to get up.

"No," he said urgently. "Only the musicians can help now. Otherwise we are in danger, all of us. Because there is tampering in the net. There is a strange thing that changes things, that wanders and doesn't respond to any of the usual actions. We know it, out at the edges, but the Venetian and New York and

Petersburg and Seoul Septs, they won't listen to us. They pretend that it's all fine. It will take a musician to hear it, to know
what it is. But we must never, ever play jazz or Stravinsky or
any of those anti-thought composers. That will destroy us faster
than anything else. That will mean the end of all civilization as
we know it."

Lina did get up this time. "I'm sure this is very serious," she
said, trying to treat him as if he had made any sense at all. "But
I can't do anything about it. I can't help you more than I am.
Now, if you'll excuse me, our break is over."

She put her plate on the service tray and retreated. Her break
wasn't over yet and she knew better than to force her voice, so
she disappeared into the changing room.

It wasn't as nice as the buffet room. There were no frescoes
on the walls or ceilings, and the floors were plain instead of decorated with tile and parquet. And there was no place to sit and
no espresso, and a touch of chill seeped in from the window.

Lina wanted to cry. She felt abandoned again, exiled from
the heart of the Pietà. She was only an orphan singer, not one
of the powers in a city of power. Her mask began to fog slightly
as her eyes grew moist, and she raised it in the privacy of the
wardrobe. No one was there, no one would ever find her here.

She wanted to tear the hanging robes that lined the wall,
wanted to put her fist through one of the diamond panes of glass
that let in damp chill. She wanted to shake that Board member
and make him see reason, that reason included other kinds of
music. He could not, they could not, eliminate any composer
that did not suit their fancy—or worse, the fancy of their system.

Even order and thought was not more important than the
music. Lina was certain of that. The end of all civilization, the
Sept brother had called it. Well, she knew better. It was the end
of all civilization if they did not play Stravinsky, if they forgot

all the music that was not approved for mental enhancement and net function.

She wanted to sing something, anything, that would make that Board member's face decently blue, as if he were properly masked in strange company. She hummed a few bars of something she remembered from the concert at Café Luna. Suddenly she wondered if that concert had been part of the reason that the meetings were rough, that the Board was unable to come to a decision on anything.

If the things Sean had told her were true, the Board's troubles meant good for everyone else. Defiantly, she began to laugh.

12

There are aliens in the net. The thought came back incessantly no matter what she was doing. It reminded her of when she had deliberately lost her virginity at the age of seventeen. After she had had sex with a foreign university student, she had experienced random thoughts that she was not a virgin any longer for the entire next week.

Only that was something she had done. This was merely knowledge—except it was knowledge that could change everything in the universe. Or everything really was already changed, only she just hadn't seen it yet, like when the anomaly had changed her nails. Humanity was already subtly different, new, subconsciously altered by the alien presence. It only looked like the world she had grown up in on the outside. Her experience of what was familiar and secure was only memory; in reality nothing could ever be the same again.

When she got out of the dreambox she could smell her own

sweat. Her hair was ratted and the makeup had streaked. She looked like a freak, and felt as filthy as the Grand Canal.

She got into the shower and ran the water on hot and as high as it would go. She washed her hair vigorously and scrubbed her skin until it felt tight. She didn't like the heavy scent of the very expensive shampoo and soap that were used in the Sept changing rooms. Now the rich perfumes seemed to encase her along with the steam, cutting off everything around her.

She could see the red and white tile pattern only vaguely through the mist, as if the bathroom did not really exist any more than any place in the net did. Nothing was clear at all, not even the drips of condensation running down the glass outside the shower.

She emerged from the steam and wrapped herself in an over-sized towel. Now her face was plain and clean, her hair hung in wet strands over her shoulders. She had to rub a place in the mirror to see her reflection, newly washed and unadorned, staring back at her.

She shuddered slightly. Even here, clean and dripping, there was the knowledge that nothing was quite what she had thought. That seemed to be a habit of late, she realized. Every time she thought she had it nailed down it shifted so that she didn't know the rules anymore. She felt as if she had woken up in a dreambox in Sept-Silence, where she would know the gross outlines but none of the subtle things, the touches of tradition and gesture, joke and memory that formed the shared culture of each individual Sept. There were underlying paradigms that gave each Sept its character and its particular abilities, as well.

Then she told herself that she was thinking nonsense, and rubbed herself briskly with the towel until her skin glowed pink. She dried her hair without any style, letting it loose and wild and then tying it on top of her head so it stayed out of her eyes.

It was late to catch a cab home. The expense was bad enough, but there was a contract waiting, would be waiting. . . . She didn't think about it. The night air was warm and she began to walk. Perhaps a night of sleep would remove all the shadows and illusions that seemed to hide behind the stone façades of the houses, lurk under the archways and shimmer in the water. Moonlight touched the canals, turning them an impossible quicksilver.

Cecilie felt as if she were walking through her dreams. The very few people on the street at this hour were part of the illusion, merging with the dark.

When she got home her parents were already asleep and the lights were turned off. She drifted to her own room, not wanting to disturb the penumbra with false gaiety. And falling asleep, she found no barrier between her waking state and the dreams that dominated the night.

Her dreams were very little different from her net.life, full of anomalies and aliens and talking suns who hunted her down through neon streets. Dreams like these brought no rest.

In the morning the bright sun streaming through the lace curtains did not make the monsters any more distant. If anything, it made them more real.

The old man's name in life had been Arturo Carlo Camerillo, and he had been born eighty-seven years ago in the palazzo where he had died. Three different dates of birth existed, but since the elder Signora Camerillo had not consulted the normal medical personnel there was some dispute. The first public date recorded outside the family was the baptism of Arturo Carlo at either three months or eight months of age in St. Mark's.

That was just a little presumptuous, but then after checking into further records, Cecilie knew that Mama Camerillo had been a social climber. She had been a singer at the Pietà and had left under circumstances that were closed to Cecilie. She ran a date check and found that the records had been destroyed on the date of the woman's marriage to Nicola Camerillo, the youngest son of a socially prominent and somewhat strapped family.

Tracing back records using credit checks, purchase dates and delivery stamps fascinated Cecilie. Of course, the Mall then had barely been built and so many purchases had been made on the old kiosks.

The woman had had expensive taste. She had bought watered silk wallpapers for every room in the palazzo, along with inlaid tables and tasseled pillows. Cecilie read over the receipts that included old-fashioned descriptions. *Twenty yards of botanical jacquard for upholstery, dark blue with matching braid and gold trim and tassels. Eighteen Murano wineglasses, blue and green with seahorse stems. Three dreambox attachments, Lorica prototypes.*

Then there were the other expense records for lessons for young Arturo. Music lessons on keyboard, violin and flute. Well, Mama had been a singer at the Pietà, after all. Private-school fees, riding lessons, soccer club, ski school and later snowboarding, trips to the beach and camping in Tuscany and a monthlong seminar in China on the history of civilization.

Cecilie was impressed. Sept education was good, but compared with this she felt inadequate. Arturo Carlo Camerillo had been groomed for the elite, carefully positioned in Venetian society.

And yet, something didn't quite make sense. His family wasn't quite rich enough to afford this kind of lifestyle. They had the palazzo because it had been inherited for generations, but supposedly Papa's elder brother held title and only permitted Arturo's family to live there. So why had Mama redecorated and where had all that money come from?

Cecilie dug deeper, following the money trail back and back again. When she reached a dead end she knew where else to go, where to skip, where records that she wanted might be held. Census and population data, tax records, credit sheets, everything was held forever in sealed files. But those files weren't hard to locate or open when a searcher knew where they were kept and under what codes.

This was the work she had been trained to do. There was little security in public records. Mainly no one bothered to go through them. They were boring, they were old, they were irrelevant to anything interesting going on in the city now—unless you knew the connections, knew how to put all the pieces together.

It took two days digging through the account and credit histories of every bank in the city to locate what Cecilie needed. And it still didn't answer the question. The uncle who owned the palazzo and the majority of the family's negligible wealth had died at the age of thirty-seven, when Arturo was five. Everything had been left to the boy.

Cecilie found the death certificate in the public records. She stared at the words for a long time because they were so bland and uninformative. Arturo's uncle had died of asphyxiation. There had been no inquest, no police intervention. He had not been married and had no children.

Cecilie looked at the description of the deceased. He had been of medium weight and fitness. She took another day going through hospital and medical insurance files. Arturo's uncle had been admitted to the hospital once in his life, for a broken leg from a skiing accident. His medical insurance stated that his regular physicals showed no signs of any disease, and that he was not under treatment for anything.

Something struck Cecilie as very wrong. This uncle thing might not mean anything at all—or it might. Cecilie didn't know, but she was curious and her curiosity had been cultivated and trained.

She went to the public housing records and found that there was someone else living in the palazzo along with Arturo's family. A man called Vittorio Longni had his address registered at the Camerillo palazzo. Cecilie began a separate check on Longni, who had been alive at the time Arturo's uncle died.

Longni had money, lots of money. The image on his ID showed a young and very attractive man with a faintly superior smile and a casual stance. Longni had money, no listed profession or trade, and a trace showed that he had come to Venice at seventeen to study at the Pietà. And, like Mama, had been dismissed under veiled circumstances with records erased in the public files.

Cecilie could taste the thread starting to emerge. Longni and Mama had been at the Pietà at the same time. At first Cecilie wondered if they had had an affair, and been thrown out for improper conduct, but that was ridiculous. Pietà singers were supposed to have affairs, with each other and with their patrons and with anyone they chose. What else would keep the gossip dailies in business, grinding out the sordid stories of who was supposedly doing what with whom? The depiction of choir life was so lurid that Cecilie had a hard time believing it. No, it had to have been something else. A simple affair wouldn't even make the daily snippet in the choir gossip file groups.

Cecilie wondered if it was something her own mother would know about. Her mother was interested in the Pietà, in the singers. Her mother was the reason she knew about the choir groups and the gossip lines and the choir chats that embarrassed her. Her mother might remember the scandal.

Then Cecilie checked the date again. It was well before her mother's birth. No, that one avenue of investigation wasn't going to work at all.

She had to get into the Pietà, into their system. If she could get to the machine that held the closed record, she had no doubt that she could find it and pry its secrets out. But she had to first get in and find it.

The problem was that she had to get in physically, because the Pietà file system was not connected in to the main net. The institution was far older than the net itself and had its own traditions, but Cecilie suspected that a large part of the reason they remained isolated was that they didn't want ten million gossip groupies accessing the source material. Cecilie idly wondered how much the choir pages paid to get their exclusive data, and how much all the groupies would be willing to pay to have their own personal download.

Cecilie knew how to open up any old-style system and make it sing, but she had to get to it in the physical world. And now that meant that she had to get into the Pietà.

Maybe it wasn't important in finding the old man's murderer. But now Cecilie dearly wanted to know the secret that Longni and Mama Camerillo shared. If they had—she had to keep her mind open to the possibility. And yet . . .

Cecilie left the public-records files. She was tired and her head was spinning. She could see possibilities all around her but she was missing the pieces to put them together. Or she was just too tired to see what was in front of her. For the past few days she had done nothing but work on this contract, tracing down the background, immersing herself in the old man's family and early world.

Now she needed to get out of it. She needed perspective; she needed to forget it all for a while. She needed to breathe fresh air instead of the recycled air in the dreambox, and to move around. Her muscles were soft and sore from the hours of inactivity while her mind wandered through the records of the

Camerillo family. No wonder so many of the most successful Sept sisters were heavy and shapeless.

Cecilie shuddered delicately and raised the hood. She sat up slowly and swung her legs over the side of the flatbed so that they rested on the step. She climbed down and found her shoes, sat on the step and put them on. Then she stretched, raised her arms overhead and stood on her tiptoes. Blood rushed to her fingers. She felt warmer immediately, and energized.

Then she realized that she was hungry. She looked at her watch and smiled. If she hurried she was just in time for dinner.

Dinner that night was served out in the courtyard and the menu was one of Cecilie's favorites. For the pasta there was penne in cream sauce and for the main dish there was roasted lamb in rosemary. Cecilie had two servings of each and finished all her salad besides. Then she left the table she had shared with the senior sisters. Julietta and Tina were already gone. They didn't have important contracts that kept them through dinner.

Cecilie walked home in the twilight. It was warm out and the stars shone in the watered-silk sky. *Jacquard for upholstery, dark blue,* she thought as she looked up.

Her father was already asleep when she arrived home, but her mother was awake and fussing with the kitchen, doing things that Cecilie could not comprehend.

"You've been late all week," her mother said, but there was nothing judgmental about her tone. "It must be a very important job you have now. I have some cake left over from dinner. I was going to have a little and some tea before bed. Would you like some?"

Surprised at herself, Cecilie agreed. Her mother cut her off a generous serving of her favorite "Grandmother's cake" and set it on a chipped plate. Then she took out tea bags and put them in the heated water. Jasmine tea to go with cake. Cecilie preferred coffee, but that was too much effort late at night and would keep her mother up.

They took their cake and tea into the living room. Cecilie's mother turned on one lamp that cast a warm yellow glow over the homey furniture. After a day full of Mama Camerillo's expenses, Cecilie noticed that the sofa she sat on was threadbare and there were indentations in the cushions from years of use. The upholstery of the two chairs could only be generously called dated and the pictures on the wall were merely common.

Nothing here was elegant or stylish, nothing about the whole apartment was gracious or well designed, yet it was comfortable and inviting. The plain and hard-used pieces told of years of family gatherings and late-night conferences, homework and visits by grandparents and relatives and friends.

Suddenly Cecilie felt sorry for the child Arturo she had spent the day researching. He had lived in a palace where everything was perfect and beautiful and keeping the furniture nice was more important than playing with toys across the floor and sitting with feet tucked up on the furniture to get a hug. She had comprehended enough of Mama Camerillo's view of priorities to know that Arturo was more a showpiece than a person.

"So can you tell me about this fascinating search you are doing?" her mother asked. "I've never seen you so involved in a project before. It must be very interesting and important."

Cecilie smiled. "Well, I don't know about important. But it is interesting. And there's some stuff about the Pietà, too, only it's really old so I guess you wouldn't have heard anything about it." And Cecilie launched into the long version of her discoveries. Her mother encouraged her to tell all the details, including the colors of the wallpaper and the whiff of ancient scandal erased from the Pietà's records. "So you see," she finished up, "I need to get in there. I need to get access through their system because their machine is isolated. I tried to jump through three times today, or maybe four. I don't remember. But there has to be some way in."

Her mother smiled slowly and patted her hand. "I don't know of any way you can get to those records, but there are a lot of people who would like to know the truth," the older woman said. "I remember my mother telling me about some incident that may well be the same one. A man and woman both dismissed from the Pietà and she married his lover's brother. There were all kinds of rumors, that they were involved in some family affairs in the south or smuggling or drugs. All kinds of stories.

"But you have to remember, things were different then. Things were changing. The Septs weren't so large or so important, didn't have the same money or influence. And things were, well, different than they are now. Freer in some ways. There were all kinds of music. Your nonna used to talk about hearing things like rock and jazz on the street played by hopeful musicians with open instrument cases for coins. And the choirs performed modern and experimental works in full concert. It was respectable in those days.

"So you might want to look into the music for the scandal. They say that's the only reason anyone's ever been thrown out of the Pietà, was for the music."

Cecilie blinked. She had never even considered that before. "Thank you, Mama," she said.

Her mother laughed. "Oh, you know, it would be fun to know what it was like then. People didn't mask, or hardly ever. And there was the story that these people were thrown out and one had a lover and the other married his lover's brother and kept it all in the family. And that the family was stricken from the roster because of whatever the musical problem was. Well, it would be very nice to know the truth. Nonna and her friends talked about it sometimes, like they talked about everything. I don't think anything ever happened in Venice that your nonna didn't know about."

Then her mother looked at Cecilie with amazement. "Of course. I never saw it before, but it all makes sense now. Your nonna and her mother and her mother before her, all of them knew everything about the city. Who was born, who died, who got married, who was seeing whom on the side, everything. You're doing just the same thing as they all did, only you get paid for it and it's respectable. In my day it was just called gossip."

"It's not like that," Cecilie protested, but her mother was not convinced.

"No, you see, gossip is information," her mother said, eyes widening with excitement. "I had never thought of that before. It's just information that doesn't seem to be very valuable at the time. Let me see, Auntie Augusta might remember something. Let me call her."

Cecilie groaned. Auntie Augusta had been her grandmother's elder sister and was almost a hundred years old, and in all that time had never had a good word for anyone. But her mother had a point. If Auntie Augusta didn't care about anything that had happened in Cecilie's lifetime, there was nothing she liked better than remembering the distant past. And this incident, which had taken place either when Auntie was an infant or not born yet, was precisely the kind of thing she would recall in full detail.

"No," Cecilie demurred. "I just need a way into the records. Hearsay won't help. Auntie might know the gossip, but I won't know that it's true."

Her mother sighed. "It will take two minutes to call tomorrow morning and it would make her happy. But I can understand that you don't want to talk to her right now. It's your first big job, after all."

Cecilie hugged her mother, who understood more than she could have hoped.

The next morning Cecilie woke late. The sun came full force through the lace curtain and moved over her eyes. She had dreamed about the Camerillos and couldn't remember anything but shreds that fell apart as she opened her eyes.

Somehow everything that was jumbled last night made sense. Vittorio was the older brother's lover and somehow supported the entire family in style, most likely by illegal means.

Anything the two ex-Pietà singers had done, they were still working together somehow, becoming attached to the Camerillos. Cecilie wondered if either of them had known the Camerillo family before being expelled from the choir. That wouldn't be so easy to trace.

But none of that really had anything to do with Arturo's death, she realized suddenly. She sat upright in her bed and threw the covers off. All her fascination with the past wasn't getting her any closer to what she needed to know.

She could sense it coming together as she showered and dried her hair, then threw on an old sweater over her leggings. She drank her coffee standing up in the kitchen, kissed her mother and ran down the stairs.

She didn't even wait to get to the Sept-House before checking in to a public kiosk and keying a message for David. He had at least given her a contact box, though how often he checked in she didn't know. She hoped there would be a reply by the time she got to her own mail at the Sept-House.

Really, it was very easy. She needed to get into the Pietà and there was no reason David shouldn't help her. Either get her in, or get in himself. His skills were not quite Sept quality, she thought, but he certainly was capable of doing a basic file search when she gave him the names and dates and the report numbers.

The way he worked things Cecilie was certain that he must have a Pietà contact, someone who could break her into the first step of the private files. From there on she could manage on her own. After all, even Pietà files were safeguarded by either Sept systems or something much older and therefore easier to break.

Given the choir's great emphasis on tradition and the physical isolation of their hardware, Cecilie suspected the latter. Between the idea of doing what was traditional and being more focused on music than anything else, it was likely they just hadn't bothered. After all, the scandal-sheet journalists didn't need any real evidence in any event, and half the traffic on the groups was debate over whether this reporter or that was telling the truth.

She practically skipped out of the canal bus and up the street. She hadn't felt so happy, so alive, since before her promotion. Since then everything good had been shadowed with either fear or a hint of corruption. Today she knew she was right, that she was doing the right thing. She would find the murderer and the Gavrillis would know and she would end up being one of the most sought-after hunters in Sept-Fortune.

She arrived and checked in while barely registering procedure. She went to the Chinese Corridor, to the cubicle with her dreambox. It was called the Chinese Corridor because large Chinese vases were arranged between the cubicle doors. They were antiques, supposedly brought back to Venice in the eighteenth century and set up in this palazzo by a collector. Cecilie thought they were ugly. She wished that she had been assigned to the Roman Corridor, which had three Roman busts and was where Julietta's cubicle was located, or the Via Veneto, which was the nickname given to the largest of the cubicle blocks, where the great majority of the sisters had their workspace.

But this cubicle on the Chinese Corridor had been hers since she had reached her adult stature when she was fifteen years old and would remain hers until she died. Or until she left Venice or became so fat that she'd have to move over to the Corpulent Corridor.

Technically, that work sector was known as the Blue Corridor, because of the blue sky painted on the ceiling, but everyone knew that each of the boxes in each of the cubicles there was for a Sept sister who no longer fit in the standard size. These had been specially designed or modified so that people like Signora Angelina could remain comfortable while getting in a full round of work. No wonder none of the cubicles on the Blue Corridor had a name displayed on the door.

Except for the Blue Corridor, all the cubicles were assigned upon arrival or full growth and never changed. In Cecilie's cubicle there was the dreambox she had customized to her own liking and would continue to change for the rest of her working life—or until the technology made another extreme leap forward and she was willing to invest in new equipment. There was also a desk with a text interface, which was useful a lot of times when she didn't need the full dreambox capabilities or didn't have the time.

She had hung a few pictures on the bare yellow walls. She hated that shade and every time she arrived she resolved to paint. Next week. When she could find a color she really liked. Or maybe she would get wallpaper, the rich fabric paper that was so popular with upper-class Venetians. She had looked at a rich floral-pattern jacquard in a dusty grey rose in the window of a specialty shop and had calculated how long it would take for her to save the huge sum she would need to buy enough for the walls. It would look perfect with a celadon upholstered divan and desk chair. Perhaps she would add sage green curtains draped in layers over the bare lace that hung there now, with heavy rose tassels caught in the folds. It would be beautiful, elegant, a place for her to be at peace and to acknowledge her own superiority at the same time.

If this contract worked out, she realized, she would be able to afford to redecorate as soon as David paid. That made her less miserable with the bare utilitarian nature of her workspace, especially since she was only going through text for the moment. She had always hated text-only for that reason, but it was the cheapest form of account anyone could buy and so there were often traces in through the text logs that appeared nowhere else.

She keyed her mail queue and scrolled quickly. Then she looked it over again more carefully. Not that he would use the name David Gavrilli, she didn't expect that. But there was nothing there from the anonymous mail drop he was using, or any of three other aliases she knew about.

But there were two addresses she didn't recognize, and both originated at the Library. Curious, she called those up first.

The headers made no sense in the mail. There was no name of sender, no place of origin. The Library was the routing and that was the only information of any use save the time and date it had passed through the Library's automailer.

Someone must have tampered with the mail. That was not so difficult. Cecilie knew that someone with David's abilities probably knew how and did if for pure amusement value. Julietta was the one who had figured it out first the year they had been thirteen, and they had used their newfound skill to fake mash notes to boys in the Brother-Septs. Naturally, they were caught and grounded for three months with a mail lock on their IDs so that the only way they could send email was by routing it through Signora Marcella's queue. Signora Marcella, not being a tutor herself, was not at all sympathetic.

She wondered who was faking headers now, and whether

they would be as humiliated as she was when the misconduct was discovered. Though, accessing the message itself, Cecile recognized nothing there as communication at all—in any language. Junk was spewed across the page, the way Kanji read in Roman alphabet systems. Cecilie didn't have Kanji on her translation list and she didn't know Japanese anyway. Besides, something from the Sept-House in Kyoto would come through Sept channels and go through prelim Sept translation anyway.

But this—this was pure and outright garbage. That puzzled her. She didn't know why there was garbage in her box. It had never happened before, and she wondered now why there was anyone who wanted to harass her this way.

Perhaps the old man's murderer knew she was looking and wanted to warn her away. That didn't make sense though. If they wanted to scare her or tell her to stop they would have a much better chance of making her understand if they had written in clear language, and just about any language would do. She dismissed her fear and was left with staring at two pieces of mail that amounted to nothing more than complete gibberish.

She thought of disposing of the two mails, and then decided against it. She saved them into a folder marked "?" just in case she had any reason to reference them. Perhaps she would have a suspicion as to who the culprit had been and use this evidence in a confrontation.

Still no word from David. Cecilie cracked her knuckles before she remembered her mother warning her that she would ruin her hands that way. She wasn't getting in the dreambox until she had a place to go there. Just to go to hang around for no reason like a deadbeat Mallrat who had nothing else to do was a waste of her time. She was restless. She didn't want to stay inside here, in this tiny space with its ugly walls and no word from David. She needed to be out, doing, walking in the sunshine, and getting something accomplished.

She pulled a mask out of a desk drawer. It was the one she had worn that night to Café Luna, the elegant black one that she had not touched again. She had forgotten that she had put it here, or even that she had had the thing.

The fine velvet of the face and the filigree pattern on the one side surprised her with its loveliness. She had forgotten this mask was here and she had forgotten how it made her feel. Slowly she put it on and watched her transformation in the makeup mirror she had fixed near the window. This masked creature was not Cecilie, she thought. She completed the disguise with the costume that shrouded her figure in rich folds of velvet accented with purple silk and touches of silver trim. Then she walked out of her cubicle, out of the Sept-House, into the harsh morning light of the street to clear her mind.

All the excitement, the expectation, was completely destroyed. She had been right about Gavrilli from the start. He was not someone she could trust. He had been raised to power but didn't play by the rules at all. He didn't play counter them, either. It was as if he had never been introduced to protocol in his life.

Cecilie, however, had been very carefully schooled. She knew how to treat Board members and musicians, how to order in a fine café and what wine went with which dish. Sept-Fortune had trained her to it since the day she had been accepted as an apprentice-candidate. Sept sisters were ladies to the core, elegant and refined, with superior taste. Cecilie learned to prefer colors that were muted and balanced between two that could be named because she had been taught to see them as refined and gracious. She could play the piano and the flute and had been taught to sing—or rather, that she could not sing—by the Maestra brought in from the Pietà twice a week.

She knew her world. While she had never been truly happy in it, she understood all the rules. There were times when it was too confining, when it chafed and limited her and she had wanted to rebel. Now she acknowledged that it also had respected and nurtured her—and formed her. No matter what she did and what she became, Sept-Fortune had created her. That was a bitter thing for her to bear.

Now Cecilie wandered the familiar streets lost, not aware of her surroundings. The ancient stone and stucco palazzos and the modern stressed-slab buildings were all the same to her. The light, the sparkling yellow light that bathed the city in gold, was an unreal wash in her eyes. All she could think was that she had been betrayed by her own hopes.

The longer she walked the more her outrage grew. She fed upon it and it devoured her, an orgy of emotion that Cecilie had never experienced before. She wanted to scream, to slam her fist into the mold-covered stone of an ancient wall, to run among a tour group crushing their evil intruding cameras under her feet, beating their unprotected flesh for being stupid and ugly and staring.

Her vision blurred and she quickly raised the mask just a bit and wiped the tears away. She couldn't let them fall on this fine velvet mask. The glue was fragile and she would hate to stain the perfect fabric.

She heard singing. It was not the usual strains of Mozart or Bach that she knew, that were parts of her daily life and events. This was something jagged, something with a time signature that was just the smallest bit abrasive and stirring.

At first Cecilie thought the music was in her head, her own private audio track for her unabashed passions. But the music took her attention and it went on in ways she could not have expected. She could feel it slide into her head, past her consciousness, and sink into the deep structures where unused neural connections had been stimulated. The music invaded deep into that part of her brain that had been carefully cultivated, where the realignment of synapses was a finely tuned art.

Everything she had learned had been at the proper window for development of a particular kind of brain, a brain that could fuse her wild talent with the disciplined rationality of the Sept. She had been given the proper genetic treatments at the appropriate times, and they had been stimulated further with drugs that made her concentrate better and absorb knowledge rapidly. She had been exposed to the right music at all times that was tuned to the erg cycle in her brain to enhance all the other abilities she had honed so carefully.

The music she heard now was beyond and beneath that. It attracted her as it repelled. Just like David Gavrilli, she admitted. But somehow the music had mitigated the rage. It was still in her, but muted and distant like the backwash in the datatide.

Then she realized that this music wasn't entirely in her head. It existed in the objective world. Other people passing by could hear it too, and someone was producing those sounds. Startled by the realization, Cecilie hesitated. Then she tried to follow the music to its source.

High above her, just to the right, an unmasked face was pressed against an ancient leaded window. The person up there was singing, singing with all the beauty and power and sorrow of the universe, with all the abandon of Cecilie's despair. She stared at the singer, unable to make out the features through the distorting old bottle glass that was as effective as any mask. Still, she could not look away.

That woman—she knew it was a woman from the range of the voice—saw her as well. The singer looked down at her, studied her, and their eyes met. Cecilie held up her hand, hoped that the other would wait. She hoped that this was not a private apartment and she would stumble into someone's personal world. But she could not resist the power of the voice.

Sirens, she remembered vaguely, they were called. Sirens,

who sang out in the sea so that Ulysses had to be lashed to the mast, to hear their song and not drown. As she felt she was drowning, overwhelmed with doubts and weirdness and fear.

Overwhelmed with knowledge that she wished suddenly she didn't have, she knew that she was engulfed. There was too much data about too many different things, all of them mixed up together and churning in her head. Never before had Cecilie desired less information, and now she realized that she had created her own private Hell.

Intensity lit up the song from within. The singer's face changed, and suddenly the distorting glass was gone as the window was raised. Cecilie could see the woman clearly now, a young woman, perhaps a few years older than herself. She was unmasked, as no one would unmask to an unknown street, and Cecilie saw there were tear tracks on the woman's face. They glittered gold in the honey sunlight, and Cecilie thought of the white masks with the tears drawn in and jeweled with garnets or painted black, or sometimes painted gold.

Cecilie wished she had a flower to throw to the window, but she had nothing at all. And then she saw the singer gesture, a slow theatrical movement with one hand, beckoning, inviting her up, asking her within.

Cecilie nodded and rounded the corner to the front of the building. It was very old; maybe parts of the structure were original and not just lightweight materials reproduction as was necessary in so much of the city. She took the steps to the door and was inside the reception hall before she realized that she had been in this place before.

Then she had been eight years old, and had been brought here to be registered in Sept-Fortune. The black-and-white patterned marble floor was the most amazing thing she had seen and the lofty pillars down the hall were gilded with cherubs and festooned with flowers. The ceiling was decorated in a typical

Baroque pattern, a roiling cloud-ringed sky full of soaring saints and angels with gold-leafed wings. She had thought it was like a dream when she was eight.

Now she found the cherubs ugly and the painted sky overblown. The gilding was chipped in places and had been patched with paint and not real gold. She no longer found it magnificent and opulent, but pretentious and undisciplined. And she was inexplicably and bitterly disappointed that the dreamlike memories she had of the place had been shattered.

This was the Septs Center, where all the records were recorded on paper as well as in Sept files, where meetings and grand celebrations were held, and where the big-industry contracts were signed. Only a few small offices in the actual precincts of any Sept-House were reserved for client meetings, and so all the major Sept business in Venice was conducted in this one shared structure that spoke of the past wealth of the city and the pretensions of those who needed to meet face-to-face at all.

Cecilie had to figure out where the window had been, where the singer waited. She felt stupid, suddenly, and wanted to leave. Maybe there was no singer and there were no archives and she was only deluded because of stress and a touch of sun-dazzle so she could ignore everything.

That would be the easy decision, she realized, to just walk out. There was no reason for anyone to know about the hidden archives. No one would believe her and no one would know. The entity that was the entire net must have been in contact for years, and it had kept silent. There was no reason to know, no reason to make changes in a life that was comfortable and safe. In a world that was complacent.

"Hello." A soft voice penetrated the room. Cecilie looked to the far staircase and on the upper landing she saw—someone. This person wore a Pietà robe and a plain white mask. That made sense.

"I thought perhaps you wouldn't know where to come," the woman said as she started down the stairs. "I waited for a while, but when you didn't arrive I thought perhaps I should look for you. I tried the buffet room first, but the meetings have begun again."

Cecilie blinked rapidly. She knew the Board was meeting. It had been posted in her daily schedule, which she had disabled and ignored. The Board. Of course a Pietà choir was there to create the right brain environment for good work. That explained everything—except why the singer had come to get her.

The singer descended to the hallway, the full Pietà robe flowing behind down the stairs and obscuring her gender, even her humanity in its generous folds. The singer took Cecilie's ungloved hand, and suddenly Cecile felt very revealed. She wore a full mask and a costume that concealed far more than the Pietà robe, yet she felt naked. Perhaps the unique luxury of that mask and costume revealed too much of her personal sense and taste, even though excellent. She had been so proud of this mask, this costume, but it made her stand out. She should have acknowledged her arrogance and worn the plain white mask with tears and the harlequin outfit with a full ruff. It was cheap and inelegant compared to this black velvet and filigree, but it would have served the purpose much better.

The woman in the regulation Pietà disguise was indistinguishable from any member of her choir. Cecilie felt foolish in all her finery next to the understated Pietà working garb. She was glad that at least her expression wouldn't give her away to the stranger.

The singer led her up the stairs firmly, as if afraid that Cecilie would run away. As if there were anywhere she could run in this place. Cecilie kept waiting for someone to appear who would announce to the whole world that she was a lowly full apprentice with Sept-Fortune and demand to know what she was doing here. The Pietà singer, who so obviously belonged and floated through these halls unquestioned, was her only excuse.

The singer whisked her past several Board members. There were even people there face-naked. They must be foreigners, Cecilie thought, shocked. But they didn't slow down, so Cecilie was unable to stare as long as she would have liked. Though if they'd stopped and waited for half an hour it might not have been enough time for Cecilie to look her fill at the elegant masks and robes, the piles of subtly colored food and the ornate gilded moldings that dripped from the ceiling between lurid frescoes and old blackening mirrors that reflected the canal shimmering through the room.

Cecilie had seen pictures of such places and such people. They had inhabited her mother's richly illustrated fairy-tale books when she had been very young, back in a life she barely remembered. Once she had found an abandoned site that, in one instant of coherence, came close to this sumptuous riot of color and design, of patterns moving to create a rich tapestry that should not exist in any reality. That belonged only in the imaginations of children and the visions of artists.

Before she had time to formulate her thoughts, she was being shoved through a small back door and into a wardrobe. It was long and narrow and there were uniform Pietà robes hanging against one wall, masks neatly suspended on hooks with each one. The other side had a series of small windows with diamond-shaped glass. It was here that Cecilie had seen the singer before. She had been singing in the cloakroom. Cecilie was glad that the woman had come for her. She never would have found this place on her own.

The singer turned to her and unmasked. Cecilie was surprised. The woman was maybe five or six years older than Cecilie herself, and not remarkable-looking in any way. Her eyes were wide enough to be pretty but the color was something drab between hazel and brown, her nose was a touch long in the old Roman manner, and her hair was the same mousy color as her eyes. In some ways her appearance was a relief, since Cecilie thought that with a voice so beautiful it would have been beyond the injustice of even this universe for her face to be exquisite as well.

Cecilie did not move to unmask herself. Perhaps that was rude, but Cecilie did not want to be at a disadvantage. She had no idea why the other had called her here, or why she had come. Only that she had heard the singing, and it had stirred something in her that she could not entirely ignore.

Besides, she had nothing better to do and had never spoken to a singer from the Pietà before. It would be another datapoint in her file, something new and interesting, and would take her mind off her disappointment in herself. And her disillusionment with David Gavrilli and his contract and his count. Most of all she was dissatisfied with herself. She knew that she could face anything, but if she told anyone what she knew to be true she would be the object of unending humiliation. She could not endure that.

"I am Lina," Lina said, her speaking voice giving no indication of what beauty it expressed in song. "And, you are a Sept sister here, in one of the major Houses? I think I recognize that mask from a Sept party, it's very unusual."

Cecilie muttered something affirmative. She had worn this mask to Café Luna. Once. And no other time.

So Lina must have been at the Luna for jazz and was mixing up having seen the mask there with some other time, a party or a safe occasion.

Unless she hadn't mixed anything up at all, Cecilie thought

suddenly. Maybe this woman wanted to indicate that she'd been at the Luna and knew about Cecilie's secret. And she wanted to intimate that she had secrets of her own.

So this Lina had secrets and those were about music. That should be no great surprise. Musicians of the Pietà were trained in all the arts from the time they arrived, just as Sept apprentices learned all the slipways through the net, how to judge the various paths and where in a veritable galaxy of data to find the one point they wanted.

Lina turned away from her, staring back out the window to the now empty streets below. "Something is wrong in this meeting. The music isn't going right and the delegates are on edge. It's as if something has cracked the shell of order and insanity is oozing to the surface."

Cecilie dropped her jaw. The language was odd, almost archaic, but the sentiment frightened her. This musician was too direct, had seen through the veils of the system too easily.

"What does that have to do with me?" Cecilie stammered.

"The Board is not going to be able to come to consensus," Lina said, as if Cecilie had not spoken. "Something is wrong. Too much bickering, maybe, I don't know about that. Or maybe it's all the jazz. We've had a few concerts recently, listened to some very complex music. Created some, too, things that don't conform to the basic system structure."

"You mean, you think that these concerts are affecting the Board?" Cecilie asked. She didn't follow at all what this woman wanted. It was as if she had entered a dream and everything was riddles. "Why, tell me. Isn't it dangerous?"

"No," Lina said. "We need this music. We need the chaos. We've been too structured for too long, and the net has to belong to us, not the other way around. But what I thought was, maybe you could tell me . . . Is it really so necessary that nothing new ever be added or done, that we have to re-create the past or we'll kill ourselves?"

"What do you mean?" Cecilie asked for the third time. This was making far less sense as she went along.

"I mean," Lina said, her voice strained, "that you know about the Septs. I need you to tell me, do we have to only do the same music all the time? Tell me, will the Septs die and our whole way of life collapse because we listen to something new sometimes, something different?"

Then Cecilie realized what it was. The woman was not completely sane. She had cracked, obviously, under the pressure of the meeting. It happened to musicians; it was one of the weaknesses that went with their talent. It was why there were places like the Pietà to keep them all protected and safe.

"Lina, at the Pietà," Cecilie said to fix the name in her mind by habit. Always keep bits of information, they always come in useful. Someday, somehow, this singer might be useful to her. Or she might be crazy or dead. Cecilie turned to leave, put her hand on the door.

Lina plucked her large sleeve. "Wait. Really. I'm not crazy. I didn't mean to sound so weird. Only this one out-of-town Board observer was talking to me about how nothing was working and the net has gotten slow. Sluggish. Like syrup, he said. And that and the way the music sounded today seemed to be the same thing and all of it went together. I don't understand it and I had to tell someone. I'm sorry. Please don't go thinking I'm crazy."

Cecilie leaned against the stucco wall. It was cool against her hand. She ran her fingers over the rough surface. Finally she lifted her mask so that Lina could see her face, could see that she was utterly, nakedly honest. "I don't know how you know this stuff. You shouldn't. I don't believe in ESP or any of that, so I can't figure it out. But there is—something—in the net. And I don't know what to do about it or about what I know. I don't know why I'm talking to a stranger when I haven't even told my Sept sisters yet."

Then Cecilie took a deep breath and plunged on. She never knew when she was going to find an opportunity like this again, and she had been trained to take advantage of opportunities. "There's this old story that has to do with the Pietà and it is somehow affecting everything. And it's in sealed records and I can't get in there. The records only exist at your site and I can't get in. Your administrative machines don't have connections so I'd have to go in to your physical plant to find it."

Lina smiled shyly for the first time, and Cecilie realized that she was indeed very pretty. "I don't believe in ESP either. I'm a singer, not an idiot. But I had to tell someone in the Septs that the out-of-town Board people are talking a little too freely about anomalies and other weirdnesses that are showing up in the music as well. And if we wait for the Maestri to do something about it, we'll be old and grey." She laughed, a deep sparkling sound that hinted at the depth of music in her throat.

Cecilie joined her. The woman was not much older than she, and now she made sense. The Maestri of either the choirs or the Septs did not ask advice from the youngest members, nor did they listen to what they called "wild speculation" and "changing the established order." Lina was right. The only reason they knew they weren't crazy was to talk to each other, to reaffirm the fact that the irregularities were showing up more and more frequently in more parts of life.

"Would you be willing to help me get in to the Pietà records?" Cecilie asked hesitantly.

She didn't have a plan yet, not really, but she knew that music—all music—was very important. It could change the patterns of the dataflow, it could re-create the net and everyone in it altogether. They had always known that, and so musicians had never been permitted into the Septs. The Septs did the few minor tasks the choirs needed done gratis, knowing that in the long run it was for the best for everyone. Suddenly it occurred to Cecilie that the Pietà might not be on line because the Septs didn't want the net contaminated with musical influences and not the other way around.

"But . . ." Lina started to protest. And then she shook her head. "I can't. It isn't just the rules. I just . . . can't."

Cecilie sighed, the fragments of her wild idea evaporated into mist and were gone. She hadn't really supposed that Lina could surf the system in any event, but there had been just the moment of hope.

Cecilie left the wardrobe room, left the Pietà singer behind. Lina had replaced her mask by the time Cecilie looked back, and so only a painted blank expression met her eyes. Her own mask didn't cover enough and she was afraid.

13

She didn't return to the Sept-House after her walk. Instead, Cecilie wandered through shops with no desire to buy, only the wish to be lost in the hordes of tourists and the throng of Board affiliates. By sunset she found herself heading closer to home and decided she might as well go. It would be early and her mother would be surprised, but it had been a long time since Cecilie had helped cook dinner. She looked forward to a quiet, uncomplicated evening at home.

For once it was pleasant to just relax with her parents and not have to talk. They asked about the Board members and the House and Cecilie would elaborate on their costumes without saying anything of substance. That was enough for her and for them.

She cleared the table for her mother and helped serve the coffee with dessert. Then she went to bed early.

"Are you sure you're feeling all right?" her mother asked. "You're not getting a cold, are you? I can make you some broth, or some tea."

"No, Mama, I'm not getting any dread disease," Cecilie called from the bathroom. "I'm just tired. The new contract and this Board meeting have worn me out, is all."

Her mother sighed but let her be, and Cecilie slept deeply until well past her alarm in the morning.

Her late arrival was not noticed in the general upheaval of the House. Cecilie was grateful for that, but disliked the noise and commotion early in the morning. She missed the silence of the halls and the lonely feel of the house, with all the little girls in classes and the older sisters still asleep, or in their offices or cubicles. Now chaos reigned in full. Various delegations shouted at each other as they tried to find their primaries, their masks and their memos. Senior Sept sisters stood with coffee cups, socializing with women from all over the world, friends they hadn't seen since their last diving vacation at the Great Barrier Reef or the Board meeting in Tokyo.

Cecilie slipped though the throng down to the Chinese Corridor and her cubicle. Curled up in front of the door was a messenger. In full formal messenger gear that made him look more like a ski racer than a hand delivery expert, he was half asleep with his head pillowed on his satchel.

Cecilie bent down and shook his arm gently. "Excuse me," she said, "this is my door. I have to get in."

His eyes opened instantly and he hugged the satchel to him. "Are you Cecilie 8 Sept-Fortune?" he asked ceremoniously.

"Yes, I am," Cecilie answered, trying to match his decorum.

He pulled himself up to full height and took an envelope from the leather bag. "Hand delivery. Please print here." He held out a thin card with a thumbprint box to prove that he had in fact delivered the document into her hands.

This was the epitome of security. Cecilie licked her lips, scared and excited at once. She had never received a secure delivery, ever, but she recognized the heavy grey paper of the envelope as being the phototight kind used to keep documents blue until the right person opened them. She had seen it on a million business programs and had even seen a blue document made once in Signora Tima's office. She had never thought to receive one—at least not until she had the title Signora and an extra desk in the business area of the House.

David, she thought, as she entered her cubicle. It had to be. No one else she had ever met would have the means and the desire to use this extreme level of secrecy.

She ignored her dreambox and dropped into the desk chair. The text reader tried to get her attention for her new mail, but Cecilie had something much more exciting on hand.

She caressed the heavy vellum across her cheek. The texture spoke of wealth and glory and all the concealed knowledge that had always flowed through Venice like the thick grey water.

Finally she couldn't stand it any longer and ripped open the envelope. The paper was indigo blue, so dark that she couldn't read what was written on it. She held the paper under the light and it faded rapidly, first to the color of the morning sky and then to something nearly white with a bluish cast.

The writing stood out clearly now, handwriting with dark blue ink that was too heavy in some places and flaked. The writing was round and feminine and a much finer hand than Cecilie had ever aspired to. It made her think of the writing in old documents, or the way legal people were trained to write official papers that would be sealed for generations.

One thing Cecilie knew absolutely. This was not David's handwriting. She scanned the text quickly to see the signature below. Then she sighed.

Lina, of the Pietà. Of course. The Pietà singers were nearly as famous for their discretion as for their music. Members of the Pietà were also well paid, perhaps on par with Sept members, and Lina was old enough to have had full status for several years now. Singers were also known to be extravagant, though certainly they were encouraged to spend in a profligate manner.

Then Cecilie read slowly, and read it through again as if the meaning of the words would disappear along with the color of the paper.

Dear Cecilie of the Sept-Fortune,

I have given much consideration to what you asked me when we met this afternoon. If there is something in the history of the Pietà that will be of use to you, I have decided that it is important that you have it. Therefore, if you can become free on Wednesday night at ten-thirty, meet me in the lobby of the Excelsior Hotel. Wear the same costume and mask you wore before. I shall find you.

Sincerely,
Lina of the Pietà

Wednesday. That was today. Lina had had a great deal of confidence in her messenger and in Cecilie.

Ten-thirty at night was late and it was last-minute. Cecilie sighed and wondered what she was going to tell her parents. They wouldn't like it. They didn't like her to go out late, as if she were still a little girl.

But she wasn't a little girl anymore. She was a full member of a Sept and had done evil things for that status and now knew too many secrets and had told too many lies. One more wouldn't hurt.

Then she giggled. There was no reason to lie. She could tell them that she was meeting a Pietà singer and her mother would approve and ask to know everything about it. They would tell her not to stay out too late and that would be all. Truly, she had

234   SHARIANN LEWITT

gotten so used to lies that she had forgotten that sometimes the truth was perfectly acceptable.

She was so excited about the possibilities that it was hard to concentrate. Her mind wandered back to the Pietà, to Lina, to the evening assignation, even when she tried to organize her plan for the day's search. Tonight would yield information, she hoped, but there was still a lot about Artos Camerillo that she didn't know, and it was still possible that nothing at the Pietà had anything whatever to do with his death.

She called up her new mail. There was, finally, something from David. But it wasn't a way into the Pietà or some stunning new revelation, it was merely a perfunctory check on her progress. There was a line at the bottom saying that he was now back at Artos's to live and wearing a tracking bracelet, so he couldn't leave the city.

She sighed. That was to be expected, but she worried that he might hold some grudge against her slowness and not pay her in full.

And there were six more garbage emails cluttering up her queue. Even the headers made no sense. She deleted the lot of it, wondering if there was some problem with the local post office. But the local post office was her own Sept, and if there were some problem then everyone would be talking about it, Board meeting or no.

She had just about finished her message routing when she got another flash in the box. It was from Zizi, an automail telling her that her request was in file. She had written the automail herself on the standard template and it didn't sound like Zizi at all. Sometime, when she had some time, she would have to customize the standard messages. If she ever had time again.

Now she would have to stop in the Library and go through Zizi's data before she got on with the search for a murderer. Or at least discover a reason for a murder that would yield a killer other than David Gavrilli. After all, that was what she was getting paid to do.

She lay down in the dreambox and wished she could just plain fall asleep, instead of starting back in search mode. Instead she set the transition to her usual spot on the Library. When she arrived she found Zizi pacing on the back of her chair ruffling his feathers.

"I found it," he crowed as soon as she took her place. "There are three main destinations in the galaxy, at least three main directions where coded information is being sent. Only I can't work the codes. They don't comply with any Sept standard."

Cecilie wondered if it was her imagination, or if the familiar actually was frustrated. "What does it look like?" she asked gently.

Zizi looked at her and put his foot up to rub his head. Somehow he stuck a toe into his nostril and sneezed wetly. Cecilie knew she hadn't programmed that, although it did look very birdlike. "It looks like garbage," Zizi said. "Absolute complete garbage. Useless."

"And where are they going?" she asked.

"Nothing at all in those directions for forever," Zizi responded. "Like I said, it's all garbage."

Cecilie studied the familiar she had created and spent hours refining. His color was precisely the way she had left it in the last upgrade, his crest and toes were perfectly proportioned, his wings fluttered just the way she'd wanted. But there was something different. His attitude was not what she had created for the bird. She had created a compliant data gatherer, not something that gave her value judgments on what it had collected.

Zizi had been changed. Subtly, like her nails, like everything around them. Zizi had been looking for the aliens and they had found him. And they made him more—birdlike. More himself. Just as they had made her nails and the whole of the Mall for the moment the collection anomaly passed through.

But how did an alien know what was essential to themselves, she wondered. And why did it matter? Why did they change things and how did they know?

Cecilie was confused enough to forget about the Camerillo case and her appointment with the singer late that night. There were aliens and they were passing through, collecting data, all the time the Board was meeting supposedly to decide the future of the net.

The Board thought they were deciding the future of the net. Now that was funny. As if the Board could actually decide on the future of a thing that was alive and growing and had large parts that were unknown even to them. The Board members didn't even know that aliens were there tucked into their sacred preserves and were collecting data and sending it off somewhere in the universe. Data went to three different points, Zizi had said. So she had perhaps discovered three alien species, not simply one.

Suddenly Cecilie wondered if she should introduce the Board to the interlopers. The idea made her giggle. Of course they wouldn't believe her—at least not at first. They would take it as a joke or a hoax, at least until they had much more data than she had. And even then they would have trouble believing it.

Still, maybe one or two would understand it the way Cecilie did. They would realize that there was a lot more at stake than hoarding even more control and wealth than the Septs already had. Some Board members would have to understand that there was an intellectual challenge here, and the opportunity to do something much greater than bicker about their profits and power.

Zizi pecked her nose with his sharp beak. She started and wondered if she had specifically created that reaction and the strength of that beak and this was only the first time she'd felt it, or if it had been enhanced like its personality.

"Something else," Zizi said, and scratched his head with his foot. "About the Camerillo data that you asked me to obtain. I have it here for your leisure, but if you would prefer a verbal summary I am prepared to do that."

"Yes please," Cecilie said, entranced. She certainly had not created this function in the creature. It didn't have the intelligence or the judgment to summarize salient points. So this was another change she could note, something she could watch in action.

Though maybe, Cecilie considered, this wasn't something improved by aliens at all. Maybe Zizi's learning functions had succeeded in creating a true artificial intelligence. There were several of them in the net, but none had ever started out as simple as the familiar. Cecilie couldn't face that possibility and so she pushed it out of her mind, prepared to listen to what her search program had gathered.

Zizi stopped pacing and stood before her. He ruffled his feathers before he began. "There is a record of contract between Artos Camerillo and the Gavrilli family dated three years ago. Contents complete in the folder. Summary, he told the family about their son, who was his student. They paid him and kept a watch on the palazzo with a hands-off policy. There is no record of what their relationship has been to David Gavrilli since. However, as per the contract, Camerillo received two thousand a month in his account from the time of the contract until the present."

Cecilie sighed and closed her eyes. Now she wasn't going to get the money from the Gavrillis for turning David over. Too bad. She would have liked that, though not so much for the fee as for the opportunity to teach that arrogant smartass a lesson, and see his face when he realized that she had outmaneuvered him. The problem was, the old man had outsmarted both of them.

"Thank you, Zizi," she said, dismissing the familiar.

"You must wait. I know more," the bird screeched.

Cecilie wished that she hadn't made his voice quite so realistic. At the time it had been a challenge. Now it was an annoyance. "What else?" she asked.

Not that she was interested. There was nothing that Zizi could have found that was more interesting than Camerillo's relationship with the Gavrillis, but she knew it would be easier to get it all at once without Zizi bothering her every ten minutes. Besides, there was something reassuring in the knowledge that Zizi had not changed so radically that he had an understanding of her priorities. That would not merely be a change, that would make her suspect that her familiar was not familiar at all and was serving some other interests.

David could have tampered with him to make her crazy, to make her think that all of her data about the aliens was as suspect as her sanity. Of all her speculations on Zizi's differences, this one made her absolutely furious. Zizi was hers, and although she knew the bird was really just a program there was a part of her that still responded emotionally to the bird as a living creature—as a friend. David deliberately tampering with Zizi's personality was akin to murder, and Cecilie imagined what she would do to him if he were at fault.

"A more important piece of information is that Camerillo was the head of a clandestine group called the Children of Dawn," Zizi informed her. "The Children of Dawn are dedicated to breaking the power of the Septs within the net and the power of the choirs through the use of nonapproved music."

Cecilie's disinterest had dissolved. She had heard of the Children of Dawn, bits of spurious reference that had been fairly meaningless. She had always thought that the so-called secret society was either entirely a hoax or really some inner circle among the Septs.

That had always made more sense, that there were sisters and brothers working together across Sept lines to insure their own superiority. The idea that this organization existed and it was truly anti-Sept was more alien than the aliens.

The old man had been the head of that. Which meant that David must be involved, and might well be the head of it now. Oh, he had a lot to answer for when she saw him next. By withholding this information he had made it clear that the organization had something to do with the old man's death.

"And the society now?" she asked, though she hoped they were too disorganized to survive Artos's demise. But then David Gavrilli had been named his protégé, which she had to assume meant his successor in the organization as well. So there was every probability that David had stepped into the leadership of a clandestine organization.

If the Children of Dawn existed. Cecilie wondered where Zizi had come up with any information at all. She was certain that none of it could actually be resident in the net. No one would be that stupid, and David was far from lax with security.

So Zizi's source was suspect—and so was David. Maybe he couldn't care less about the palazzo or anything else, and Cecilie was certain he didn't. But maybe he did want the leadership. He was arrogant enough to desire it, arrogant enough to think that it mattered. Cecilie wondered whether he thought it was important enough to kill for.

"Give me the site references," Cecilie said to Zizi. Wherever Zizi had found this, it had to be in the net. Zizi did not exist anywhere else. But Cecilie was bemused by anyone storing anti-Sept information in the net. That was just plain stupid and nothing about either David or Camerillo was stupid. There was nowhere in the net that the Septs could not go, no security that could hold them out. She had proved that herself, and so Cecilie doubted the existence of the site even as Zizi told her.

She had not planned to spend the day here. There were other things to do, with the Board meeting and her appointment with Lina. But she couldn't ignore the strangeness of a net site where the Children of Dawn openly proclaimed their anti-Sept message and propagated jazz.

She looked at the site coordinates in her folder, written in red glow on the brown report cover Zizi had submitted. That was also new—usually Zizi just left things in the folders she had created in her own personal strongbox, not new files left out on a Library table. She automatically decoded the abbreviation string to visualize the location and she started.

The location indicated was right there in the Library. It was in that basement that no one ever used.

It seemed to be getting very crowded down there, with aliens and cabals competing for space. She found the image funny, especially since there was so much empty space in the net. And still more space could be created simply, at will, by anyone who knew how.

Cecilie was willing to think that maybe aliens didn't know how or didn't want to bother. That finding free, already-created space was useful to them and made life easy. Fine.

But the Children of Dawn were supposed to think of themselves as net.ninja. Much as Cecilie thought they had been absurd to claim a site in the net at all, taking up a Sept-created room in the Library itself was ridiculous—unless they were taunting the Septs. Or if they were on a suicide ride.

Well, at least it was convenient. Cecilie arrived at the designated door in two seconds and bitched at the delay. The Board meeting was taking up way more than its share of bandwidth. The door was between two that she investigated, and both showed alien presence. She only glanced briefly through the smallest opening she could manage to confirm her suppositions and then went back to Zizi's site.

She knocked. It was polite and she didn't want to surprise anyone. There was no answer. She tried the door. It was locked. She snorted and began with a series of lockpick programs she had written as a third-year student, when she was still flat-chested and wore jumpers because she was too young for a blazer. She got through their primitive barriers on the third try. One thing this proved to her was that the Children of Dawn, no matter how they styled themselves, were no true net.ninja.

At least the room had been created by a human sensibility. She could recognize the desk and the files and the toolbox all arranged in the same sequence as came in midrange commercial software. This was the kind of setup a larger maskmaker might have, perhaps, with unused places for inventory and payroll.

Cecilie had to suppress the desire to giggle. She was at the heart of the great conspiracy and these were the resources of the people who thought they would bring down the Septs. She could have scrounged and written better over lunch waiting for her soup to cool.

The only thing that stopped her short of complete contempt was David. She had met David in the net, and she knew what he could do. And he could have written better over lunch too, she was certain of that.

She went through the files, which were boring and useless. There was nothing at all about the activity of the Children of Dawn, though given what she had seen so far she would not be surprised if their entire activity was setting up this site. There were no records, no address lists, no capture files full of sensitive Sept data. The only thing Cecilie could find were business accounts of something that looked like an importer's.

Cecilie perused the accounts quickly. There was nothing at all untoward on the surface of the records, and to really get into them she would have to spend some serious time, but she didn't expect to have to do that. She thought that probably there was nothing at all amiss with the accounts.

This was Artos Camerillo's business, his uninspired office transported to the Library for some reason. Probably, she suspected, the office was dull because Camerillo didn't put his heart into the business. His passion was music, and maybe the net, but it certainly wasn't importing luxury foodstuffs. Cecilie had barely heard of and had never tasted most of the things on these invoices.

She wanted to leave this place, leave the net entirely and get out of the dreambox. She requested a chrono read and the numbers showed up in blue in the lower left edge of her field of vision. It was almost dinnertime and she became aware that she was hungry. But still, she decided to do a quick scan with a filter for the Children of Dawn string before she left. Just to make sure, just to be thorough.

Three items triggered the scan. The first was a bank account, innocuous in itself, but the check record showed a large number of payments made out to Children of Dawn. Cecilie forgot that she was hungry. The other two documents would appear equally ingenuous to someone who was looking for tax purposes or personal credit. There was an appointment tickler with certain dates and trips marked CD. Cecilie immediately transferred that to her own account and then erased the trace that would have shown it to have been copied. Maybe Zizi had included this file in her investigation folder, but she didn't want to take the chance. The familiar was good, but since he had gotten uncanny she didn't entirely trust what he would or could do—and what he wouldn't.

She was excited about the appointments. She might be able

to correlate the trips and meetings to other events. Maybe there was some pattern to the movements that would lead to a killer.

Suddenly Cecilie realized that she didn't want David to be the killer, and that was why she had accepted the contract. She wasn't sure why it mattered to her. Maybe just that she had met him and she couldn't bear to think that a murderer wouldn't be marked in some easily recognizable way. There should be something about his speech or his face or his way of sipping coffee that would proclaim that this was a bad person. A killer. A pariah. A person beyond the pale of his humanity.

Beyond humanity. Cecilie whistled through her teeth. That was why the office was here. It had not been put here by the old man or David or some fanatical idiot in the Children of Dawn.

It had been brought here. It was an intact image, abandoned and complete. It must contain much more data about context than they could acquire in a populated area, where things were always changing and they had to stay hidden. Here the aliens could take their time to study a complete working system from the subject group.

Cecilie felt dizzy. There was too much and it was too weird and she wanted dinner. She wanted normalcy, she needed Julietta's inane conversation to prove to her that not everyone saw conspiracies in the subterranean dark.

But there was still the third record. She had to at least see what it was before leaving for the day, even though she had a copy safe in her own private files.

The third document that mentioned the Children of Dawn was an insurance claim. Cecilie puzzled over that for a moment and they saved it. She would think better after she had eaten, and she had entrée to the Pietà systems tonight. That would solve a number of mysteries, even if they were irrelevant to her investigation. She still needed, wanted to know. Curiosity was a characteristic that had been duly encouraged in her Sept education. Fortunately, so were common sense and a healthy dose of self-preservation.

She did not ignore those two qualities entirely. She left the office, left the Library entirely, and returned to Real Life. She had downloaded the appointment book and the insurance claim and could peruse them in text environment while she ate a sandwich and waited for ten-thirty to come.

In the end, I am frightened. The Septs are more than I feared them to be, completely without ethics or concerns past their own interests. Most of all I fear Sept-Sorian, as I have always known their true place in the hierarchy. Even if it is nearly illegal to even think the truth, I cannot help but know. I fear that they will find me and my Children and destroy us, as they have destroyed all opposition in the past thirty years.

I remember a time when the net was free. When multitudes would go to extreme lengths rather than forfeit that anarchy. When even the most powerful had to abide by prevailing tradition and common usage. Over the years this has deteriorated so that now the Septs run everything of consequence and the rest of us have kiosk accounts where we can spend our money and chat to friends. We appear to be free—so long as we don't try to touch anything that matters.

Cecilie read the old man's words over and over again. She tried to believe that she was wrong and that Camerillo was too. She was infuriated and insulted and afraid that there was more than a shred of truth in the old man's paranoia.

. . . completely without ethics or concerns past their own interests.

Cecilie shuddered. She knew what had happened to her in even a few weeks. Step by step she had been enticed. She had done things that violated her entire moral center and in so doing she had changed. Things were no longer quite so clear or so meaningful and she did what she had to do to satisfy the Sept. Doing whatever the Sept required had even begun to feel right to her.

Bit by bit they were changing her. They had created her in the first place, embedding values like loyalty and the search for truth. Then they twisted those scruples, forcing her to abandon any meaning other than the Sept's.

They had done it well. Cecilie knew that she hadn't felt right, hadn't felt clean, since the day Signora Tima had explained what she had to do to pass her promotion to senior apprentice. She hadn't felt really alive since then. She was all weighted down and wrapped up in some fog of necessity that the Sept had convinced her she would eventually come to accept.

Only she couldn't accept it. Her own acquiescence had sucked the life out of her. Looking at the elders, at the women who had invaded Sept Fortune for the Board meeting, Cecilie knew that none of them seemed fully alive, either.

Even her mother had more vitality, more sparkle, than these privileged and educated elders who appeared utterly enervated. Cecilie wondered if all the wealth, the ski vacations and the elegant beach houses, the large apartments in the Sept-House and the retirement House in Hawaii, if all these things made up for becoming part of the conspiracy. She suspected they didn't. Or why would the Septs need this Board meeting, crave even more power than they already wielded and seek to bring the whole world under their sway?

Somehow it made a kind of sense to Cecilie—a sickening, scary sense. There were large pieces missing, and Cecilie realized that she wasn't certain that she wanted to know what those pieces were. Every time she had uncovered new data everything became uglier and more immediate. There was no reason to think that this would change, that the downward spiral would stop suddenly and she would find the light.

They had corrupted her that deeply, she realized wearily. She no longer expected good. She no longer had hope. And she was running out of time.

Cecilie had been inside the Pietà many times, through the grand door that gave onto the stone wharf. Beyond this door was the concert hall with its gilded ornaments and sky blue velvet hangings and its many chandeliers. She had worn her best costumes here and had filed in clutching a program printed on heavy paper, had mingled in the soaring sky blue lobby with a ceiling painted with bare-breasted angels. This had always been a place of hush and awe and pleasure, a symphony for the senses.

Lina did not take her to the familiar door. Instead Lina led her to a much smaller door on the street. Here there was no fine art on the ceilings and no gold and silver leaf on the flood-stained walls. The smell of dust and chalk and musty robes lingered in the dark. Lina led quickly down the corridor so that Cecilie didn't have a chance to see what was behind the scenes of the Pietà. "Classrooms, rehearsal rooms," Lina said, waving her hand vaguely.

They turned several times and came to an elegant if small parlor with French doors that Lina opened with an old-fashioned key card. "The office," she said with a flourish. She told the lights to come up to two-thirds; full bright would have seemed harsh and threatening compared with the shadows through which they had passed.

There were only two workstations. Lina sat down and whispered a series of commands in a sequence that meant nothing at all to Cecilie. It must have been the Pietà's private code set. The text readers looked ancient. Cecilie was certain that they hadn't been replaced since just after the last flood. Which had been when she was two years old. Interfaces had improved since then, and besides, these old things looked like antiques.

Well, she thought, *at least they fit in with the rest of the office.* Everything there was antique, some of it very fine and most of it too scarred and flood-stained to have any serious value.

"It's ready for you now," Lina told her, and then got up from the narrow-legged gilt chair that matched nothing else in the room. Cecilie perched on the tapestry seat cautiously and looked at the display.

She was in a file system that resembled no file system she had ever seen before. Slowly, experimentally, she worked her way through the year and the names where Lina had left her. Whoever had kept these records had done so in a highly idiosyncratic manner. Without Lina setting her in the correct year and at around the proper placement, Cecilie honestly thought that she might not have been able to find even something fairly easy to access.

"Do you know why these were taken off the net?" she asked Lina casually.

The singer shrugged and looked up from her folio. "I don't know. They said something about our record system being incompatible or something and that the site wouldn't carry anything in an exotic format."

"Yeah, I can see why," Cecilie muttered to herself. "This is a mess."

Lina looked up from her sheet music again. "No it isn't. It's organized on the same principle as a symphony, is all. Some of the records, the more personal ones, are structured around other musical forms. But all our serious records are symphonies. That makes it easy for anyone to access them."

Cecilie groaned. She didn't know anything about the structure of symphonies, but what she found really absurd was Lina's naïveté. As if just anyone could use the structure of a symphony, indeed!

Suddenly she flashed on the alien catalogs in her mind's eye. Their structure was only somewhat less coherent for her than a musical form of organization. The aliens were completely alien, but that didn't mean that there weren't plenty of her own species right here in Venice who lived in a different world entirely.

Maybe being alien was only a matter of degree.

Suddenly Cecilie wondered if Lina might be closer to understanding the alien archives than a Sept sister could be. Maybe there was something in their patterning that was closer to the organization of music the way Lina had studied it than to a more usual cataloging of information. The idea excited Cecilie. She wanted to ask immediately if Lina would be willing to enter a dreambox with her and go to the alien sites. If Lina couldn't see any underlying structure, Cecilie could find someone else who thought very differently from either of them.

The implications were huge and important. To be able to identify any form of alien organization would mean to begin to communicate. Once they were able to communicate and everyone knew, who knew what then? Even if they could never do more than exchange information, who knew what techniques and technology the aliens had?

Something more than that moved Cecilie to want to act. It was the idea that they were not alone, that there were others out there, wondering, looking, curious, aware. Others so far away that she could not pinpoint their star of origin were aware of humanity. All that humankind were and had been would not be isolated on one single rock and extinguished alone. Something of them would live on elsewhere and someone would notice when humanity as a race died. Maybe someone would even mourn.

It was like imagining her own funeral when she was fifteen, Cecilie thought. It was Valentina's idea to wonder about who would be there and wallow in the image of their grief. Only Cecilie had always thought that when the end came for her species everything would cancel out. That there would be no memory, no grief at their passing. Now, perhaps, that was not true, and that alone was a tremendous comfort.

She couldn't work on the big picture while the smaller one was so urgent. The aliens had been there for a long time and looked fixed to stay. David Gavrilli, however, was wearing a tracer bracelet and could not leave the city. David Gavrilli was much less important than the aliens, but his signature was on her contract and now that had to take precedence over the greater revelation.

Besides, she didn't have the luxury of time to waste in these records. Lina could not hold this open forever. Instead of trying to understand any of the organizational principles, Cecilie merely asked Lina where she would find information on two members' dismissals. Lina asked if she wanted text or visual or interactive. Cecilie decided on text. It would be the fastest format, though she didn't know why she felt so pressed for time. Lina did not seem rushed or worried.

Lina sang a couple of notes and text appeared. Cecilie tried not to appear too overwhelmed. What perfect security for the Pietà! It truly was unbreakable by many of the Septs, which did not include musical training. Cecilie herself could not carry a tune. Some of the Sept sisters at least could hit notes when they wanted to, but Cecilie couldn't conceive of breaking this system alone no matter how much she knew about it—not that it would ever have occurred to her or to anyone in Sept-Fortune to use that kind of barrier. She was impressed, the more so because it was so very simple.

No one at the Pietà would have the least problem getting in and no unqualified person could follow or reproduce the code. Oh, maybe if she knew the sequences and got a singer from one of the other choirs she would have a chance. But Cecilie thought it very likely that the choirs would stick together the way the Septs would in the face of an outsider. Just like the Septs, they might argue all they like among themselves and treat each other as bitterest enemies and rivals, but no doubt they would close ranks immediately if someone completely outside their system confronted them.

Then Cecilie shook her head to clear it. There was too much to do and very little time. Priorities. She glanced at the text that Lina had brought up, and nodded. This was what she had been searching for. She began to read the files avidly.

When she reemerged from the Pietà files it was nearly two in the morning. Cecilie was shocked. She didn't feel like she'd been that engrossed in historical reports that had nothing at all to do with the old man's death. At least, she didn't think they could have any relevance.

Lina was sitting hunched over, her face in her arms and her breathing regular. Asleep, Cecilie thought, and no wonder. She touched the singer lightly on the shoulder and Lina's eyes fluttered.

"Did you get what you want?" the singer asked, her voice slurred with sleep.

"Yes," Cecilie said, not certain it was the full truth.

Lina closed her eyes, leaned back in the chair and stretched. "Then I guess I'd better let you out and you can go home," she said, rising.

Cecilie followed her back through the empty classrooms and rehearsal halls to the small side door. This time the place felt truly dead, as if there were no one alive but the two of them in the whole pile of stone or in the whole of the world.

"You'll be all right?" Lina inquired as she opened the heavy door.

"Sure," Cecilie reassured her. And then Cecilie slipped out into the night.

There were no taxis in this neighborhood. She had to walk several blocks to the vaporetto stand, where she was alone for the full twenty minutes until a small boat came her way. She paid and got in. There were perhaps five other people in the boat, three of them quite definitely drunk. One had his mask raised over his mouth so he wouldn't vomit into it and choke himself. Cecilie positioned herself as far from them as possible.

The late-night rides were slow. She didn't get home until after three, and she was exhausted. Her mother was awake when she got in, but Cecilie was too tired to argue. "I'll tell you everything when I get up," she said, staggering off to her own room.

"And what about work?" her mother demanded. "How are you going to get up tomorrow?"

Cecilie shrugged. Right now nothing seemed so important as getting to bed. "I'll go in late. With the Board meeting no one will notice anyway." Then, not listening to anything more, she stumbled into her room and barely pulled off her clothes before she was asleep.

"Where were you last night?" her mother demanded over coffee. It was midmorning and the building was quiet. Everyone was off to work or school and only a few retirees were left. Except for Cecilie and her mother.

"Don't you have to go to work?" she asked.

Her mother sighed and shook her head. "I called in sick this morning because I need to know what you've been doing. I am sick, staying up worrying all night long, wondering if you were murdered or abducted and the police would find you floating in the Grand Canal in the morning."

Cecilie tried not to giggle. "It wasn't anything like that," she said. "I was working late and got involved in what I was doing and lost track of the time, is all. You'd be interested. I was at the Pietà."

Her mother's eyes widened. "The Pietà?"

Cecilie nodded. "I got into their records. And I found out about that scandal that you thought was so romantic."

Conflicting emotions animated her mother's face. "That isn't right," she said finally. "Don't you have a code of conduct, where you took an oath to the Sept? Those records are private."

Cecilie tried very hard not to laugh. If her mother only knew what the Sept had asked of her, breaking into records would sound like the most minor infraction. But her mother didn't know. Her mother didn't see the change in her, didn't know the things she had done. To her mother, privacy of Pietà records was sacrosanct. Unless, of course, it was broken by a tabloid journalist.

So Cecilie did the only thing possible. She told the truth. "I didn't break in, I was let in," she said easily. "But if you don't want to know what happened and why those singers were dismissed, I will consider it privileged information."

Her mother turned red and gasped. "Cecilie!" was all she said, but that said it all.

Cecilie giggled. "Yes, Mama. Okay. Well, Signora Camerillo was known as Laura Marghetti in her Pietà days. She was a lead singer with a special flair for opera. And Longni was also a lead singer, with an even bigger reputation at the time. Anyway, they were both introduced to jazz through the elder Camerillo brother, Longni's lover. He also played keyboard and loved jazz. They met him at the Pietà, where he was a rehearsal accompanist. The younger brother was a musician too, by the way, played the drums. The four of them began performing new music and drawing pretty serious crowds given the Pietà reputation.

"There were a lot of venues in those days and they were very popular. That's where a good bit of the Camerillo money came from, it turns out. That isn't important. What is important is that they were asked to stop. Sept-Sorian asked them to stop, and not too politely if I read between the lines.

"It's all in the records, right down to the scans of the hand-written Sept-Sorian notes that sound like demands written by criminals or kidnappers, not a reasonable request to a choir."

"That's absurd," her mother interrupted. "The Septs don't have anything to do with the choirs."

Cecilie blinked. It was not possible that her mother was so naive. "Of course the Septs have everything to do with the choirs," she said, wondering if she was going to have to spell it all out. "The Septs have supported the choirs from the beginning, from when it was first proven that certain forms of music increase intelligence and effective thought. It has to do with the erg cycles of the brain. The work of certain composers enhances those cycles.

"And it has never been proven that any other music makes you stupid," she continued. "But the Septs worry about that. There was a study done around the time that this jazz group was getting popular, though, that different kinds of music do affect the patterning in the brain that dictates behavior and that some of the forms of music were directly associated with how people regard authority. Someone wrote a study that jazz made people more independent and that rock made them more aggressive. I'm not sure that the study even was done at all, let alone that it was valid. But it is still quoted to this day.

"So the Septs have always paid the choirs to keep us working at top efficiency and the Septs have been very influential in choosing the music. That is the reason that Mozart is so popular with the choir recitals and rock and jazz are discouraged in the city.

"It's usually Sept-Sorian's duty to deal with these matters.

Their specialty isn't really the net work. They're more generalists and they tend to take care of a lot of the Real Life interface for the Sept Board. When the Board agrees on anything, which usually they don't. Like now. It makes sense that Sept-Sorian took care of the matter.

"They threatened the Pietà financially, said that unless the jazz players were not only dismissed but discredited the choir would no longer receive Sept patronage. Believe me, Mama, that counts for the main share of their revenue. I've done the accounting and I know.

"And that wasn't all. There are provisions that the four of them would not play in public together again."

"And what did they get for that?" her mother asked.

Cecilie chewed her lip. She hadn't realized it before, but now it was obvious what had been missing from the record. The quid pro quo for the singers' silence was not delineated. There must have been something, something that would really hold them. Because from everything else Cecilie had accessed, they had indeed lived by the terms of the agreement.

"Perhaps money," her mother mused. "People will do a lot for enough money."

Cecilie jumped up and hugged her mother. "That's it, that's got to be it. I've been trying to find out where the money came from."

Her mother only smiled. "You've been working too hard and staying out too late. And probably not eating proper dinners, either, when you're not home. I know there's a nice dinner at the House and I'm certain that isn't where you were. You have to slow down a little, Cecilie. Have some life. Enjoy everything you can. You're young, you're beautiful, you can't live just to work. That will keep until you're older. There is always work and finances and advancement. Now you need to sleep more and go to parties and have fun. And eat. You're not eating enough, I can tell."

Cecilie shook her head as her mother set another roll and butter in front of her. There was no resisting, and though she wasn't hungry she buttered the bread and broke it and nibbled at the crust. Eating relieved her of talking, which meant that she could think more effectively.

The Camerillo money had been the settlement for the end of the jazz band. They had been making decent money all along, so it would have had to be a substantial sum. But this was back in her territory, and Cecilie knew how to find exactly how much had been paid out.

So it came to both sides of the family and eventually all to the only heir, Artos. She had done a full day's work in an hour. Maybe her mother had done half of it for her, she wasn't sure, but sometimes she was proud that her mother was so smart.

14

Lina only got four hours of sleep. She was on the early shift at the Board and she cursed as the alarm woke her. The night with Cecilie had been miserably long and she was still cramped from hours dozing in the desk chair. She had forgotten that she had the early session.

She stood under a torrent of hot water hoping that it would help her wake up. Cold would do a better job but she couldn't even face tepid on a normal day. Exhausted as she was she couldn't consider the idea without far more misery than it was worth.

Getting dressed was an ordeal. She wore the usual Pietà blue robes and the Pietà mask that left her nose and mouth free to sing, but it took her at least ten minutes to decide what to wear under the robe.

Her hair looked awful but that didn't matter. The traditional Pietà turban that matched the robe would hide it, though usually she liked to wear her hair down, flowing over her back with the turban on top. She was often criticized for that. The idea of the robes and masks was that all the singers looked perfectly alike. One could not be told from another. She knew she should keep her identity decently concealed, but the hair was a fashion statement and had become popular with men and women alike. It had been quite daring on the streets two years ago, and the Pietà did have a reputation to maintain. These days only old stick-in-the-muds like the Maestro or the Sept members would refuse to ever show a lock of hair in costume.

Maestro was fighting a losing battle as more and more singers showed off their tresses. One day after she had heard the argument for anonymity for the third time in an afternoon, she suggested that a fall be attached to all the turbans of singers who didn't have beautiful hair to display. That shut the questioner up quickly.

Today, though, she wound her hair on top of her head and pinned it so that it wouldn't fall out of the headdress. No one would see that she was bleary-eyed and that her skin was pasty. There were definite advantages to wearing a mask.

She couldn't wear the mask to breakfast, though, and it dangled from the little invisible hook inside her large sleeve that was made for the purpose. Everyone could see that she looked like she could barely make it through breakfast, let alone perform a full program for the Board.

At least there was plenty of coffee. The breakfast room was laid as always, with the giant coffee urns on both sides of the table full of baskets of bread and sweet rolls. Normally Lina took one cup of coffee and bread and butter. Today she went back to the big urn twice and took two of the breakfast pastries with lemon curd. Between the coffee and the sugar she might possibly get through the morning.

She resented it even as she finished up and prepared to leave with the group. The early choir wasn't very important. Very few

Board members arrived for the breakfast or to work out alliances before the meetings began. Most of that was done late at night and under the influences of varied and unregulated music.

Lina hated the fact that she had to wake up early, had to perform complex and inspiring music for only a few who drifted in and couldn't care less that their mental and emotional needs were being as carefully coddled as their physical requirements. No, these arrogant Board members would talk to each other loudly, as if the music meant nothing to them. They would rattle their coffee cups and spoons, ask for jam or butter, and generally ignore the delicacy of expression Maestro had worked so hard to achieve.

And that was only the ones who came. Most of them didn't. After the night Lina had spent, she wanted nothing more than to absent herself from the whole meeting. Forever. She wanted only to sleep and never to see the inside of another Sept function again.

If her pride would not let her ask to be excused, all the traditions of the stage were on its side. Those traditions meant that she had to perform no matter how she felt, even if she were dying. She had heard of an opera production where three different tenors had sung in three different acts because the first two had died as the curtain went down.

She trailed the group as they got into the choir vaporetto and took the last place to stand.

"Did she come last night? Did you do it?" someone whispered to her from behind a mask.

She recognized the voice and started hard enough that she was practically awake. It was Sean.

"What are you doing here?" she hissed at him.

He smiled, slow and sardonic. "Yves was taken sick early this morning and rushed to the hospital. I suppose you didn't

hear the commotion? No, of course not, you're in the far building. They needed another tenor who knew the music. So here I
am. For the duration, it looks like."

"What did you do to Yves?" Lina asked.

"What do you mean, what did I do?" Sean asked, his voice
full of wounded innocence. "Yves has acute appendicitis. Believe
me, no matter how good I am I can't pull that one off. He'll be
back home tonight or tomorrow but he won't be able to sing
for a week. That's what Maestro told me when he asked me to
take Yves's place."

"You mean when you volunteered to take his place," Lina
corrected him.

Sean shrugged, but the gesture was nearly lost beneath the
yards of robe. "I'll admit to that much. But you didn't answer
my question about the Sept sister. Did she get in? Did she get
the information?"

Lina closed her eyes and wondered why she had agreed to
help him. She had liked Cecilie and trusted her in a way she
didn't trust Sean.

"Yes," Lina admitted, looking at the choppy grey water so
she didn't have to look at Sean's face. Even with the mask she
was sure she couldn't avoid his arrogance.

"Good," he said, turning to the water himself. "David will
be pleased. You've been very useful, you won't regret it."

Lina decided not to tell him that she already did regret it;
she hated the idea of helping him even if he was right. And she
wasn't so sure he was right. If Cecilie hadn't been so certain,
Lina would have let it drop. After all, things like the Septs taking over the net had no effect on her life. Why should she risk
herself, her position in the choir, her whole future, for something
she didn't think would matter?

But Cecilie had changed her mind, far more than Sean, more
even than the jazz. Cecilie, and the things she had heard and

overheard from the Board meeting. The bits of conversation she picked up during her breaks were alarming. She had realized how often there was one more whisper, a glance over a shoulder or toward the door, the tiny gestures that spoke of secrecy among certain of the Board members.

The boat arrived at the dock. Lina stood up straighter to live up to the image of the Pietà singers. They were a long, proud lineage, never seen to be weak or unable to perform, inviolate acolytes of their muse and serving none other.

Though they had always served the Septs and always would do so, Lina thought. Unless something happened. Unless they all learned to be free again.

They marched into the great chamber and took their places on the risers that made a backdrop for the main panel of speakers. Before the Sept sisters and brothers arrived, the main hall was impressive. Above, the ceiling was coffered in gilt with frescoed panels. Two walls were papered in the rich, Oriental green that was often thought of as Venetian. The other two walls were covered with paintings, allegories of the four seasons divided by carved mahogany moldings.

This morning Lina noticed nothing. It was hard enough to just stay awake. She opened her folio, though of course she knew the music by heart. The only thing she noticed was when Maestro brought his baton down.

Two hours later she staggered out for coffee. The buffet room was as elegantly set as before, but food didn't tempt Lina. Her stomach churned both from her conversation with Sean and her only partially successful attempt to counteract the long night. The place was stuffy and crowded—in the past twenty minutes most of the Board members had arrived. Lina glanced at the ormolu clock that sat on an oversized mantelpiece, and it already read nine. No wonder everyone was already here; she hadn't realized that so much time had passed.

She took another espresso and sat down on one of the narrow chairs upholstered in antique green velvet. It was miserably uncomfortable, made for ladies with big skirts to perch on rather than for exhausted singers to make up a lost night's sleep. She was staring deep into her cup in a daze when she heard a very soft voice just behind her.

"You really should be more careful of your security," said a man in a dark red mask. Lighter red twinkled around his left eye, subtly and not overdone. The work of a master maskmaker, Lina noted dully.

"Sept-Sorian has already guaranteed Pietà security," the man continued. "But what you compromise cannot be guaranteed in the future. Do you understand?"

"Yes," Lina muttered, not sure exactly what she had heard. Compromised security? What did a Sept have to do with it, anyway? Her brain was fuzzy and moving slowly. The man in the dark red mask disappeared and Lina forgot about him. She finished her espresso and returned to the hall for another hour of singing before her next break. It wasn't until they filed off the risers for the second time that she realized she couldn't spot Sean.

He probably was there and she was just too tired to pay attention. That happened when she didn't get enough sleep. She missed things and couldn't think.

It didn't matter, she told herself. Sean was there. Maybe he was farther to the right than she had realized. Maybe he had ducked into the rest room before they got to the buffet room. She was being silly, that was all.

She felt a hand on her shoulder and herself steered away from the food. "What?" she started to ask.

"You little idiot," a voice hissed. She heard his voice and his accent and recognized her abductor, the foreign Sept brother who had spoken to her so pleasantly the day after the meetings had opened. Only now he wore a refined mask in a subtle pattern of midnight blue and indigo, with a matching costume and all his hair tucked into his turban.

He didn't let go of her, but pushed her through the narrow back hallway through the old-fashioned cloakroom and down the back stairs.

"What are you doing?" Lina demanded, holding the newel post against being dragged any farther.

"Saving your life, you stupid little chicken," the Sept brother whispered in her ear. "That was Tano, the chief of security at Sept-Sorian. Talk about someone who's attention you don't want to attract. Now come along with me as if you meant to show me where to buy some souvenirs or something, like it was the most natural thing in the world."

Lina was too tired to hesitate or even evaluate rationally. It was simply easier to go along with the Sept brother than try to fight to get back upstairs. Besides, the second sopranos had only a tiny part in the upcoming section and she didn't know how she was going to manage to stay awake for two hours to sing for three minutes.

He never let go of her arm. Even through the heavy fabric she could feel the insistence of his grip. They walked several blocks to the public vaporetto stop. There they paid the fare and boarded in the middle of a Japanese tour group, who stared at them. Yes, indeed, a Pietà singer and a Board member abroad on public transportation were very interesting sights indeed and the tourists spent the entire ride taking pictures and grouping this or that family member with these friends with the masked Venetians.

They disembarked near the Basilica. The tour guide seemed to have some trouble getting her group to follow the planned program instead of taking off after the local celebrities in their midst—or at least getting pictures of their typical costumes.

They walked briskly. The Sept brother led her wildly through the streets in such an order that she could not have re-created the route. Finally they came to a once fine but now crumbling palazzo on a back canal. They didn't go in through the main door, which was to the water, but through a small service door on the side.

What little she saw of the entrance floor looked to have been badly affected by flood damage, but she didn't get to see much. Her kidnapper—or rescuer—steered her up the back stairs and then through what had once been a servants' corridor to an upstairs parlor.

Even unaware as she was, she realized that the furnishings showed both good taste and originality. None of the usual gilt and moire adorned the plain surfaces. It reminded her almost of Café Luna, only the chairs were elegantly covered and abstract canvases hung on the oversized blank walls.

In the corner a man waited. Lina recognized him, too, from the Luna. He was one of the musicians. He was unmasked, which made sense if this was his own home, and appeared at ease. His hair was dark brown and his features were cosmetically perfect but not particularly interesting. Lina recognized the results of the more popular forms of surgery from those places where people didn't mask. She thought it a pity, really. Masking meant that Venetians could remain themselves beneath the masks instead of pretending they were barefaced and honest. When in truth everyone masked and those who learned to do it with their faces showing to the world were merely creating another mask, a more dangerous one.

The man rose gracefully and held out his hand to her. "I am David Gavrilli," he introduced himself, and his voice was deep and musical. Lina wondered if he could sing.

"Sean has told me a great deal about you," he continued. "You've helped us greatly, so we couldn't leave you in danger."

"I'm not in danger," Lina said.

"I'd better go before I'm missed," the Sept brother told them. David nodded and the foreign brother left.

Lina slumped down on one of the chairs uninvited. She was tired and she was a Pietà singer so she was used to the privilege. David merely sat beside her.

"What is this?" she asked. "I went along, but I could really use an explanation. Or I'll leave now."

David did not try to restrain her. "Sean told me what you did for Cecilie last night," he said. "We owe you. You might not have wanted to help us as such, but you have. And when your actions came to the attention of Sept-Sorian we had to take steps to protect you."

"But they're just a Sept," Lina protested.

David shrugged. "They are dangerous," he replied. "We don't know what their connections are, but it's better that you're out of there for a while. At least until after the meetings are over."

"I can't," Lina said. "I'm in the Board choir, it's a special position. I can't just disappear, it will be noticed."

David hesitated. When he finally spoke his voice was not nearly so authoritative as it had been before. "Why not stay here today and tonight? You are too tired anyway, and your shift for the day was almost done. So wait until you are rested and can evaluate the situation properly, with a clear head. We have a lovely guest room set up for you."

Lina nodded. She would have agreed to almost anything to go to sleep. David led her to an airy bedroom full of flowered prints in soft greyed pastels. A fresh nightgown had been laid at the bottom of the bed, crisp white cotton edged in lace. David opened the door and she cared about nothing at all except sleep.

No matter what her mother recommended, Cecilie did not stay home all day. She had to report her findings to her employer, and check that he sent the payment due. She still hadn't found the killer but she was close. She could feel it, she could smell it. She knew she was close the way she had always known before when she had first learned to do data searches through the whole of the infosea.

Others would get lost and they were the ones who did not last. The next morning a place would be empty at breakfast and even the littlest girls knew that someone had failed. Then there were those like Valentina and Julietta, who had a specific plan of action and could negotiate through the dataflow by diligence and organized force.

And then there was Cecilie, who had somehow found ways to pick through and come to a final comprehension without knowing quite how she'd done it. It was intuitive talent, Signora Angelina had said, but that didn't mean that Cecilie didn't need to study and learn the same techniques as the others. Talent alone was useless without training and discipline and lots of hard work.

That talent was even more useless without a dreambox.

At least the House was deserted when Cecilie arrived. All the delegates were likely off at the Board, and everyone else was in their cubicles. She didn't see anyone as she crossed the Main Hall and passed the girls' school before entering the Chinese Corridor. Everyone in the Sept could be dead, and the thought didn't disturb Cecilie much at all.

She didn't bother checking her mail in text. What was there could wait; she had better things to do.

She lay down on the dreambox and hooked in the leads. The cover lowered and colored, first a pale blue swirled with green and violet and then blanked into red. Then she saw the Library form around her, in flat two-dee before the connection solidified and she transferred consciousness completely to the net.

Only things had changed in the Library. Someone was sitting

in her usual spot at the table reserved for Sept-Fortune and this was not a sister of the Sept. For one thing, the figure was male.

Nor was it anyone she knew. He looked at her and gestured for her to be seated. There was something about him, even here, that she didn't like. His costume was usual enough, a harlequin in black and orange, the colors of Sept-Sorian. He seemed neither imposing nor strange and showed none of the signs she had learned to suspect when she was inside. Yet, just the fact that he sat at her table in the Sept-Sorian colors frightened her. She sat down facing him and neither of them unmasked.

"Little sister," he said slowly, "you are very young and very naive. We know that and we are willing to make allowances for these things. But you should know when to retreat, when it is better not to know things. Your teachers should have instructed you. Sometimes you cannot know the whole story. Sometimes it is better for things to remain silent, to remain buried. Do you understand?"

Looking at the cold eyes that no mask could hide, she did understand. She understood all too well.

"Someone innocent should not pay," she replied.

"No one innocent ever pays," the Sept-Sorian brother told her. "The one you were hired to clear, to protect, he is not innocent. He may not have killed Artos Camerillo, but he certainly is not innocent. You will have to trust us. And trust that his— elimination—is also to our benefit. All of our benefit."

Cecilie felt frozen, as if the ice in this brother had reached out and chilled her as well. "I understand you," she said.

"Good," he said. "You will let this matter drop completely. Your superiors will be informed."

He got up and walked out of the reading room. Cecilie moved around to her usual chair, which he had taken. She looked down and then the tears came.

Zizi lay twisted and broken on the floor. No matter that it

had just been a program, and one she had created. It had still been her familiar, warm and friendly and part of her world. That small body with its neck crushed and feathers strewn about the legs of the chair was a threat that was more cruel and telling than anything the brother had said.

Cecilie realized that she was crying. She hoped that her Library mask held, that no one else could see her tears. How could he have hurt her familiar? The bird-construct had done nothing at all.

Oh, she understood all too well and it made too much sense. Everything fell neatly into place. What the singers had gotten that was not listed became clear. They had been allowed to live. As Artos Camerillo had not. As Zizi had not.

As she would not if she reported her findings to David.

Information was power. But Sept-Sorian wasn't stopping at information, and hadn't stopped there for a long time. Now the Board just wanted to go public with the arrangement, and force the Septs into some kind of cohesive whole so that Sept-Sorian could keep them in line as well.

Once upon a time she had learned that the Septs, being systems experts, were helpers to all humanity. She had believed those stories, had been proud of her contribution. All the promises of wealth and privilege hadn't made her proud of her vocation. Then she had been so full of righteousness, of moral fervor. She had been so stupid. She had been so wrong.

Now Sept-Sorian would kill her, too, the way they disposed of anyone who got in their way. Cecilie wondered if that was what Signora Tima and the sisters from San Francisco and the other major Houses had discussed in their private meeting. While Cecilie could easily believe that Signora Tima was out to take over everything, she would take it for Sept-Fortune. There was no love lost between Signora Tima and the bullying brothers who tried to force her hand.

Gently Cecilie picked up the pieces of Zizi that were scattered on the floor. The body had weight and there was still a little warmth—she had been so pleased at how well it had mimicked Real Life. She gathered the feathers into a pile. There were the long curving feathers of the tail and the crest, the near iridescent flight feathers.

She would never make anything like it again, she swore. It was stupid to be so attached to a program. Why had the brother killed it? It was only a familiar, a funny, useful thing that every Sept sister and brother had.

Zizi's demise might not have been entirely symbolic. The familiar might have discovered something. If he had unearthed something he would have downloaded it before arriving at the Library. She had written that in when she was very young, before she could trust Zizi's effectiveness in finding her.

She could regenerate her familiar if she decided to. The idea of living without Zizi was bleak and humorless and she could not bear being without him. Much as she did not like to admit it, she was very fond of her virtual bird. But that decision could wait; what Zizi might have gathered could not.

Now that she knew the reading room was not safe she had to find someplace where a brother of Sept-Sorian wouldn't look for her. There had to be someplace where she could just disappear. She was certain that Sept-Sorian had passive telltales on all the level entries in the net. That must be how they knew she had arrived in the Library, which meant that she had to slip a level or two without going through any of the approved gates.

Well, there was the story that all water on every level was entry to the infosea, if only one had the courage to enter it. Cecilie knew of only one body of water large enough for immersion on this level. Grimly she made herself leave the Library and cross the few blocks to the Mall. The Mall was the last place in the universe were she wanted to be right now. She wanted to be alone, to mourn and to cry and to be afraid and think and eat ice cream while she took a time-out from life. Only in Real Life there were no time-outs, and virtual ice cream was useless, she reminded herself. Though it wasn't fattening, as Julietta always reminded them.

At least the Mall was in its white pseudoclassical phase. She couldn't have borne the neon, or anything too cheerful. As it was, she felt that her slow pace and hunched posture must make her obvious among the chattering, shopping crowd. They were all so happy, so oblivious of what was around them, that she wanted to hammer their virtual heads through the illusory plate glass.

She ignored all the shops, the piles of colored goods stacked seductively in the entryways, the salespeople and pitches every three meters. She stayed on the main level and headed inward to the center, to the big fountain.

In pseudoclassical phase, the fountain was half surrounded by a pillared arcade. There were stairs leading into the basin as if this were some naiad's pool. Cecilie sat on the marble ledge and dipped her hand into the water. From this perspective she could tell nothing. Maybe the blue floor was really just a floor and no one could use this place to change.

She swung her legs over the ledge so that her feet were on the steps, squarely in the water. She began to walk down. There were only five steps and she was on the bottom. It was barely to her knees.

"Wait, get out of there, you can't go in there."

She turned. A uniformed security guard was running toward her. She knelt down and then held her breath and ducked her head under so she was completely immersed. For a moment the blue bottom and white steps of the fountain in the middle of the Mall lingered; and then opened out into the whole of the infosea.

There was very little here. The Mall was a wasteland on the inner levels. Experimentally, Cecilie kicked out and headed for a darker eddy she could see nearby. Most likely the Library analogue on this level, though she had always seen the image before as a brilliant sparkling green reef abundant with life.

This was swirling indigo like the deepest and most secret parts of the level. Nothing seemed alive in there, though glints of light were visible in the whirlpool. Everything spiraled downward. Cecilie wondered if it was the aliens, sucking all the life and knowledge from the net, from humanity. In the end they'd be left with nothing, a structure that was perfectly clear and void.

There were quiet pools near enough the eddy that she could see, but far enough that she would not be dragged down. Cecilie found one with a marker buoy and clung to it, afraid of being dragged into the maelstrom. As she caught her breath and adjusted to the quiet pool she realized that she was not alone. There were other things there, tethered to the buoy, data present on a site.

She looked more carefully. It was an oddball assortment. There was part of a working office that looked vaguely familiar, a ballet dancer, a baby whale, a swirl of autumn leaves and what appeared to be an entire field of tulips. Some of the things were more familiar, the Mall in each of its phases, the flavor list from a nearby ice-cream parlor, sidewalk stones, street signs and an assortment of vehicles, many of which Cecilie couldn't name. At least there was some basic sense in the collection.

There were a few animals grouped together, too, net constructs, things that didn't exist in nature. Unicorns and griffins, dragons and basilisks had been among the first things created for profit as well as pleasure. And at the bottom of the heap Cecilie saw a shade of iridescent blue that she knew only too well. No, whoever was here couldn't be that cruel. She couldn't avoid looking to be certain, knowing that she was right. Though she couldn't have been anything other than right.

It was Zizi, as she had found him lying on the reading-room floor. The sight of that broken little body made her sob with unrecognized grief. She reached out and the image wavered in the medium. It was not the real Zizi, her Zizi, merely a recollection of him. Somehow that made it easier.

She felt as if someone were watching her curiously but benignly. There was no figure she could make out, but on this level that didn't matter.

The collection in front of her had changed, and this time there were no familiar things, no ice-cream lists or bird-familiars. She was thankful for that and wondered if whoever had placed Zizi there in the first place felt badly about that. Now there were only people, faces that she couldn't recognize for the most part. In each face field there was an icon. Some of the icons denoted Septs, some nationalities, and some were family crests. She gestured to the icons with her eyes and the whole thing shifted quickly. Now the people were sorted by icon.

Cecilie went through and touched the Sept icons. She didn't know why, it seemed very silly and yet important. The other groupings disappeared, and now she had an arrangement of Septs. She was surrounded by all the familiar symbols for Sept-Fortune and Sept-San Marco and those foreign Septs she couldn't pronounce correctly. And in the center, larger than the others, was Sept-Sorian.

She stared at the arrangement. Something glittered on the buoy and resolved into a crude harlequin shape. She understood. This was one of the aliens. It was trying to communicate with her, though whether it was trying to tell her something or ask she couldn't comprehend. But this time it had come with far more organization than she had seen before in the rooms, or some organization that she could follow. Obviously it was learning something, grouping data in meaningful ways.

It was trying to communicate, in as close to her language as it could manage. The event would have been amazing, historic, had she not been so sunk in her own concerns. She gestured toward the dark whirlpool. "The Library," she said, feeling foolish, knowing that her words were incomprehensible and yet not comfortable without them. "There's a lot more there once you know how to use the resources."

The glitter turned dark and ominous and suddenly there was a shimmer throughout the quiet pool, and she was encased in a bubble that was tied to the buoy along with all the rest of the collection. Gingerly she tested the bonds. They dissolved when she pulled them. Not real, then, either, and not meant to be more than an impression here.

That was communication, she realized, but she didn't know what it meant. Did it mean the alien didn't want her to go or did it mean there was danger where she was headed? Or did it merely want her—or her image—for its collection, and it was asking politely?

The whirlpool was getting darker, and streaked into the indigo were long plumes of red. She found herself pushed from the pool, propelled through the datastream into a fast-moving current and hurried down that to the nearest exit. Whatever had brought her had not given her any choice, and so her focus was suddenly thrust back into her cubicle, where the surround screen of her dreambox went blank.

There were no exit codes. That had never happened before. It seemed as if the box were dead or had been disconnected. The top swung up too easily, as if detached from the controls.

Cecilie was afraid. She'd never heard of anything vaguely like this happening before. Something was very wrong. She slipped off the dreambox and crouched at the base. There was no place to hide in the cubicle.

That was ridiculous. Why should she think of hiding in her own Sept-House? She belonged here, she was safe. It was absurd to think otherwise.

Slowly she straightened up and forced herself to walk to her door. She didn't hear anything and opened the door onto the Chinese Corridor. There was nothing there.

The tension stayed with her. She was almost halfway down the hall when she heard something that sounded like marching. Heavy steps muffled by thick carpet carried through the floor, steps that were never made by a Sept sister in expensive pumps or athletic shoes.

Cecilie glanced around quickly for someplace to hide. Glad for once she was in the Chinese Corridor, Cecilie climbed onto a bench and into one of the flanking porcelain jugs. Once upon a time, when she'd first been assigned a cubicle here, she and Julietta and Valentina had played hide-and-seek down the hallway. It had been a very long time ago and she had grown since, but the jars had been more than spacious. She hoped she fit now.

She folded herself down and found that, while her legs were cramped, she could crouch low enough to remain hidden. She couldn't see anything and that made her more nervous. It also made her feel sillier, if that was possible. Hiding in the Chinese jars was something the little girls did and outgrew by the time they were old enough to wear blazers.

Well, she thought, *if it's one of our own Sept sisters, I can always say I'm playing with the little ones. It won't go over well but at least it's believable. I hope.*

"This really isn't necessary," she heard a familiar voice say. "This is her cubicle, but honestly, I think that you could give us the courtesy to take care of our own. We wouldn't presume in your House. And even your Sept doesn't have authority over us."

Signora Tima was speaking, Cecilie realized with a start.

"That will all change very soon, Signora," a man said. His

voice was also familiar and made Cecilie's stomach clench. The Library, that was where she had heard his voice. He had threatened her. He had killed Zizi. Fury fought with fear and it was all she could do to stay inside the painted porcelain jar. But she ignored the emotions to listen to the conversation, which she thought had to be about her.

"We have the mandate from the Board's Advisory Committee. It is unfortunate that one of your apprentices got mixed up with these rebels, and certainly the Board does not hold Sept-Fortune responsible. We have all had our troubles, which is why we're here to help you. Just as we know you would help us if the situation called for your expertise."

Signora Tima sighed hard. Cecilie had heard that sound many times after a serious disappointment or an apprentice's extreme stupidity. "This is her cubicle. I can't stop you."

They would know she was not there. Cecilie was rigid with fear. Any reasonable person would look in the jugs, they were too obvious to overlook. Not a single girl who entered Sept-Fortune ever ignored them.

"Cecilie, get out of there and get out of here now," Signora Tima hissed over the lip of the jar. "I can hold them for a minute or two in your cubicle, but you have to get out of here. Now!"

Cecilie didn't hesitate to do as she was told. She pulled herself up and stepped onto the bench and then ran down the middle of the carpet while Signora Tima entered her cubicle. To talk to the Sept brothers who were looking to kill her.

She took the side door, the closest one, and tried to get lost on the street. But she hadn't brought a mask and here she was face-naked in the quiet Sept district.

She ran toward the vaporetto stop. This time of day there should be a crowd waiting for the next boat and there was. She had never been grateful that she was petite and looked much younger than her classmates. On this dock she was just another one of the schoolgirls who were waiting to go home for lunch.

The crowded vehicle crossed the grey water and Cecilie thought only of salvation on the other side. She wanted to go home, where there had always been safety. Her mother making shrimp for lunch and she could go to her own room with her soft sheets and the blankets she could pull over head against the closet monster. Against Sept-Sorian.

Then she realized just how crazy that was. Sept-Sorian would already have her home address. They might be waiting for her and they might threaten her parents. They might even kill her parents. She couldn't go there.

She couldn't go anywhere. No place was safe. She wanted to sit down on the corner and cry. She wanted to be a little girl again and safe, believing that there was only good and honor in her world.

Wishing didn't help. She had to find someplace to go.

If only she knew where David lived. Not because she wanted to run to him, but because she wanted to kill him. This whole mess was his fault. If he hadn't hired her she would be just like Julietta and Valentina, happily working away as Sept sisters and waiting until their own day to reach the Board.

That wasn't really true, either, and she knew it. She had never been like Valentina and Julietta and she would never have forgotten the things she had been asked to do. In the end she would have discovered the deceptions and would have been in the same position. Only then she might have been older and more knowledgeable and had some idea of where to go.

All this time as she had considered and let herself be afraid, she had wandered through the streets of Venice. She had left the Ghetto and gone through the older sections away from where the tourists went. Now she glanced up and found that she recognized where she was. This coffee shop was the one she had stopped in with David. She was near Café Luna.

By daylight the neighborhood was drab. Stains ran down the façades of buildings, and people yelled in the street in uneducated accents. The coffee shop looked sad, the sandwiches wilted and the jars on the counter scarred. The few men standing with their coffee cups looked drawn and grey. Cecilie looked through the window and found it too depressing.

She walked on to Café Luna, though there was no good reason to go there. The place would be closed now, she knew. But it was one of the only places she knew where she could go, where she didn't think Sept-Sorian would connect her. Maybe the bored ticket taker would be there and he would take pity on her. Not likely, but her brain was frozen and she felt numb.

In daylight the heavy black door was closed and forbidding. The whole building looked like an abandoned garage. Probably there never had been anyone there at all, and she had only dreamed the jazz. She stood and looked and turned away without knocking.

"You looking for Benno?" a woman yelled at her from an upper window across the street. "He's eating lunch, I'll send him right down."

Cecilie started. The woman didn't seem to expect an answer. Cecilie didn't even get a good look at her, only that she was wearing a faded pink kerchief on her head and a housedress that matched. The old woman looked as grey and stained as the neighborhood.

Cecilie sagged against the door and wondered about Benno, and if she should stay or bolt again. Maybe Benno was Sept-Sorian? No, that was completely ridiculous. No Sept brother or sister would be down in this place, let alone known to a woman in a worn pink housedress who lived on this street. If any of the sisters in Sept-Fortune had come from such a background, her parents would have been moved to a proper place years before. Sept-Sorian couldn't be that different.

As Cecilie considered her lack of options, the ticket taker appeared in the shadows of the entryway across the street. "Yeah, what do you want?" he asked her, wiping a bit of orange soup from the corner of his mouth.

"I, I needed a place to go for a few minutes," Cecilie improvised. "There's something happening and I need help."

Benno turned away without a word. Cecilie slumped against the pavement and the tears started. She couldn't stop and she couldn't help herself, and she had no idea of where else to go.

The woman poked her head out the window again. "You want some soup, girl? That boy of mine, I taught him manners. But he's like any man, his brain goes null when a woman cries. Come on up, apartment thirty-one."

Cecilie went into the dark entryway. She found that the light had been broken and there was no security gate on the door, which stuck halfway open. She walked up the stairs, long dark flights where only every other fixture worked. The landlord here was cheap and so there were shadows and the smell of mold and old dinners everywhere.

When she got to the door with 31 painted in chipped cream on dark brown, Benno opened the door before she had a chance to knock. "I don't know what's going on," he muttered to her. "But if you even think of ripping off my mother, you're gonna turn into ribbons. Promise."

Cecilie had no doubts that he meant it. She slipped by him into the large kitchen, where the woman in the pink kerchief ladled soup into a chipped plate with tiny blue flowers painted around the rim. In this kitchen Sept-Sorian did not exist. Here there was only calm and peace, the mingled smells of lemon cleaning liquid and rich lentil soup.

The woman sat down opposite her and smiled. "Eat, baby, you're too thin," she said. "And whatever is making you cry like that, it won't look so bad with some nice hot soup in you, and some chocolates afterward if you finish it all up. And then you can tell me what terrible thing was making you so upset."

Cecilie finished her soup in silence. The woman was right. The bright tranquility of the well-scrubbed kitchen and the simple meal, as tasty as anything she'd ever had prepared by the Sept chefs, did comfort her. She wanted to tell this plain woman with reddened hands all about her betrayal and pursuit and she knew she couldn't. Those things did not belong in this world. Even the words in her mind hardly made sense so far out of context.

What seemed reasonable, logical, even normal in the Sept-House with its dark corners and silent corridors was absurd now. This woman might well believe her, but would not be able to comprehend the reality. Even Cecilie found it difficult to acknowledge reality here. It belonged to some other level of existence, some other universe. Maybe where the aliens belonged it made sense. But not here with the sun shining on the basil pot that sat on the windowsill.

So Cecilie spent her eating time figuring out a way of saying something that might get her some real help within the confines of possibility in this neighborhood. Something with no Septs, no betrayals of trust, no stalking the innocent and no Board trying to take over the world, all of which sounded completely insane right here.

"I need to find this musician who was playing with the jazz band that sometimes plays at the Luna," she said. "He has to help me. There's nowhere else to go."

"He got you in trouble?" the woman asked sympathetically.

"Yes," Cecilie whispered, thinking just how true that was.

"Benno can find him. Benno knows all the musicians," the woman mused. "But what about your mother? Have you told her? She might help you."

"I can't," Cecilie said. "I don't dare even go home now. I'm afraid. I couldn't stay there. I need someplace to stay, someplace no one except maybe David can find me. I don't know, maybe I shouldn't see him, either."

The woman patted Cecilie's hand. "It's not so bad, really. You should see him. He has the right to know. But if you can't go home, at least not now, and you don't know how to talk to your mother, there are people who can help. I know that when the Melio girl was in trouble like you are she went to the nuns at Holy Innocents in Padua. Let me see, I should be able to send them mail and we'll know if there's a place for you."

"No," Cecilie protested. The idea of spending time in a charity hostel for unwed mothers insulted her. But then she realized it was a perfect hiding place. Sept-Sorian would never look for her there. No one would ever look for her there. It was perfect.

She thought fast. "I don't want anyone to know where I am right now, and if you mail from here someone might guess."

The woman smiled. "I'll ask Benno to ask Father Alberto to mail from the church, under the seal. How would that be?"

Cecilie smiled. "Thank you," she said, with profound gratitude. The seal of the Church was one thing the Septs didn't violate. Even Sept-Sorian respected it, Cecilie believed, though she didn't know how long that would last.

The woman left the kitchen and went into the dark front parlor, where Benno had turned on the soccer match. The kitchen window was open and sounds of the street filtered up. There was some shuffling, and then Cecilie heard a voice from below: "She's not here. You see, it was a waste of time."

"She couldn't have just disappeared. And she's known to know those jazz people so she might have come here. It makes sense. You'll have to track the rest of them down."

"Me? What about you? And why aren't you going to search the neighborhood more carefully? She could be somewhere around here."

"If you let me finish, that is what I was going to do. This is not my first contract, you know."

They grumbled and she heard footsteps that passed the downstairs entrance. Obviously the Sept brother searching the area was not going to comb the buildings. Cecilie let out her breath, took the soup plate to the sink and rinsed it. Only then did she dare glance down through the window to the bolted entrance to Café Luna.

The street was empty. There was no sign that the Sept brothers had ever been there. Two teenaged boys came around the corner shouting and jostling each other. She saw Benno come around the corner and a few seconds later heard his heavy steps on the stairs.

The door creaked as he entered the apartment and he spoke in low tones to his mother. Cecile could hear that they were talking, but their conversation was mostly masked by the announcer calling out soccer plays. The woman came back into the kitchen.

"The nuns have space for you," she said. "You'll have to follow their program, and they are very strict about schooling and work and learning child care. But you are accepted, and Benno will drive you out."

The drive was not long, but very uncomfortable. Benno showered her with disapproval. "It's only because my mother's a saint that I'll help her," he grumbled. "I think you should go home and it's none of our business. At least you didn't take any money. The last person my mother helped out, she gave him a week's worth of grocery money. Then what was I supposed to do? I had to borrow against my pay, but do you think my mother thought of that? Well, she's one of the blessed ones, not like you and I. But let me tell you, you are damned lucky. I only do this because my mother asks, not because I have any sympathies for some tramp who thinks a musician is going to take care of her. I lose girls all the time to musicians. The girls, they always ask me to let them in backstage, for this one's address and that one's favorite coffee, and do they ever talk to me? I get sick of it and I think that all you stupid little whores aren't worth anyone's time. But my mother, I can't say no to her. So here I am driving you out to the country and I'll even try to find your boyfriend. Because the nuns think it's a good idea, and who am I to tell them that musicians are useless fools with more bastards than a nun's got fast days?"

Cecilie could not even enjoy the scenery, the sunlight on the trees and the neat farmhouses with Benno's nonstop litany. She tried to tune him out but she couldn't help registering the words. The anger, the underlying resentment and the threat all came through too clearly.

She was relieved to see the sagging stone convent, to be greeted at the front gate by a woman dressed in a habit exactly the color of the building. It made her think of the Sept-House, which for all its danger was still familiar and home.

Benno let her get out by herself and roared off as soon as she had shut the door behind her. The nun who had admitted her spoke as they walked down the polished floors to the office. "You will not find life here easy, but you will be able to live and take care of your baby. And if you decide to give him or her up for adoption, we can help you find excellent parents. It is entirely your choice. We don't try to influence you that way. But you must tell your parents where you are and we think it is only right if the father of the child is informed."

They arrived in a place that was very far from any Sept office Cecilie had ever seen. This was as sparely furnished and as serene, but that was where any resemblance ended. There was no silk, no rich color and no lush upholstery here. The furniture was plain, none of the wood inlaid though it shone as perfectly as Signora Tima's. The only decoration was a crucifix on the wall, and while it was certainly a fine piece of art, Cecilie doubted that it had been placed there for aesthetic consideration.

The nun took her seat behind the desk like Signora Tima and called up a large registry form onto the old, utilitarian flat screen. Cecilie bit her lip and considered again. It was one thing for the woman who sent her here to be mistaken. It was another for the nuns to believe that she intended to stay more than a few days and to inform her parents where she was. No doubt their kiosk mail accounts were under constant observation.

Worst of all, the registry form was one she had seen before. It was in the datalink. This convent did not have its own physically secured files. Everything they thought was private was easily accessible to the Septs. How else would the Septs ever perform contracts on tracing families for adoptees, medical records for children who never knew their fathers, family histories for those who no longer wanted the secrets protected?

Cecilie knew seven easy ways to break this system and ten ways to make it yield information that the nuns barely knew how to access. No, having her on that registry form was as dangerous as standing in the front hall of Sept-Sorian and inquiring where the brothers who had her contract were. It was time to tell the truth. Besides, the truth didn't seem quite so alien here with the sunset shadows falling on the whitewashed walls and the far hills already obscured.

"Sister, I am in trouble but not the kind you think," Cecilie began. "I'm being pursued. I know a secret that is dangerous and there are dangerous men who would prefer that I weren't free to tell it. My parents' house and mail are being watched. And if you put my name into a public registry they'll find me. I only want to stay a short time, until I can contact the people who can help publish the secret. And then I should be safe again."

The nun looked at her skeptically. "We don't have facilities
for dreamers, storytellers or radicals. If you can't contact your
parents or put your name in our registry you can't stay. Our mis-
sion is to young women who are not prepared to care for their
new children, not for girls with paranoid delusions. I'm afraid
you'll have to leave."

Cecilie began to cry. She didn't know where the tears came
from, only that they kept coming and she couldn't stop them.
She hadn't had a chance to acknowledge her situation, and suddenly she realized that she was going to be cold and hungry and
there was no place she could go to spend the night. It was late
in the afternoon and soon the sun would set and it would be
dinnertime and she had no where to go and no one she could
trust.

"Please, can't I stay here just tonight?" she begged. "I'll go
in the morning, I promise you. But I need a place where no one
will look for me tonight."

"Isn't there anyone you can ask?" the nun asked awkwardly.
Obviously she was ill at ease with Cecilie's display.

Cecilie shook her head.

The nun looked distraught. Then she seemed to make up her
mind. "Only one night. And that's only because it's too late to
take the bus into town and I just can't turn you out on the street.
And we do have an extra bed. But you'll have to leave tomorrow. You may use my mail, if you like. If you think yours is being
watched," the nun offered. "You can stay here in the office and
wait for replies."

Cecilie nodded her head, afraid to speak. She wanted to
throw her arms around the nun and sob into her faded blue
workshirt. At very least with the convent header rather than her
own, she could contact her parents and David. She was safe. At
least for the night.

She wrote the message to David first, hoping that he'd have

some idea of where she could go. Then she wrote a longer note to her mother, explaining that she was okay and out of town for a few days on business and that she would be leaving this convent very soon.

She reread the letter and was disappointed. She hadn't managed to say what she wanted to say and she was afraid of giving too much away. She tried to fix it, but the changes only made the thing worse. Finally she gave up and sent it. When Cecilie looked up the nun was gone.

A girl in a neat white dress brought up a tray with coffee and a sandwich, tomato and cheese on crusty convent-made bread. The girl set it on the desk. "Sister Paul said she thought you'd be hungry and couldn't wait for dinner. That's at seven. But the nuns are really nice here. They've helped me and Aemilia a lot. I didn't know what I was going to do, my mother kicked me out of the house. Said I was a tramp. And Marco, well . . ." The girl made a face.

"Anyway, Sister said you might be hungry waiting for your messages, since you didn't have lunch. Don't fill up, though, because we're having rabbit and tortellini tonight for dinner. Sister Maria Francisco is doing it in rosemary now. She's the best cook."

"Thank you," Cecilie said. "I'll look forward to dinner. It's been a long time since I've had rabbit in rosemary." Then she hesitated. She couldn't believe that the convent would really have a dreambox, though it was the only thing she had been able to think about since her arrival. But if it did she could probably steal in through their keys and get hold of David. Or get hold of somebody.

With a convent origin she might even be able to penetrate certain of the Sept-Sorian files she remembered. They wouldn't have a flag on an obscure convent catering to pregnant teenagers.

The girl stood and studied her. "You know, I don't have any

idea," she said slowly. "I can't imagine what the nuns would do with one. But ask Sister Theresa, she's the extern sister. And she's really nice. I'm Bianca. If you want to come out tonight, Tonia and I are going shopping at a mall nearby. You could come along if you like."

Cecilie shook her head mutely. She couldn't imagine taking a ride with this girl any more than she could face the fact that she was out of Venice. Out of Venice for the first time in her life, except on a properly arranged holiday. This was her very first real adventure and all she wished was that it had never happened, that she would wake up in her own bed and this would all be some idiotic dream that would fade out of her nice everyday life. And she knew that she might as well wish to be the Queen of England.

The girl left. Cecilie sipped the coffee, which was weak. She nibbled on the sandwich, which was good. She wasn't hungry, but attacking the food was something to do that would use up time until she got her replies. Soon the tray was empty. She nosed around the office, but there was nothing lying out on any of the surfaces, not a book, no pictures, nothing at all to take her mind off the lingering seconds.

Images of the Sept brother following her formed in her mind. She had to stop it now or she'd be lost, crazed, too frightened to think or to move. She tried to calm herself and it was no good, all she could think about were the killers after her and after all of them. Visions of the Board meeting with Sept-Sorian in strong attendance haunted her. She thought Signora Tima would be in danger for delivering the Sept-Fortune position.

What was the Sept-Fortune position? Cecilie wondered vaguely. She had no position at all, and no one had talked about one in her presence, as if it were a foregone conclusion that the Board would be able to coordinate the various specialties of the

Septs into a single unit. As one they would not have to listen to anyone. They would be ultimately free—or so the story went.

What really would happen was that Sept-Sorian would take over. Cecilie did not doubt that Signora Tima recognized that goal and did not approve. Signora Tima and Sept-Fortune would lead the opposition to Sept-Sorian, and they would all pay for it.

The tone of a deep bell called Cecilie from her reverie. At first she ignored it, thinking that it must mark the Sisters' chapel duty or some esoteric convent thing. When it chimed again she realized that it came from the interface speaker. Obviously the nun had changed the usual biffs and beeps into something more suited to the environment. Cecilie smiled—the nun must not have been a complete recluse all her life.

Cecilie looked at the text scan. Two messages. One was from David. She'd hoped to hear from him; hoped harder that he'd have something useful to say. He'd gotten her into this mess. It should be his problem.

Meet me in the ocean place where I first met you and you hated me at ten tonight. We can plan from there.

Grudgingly she approved. He had given nothing away to their enemies. Only how was she going to get out there by ten? Did the nuns have a dreambox? She doubted it seriously, but she would ask. If they did, who knew what kind of shape it was in? She would be lucky if they had one at all.

She sighed. It all felt stupid and difficult and she wished she hadn't gotten this far away. She wished that Benno had delivered a message on paper and that she was somewhere she could rest. She stood up. Her jeans bagged around her knees and her blouse looked like she had slept in it. She dragged her fingers through her hair, trying to separate the knots. They wouldn't give.

The computer chimed again. The other message didn't like

being ignored. It had no origin in the header—something that a Sept brother or sister could forge without thinking, but would be impossible for anyone outside to manipulate. Or so Cecilie had thought. She herself had learned to forge headers by the time she was twelve. It had been great fun for a while.

She was afraid to open the mail. It could be a trace, set to alert the sender when it was accessed, and where. And Cecilie had no doubt that it was from Sept-Sorian.

But it was safer for her to erase it here than to let it sit and fester in her queue. After all, it could be rigged to log the rest of her mail too. Certainly the Sept brothers on the other side would see how long it took for her to read it. Better to read it here, where she was leaving very soon, rather than wait until she was in some place she might stay long enough to be found.

The letter did not resolve into text on the screen. Instead it showed a series of graphics, strange juxtaposed images that almost made sense to Cecile. A seascape with buoys marked with numbers that changed, filled the space, and then the fish and data packets convened around a lighthouse that Cecilie recognized.

Not one she had used in many years, but a secret meeting point she had had with Julietta when they were going through a phase of hating Valentina. A lighthouse in the infosea that was half torn down and where unclaimed bits lay resident for ages until they were summoned again. It had been an eerie place.

Once she had thought of making it scarier, and maybe adding a ghost or two, until she learned that the underlying programming for this level had been burned in. There was probably some way to change it, but at fifteen it had been hardly worth the effort just to add a finishing touch to an already exquisite atmosphere.

The image shook her. Was Sept-Sorian telling her that they knew her most intimate secrets? That they knew more of her history than she cared to remember?

But then, why was her mother's kitchen table in the scene and what was an entire collection of doorknobs doing arranged on the walls like a museum display?

Museum display. This message was not from Sept-Sorian at all. This had to be the aliens.

Cecilie was disoriented. She grasped the corner of the desk to steady herself even though she was quite firmly seated in the hard-bottomed convent chair. The anomaly, the aliens, had contacted her. What did they know of her and what were they trying to do? She didn't understand what the message meant and she didn't understand why they had sent it at all. But there was more communication here than before; clearly the visitor was learning rapidly.

She searched the image, turning it this way and that trying to get a new angle, trying to see what the various additions to the scene could possibly communicate. Besides the kitchen table and the doorknobs were randomly placed feathers. Zizi's feathers. She had collected them and saved them but she didn't know how they could help her.

Or maybe the image meant Zizi himself. Only Zizi was dead and gone and there was no other. But Zizi had known things and had hidden them.

Then Cecilie began to smile. The message was a pointer and it made perfect sense. Either the aliens had made far more out of her visits than she had realized, or they knew more about the human organization of thought than she recognized from their own levels of organization of data. In any case, they had contacted her and told her something that could be useful.

Zizi had known everything about her, had known all her haunts and habits. And Zizi was a bird, which meant he had liked to take small shiny things and hide them away. A lot of packets on the datastream level were bright and small, perfect for Zizi's beak. The familiar would have hidden them some-

where she could find the data, just the way Zizi always put findings into a folder in her private space. The bird program had
been her familiar and had known her better than any other
being in existence.

She had never known that Zizi had instincts to grab random
data. Or maybe it wasn't random at all. Maybe it was bits of
things she had asked about and had not bothered with again,
things that she had not pursued.

Suddenly she was anxious to get to the infosea and find
what treasure the alien pointers had indicated. Perhaps it was
nothing. She told herself this to try and calm down, to think that
maybe the answer was not waiting perfect and whole hidden in
the datasea.

She turned off the text reader and went in search of Sister
Theresa, praying only that the convent had a dreambox. That
was the only way she could do everything she had to do and
cover her tracers. If only the nuns had a dreambox.

Wishing alone was pointless. She would find Sister Theresa.
If the convent didn't have a dreambox then she'd figure out the
next thing to do.

15

The Pietà robes were so full and loose that he could carry anything under them. Once upon a time he could have carried enough weapons for an entire squad hidden in the massive sleeve. This time all he had was a soft package taped to his ribs, the way he had learned from his mentors back home so very long ago.

He waited through the first break and the second. Better to see Lina disappear. She had been some help and so she deserved a chance, at least. For himself, he wasn't worried.

He sang. He sang better than he had ever sung in his life, his clear, pure tenor shimmering with emotion. Perfectly disciplined, his voice was like water, underlying the weave of the music. He let himself drown in the music to forget his plans and his hopes, to forget everything but the glory of the song.

He soared. He had been promoted. For a warrior people who honored bards above kings, he had made the ultimate leap into the priesthood. He was that perfect fusion of what a person should be—warrior, artist, seer. He could tell the future because he was going to create it.

The third break came. Now it was almost lunchtime. Today's opening statements had been made, the Assembly Hall filled with senior members of every Sept. Attendance had been taken and they were all accounted for, or at least someone had whispered that when Sean went for coffee. He had been too intently focused on the music to notice.

He didn't need the reassurance, since he recognized all the extravagant masks and costumes massed together. Maybe one or two were missing, lingering in a Sept-House or more likely a coffee bar for some private consultation. That was not important. In the end the act itself mattered more than the result. He didn't care who survived and who was absent. Only that they would understand that their goals were—not acceptable.

That's what David had said. Over the years they had taken too much power bit by bit and no one had noticed. Now there was nothing less than the terror squads of Sept-Sorian that David called blackshirts.

Sean understood all too well. He had fought an enemy like this at home. He had grown up caught in the ebb and flow of their power and he remembered how, when he was very young, his parents had hoped for a peace that never came. The enemy became more dangerous in the quiet of the negotiated cease-fire that they didn't quite trust. Sean had experienced only too personally how they finally relied on brutality to assuage their fear.

He knew it, nor could he ever forget. The long white scars on his chest and the uglier ones that curled around the insides of his thighs had faded over the years, but they were still clearly visible, as immediate as the memory of the random violence that had caused them. After he had been in Italy for several years he thought about having them removed. In the Pietà he could afford it and too many would-be lovers had turned away. Then he had met David, who had caressed the marks and kissed them and called him beautiful and brave.

There was the center—David. There was nothing at all Sean would not do for David, and in a very short time he would prove it. David had not given him any orders. Sean knew that these people were not used to fighting, not the way his own people were. His only hesitation was that David might not be as thrilled with his gift as Sean would like, and though Sean was perfectly content to die for David's causes he thought it possible that David would be angry if he was killed in the attempt.

David, like the rest of the people here, was still naive. His only experience of repression was words and difficulty, not casual murder in the streets or police searches in the middle of the night. Those would come later, Sean had no doubt of that. Sept-Sorian was already starting.

This must have been what it had been like at the first invasion, he thought. Once his people had believed that their music and their art and their honor and their god were going to save them. They found that the presumption of the invaders was so ludicrous as to be laughable.

It wasn't laughable. Sean knew that better than anyone else and he certainly knew it far better than David did. So he knew what he had to do to save them all, and to keep David's reputation clear. He had to make everyone understand that David was stronger and larger than these plotters so they could win a decisive victory early. That was crucial in Sean's overall strategy.

During the break he took a coffee and greeted a few of his choirmates and then excused himself to the toilet, which was perfectly reasonable. But since he hadn't been here before he took the wrong door and found himself in the half-empty Assembly Hall—precisely as planned.

No one noticed him in his blue robe and his white mask. He

slid his hand under his working uniform and pulled the soft pack from under his clothes. In the voluminous choir robe with no one paying any attention to him it was easy. One of his earliest lessons had been that no one pays much attention to anyone's actions. Most things can go unnoticed. People edit with their minds, make things normal, make them fit a common pattern. People often did not see anything out of the ordinary even when the event was not common at all.

He concealed the packet in his hand, the tape still dangling from it. He walked to the podium with assurance. Once there he used the tape to secure the few grams of explosives and the timer to the underside of the speakers' table.

The exercise took barely two seconds, but his heart was racing and his breathing was shallow. It had been a long time since he had felt this exhilarated, this afraid, this alive. Like sex and better, the fear of getting caught and the knowledge of what he was about to do made him feel superhuman. There was nothing he couldn't do, nothing beyond him.

A Board member in an extravagant costume came up to him. "Are you looking for something?" the member asked with a slight accent.

"The toilet," Sean answered, putting just a tiny hint of confusion into his tone.

"Go out the main doors and then it's past the corridor. Everything around here looks the same."

Sean thanked the Board member and left. The doors did not look at all the same. He went upstairs to a smaller rest room he had found on earlier forays in the building. This one was empty.

He slipped off the blue Pietà robe. Underneath he wore a loose dark red tunic to his knees and black pants. They concealed enough. He put on the plain Pietà white mask and a black beret to cover his bright hair. Now he looked like a Venetian out for a casual stroll, or maybe a tourist trying to be sophisticated and partake of the liberty of the masks. The important thing was that he looked nothing like a Pietà singer or a Board member or anyone else to be noted or acknowledged.

He waited until he heard the music again, soft strains under the thick insulation of the old floors and walls. They were back in session, which meant he didn't have much time left.

He left the building by the back stairs and disappeared into the maze of alleys that Venetians called streets. He was not terribly familiar with this area and so he headed only one way. When the narrow passages turned on themselves he always chose the right turning. He had seven minutes to get away.

He arrived at the vaporetto stop to find it empty. The boat-bus had just left. He had three minutes, and while he thought he was probably far enough and there were enough structures between him and the Board building, he still would prefer to be across the canal.

He hailed a taxi that refused to stop on the vaporetto quay but made him move down so that it was a legal taxi stand. He got into the small motorboat and settled on the seat when he heard the muffled blast.

"What was that?" the driver wondered aloud.

Sean just shrugged and told him how to get to the Camerillo palazzo.

Venice knew intrigue as a Pietà singer knew music. It was in the bones of the city, it ran like the water that was her blood. The houses of the rich and the powerful had been built with the idea of betrayal and escape as the status quo.

David Gavrilli did not think staying in the old man's home was prudent, not for himself and certainly not for Sean and Lina. And especially not for Cecilie, who was now being hunted by one of Sept-Sorian's top contract brothers.

But there was no place else to go. There were the mazes and

side entrances, and the hidden room where David had lived for a year before he had felt comfortable enough to take a proper bedroom, but David did not believe the old tricks were good enough to withstand a serious hunter armed with the latest technology. Still, there was no place else he could hide them quickly. Lina was already up there, shivering. Sean had come in by way of the old back entrance that now was part of another apartment building. That had once been part of the palazzo but had been sold off separately, and while the space could be divided, the entrances all still worked.

Sean paced across the upstairs parlor floor, ignoring the coffee that David had put on the table. "I did it, it's over," Sean muttered. "The Board is dead, the Assembly is gone, the Septs are headless. All of them. It's over. The net is yours, all yours."

David shook his head. "What do you mean?" he asked slowly, enunciating carefully. There was something manic about Sean that worried him, something he had seen hidden in the singer before that had lain dormant all these years. It had frightened David when he first noticed it, though that fear was part of Sean's appeal. But he had never considered that the seductive power of Sean's past could still affect him here, so very far from his own history.

"It was very easy, really. Just a little explosive, we learned how to do it back home. I was training to be a bomber back then, before I got sent here when the factory went. Funny how things come back to you. I would have sworn I'd forgotten how. But you know, it just comes back. And it wasn't hard at all."

"What are you talking about?" David asked.

"The Board," Sean answered. "I blew it up." He came over to David and stroked his shoulder. "For you. As a gift. I know what they've done to you, I know what you wanted. So I did it, that's all."

David jerked around and pulled away from Sean's hand. "You did *what*?"

"I blew it up," Sean repeated. "I told you that. For you. Just for you."

David stood. Nausea washed over him. He was horrified, shocked. Sean was crazy. David never wanted to see him again.

At the same time he was overwhelmed. Sean had done this for love. He had never been given a gift quite so—unworldly. And so unwelcome.

David had touched one corpse. The idea of being responsible for hundreds more horrified him. The old man and the Septs and all of them could keep their callous ways. That didn't mean that he had to become part of them, become like them.

He wanted only music. He wanted freedom and beauty and civilization. He wanted exquisite bliss and perfect innocence.

He had wanted love and he had been given love, and love was a harsh and unrelenting thing. Love was the look in Sean's eyes, the hard cold adoration that made him present the Board like a cat presenting a headless mouse as an act of adoration.

Looking at Sean, David wondered if being loved was worth the price. And yet, he couldn't look at Sean without desire or pity, without wanting to protect Sean, and without seeing the essential innocence that lay within the violence in his soul.

He had been right: Sean was like a cat. He was just as guileless and pure, and just as casually cruel. His vengeance was elemental and clean. David had to admit that this quality was one that he cherished about Sean, the otherness that made Sean utterly fascinating.

David could be cruel. He knew that, he'd done it. He could be cold. But he could not remain clean and virtuous with the purity that shone in Sean's eyes when he acted. The violence that was a single clear component of Sean's essence in David was twisted and frightened and crusted in guilt.

"Damn," David said softly. Sean turned away and hid his face. David went to him and put a hand on his shoulder, but didn't look at him. "We're not safe here anymore. Not with the Board blown up. They'll be looking everywhere in the city for you, and for Lina. And Sept-Sorian is looking for Cecilie and I have to find her first." He shook his head.

"Where else can we go?" Sean asked. "I'd rather be with you, anyway, no matter what happens."

"I don't plan for you to be dead that soon," David snapped. "I don't plan for any of us to be dead soon and that will happen if we're all together. Damn. Let me think."

"There should be confusion for at least a few hours," Sean offered from his training back home. "The Septs don't know who I am or who set off the bomb. I was masked the whole time. And they won't be able to organize quickly enough to get anything done for hours yet. All the leaders were there."

"There'll be new younger leaders is all." David dismissed the idea. "But since you've been masked the whole time we might have a chance. Maybe this much will work."

He sat down at a secretary so delicate it seemed absurd for it to serve an honest purpose. David pulled out several sheets of wrapped security paper, and one piece of formal ivory vellum. He wrote on the vellum quickly, then set it aside and hand-wrote a much longer missive on one sheaf of the security paper. The other sheet he pondered longer and wrote less, but more slowly and carefully. Then he broke the seal on both security blue sheets, unwrapped them and slid them both into a grey photo-block envelope.

He turned to Sean and handed him both documents. "The secure letter is to my family, explaining a certain amount about who you are and my activities. The other is a legal document to formalize our relationship so that no one in my family can deny your rights." He ignored Sean's dazed look and handed him the vellum paper. "This is for you. It is a kiosk account number with the passwords and verifications you'll need to draw funds for you and Lina to get to my family, along with the address and information to get you past the gates. You'll be safe there. I'd suggest leaving the house now and going to the kiosk station down in the Ghetto, then taking a taxi to an intercity rapido. Buy your tickets on the platform, not at the counter, and use this kiosk account to do it. That way you won't leave a net trail. Or rather, you'll leave a trail for one Michele Turbindo, who should not light any flags except family ones. That means my parents will be waiting for you and you'll be in the uncomfortable situation of having to explain. But at least you'll be safe."

Sean held the papers gingerly. "You mean you're formalizing our relationship? You mean just until you can leave here. You don't mean for real, do you."

David looked at his hands. He had never considered it before. Even now, he only wanted to protect Sean and Lina, whom he saw as his responsibilities. And he wanted to name an heir, any heir that was not his parents. Sean as his heir would give his parents even more grief than David had, and that was good enough.

He had never considered what this might mean to Sean. Now he looked into the utterly guileless blue eyes and he knew that he was truly guilty. He wasn't sure how he felt about Sean, and in the present circumstances he didn't think he could sort out any emotions anyway. It had never occurred to him that Sean might be enough in love with him to kill for him, or to have intense hope at the thought of formalization.

"I don't know," David said honestly. He wondered why he didn't lie. There was a chance that none of them would survive, and why not make it easier, but he couldn't mange the words. After all the things he had done, the deception he had pulled off, he couldn't lie to Sean about something that meant so much.

And that made David confused and angry and strangely contented all at the same time.

"I don't know. We'll see what happens later. Right now I can't think of anything but making us all safe. And I can't leave this city or even the house without the police knowing." He took Sean's hand. "Later. When we're all past this."

Sean took the papers and left the room, saying nothing. David stood at the top of the stairs. He heard Lina join Sean, heard the door open and then bang shut.

He hoped both of them were masked. They might both be crazy singers, but neither of them was stupid. They could be trusted to mask without him telling them so, David told himself, but without seeing it he didn't feel entirely secure.

He wasn't sure how he felt about running back to his family, and being a coward at that. Not facing them himself, he had still sent Sean and Lina to them for sanctuary, for a kind of protection he couldn't provide.

He should be able to provide it. He resented having to turn back to the Gavrilli power, having to beg them for protection. But he had to take care of his people, he told himself. Even if it meant begging his family. It was the first lesson his grandfather had taught him and his father had reinforced. Part of what made the Gavrilli powerful was that they always took care of their own.

When he had left home he had hated them, he remembered, but over the years in Venice the hatred had grown cold and bits of it had been forgotten or crumbled away. Now he remembered that his parents might be not only helpful to Sean and Lina, but kind as well. There had been the first time his father had taken him out in the net and had shown him the Gavrilli files. He remembered the years when his mother had listened to him practice piano every day and played duets with him.

Not everything he remembered was bad. Maybe they would

help his friends more than he had requested. Maybe they would treat Sean like part of the family and not an interloper. Maybe, just barely maybe, he could consider returning to them, coming to his sister's birthday party or to hear his mother sing.

His eyes felt damp and his shoulders hurt as he recalled things that he had so carefully erased. What seemed so hideous, so very repressive years ago now just seemed like people who didn't know what was best but were trying. He didn't know what was truly best for Sean, certainly not for Lina. Perhaps disappearing from the Pietà would be worse for them. Maybe they could just slip back inside and no one would ever suspect them, and they could carry on the lives they had chosen.

He hadn't given them that option. He hadn't even asked. He had decided and dictated and they had followed his orders. He remembered how much he had resented following his father's orders, made with as little consultation. Which, he suddenly perceived, had not been made without consideration. Only his father always thought he knew best, had always acted just the way David realized he was acting now. As an absolute dictator.

He was no different from his father.

The revelation startled him.

And he had to do something about Cecilie. He didn't know where she was and he was afraid that the Sept-Sorian brothers might have gotten to her already. And while he was good, and not afraid of much in the virtual world, he wasn't quite ready to try to crack Sept-Sorian's security system. At least not yet.

Then he realized that he was planning by fiat again. Deciding that he had to take control, had to make all the decisions, was exactly what had driven him out of the house when he was eighteen. Just the age Cecilie was, and Cecilie didn't particularly like or trust him. In a way it was harder to made decisions about her life than it was for Sean, who would walk into Hell for him, who had killed for him.

Cecilie was altogether another matter, and maybe he could practice listening to her before he saw Sean and Lina again. But first he had to find Cecilie. Sean and Lina should be safe—the kiosk account would light up a red flag in the Gavrilli security system everywhere there was an office. The ticket purchase would alert the family and there should be someone coming to meet them. The rapido between Venice and Roma was nonstop sealed. If they made it to the train even Sept-Sorian couldn't get to them.

Once they arrived in Rome and were acknowledged under Gavrilli protection there would be nothing Sept-Sorian could do. For all the Septs believed that they already did rule the world, they couldn't get past the kind of wall a major family like the Gavrillis had lived behind for generations. It had been written by a hodgepodge of programmers living in different times and from different Septs and from the time before there even were Septs. It wasn't that it was too elegant to break, merely that it was too messy and massive.

Even David Gavrilli hadn't been able to break through, and he had tried. Sean and Lina would be safe, he told himself. He didn't have to worry about them now. One thing at a time.

16

He had to find Cecilie. She might not even know that Sept-Sorian was after her and she might already be dead. No, just one thing at a time. Find her first. Then consider the next step.

He couldn't go in through the house dreambox—there was a flag on it along with his bracelet—but he could use the text environment. Besides the fact he wasn't flagged in text, he could remain invisible this way. Text was passive and showed nothing on the net.

So he began the search pattern, looking for the easy trails first. There were none. Cecilie had disappeared from the environment yesterday and had not reappeared in any of her usual configurations. He checked again. He wasn't sure if that was a good sign or a bad one.

Quickly he flipped through the day notices and the public-file police reports. No record of anyone like Cecilie found dead or admitted to a hospital. Terrorism at the Board meeting was just coming up on the newsfeed, though, and he paused to read it.

A bomb was detonated today at noon in the middle of the Sept Board Assembly Hall. Over fifty delegates to the current meetings were killed outright. One hundred and six have been injured and are currently awaiting treatment at seven area hospitals. Eight Pietà singers were also injured, one was killed and two are missing, presumed injured or dead. It is believed that the perpetrator gained entrance to the building disguised and masked as a choir member. Police are searching the area for physical evidence and questioning witnesses. As several of the delegates killed and/or injured were foreign nationals, Interpol is acting in cooperation with the local authorities. Anyone who might have any knowledge about this crime is asked to report it to emergency@interpol.gov.

David smiled. Horrified as he was, he couldn't help but be pleased that Sean had pulled it off. He and Lina were listed merely as missing, presumed dead, and not as suspects at all.

He was impressed. Even if he didn't approve of the action, was appalled that it had been done "for his benefit," he still appreciated a thing done well. Competence was always admirable, and David had never thought of musicians as particularly competent in any other aspect of life.

He didn't have time to dwell on it, either. Hours had passed since noon and Cecilie had been missing all day, so David ignored the rest of the news to resume his search.

He went to all the usual places. The Library, the Mall, nowhere was there a record of Cecilie passing. And there would be a record, there would have to be. If she wasn't in the net there was nothing he could do but sit and wait and hope that she contacted him.

Doing that was truly dreadful. Ten minutes later David was pacing the antique rug that was already worn in the pattern he walked. There had to be something else to do until she reached him. She had to reach him.

He set his mail on alert, so that it would ring when he got a message, and went to his piano. This was the smallest electric keyboard he had in the house. The four others were larger, more sophisticated and offered a wider range of options. But this was his favorite for practice, for the half hour of scales and then the hours of music that he had neglected in the recent months. He had already missed a day this week, and probably had missed an entire week of daily exercises since he had begun to try to do something about the Septs.

He didn't feel like practicing at all, but the familiar normalcy of it calmed him. After the scales he started the exercises, and suddenly he was lost in the music. He couldn't think or plan or worry when he was working like this, and time had no meaning. There was only work and music, trying for just a little more resonance here and a softer interpretation there. Different tempos, different phrasing were discarded as David delved deeply into his playing.

He was so lost in the music that at first he didn't hear the buzz indicating that he had new mail. The alert had to go off twice before it penetrated his concentration. When he looked up he glanced at the time and was shocked—hours had dissolved while he had played and it was now nearly evening.

The text of the email was short and careful. *I am currently at the address at the header,* Cecilie had written. *But I cannot stay here. They are asking me to leave immediately and I need someplace safe to go.*

David felt such vast relief that he forgot that he hadn't made up what to do next. He should send her to his family, he thought. They already had Sean and Lina and it would make sense for everyone to be together. But Sean and Lina had left hours ago and they were either already there or arriving momentarily.

Meet me in the ocean place where I first met you and you hated me at ten tonight. We can plan from there. He wrote slowly, considering the words. At least there was nothing Sept-Sorian could use if they intercepted the message. That left him with more empty hours. In the midst of action he had nothing to do but sit and wait. He was frustrated and furious. Nor did his fury abate when the doorbell rang.

It rang twice and then there was insistent pounding while he went down the stairs. From the incessant noise he knew this was not someone who meant him well. He wondered vaguely whether he should open the door at all, or if doing so would mean that he died. He opened the door anyway.

Two men and a woman stood there. The woman and one of the men flashed credentials. The man was local police and the woman was Interpol. The second man who stood in the background did nothing at all.

Nor was he dressed like the other two, though the difference was subtle. The man without credentials wore a more expensive, better-cut suit, and his shoes were perfectly shined. Sept-Sorian, David thought. A Sept brother could afford clothes well outside a policeman's budget.

David invited them in graciously. The two police officers were polite, thanking him for his offer of coffee and sitting where he indicated. The Sept brother stayed in the shadows and acknowledged nothing at all.

"We are here to check on your whereabouts today," the local policeman said without preamble. "You know about the bombing at the Board. Where were you?"

David smiled and held out his wrist. "You only have to contact your own department to find out that I never left this house
today. If I was anywhere near the Board Hall you would have
a record of it, so I can only assume that you are looking for
something further."

Inside he was trembling and terrified, but he heard his own
words as if they had been spoken by someone calm and urbane.
He sounded like someone with nothing at all to hide. Then he
realized that the assumption of control and complete lack of
anxiety he projected made him sound just like his grandfather.

"We're looking for a Sept sister, Cecilie 8 Sept-Fortune," the
woman said. She had a slight accent, perhaps Swiss, David
thought. "We have been told that you have had some contact
in the net. She's been reported missing and of course we are following up on any missing Sept sisters and brothers, to take
them off the casualty lists. So if you have seen her this afternoon,
or if perhaps she is here, you would be doing us all a great service in letting us see her and know that she is alive."

David spread his hands, palms up. "I wish I did know that.
It would set my mind at ease, too. I did not know she was
among the missing. Now I'm worried as well."

The police officers looked at him oddly. Then the Sept
brother spoke for the first time. "We know you received email
this afternoon, maybe half an hour ago, from this Cecilie. If you
have and you're withholding information you will be charged
with perjury and no longer have the luxury of house surveillance. We know you killed Artos Camerillo and now maybe
you've killed this girl, too."

"Please, you are welcome to search," he said. "As for my
email, it came from a convent outside the city. You wouldn't be
looking here if you had proof that she was alive elsewhere. At
least I think not. And so I assume that your concern is making
you grasp for straws."

The Sept brother grunted. The police went through the house while David stayed seated in the library. His main concern was keeping his breathing even and not bolting. This was utterly absurd, and yet he could see the logic to it clearly. He was being set up by Sept-Sorian, though why he couldn't fathom.

He certainly was opposed to the Sept power, but Artos's little organization was no threat to the Sept system, even with the Board blown to pieces. There was something else going on here, something bigger that he didn't have enough information to understand.

His text reader sounded that he had new mail. He got up to read it, knowing full well that both officers and the Sept brother would join him. He only prayed it wasn't from Cecilie, or Lina or Sean. There was plenty of innocuous email he could have gotten and he prayed without hope that this was one of them.

The header indicated that the mail came from his family compound, but the personal line said nothing about either Sean or Lina. Instead, it was his mother's name and the codeword she had given him when he had been seven years old to authenticate any communication from her. Sean and Lina must have gotten through, then, because otherwise there was no way for his family to have gotten his address. He had made certain of that.

He cursed silently. No doubt she would tell him that they had arrived safely and ask his plans and that would be all the Sept brother would need. The location of the missing Pietà singers would be more than enough to incriminate him.

There was no choice. He opened the mail and watched as the text appeared on the screen. He skimmed the body of the letter twice, not certain that he was reading correctly. This was impossible, was insane.

Your father died at one this afternoon, his mother wrote. *He had been ill for several months and the doc-*

tors knew it was terminal, but Papa only admitted it to the rest of us six weeks ago. We wanted to get in touch with you, to beg you to come home. You are now the only one who can lead the family. I have never cared for these matters and am barely able to survive as it is—the idea of living without your father is beyond me. Perhaps I shall enter a convent. Living death is at least acceptable there. I have done with this life. Verification in security blue will follow by messenger.

It was unsigned. It didn't need to be signed. The two police officers made sympathetic noises. The Sept brother regarded him suspiciously, as if he had engineered this turn of events.

David was stunned. His father couldn't die. His father certainly couldn't be dead today. That was too much coincidence.

Or maybe not. Suddenly he understood why Sept-Sorian thought he was dangerous. They could get into medical records, and the records of someone as important as his father would be regularly monitored. They knew that his father was dying and that he stood to inherit the Gavrilli fortune and economic power, which could be a threat to them. Especially now, after the bombing, with the Board in tatters, they were vulnerable.

Suddenly David wondered if the old man had been killed on the day Sept-Sorian found out that his father was dying. How very apt. David was beyond words. It was airtight and yet he was in no position to accuse the Sept—not until he had managed to return home and take over the Gavrilli holdings.

He was going to assume the power he had been raised to wield. Now he knew that he wanted it. He had always wanted it, he realized, and that was really why he had run away. His life as a freelance net.walker was irrevocably over.

"It is good that you are all here and could see this," he said, his voice as calm as if he were enjoying a springtime afternoon. "Now perhaps you will tell your superiors and I will be permitted to return home for my father's funeral. With the bracelet if you insist, but I know that prisoners already convicted are permitted to attend a parent's funeral. Besides, as you can clearly see, my mother is distraught. She isn't able to cope. She needs all of us."

"And your siblings?" the Interpol woman asked.

David shrugged and tapped the side of his head. "Not all quite there, if you understand," he said, knowing full well that she already had a file on his family read into memory. She probably knew more about them than he did at the moment.

"Mmmmmm," the Interpol officer said, nodding slightly.

"This is a waste of time," the Sept brother told them. It was the first time he had acknowledged either of the police authorities. "Either take him in for the murder that we know he committed, or turn him over to us. We've already given you more than enough evidence to convict him."

David closed his eyes. That was the final piece he needed. Sept-Sorian, or the Septs in general working through Sorian, wanted him out of the way. He wondered vaguely whether they would feel the same if he had been more true to the mold, had not participated in disapproved music and hired Sept brothers and sisters to handle the net.

Now it was all so simple, so straightforward, that he couldn't believe that he hadn't realized from the start. He thought he could get away from his family, create himself entirely anew. He thought his father would live twenty more years and that his mother would want to take over the clan. Maybe if that had happened he would have had the life he'd envisioned, being the ultimate disaffected rebel.

The Septs were too powerful to worry about some fringe crazies. David understood only too clearly that was the way they viewed Camerillo. They saw Artos as just another ineffectual nut that threatened them no more than a flea threatened an elephant. But when the flea infected a lion and the lion could hunt the elephant, then the whole game changed.

"I should like to know what evidence you gave," David said coldly. "I have given the police every cooperation in this matter and I would be more than happy to provide additional resources, but I suspect that any evidence given by any Sept against me may not represent the whole truth of the matter. The Gavrilli family will be most happy to assist in any way we can, with whatever resources we have."

His voice sounded like his father's, the controlled threat veiled inside the masterful tone. He sounded so sure of himself, so perfectly composed, that David was not certain that he had spoken the words.

"Unless we are prepared to bring charges, we must permit him to attend the funeral," the local policeman said.

"If you let him go back to them, he'll be untouchable," the Sept brother retorted. "Even we can't get through their security wall."

The Interpol agent seemed mildly amused. "No, and you don't have the authority to demand either access or a prisoner, either." She shrugged. "We do."

David tried not to smile. The Septs had forgotten that there were other authorities in the world, and other forms. That being able to manipulate the net might be the center of power, but that there were other forms of power. For all their expertise in creating and breaking security systems, the Septs didn't have any mechanism to just ask.

Sept-Sorian might behave as if they already owned the world, but not everyone in the world was going to lie down and accept that. David enjoyed watching the Sept brother's face smolder and the Interpol agent remain completely oblivious of his anger. Obviously she hadn't thought that Sept-Sorian represented the ultimate power in the world.

"We can't charge him," the local man said. "We don't have enough hard evidence. What we do have is merely speculation and circumstantial."

"You have DNA matches, fingerprints, all the physical evidence you could want," the Sept brother muttered.

"Yes," the Interpol officer said. "And that's entirely reasonable given the fact that Mr. Gavrilli admits to having been living here at the time. And the fact that he found the body. There is nothing at all inconsistent with those findings." The local officer hesitated. "In fact, your insistence sometimes makes me wonder whether you would like us to close this matter in some way because of something you expect to gain or want, rather than simple justice. Our records indicate that there was little local approval of Mr. Camerillo's activities."

"Are you accusing us?" the Sept brother asked, incredulous.

The policeman remained perfectly bland. "I am just pointing out the obvious," he said.

Then the Interpol woman snapped open her datalink. She studied it for a moment, touched the pad with her long fingernails and clucked her tongue. "We have no sound reason to hold this person at this time," she said to the local police officer. "Unless you have any compelling reason for holding him, we cannot justify it on the basis of what we have at the moment."

The local policeman's stone expression did not change as he brought out the keytouch, and applied it to the sensitive spots on the bracelet. The surveillance bracelet opened and fell away.

The policeman scooped it off the carpet and put it in his pouch along with the key. "You're free to go," he said.

David thanked them, not because he thought it was more than simple justice but because it was good policy. Courtesies cost little and repay a lot, he remembered his mother saying when he was young. He had forgotten that she had taught him that, and that he had never stopped practicing it.

The three left, the Sept brother giving him a poisonous look in the end. David was just as glad that one couldn't keep his feelings completely in check. This way he was armed in advance.

Besides, there was something else David suspected. He had not looked or tried before because he had been afraid and under surveillance and preoccupied with other matters. For the first time since the old man's death, David entered Artos's suite. Artos had had three rooms in the corner of the third story that overlooked the garden and the canal. They were large rooms with high ceilings decorated with ancient plasterwork and paintings, as David remembered.

Or at least what he had seen of them. He had only been invited into the outermost room of the suite, the old man's music room. Here were keyboards and drums, guitars and amps and long snaking cords from one piece of equipment to the next. Dark teak shelves lined the walls and these were filled with music, both written and recorded, folios and chapbooks and periodicals with tips on getting more bend on a note. He had only ever glanced in through the doors to the bedroom and the third room, which he had always assumed was a library or dressing room, or something of that nature.

The palazzo was his now, and it was time to enter the old man's rooms and find out if he had left David something extra—something more useful than the house itself. The music room was exactly as he remembered it. Busty nymphs cavorted on the ceiling and dust had settled on the piles of sheet music in the shelves. He ignored this room and went on to the bedroom.

The bedroom was magnificent in the old sense. A canopy bed covered in bottle-green velvet stood on a dias near the wall. Sofas of matching green leather faced each other in front of a fireplace that sported a Baroque carved marble mantelpiece. In lighter colors and more delicate fabrics, this style would have suited his mother very well. The marquetry tables scattered throughout the space had been created for some eighteenth-century princeling, and the golden tones of the woods and the deep greens shimmered and came alive in the deep butter light of late afternoon. David had never thought that the old man was such a sensualist.

Still, the revelations here were personal. And while they were interesting, they had little to do with his immediate quest. He went on to the third room and was shocked.

In the middle stood a dreambox. It had to be unauthorized. David cursed under his breath. He could have come here any time for interface, instead of begging Sean or respecifying the dreambox in his own quarters. He slid his finger over the slab steel table. It came away dusty.

He turned away and then he saw what he had been looking for. Against the far wall, hidden by the box lid, was a functional workstation with a set of channel receivers. If what he suspected was true . . .

David sat down and turned on the receivers. A hum filled the space, and then he adjusted each one delicately. Voices. There were voices. He did another set of adjustments and he could hear what they were saying.

"It was Interpol. If it wasn't for them being in on the case we'd have him by now, and it's only because of the Gavrilli connection that Interpol's involved. Any normal murder they'd have just left to the locals," a familiar voice said. David had heard it only an hour earlier. It was the Sept brother who had been there with the police.

"Well, what should we do? We don't have the singers, we don't have the sister, we don't have the Gavrilli. This is absurd," another voice, more authoritative, said.

"It's less important than the Board," the familiar voice whined. "We've lost seven brothers, including the three brother executives. So why should we bother with something as minor as Gavrilli and friends when there's revenge for the Board to be collected?"

The more refined voice coughed softly. "We can afford to waste one brother on Gavrilli. Besides, I have a feeling this is all related. It's an instinct, I feel it in my gut. My gut has rarely been wrong."

"Like your gut instinct that you will be one of the next brother executives?" another voice sneered.

David smiled broadly. He had thought that the legacy to Sept-Sorian was too generous. The old man had hated all the Septs, but reserved his particular venom for Sorian. His gift had been a perfect way to introduce telltales into the House. He had been very good at those things, Artos Camerillo had, and David was glad he had had the opportunity to study with such a master.

". . . so follow him and find the others. He'll lead you to the girl and she'll lead you to the data. But let them think that you've gone, that you've lost interest, that we've called you off."

There was a grunt David took for grudging assent.

It was not just luck, David thought. He had always had this kind of luck, to find out what he needed to know, to find the right people at the right time. It was destiny, his destiny, and he was going to make everything of it. There was some Divine

Providence that was as offended by the Septs as he was and was giving him every opportunity to destroy them.

So the Sept brother would be watching him? There were other ways. He went to his text reader and sent a private message to a kiosk box. He was going to stay in the house until it was time to take the morning train to his family, but by then everything should be over.

17

Sister Theresa wore workboots and a heavy canvas apron covered with oil stains from machinery, not the kitchen. Cecilie knew she wouldn't attempt to eat anything Sister Theresa cooked, but the nun did look like she could fix machinery. And work it.

"A dreambox?" Sister Theresa asked. "Well, we do have a very old one. I haven't checked it out in ages, though. It might be junk now. And I can't get to it until I get this mower fixed. You'd think those girls had never seen a riding mower before in their lives."

Cecilie thought it very likely. She had never seen anything like the contraption that the nun was working on, and she hadn't grown up in the cramped streets of the poorer city neighborhoods. A riding mower indeed. As if there were any grass in Venice.

"So I'll take a look after dinner, how's that?" Sister Theresa stood up and wiped her wrench with a plaid handkerchief.

"Thank you very much, Sister," Cecilie answered sincerely. "It will help me get out of your hair sooner, and if you have the thing it doesn't hurt to find out that it's functional."

"I don't know how we came by it," the nun replied. "Before my time. It's really old, even if it is still working. Maybe it was just here when we got the house. Some rich old man left the house to the order, and we figured it was a better environment for the girls with babies than the older building we had on the adjoining farm. This place needed a little work, but it's bigger and has nicer windows. Babies need lots of natural sunlight. So now the old building is our convent and this is our mothers' residence. It makes things much easier."

Cecilie had nothing to say. She went back to the house, which she now knew was the mothers' residence and not the convent building proper, where there was nothing to do for the hour before dinner was ready. Two teenagers in clean cheap clothing set the plain plank tables in the dining room. Others rocked infants and sang songs Cecilie vaguely remembered hearing her mother or her grandmother sing. She went outside and stood in the driveway, certain that every time she heard a vehicle pass it was from Sept-Sorian coming for her.

Mostly the traffic on the road passed the big farmhouse by. The one time the gate was opened it was for a milk delivery from a nearby farm, young strapping men in work clothes wrestling the raw transport canisters off the platform and through the kitchen door. The sun set and dinner was announced with the laughing peal of a small bell. As a visitor, Cecilie had been set a place near the head table. Somehow the plain white napkin and white china on the bare golden wood of the table managed to look elegant and designed, not merely functional.

The rabbit in rosemary was delicious, just as Bianca had promised. Cecilie smiled at the girl across the room, and Bianca waved back cheerily, but there was no conversation. After the

meal was over and the girls were gathering the plates and sil-
verware onto large trays, Sister Theresa collected Cecilie and led
her briskly through the silent halls of the convent.

They passed through a small door and went down a flight
of stairs into a dark basement. It smelled of damp and root veg-
etables and the apples that must have been stored here for hundreds of years. Sister Theresa turned on a light and Cecilie saw
the shelves that lined the walls from floor to ceiling, all stacked
with neatly labeled jars of preserves and pickles.

Up ahead were voices and soft laughter. "The girls' lounge,"
Sister Theresa told her. "The front part of the basement is finished off."

They passed the door that spilled light and music and went
on past odd bits of farm machinery and a huge stack of wood.
Several small doors led off, recessed in the endless shelves.
"Storerooms," Sister Theresa told her. The nun unclipped a
huge ring of keys from her belt and searched before finding the
right one. "Now, I'm not sure which room the dreambox is in.
Though I think I saw it around Christmas, so it probably is in
with the decorations. Here." She opened a door that desperately
needed to be oiled. And, just as the nun had promised, there was
an antique dreambox shoved against a wall and covered with
loosely packed boxes, each clearly marked for the creche or the
tree or the table decorations.

Cecilie felt her hopes smothered in dust. The dreambox was
ancient, as advertised, and obviously had not been used in
decades. The flat table was being used in place of a storage shelf,
and the upper half, suspended from the ceiling, was opaque with
dirt. The workings were probably all mucked up, the connec-
tors corroded, the relays and neural interfaces completely worn
away.

"Well, get some of these boxes off of here and we'll see how bad it really is," Sister Theresa said in a voice that didn't hold too much hope.

Cecilie started lifting boxes, piling them higher against the adjoining wall. She could feel the contents shift and hoped nothing broke as she reached with her fingertips to balance them on the already staggering heap.

Sister Theresa was already studying the connections on the overhead unit, standing on the flatbed surface and poking around with her handlight and a screwdriver. "Hmmmm, this doesn't look too bad," the nun said, surprised. "I'd have thought it was worse. Well, this basement isn't damp, it's pretty well sealed. But still—I'll bet no one has used this thing since way before my time."

The nun took several fine electronic adjusters out of her worn leather tool belt. Cecilie recognized the tools from her own required hardware design and maintenance classes and wondered what a nun was doing with a full set. Sister Theresa started testing each of the neural connections the same way Cecilie had been taught, only the nun managed to hold a flashlight under her arm as she worked. Cecilie's Sept-sister teachers never expected her to use any less than the finest, the newest, the most advanced hardware. She had never considered how hard it would be to read the status board with only the one halftone light dangling precipitously over the stacked boxes.

Sister Theresa began to whistle a tune Cecilie only half recognized. "Can I do something?" Cecilie asked. "I mean, maybe I can check the relay panel while you're doing that."

"You can?" Sister Theresa asked, surprised. "Sorry, I'm used to girls who have to be taught how to brush their teeth. I'm not used to skills in a visitor, let alone anything technical. Sure, come on, there should be another flashlight in the toolbox. I've got the big one, but there's a smaller one in there. It's yellow."

Cecilie went through the nun's neatly arranged toolbox. The yellow flashlight was near the top. She had to squeeze into the space at the head of the table and wipe off the view panel with her sleeve before even the additional light would do any good.

She pressed a few of the diagnostic keys. There was no response.

"Try turning on the juice," Sister Theresa said from above.

Cecilie felt like an idiot. She traced the connection back to the wall box, where the power had been turned off. The switch looked rusted. It took Cecilie three tries to move it, but even from here and without the extra light she saw the panel blaze and start to run its own start-up test.

She ran the diagnostics carefully, twice, but according to the status bar everything on the table side was in working order. Ancient and probably rather crude, the thing was still functioning. Maybe it still worked because convents were so clean and careful, or maybe because there was some deity that looked after her.

"Yeah, it's all working up here," Sister Theresa said. "I had to replace a couple of synapses that had dried out but everything else checks out fine. Looks like you're in business."

Cecilie took a deep breath. The nun had already clambered down from the tabletop and was replacing her tools and belt in the tidy toolbox. Then Sister Theresa left and Cecilie was alone with only the single dim light and the dreambox.

She dusted off the rest of the table with her sleeve, wishing that the nuns hadn't been so perfectly organized not to have left a single rag lying around.

It was after eight. She looked at the box. It was old and even checked out it could die in the middle of interface. That wouldn't kill her, Cecilie told herself. It would be uncomfortable, and perhaps disorient her, but she'd survive. And she wouldn't survive Sept-Sorian. Just because she felt so safe, so otherworldly here, was no reason to abandon the future. The nuns were going to throw her out in the morning and give her bed to a girl in a more traditional definition of trouble.

She had to contact David before she ran again and she had to find out what Zizi had left and what the aliens meant. Somehow she had managed to forget all these things while she enjoyed the convent's timeless serenity and connection to the earth. Without further thought she lay down on the table and keyed the telltale under her left hand to lower the top.

The interface looked/felt odd. Colors were greyed and blurry, and Cecilie thought that she would never be able to make out text here. Movement was ragged and she felt more as if she were lurching rather than moving smoothly through the medium, but there was no doubt the interface connected. She was here in the middle of the Mall dressed like a medieval nun in an old-fashioned habit.

She giggled. The default must have been programmed by the previous owner of the house. No real nun would ever wander around in these layers of black robes and heavy veiling. She had worn costumes this constraining, but not for long.

The previous owner presented this image in the net and then left the house to an order—maybe she had wanted to be a nun and had been rejected. Then Cecilie told herself to stop wasting time and being ridiculous. She had no reason to care about the person who had owned this interface and she had plenty of reason to get moving. She checked chrono and it was nearly half past ten. She wondered how long David would wait for her, and if he'd leave a telltale in the lighthouse if he couldn't.

This time she took the traditional route to the deeper levels. She went down the elevator past the subbasement green. There she whispered "Water" to the system, which responded by creating a water icon along with all the other options on the menu. She touched the water icon, a scene of blue curling Japanese waves.

Nothing happened for a moment, and then the elevator doors slid open to the primal datasea. She began to swim. The transition was immediate. She could breathe and move easily here but the full habit and veil weighed her down. She slipped off the veil first, and then the confining wimple and cap before taking off layers of dress and petticoats. From her own dreambox she could have transformed to a mermaid complete with tail, green hair and coral crown, but that option wasn't available now. Too bad; the mermaid swam much faster than the human did.

She swam through the bright green water, sparkling with living representations of packets zipping to their assigned sites, or to someone's call-up or queue. She watched the orange buoys, noting the numbers, as she made for the lighthouse. It had been her lighthouse, but that had been ages ago when she had been a girl apprentice and innocent. In those days she knew that the Septs were right and honorable and dedicated to keeping the net usable and free. The lighthouse could have changed along with everything else.

The swim seemed longer and the water heavier than before, though maybe without the mermaid guise she was just that much slower. Or maybe it seemed slower because she was so scared, so certain that David wouldn't be there and that Sept-Sorian would.

They couldn't kill her here. Not really. The old saw about a charge that entered the receiver's brain and fried it was just one more net.legend, like the little kid who still wanted postcards or some strange cookie recipe that floated around and showed up at random intervals. But they could trace her if they found her and she had been confident enough that the weird old dreambox was unregistered that she hadn't bounced around the nodes to obscure her origin.

She had been too scared to think straight and so she was here in the clear, though through a box that was old enough that their great-grandparents might have used it. If it ever had been registered then the registration would have lapsed ages ago. Had they even registered boxes back then? she wondered, and then realized how absurd the question was. She had better things to worry about than changes in registration laws over the past hundred or so years.

The lighthouse looked different than it had before, even the last time when David had found her here and demanded the banking data from her. That memory seemed a shred of fantasy from another life, one she could hardly remember in the distant past. The lighthouse seemed disheveled somehow, as if it had aged a century since she had seen it last. It was not precisely in disrepair, but seemed on the verge of abandonment.

She went inside and she understood why it was all changed. It had been ransacked. Sept-Sorian, or maybe some other Sept, had gone through all her personal files. Things were torn out and open, floating in the shadowed water. Bits glittered like jewels ripped from their settings. Nothing was whole and nothing would make sense.

Cecilie wanted to cry. She wandered through the heap reaching out to a glitter here, a shred there, knowing that nothing would ever put them back whole.

The brothers had done their job and left the lighthouse. Utterly, perfectly still, there was no sign or sense of any other being there. David was not here. Despairing, Cecilie doubted that he had ever come, even at the appointed hour. He had abandoned her like the infosea had forsaken the lighthouse. Or maybe he hadn't been able to come, had been traced and tagged or even killed. That was all possible. Maybe he wasn't completely unreliable but she hadn't expected him to make their appointment in the first place.

So she was surprised when she arrived in the top tower

room. David was not there, but there was a pristine zipped
folder with her name on it, seals intact lying in the center of the
otherwise trashed floor.

She had to try several passwords to open the folder. *Sun* was
the one that finally worked, which irritated her. David would
have to choose something for himself, not something that would
be immediately obvious to her. He was nothing but an arrogant
rich kid, right to the end.

Inside she found instructions, a train reservation and a kiosk
account complete with password (*lighthouse*—how very original) and ID numbers all set. The reservation was for a local train,
second-class, from Padua to Rome. Local. Second-class. That
wasn't at all secure and he was being a cheap jerk, she thought
angrily.

Then she thought again. It made sense. They wouldn't expect her to travel second-class, and certainly not on a local. A
Sept sister would fly, or at very least have a first-class ticket on
the rapido. They would never look for her here. This was safer,
but she wondered if David had really just been stingy.

There was also the kiosk account and ID. She could access
it from here, but she didn't want any traces on the record to
show that anyone could get in through this level; it would give
away too much. So she didn't know how much he had given her.

And Rome. Why would she go to Rome? She'd been to
Rome twice, once for a holiday with Julietta and her family, and
once as an apprentice with Signora Angelina when the signora
had some specialized work to do. She had found the city over-
large and not charming. She sincerely hoped that David had a
plan or a place to hide her, because outside the Sept-House in
Rome she knew no one.

Still, it was her only option. And it was far better than if
David had not come at all, which was what she had expected.
She took a minute to memorize the passwords and numbers and

the confirmation on the ticket so that she could call it up from the kiosk with all the other arrangements.

She sat in the middle of the lighthouse floor surrounded by debris of her life and tried not to see it. Somewhere in here Zizi had stashed something secret that she would never find. She felt strangely sad, missing the bird that would normally have flown around here as if the level were air and not water, and chattered constantly about what it had found. She missed that stupid program more than she missed most people in her life.

She destroyed the documents, ripping them into component bits and scattering them for reuse. A school of neon pink and yellow fish came and ate the scraps. At least there was no record outside her head of the kiosk account or the train ticket.

Sadly, she descended from the top room of the lighthouse. She would never come back here. There was too much memory in this place, too much she could never restore.

She was so deep in her thoughts that she didn't watch as she exited the structure, and so the Sept brother took her by surprise. "So you are here," he said, throwing a fine-knotted fishing net around her. "Well, what a catch today."

She struggled against the net, but the more she pushed against it the more deeply entangled she became. The brother was young, probably still an apprentice, and he was laughing.

"Brother Michele said not to bother," he said carelessly. "Is he ever going to be surprised when he finds what I've caught and tagged. And now we'll just be able to trace your registry and collect you tonight. And I'll get all the credit, too."

The net dissolved. She could feel the tracer attached to her in such a way it couldn't be deceived. She couldn't outrun it, couldn't leave the trace. It was worse than the net. It was like being dead.

Only she wasn't going to give them the satisfaction. They would try but at least she was far enough that she could get back to Real Life before they could come and take her physically. She had to leave immediately and she'd need a place to stay tonight and far from Padua. There was the kiosk account David had left her. She wondered if there were trains running out here late at night, or if service was limited to heavy-use hours. Padua was not a center of the universe like Venice or Rome or Paris or New York or Tokyo or ten million other cities she could name. She could be stuck for the night, and once Sept-Sorian knew she was in Padua she would be too easy to find.

No, she had to do something, but she couldn't think of what. Even if she bounced through a dozen nodes the tracer wouldn't lose her. She couldn't stay in the net all night.

Well, why not? she wondered. If she could stay until just before her train, then they wouldn't be able to trace her easily to Padua until she exited the net and hit the dreambox. Since the interface wasn't registered the header would give only the box address without any of the standard attachments, so they would have to wait until she was ready to leave. By the time the trace could give them her location after she connected to the physical box, they wouldn't be able to get there before she had left. They must assume that she was still in Venice, and tracing this ancient illegal would not be trivial.

It wasn't an elegant solution. It wasn't even a reasonable one. She didn't know what staying all night could do to her. In the Sept-House there were limits, and she was beyond all of them now.

She swam aimlessly, thinking of how long she had to remain here, awake and conscious. If she fell asleep the connection in the interface would automatically be broken and the trace would go off. As soon as she realized how long she had to remain awake, she realized how very tired she was. Everything here exhausted her. Swimming was great effort, evading Sept-Sorian took too much trouble. It would be worth death to sleep.

Silly, she told herself, and tried to shake herself more awake. Maybe if she got out of the level and went somewhere more lively she would manage.

She started paying attention to the buoys and went for the elevator station. There she pressed the elevator icon impatiently. This was not real; there should be an elevator waiting. As soon as she thought that the doors slid open and the menu glittered on the back wall. She looked at her options.

There were the hangouts and the public parties. She queried for a list and got over fifty thousand topics, half of which were somehow related to sex. She eliminated those, even though many people thought that channel sex was better than the real thing.

She found a group called "Revenge" and pounded the icon with her fist. Revenge was just the way she felt. Running was bad enough. What she really wanted was to get even.

The elevator doors opened on Revenge, which turned out to be rather sparsely decorated with heavy Jacobean-style furniture and a parlor that could have served Catherine de Médici, whose picture hung on the wall. Only three participants were on channel. Two were dressed to match the place, a woman in wide skirts and gloves and a man in a brocade frock coat with long curls. Cecilie thought they were probably the bots that kept the place going when there was no one around. In the corner sat another figure not dressed in period at all, studying a book.

She walked up to it. "What are you looking at?" she asked.

The figure looked up at her. She couldn't tell if the being was male or female. It had an androgynous look that changed depending on the angle and the light. "A book of poisons," the androgen said softly in a voice that was as indeterminate as its face. Indeterminate, but not sexless, Cecilie thought. Whichever gender the being was, it was seductive. Being difficult to identify made the individual more attractive and more disturbing.

"You know, poison is rarely used these days, and very often not used well at all," the androgen went on. "Think of de Médici. She is my goddess, the ultimate poisoner. It is said that she is the inventor of the poison ring. She used everything as a medium of death—cosmetics, a book, a cross, a pair of gloves. The gloves were most subtle. And nothing ever proved, of course. Today we are so crass. We kill, we trace in the net, but we lack elegance and creativity. Revenge is an art form more than a simple act of fury. People don't understand that anymore, and so the art has been lost. It is not about death, it is about making your enemy suffer."

The dark face with the angel eyes smiled beatifically, and Cecilie shuddered. Revenge was art indeed. She wondered what the monitor at Sept-Sorian thought on experiencing it at one remove through the trace.

And then she smiled. The tracer could see whatever she saw, hear whatever she heard. It could not see what she thought or planned or what she knew. No, it could only pick up what was out there to be seen.

Revenge was indeed an art and she knew what she was going to do. It was dangerous and she was afraid, but fear was less important than fury. She knew hate, and she was willing to sacrifice whatever was necessary on its altar.

She was anxious to go. The stranger had turned back to the book, ignoring her. She returned to the elevator and pressed the icon for the Library. This time she knew exactly what she was about.

She ignored the main reading room altogether and headed directly for the basement. She flung open doors one after the other until she found what she was looking for.

Behind this door lay insanity. Images crossed each other out of context, everything disheveled and beyond recognition. Here was the antithesis of all order, that which defied categorization.

On top of the images were the twisted images and nauseating angles, things that disregarded all human sensibility.

Cecilie stepped into the room. Data flowed around her, tumbling inchoate, moving crazy. Even braced for the disorientation, she found that it sickened her. She closed her eyes and blotted out the madness around her. And she smiled grimly, knowing that whoever watched the other end of the tracer didn't have that luxury. Whoever was on the other end was receiving the full live feed and couldn't look away. Revenge was art.

She stayed in the room with her eyes closed for what seemed like eternity, and then she waited for a second eternity after that before she exited. She called up the chrono and the readout appeared in the lower right side of her vision in blue superimposed on the cool basement wall. There were hours left to go. She set a limit on the timer to jolt her when it was time for her to return to the convent and leave Padua. This was not a thing the tracer could read. It could only follow her and see what she saw. It could not know that she had set an internal alarm in her mind.

Grimly she went on to the next archive, and then the one after that. Each had its own brand of dementia, its own inhuman twist to human life and a human world. Each curled the net around itself in a different flavor of anomaly. As soon as there was any hope of sense, Cecilie moved on.

Each alien archive threatened Cecilie's grasp on reality just a little bit more. Though she tried to tear herself out of the strangely contorted information that made up the alien catalog, she could not completely disassociate from it. Every movement jarred her sense of center, her stability. Finally she could not be sure she felt floor under her feet, that there would be calm and emptiness in the corridor, that the Library had not dissolved into some melted conglomeration that had once been knowledge but no longer made any sense whatever.

She lost track of herself. She no longer existed in this jumbled psychosis. She would have lost herself completely in the sensory lunacy had not her alarm indicated that it was time to go. Finally she staggered out of the last room. Keeping her eyes closed had not been enough and she was so badly disoriented that she could barely get back to the dreambox.

The tracer was with her until she broke the neural connection with the box, but her train left in half an hour and while they could get here quickly enough if the person on the other end could report easily, Cecilie had an idea that he would waste that much time trying to disconnect himself and get to his superiors. By which time she would be on her way to Rome. With a second-class ticket on the local. And they would never find her.

18

David waited at the platform in Rome for the local to arrive from Padua. He didn't know if she was on it; he hadn't had the time to access the account and double-check. Besides, that would be dangerous. He had arrived over an hour ago and had spent the time drinking coffee in the waiting room and trying to avoid the beggar girls with dolls swaddled to resemble real infants. He had forgotten this part of Rome, though he had not known it intimately. A Gavrilli, he had always traveled privately, been flown or driven wherever he wanted to go. He had only been to the train station twice before, and had not remembered it as this unpleasant.

He found himself enjoying the irritation. If beggars and pickpockets could worry him then he was in a very good state. Gavrilli Security/Transport should arrive just as Cecilie's train was due in, and then they'd be safe. Sept-Sorian might be stronger in Venice and on the net, but he was certain that they could not penetrate the defenses of his family home.

They were almost there. Almost. Safety was so close he could taste it, but the danger was not over yet. He paced on the platform. The train was due in two minutes and the local was as reliable as the rapido.

He saw a man and a woman in Gavrilli Security uniforms, crisply tailored and dark authoritative red, and he felt just a touch easier. They appeared unarmed but David knew better. They waited for the train he had said he was arriving on with a friend. These two must be newer members of the security team since they didn't know him on sight.

Though maybe even someone who'd known him at eighteen wouldn't recognize him. He thought he looked the same, but he had both more assurance and more apprehension. His style had changed in the years up north and now his clothes were Venetian, more subtle and fashionable than was usual in a Roman crowd. He had forgotten.

The train appeared in the distance, slowing as it came to the station. David was anxious although he could think of no reason anything should be wrong. Cecilie should be fine and exit from one of the red-painted second-class cars in a minute. He hoped she wasn't too angry about him booking second-class, but he had thought that it would be harder to find her in the more crowded compartments.

The train slid to a smooth halt. Doors opened and people poured out. Some struggled with luggage and others gripped small children's hands tightly. Business travelers in conservative suits carried leather briefcases, and students were festooned with backpacks and books, but there was no Cecilie.

He waited. The crowd on the platform subsided and now there were only the stragglers, the ones who couldn't reach their luggage easily or who hadn't wanted to endure the crush.

A young woman with Cecilie's mass of bright red hair came off the train three cars away. She walked slowly, as if she were very old, and she carried no luggage. He ran up to her and took her elbow. She flinched.

"Come on, the security guards are at the end of the platform and then we're safe. You're out of it. You're okay now. It's all over." He tried to be comforting but she didn't acknowledge him.

Then he looked at her face. Her eyes were blank and dull, as if she had stared into Hell and would never see anything else again. Her face was slack, emotionless. All the passion was used up, inward, that had buffered her from whatever had rendered her this lifeless. It had not been enough.

This was not the Cecilie he had known. That person had died, murdered in the night. He wondered if her brain was permanently damaged, if she was going to be like this forever. And he wondered what had left her so scarred.

Then she turned to him and smiled. That smile was more frightening than the blankness. It was filled with cruelty and triumph, and he wasn't certain if the cruelty wasn't aimed at herself.

"Revenge is an art," she said. "I always thought that what I did best was collect data. I was wrong. You know, David, you always were so superior to me because you were an artist and I was merely a Sept-sister net.ninja. But you're wrong. I'm an artist too."

They said nothing on the short hop back to the Gavrilli compound. The security team was efficient and not too familiar, and they wore black armbands to indicate that the head of the household had died. They had brought armbands for David and Cecilie, as if it was unthinkable that anyone connected with the family would be without some overt symbol of mourning.

As they hovered over the landing pad, David fought a flood of emotion. He was back here now, behind the walls and the electronic guards, with all the expectations and roles he had despised. The last time he had seen the house he had only desired never to see it again.

Now it stood ominous in the brightness of the afternoon, deceptively calm among the terraces and flowering trees and the tiled fountain that stood before the door. Silent, waiting, all that it had once symbolized threatened to swallow him whole. He looked back at it and felt his whole youth screaming at him to run. He had been an idiot to return.

But he was now the master here, he reminded himself. The house could no longer prevent him from doing what he wanted; it was merely one more resource in his portfolio, and a minor one at that.

Once upon a time he had wanted to fight the Septs, and now he had the power to do it. Money, expertise, influence were his for the asking. He had earned it and now he could wield it as he desired.

He was certain he could stop Sept-Sorian cold. The bully-boys could fight a bunch of nobodies who had only music and desire as weapons. They had never been challenged by the head of one of the great mercantile houses in the world.

He motioned to his escort to pull the vehicle to the side, and he got out to walk the last few hundred meters. The flowering trees were not in bloom and the giant cypress stood guard over all. The air was still as David breathed in the scent of the gardens. He walked slowly, approaching the silent house with the black wreath on the door reluctantly but inexorably. He could not avoid his fate any more than the fly being seduced into the spiderweb.

Ghosts remained. They fluttered behind the closed curtains, the shadowed door. The ghost that haunted him most was his own, his memories of powerlessness and restraint, the family that had torn him from everything he had enjoyed and done well to play Crown Prince of the Empire. With the expectation that his father would live for many years and that he would be an errand boy until he was a grandfather himself, he had felt suffocated.

Why hadn't anyone ever told him that his father was sick? That his father wanted to insure the dynasty when his mother really had little interest in the day-to-day workings of the Gavrilli concerns and his sister was not capable. From the time he had been twelve he had hated his father with an intensity reserved for those deeply loved. Now he wished that he had known, that someone had told him, that he could have told his father that he understood.

Or maybe at fifteen, or eighteen, he wouldn't have understood. Without the old man, without the music, he might never have learned. As he walked toward the house he was surprised to find that he was weeping. He mourned the fact that he had never been able to come home before and reconcile and recognize exactly why his father had made his life so harsh.

That was then. This was now. The cavernous door opened and his mother stood, a frail figure alone, dressed in black, framed in the oversized foyer. He went to her and she hugged him hard, wordlessly. Everything was so different from the way he had imagined it, and yet so utterly familiar that he could have seen it a hundred times.

"Your sister is resting," his mother said softly. "It's been very hard on her."

David only nodded, remembering the overwhelming jealousy he had had. His sister, who could never function fully in the hierarchy of the family, had always been their father's favorite. She had had all the love and attention he had wanted, while he thought there was nothing for him but disapproval. And now that he had some glimpse of why decisions had been made it was all too late. Still, he did not want to see Lucia immediately. Better that she get her rest and let him assimilate his ghosts alone. No reason she had to pay for his emotional blunders, which she would never understand anyway. She was not capable of understanding, but she was fully able to express anger and recrimination and love. He realized that he very much wanted the latter.

"My friends?" he asked when the embrace was over.

His mother nodded. "They are waiting for you. But I wanted to see you alone first." She hesitated. "And the friend you brought with you?"

"Cecilie Sept-Fortune," he answered quickly. "She's had some trouble recently."

His mother nodded but said nothing. She turned and led them into the family parlor, where Lina and Sean waited. They both sat formally on straight-back chairs and wore dark clothing. Sean wore full black as an acknowledged member of the family.

"So, finally, we're all here together," David said heavily.

"I want to get some rest," his mother said, excusing herself. David nodded, certain merely that she wanted to leave them alone. He was just as glad of it.

"What happened?" Sean asked.

"I don't know," David said. "Cecilie will have to tell us."

Cecilie told them about leading Sept-Sorian through the alien archives. Her words were spare and lurched forward, as if she couldn't encompass the entirety at once. "And so," she concluded, "maybe one of them is mad, or maybe I am. Or maybe they're on the way here now. But revenge is an art. And if I drove one of them mad, then I've proven something. I've shown them the power." And she began to laugh, her tone tinged with hysteria.

Lina patted Cecilie's hand. "We'll have to find out just how much destruction you and Sean together caused," the singer said softly. "But I would think that the heart is torn out now. The Sept Board will try to reassemble, but they must be terribly weakened. And even if you didn't drive anyone mad, Cecilie, not even yourself, you have forced them to publicly confront something much more difficult. There are aliens. We could ignore anomalies in the Mall, and debate whether or not we were alone in the universe. The fact is that now we know and no one can retreat from that knowledge. That is a much greater revenge than insanity. Everything will have to be different now. We know they are here. Somehow we will have to deal with them, learn to communicate, learn to exchange information. We will need to or we will have to destroy them. There is nothing else. We aren't capable of simply recognizing that we can't possibly communicate and let each other go. I wonder if they feel the same way?"

"What?" Cecilie asked from within her daze.

"They're here because they can't ignore the fact that we exist," Lina said. "They can't simply pass on the idea that we can't understand each other and let it go at that. They also need to try to understand, somehow. It's all like music. Even if you try to eliminate jazz, it is still here. It can't die, it can only transform itself. But the things that we are not permitted to hear seep into the cracks in our consciousness and we can't escape them. Maybe music is information, I don't know. Certainly they behave the same way. Neither can be suppressed, they both are alive and re-create themselves everywhere. Maybe it is part of our nature, or maybe it is true everywhere. I wonder what the aliens think of that, if they find that music and information are almost impossible to contain?"

David blinked. He had thought of Lina as no more than a singer. Now he understood why Sean had approached her.

"We're safe now," David said. "Sept-Sorian, none of the Septs can do anything to us here. So I suggest that we find out and evaluate exactly what kind of damage Sean and Cecilie have done. That's the first step. Then we'll take it farther."

"Why don't you stay with your family?" Lina suggested. "For any of the public information, I can handle a kiosk account. Sean and I can pull together the public picture. And later on either you or Cecilie, if she is able to, can go in and look at the Septs from the inside. But she needs to rest now and you should look in on your sister."

Lina stood as if it were all arranged. Sean looked at David with a question in his face. David nodded. Lina was right, they could do that. And Sean would enjoy seeing just what havoc he had created.

Lina took Cecilie by the hand. "Come on, there's a room made up for you and a wonderful tub. You'll have a hot bath and then a good long sleep and you'll feel much better."

David doubted that, but let Lina lead Cecilie away. Sean turned back and studied David for a moment. "You'll be all right?" he asked. "You won't do anything stupid?"

David sighed and shook his head. "As if you're the one to ask," he said, but there was only admiration and warmth in the statement.

He was alone. In the Gavrilli house he was blessedly alone for the first time. The family parlor was just as he remembered it, but he liked it better. Maybe after all the silk and heavy watercolors of Venice, he found the restrained design and muted palette restful. Things were less ornate by style, permitting the contrast of materials—of marble and aluminum, steel and tile—to provide the interest.

He had been wrong about a lot of family things, he thought. Maybe he was more wrong than he had known.

He left the parlor and went to his own suite, not because he wanted to revisit memories but because his dreambox was there. Or should be there, if it hadn't been ripped out and discarded when he had left.

His whole suite was exactly as he had left it. The dark reddish brown marble set off the blond wood furniture throughout. Everything was simple and clean the way he liked it, the way he had forgotten in the years in Venice where everything was decorated, adorned and embellished. Sean's things had been unpacked into his closets, which startled him at first, and then silently reminded him that his family had taken his documents to be true in spirit. Strangely, David realized that he was pleased.

His old dreambox was in the last room, in an alcove in his study. He decided that if he stayed he wanted to keep these same rooms. He didn't want to move to his parents' wing, which in any case had been decorated by his mother and was far too pink and white for his liking.

The dreambox was exactly where it had always stood, dusted and polished and even recently inspected. There was a date on the inspection panel that was only a week old. Maybe they were expecting him home, or maybe it had just become part of routine maintenance, he didn't know, but he was glad to have this interface again.

He had no intention of waiting until Sean and Lina gathered a report. He had to know, now, precisely what effect Cecilie's strategy had had on Sept-Sorian—and Sept-Fortune.

This time he did not don his sun mask inside. He went with a harlequin, utterly indistinguishable except that it had come from the best of the Venetian maskmakers and indicated that he knew what he was doing. He could not interface directly into the Library so he took a more circuitous route, but ended up in the main reading room.

It was mobbed as he had never seen it before. He blended into the background, trying to appear as a junior Sept brother who was merely there to observe and learn. There were surely enough of them, it seemed. If this had been a physical space they wouldn't have all fit.

"They've been gone for an hour at least," someone near him complained. "It doesn't take that long to go to the basement."

"It isn't that long, and they had to find the aliens," someone else replied.

David realized that he had no way of telling people apart, not by Sept or gender.

"I still think we should have had a joint committee go," the original speaker groused. "Sept-Sorian has been just a little too important lately, you know? Pushing us all around as if they were in charge all the time. I mean, what about that Sept sister who disappeared? The one who they said went renegade and all? Why shouldn't she get protection and to bring her case before the Board? Where does Sept-Sorian get the idea they have the right to decide what's good for all of us?"

"Because there isn't any Board," the second speaker said. "And with so many senior people dead or in the hospital, and the danger to all of us, someone had to be in charge. So Sept-Sorian showed up and did the work, and if they're taking the brunt of the hits now we have to support them. Or else there wouldn't even be a Sept system anymore. We'd all be dead."

A third person masked as a red harlequin chimed in. "No, we wouldn't all be dead. We'd be restructured some, and probably more consolidated, which was the whole point, right? We would all be standing around here now just like this, but we'd have some say about was going on. Do you really believe all that alien stuff?"

The others in the general vicinity shrugged. "It doesn't really matter, does it? Aliens are not responsible for the bomb in the Board room, and that's what's important now. Not this damn idiocy." This speaker had a firm voice and some charisma. David tried to take note. "Sept-Sorian suffered the loss of two brothers and they want Sept-Fortune to pay. Sept-Fortune suffered the loss of a sister, who was protecting herself against Sept-

Sorian. If this is what we've come to then we're pretty sorry."

"But didn't she set the bomb?" someone else asked.

"Who knows?" the firm speaker said. "That's what Sept-Sorian says, but since when have they become the single arbiters of truth? No, they just want us all to fall into line, do what they say because they want to be on the top of the heap. And they're using this crisis to do that."

"You think they caused it for their own benefit?" someone said thoughtfully.

David jumped in immediately. "It makes some sense," he volunteered.

"More than some sense," the leader agreed heartily. "After all, how long have they been going around trying to run everything and all of us? Trying to tell us which contracts we could accept and which we couldn't? That we weren't allowed to work for any corporate sponsors anymore without paying them a commission, which cut revenues pretty badly? And whose idea was this meeting, for us to consolidate firmly under one single leadership, so that we could combine our strengths?"

"Well, it was Sept-Sorian's idea," the first speaker said. "We all know that. I thought it was weird that they picked a city where there wasn't one of their larger or stronger Houses."

"They never liked the sister Septs," an unmasked woman volunteered. Her net.face was young and beautiful but her voice carried the authority of experience. "Especially Sept-Fortune. We were told more than once to concentrate on the work that was our place, not what we wanted to do. Or the higher-paying contracts we were offered. Frankly, they tried to bully us and we didn't want to listen. So they attacked us through one of our newest members. Very brotherly."

David thought that this might be Signora Tima. Cecilie had said she was fearless. He wasn't sure that "rash" wouldn't be a better word to describe her. In any case, she was not in the least subtle. David wondered if she had ever really studied Machiavelli, and what benefit that study had been to her.

As they talked David noticed that the Library changed. It was subtle at first, like the anomaly had been. The heavily burled paneling seemed to soften and drift, the deep gloss of brass became shiny and cheaper. Then the others caught it and everyone became very quite as the Library lost the extra layers of solidity and fine detail that marked it as Sept more clearly than any designation.

The illusion of walls and tables, reading lights and leather chairs wavered. Everything became gossamer and insubstantial, the plan of the Library and not the place itself.

"Go back to the real world," a voice proclaimed. "The Library is contaminated and condemned. We are ridding it of the pestilence now."

Anger rippled through the crowd. The speaker had stood by the door, looking much more concrete than the shreds of Library that remained. The speaker removed a black hawk-nosed mask, though it was not by face that David recognized him. Rather it was the arrogance and the way he behaved. Sept-Sorian. And probably a senior brother.

"What gives you the right?" an older woman challenged him. Small and determined, she marched through the crowd and confronted the brother. She had been the first leader in the discussion, not the second, and David realized he had been wrong. This woman who was a cross between a grandmother and a witch was Signora Tima, and he had no doubt that she could be as subtle as she was forthright. Something about her reminded him of Catherine de Médici, the Florentine girl who split and terrorized all of France. "The Library has always belonged to all of us. Not to you, not to any single Sept or generation. You have no right to destroy it."

The brother shrugged. "This place is infested. There are

aliens here digging into the basement levels, building archives with an architecture that will drive any human insane. You've been fortunate to avoid this reality. We at Sept-Sorian have more experience, due to your Sept sister. Whom you're protecting even now. Believe me, we know that Sept-Fortune is obstructionist to our combined benefits. You have always stood with those few sorry Septs promoting forbidden music, teaching apprentices to respect authority other than what is properly constituted among us. You have been a problem."

A deep hush fell over the group as the walls started to disappear. The furniture was already gone. The Library was almost entirely erased already; at this point protest was merely impotent fury.

But Signora Tima did not explode. There was no anger in her, only the wisdom of the adult watching children rip apart a favorite toy. "No, we have not been a problem. You have been a problem," she said. There was no defiance in her tone, no flight of inspiring oratory to her style. There was only a bare discussion of the facts. "You yourself are not old enough to remember what things were like once, when the choirs played any music they liked and the Septs were all independent. It was Sept-Sorian and a few cohorts who pushed through the idea of change. Change is good, people said. Change or die. So we changed, and we left ethics and competition and honest work behind. When I was a young apprentice, the function of the Board was to mediate disputes between Septs, not to take over the net. No, Brother, you have tried to create some new and different world and unless you eliminate all of us you can't. You'll tear down this Library, which is more important and was more substantial than the Board, and you'll dissolve any hope of unity we ever had.

"And you can't win anymore. Septs fighting septs. You won't have time for the rest of the world. You'll have to watch your traces too much. Your dreams are all gone and we didn't destroy them. You did. You went too far, though I don't suppose your Sept believes in classical education so I don't think you would understand that you are guilty of hubris. Which is more than just 'pride' in classical Greek; it means challenging the gods. You and yours are no longer welcome in any house of Sept-Fortune."

Then quickly, as if she were trying to catch up with the rest of the Library, Signora Tima dissolved into nothingness.

David did not need to listen to any more of their talk. He wondered where the aliens would go now, whether they would remain at all, or even knew what was happening to them. Thinking of the aliens made him sad. They maybe could have learned somehow to communicate, someday. And the information they could have shared then . . . Just knowing there were other people out there somewhere was important. David wished they'd known where the aliens were from, how far away they were. And if they could ever be more than collectors and archivists to each other.

None of that mattered now. Sept-Sorian was set on barring aliens from the net and Sept-Fortune would oppose them and the power lines would be drawn. The Septs would fight each other and the Gavrilli clan would sit back and pick up the business. It would be easy, maybe too easy. And he could get everything he had ever hoped for. Only the victory tasted hollow.

One more death. They had just buried David's father a week before. The ceremony had been beautiful, moving. The music provided by Lina and Sean had been breathtaking and had brought everyone near tears.

It had been a good funeral, Cecilie thought. She was no connoisseur of the form, but she recognized the stately presence of death and the majesty of loss inherent in the ceremony. The public service would come later. This funeral had been only for those who mourned a man, not a symbol.

David had stayed with his mother and sister throughout. That was only proper. Sean was included in the family group, but placed behind David in the order of things and not in the row of the principal mourners. That, too, was proper. Everything was ordered and choreographed and people moved in their assigned places.

Cecilie had stayed well in the back with Lina. They had felt like interlopers, and yet it would be impolite not to attend. So they agreed they were there for David's sake, which made sense in some strange way.

The time before the funeral, and the week since, Cecilie had spent healing. The shock and horror she had absorbed during her revenge was muted by days wandering the compound gardens, swimming, playing tennis in the sunlight, all the helpful and restorative things the therapists prescribed. She listened only to light music in the evenings and spent a lot of time outdoors, where nature helped her gain some balance and sense of order.

She was not permitted back in the net, not even through a kiosk account to go to the Mall. When the therapists agreed that a shopping trip would be a good outing, Cecilie went with Lina and two women guards in plain clothes into Rome. There they went to the finest stores and tried on expensive outfits that they could afford only because the Gavrilli account had been opened to them. Cecilie hadn't planned to buy anything. "But you weren't able to pack anything," Lina pointed out. "At least buy some nice lingerie and a change of clothes. Too much washing and those things will be rags soon."

Lina was right. So Cecilie used the account and bought a pile of lace and silk underthings, several dresses and a few casual outfits. Lina bought lipstick and a fancy dress for performances as well as everyday clothes. The guards never looked at the goods for sale at all.

She was better, they all agreed. Not the way she had been before, but better. Recovering. That level of shock was not absorbed quickly, and some might not be absorbed at all. There was some talk of memory surgery, to remove the worst of it, but Cecilie refused permission. They were her memories, after all, her scars. She had earned them.

So the days followed each other with mind-numbing sameness, dull and wholesome and unproductive. Privately Cecilie thought she spent far too much time doing nothing. If she had some project, something to occupy her mind, she would have little opportunity to dwell on the insanity that played around the edges of her consciousness. But the therapists had said that she wasn't permitted back to the net and there was nothing else she could do. She hadn't been trained or fit for anything else at all.

David gave her a job doing something with shipping reports, but she couldn't make sense of it and quit less than a day later. "We're just waiting, all of us," David had said when she had told him that she didn't want a charity job that was completely useless. "When the Septs begin fighting among themselves, we'll be able to go in and keep them from tearing the net to pieces. And then we'll emerge in exactly the position Sept-Sorian had envisioned, only we'll do it right."

She had heard his words but she doubted him. Sept-Sorian thought that they could do it right once, and they were wrong. She was also proud of what David had told her about what Signora Tima had said to the Sept-Sorian brother when the Library had disappeared. Signora Tima had not taught her ethics for nothing. Everything that had twisted when she had become a full member of the Sept had unraveled, and she believed again what she had believed as a girl. Sept-Fortune was there to serve those who could not navigate by themselves. They were there to provide security for those who needed it, they were there to keep the net free. Not make it a fiefdom for Sept-Sorian.

She had dressed for dinner slowly that evening, watching herself transformed in the mirror. She pulled her unruly hair back severely and pinned it firmly in place. The girl, the fugitive, the convalescent disappeared. In her place emerged a woman of strength and reserve, determination and power.

The letter had changed everything, and it seemed to Cecilie that the change appeared on her face, in her hair, in the way her formidably tailored dress armored her figure. She was already the woman they had invited home, not the rebellious girl who had run away. Still, she was worried about telling David and the others.

"I have to go back to Venice," she said that evening. She had waited until after the dinner dishes were cleared and David's mother and sister retreated to their own misery. Coffee and brandy was served in the library, a place far more forbidding than the Sept Library that was now a ghost in the net.

"Why?" David asked, putting down his espresso cup. "You're part of the new world here. You can create anything now. Why go back?"

"Because," she said, and she stopped. She knew she couldn't share the contents of the blue-paper letter she had received from Signora Tima that afternoon. The letter had shaken her deeply. Signora Tima had not only found her and was inviting her home, but was also promising to make Cecilie her protégée to take over Sept-Fortune. In the coming war between the Septs, Signora Tima and Signora Angelina had decided that Cecilie was the most likely leader to counter Sept-Sorian, and they had decided that she had to begin a new phase of training immediately.

Ordinarily we would have waited until you had made journeyman to tell you what our plans were, and take you into our confidence, the note had read. *You were al-*

ways our choice of your generation, which is why we made things so difficult for you. No doubt you understand now that everything we have done in your special education was to prepare you for the role we have chosen you to play. Cecilie 8 Sept-Fortune, the elder sisters and signore decided more than five years ago that you would be groomed to become the signora executive of the Sept. That was before we were threatened by Sept-Sorian. Now that we are fighting for our survival it is necessary to begin your instruction in the art of diplomacy and negotiated combat far earlier than anticipated. You are expected immediately.

It had been signed by both Signora Tima and Signora Angelina. Cecilie was thrown by the implications in that letter. She had never desired this role, and wasn't certain even now if she wanted to accept the decision of the signore.

But Sept-Fortune had the resources to win the coming conflict, and Cecilie knew that she wasn't afraid of a fight. Nor was she so innocent that she could not win against a treacherous enemy. She was a Venetian, after all, trained in Venice and twisted to the purpose of her Sept.

Were there any other options, anyway?

She looked at David Gavrilli. He had changed since she had first met him playing jazz. Now he wore the silk suits he had eschewed in Venice, the handmade shoes, the buffed nails. Everything about him was perfect, verged to take over the world.

He was no different than the brothers in Sept-Sorian.

She had never entirely trusted David Gavrilli, and now she understood why. He had been trained to authority and he wanted it. No matter how badly he denied the fact, he had been raised to power and it was in him deep as his DNA and he couldn't resist it.

She could. She wanted nothing more than to return to her old life. Only that life was gone, and Cecilie realized that she knew more about the one that was coming than most. She had lived here, she had seen them all up close and knew how they thought. If she did not accept the mantle of authority, someone else would.

The power was there for her just as it was for David. He was Gavrilli. She was Sept-Fortune. Like David Gavrilli, she was also the heir to great resources and power, and like Gavrilli she had been prepared all her life to wield them. They were no different, she realized. She and David were precisely the same in far too many ways, and that made her sad. But she could not escape that fact any more than David Gavrilli could escape being Gavrilli.

Now she had to tell that to David. He had used her, she knew, but he had also tried to protect her. And he had given her jazz, the freedom of mind that would make her stronger and more creative than any member of Sept-Sorian could ever imagine.

She closed her eyes and composed her words carefully. "Because I have been called back to Sept-Fortune," she said quietly. "What you need to fight is a particular attitude among the Septs in Sorian's camp, and I have just been drafted by the opposition. I will be leaving on the evening rapido."

David studied her thoughtfully, then smiled sadly. "I had hoped you would join us," he said. "But perhaps it will be a very different future when there is the possibility of a Sept bringing down the Septs. We've been allies before. I hope we can remain allies in the future."

Cecilie shrugged. "We don't know what the future will bring," she said. David seemed to accept this, but she realized that she wanted to give him something more. Some hope, a hand held out after all they'd done. Now that she was leaving, she doubted that she would ever see him again, except perhaps on the opposite side of a negotiating table.

"Don't stop playing," she said. "And I'll never stop listening to jazz. It will always be part of Sept-Fortune, and it will always be part of you. So there will always be a reason to talk."

David smiled and held out his hand. She took it firmly, then kissed him on both cheeks goodbye.

*   *   *

The world wakes up to syncopated sunlight. Music shimmers between dawn and daylight, the sad time to go to sleep and the hope of a new day. They come out to sit and sing and play on the bridges and in the squares, students and young players trying an improvisation or a long slow sorry line of the blues. Their teachers have already staggered to their beds unimpressed with what the night has brought.

Night lingers in the smell of old coffee and the hurting strains of dirty Delta blues, whisky voices and raw desire. But it is daylight and time for the ordered music of the light. So the players pack up their instruments, their keyboards and saxophones and drums and guitars, their horns, their basses, their jugs of cheap wine, and go home until the shadows grow long again.

They go back to the large schools where they wear the sky blue robes of the Pietà and study Mozart and Stravinsky and rock and jazz. In their sacred calling they know that they keep the city, they keep the minds of the Septs and the world in the music.